CELEBRATION DAY

THE LED ZEPPELIN ENCYCLOPEDIA

First published in Great Britain in 2010 by Cherry Red Books
(a division of Cherry Red Records Ltd.), Power Road Studios,
114 Power Road, Chiswick, London W4 5PY

ISBN: 978 1 901447 81 1

*Every effort has been made to locate the owners of some of the images in
this book, with no success. Please get in touch if you are one of these
copyright holders.*

Design: Dave Johnson

CELEBRATION DAY

THE
LED
ZEPPELIN
ENCYCLOPEDIA

MALCOLM DOME AND JERRY EWING

THIS BOOK IS DEDICATED TO TH!

MEMORY OF MICHAEL BONHAM

INTRODUCTION

There is something mythic and altogether extra-dimensional about Led Zeppelin. In fact, not only is it sometimes difficult to realise that they did once exist, but just how massive they were.

We now live in an era when easy access to information means that no band can attain the sort of status Zeppelin enjoyed, and endured. When they were the subject of stories which proved to be the fuel which constantly inflated their own sense of deification. This wasn't just a huge rock band, but something far more.

In America, especially, the iconic celebrations of the Zeppelin aura has continued at a fever pitch no band since has come close to emulating. Because this isn't just about the music, or the personalities who made it. This goes much further, and ensures that not only Zeppelin stand alone, but that their importance also increases every year.

As we write, it's 30 years – count 'em – since they decided that the death of drummer John Bonham marked the end of the band. Occasional one-off reunions notwithstanding, that's the way it's stayed. And if you wanted to know which reunion would dwarf them all, then this was the one. Over a million fans applied for tickets when Zeppelin last played, at the O₂ Arena in London in December 2007. People flew in from all parts of the world, just to bear witness to the return of the Timeless Lords.

When anyone has such an indefinable impact, any book must by definition be only able to capture part of the intensity and the story. But that's not what this is about. What you have here is a reference work, a way of dipping in and out and seeking relevant facts and information. It's not meant to be a detailed biography of the band; if you want that, then there are numerous books by the likes of

Dave Lewis and Mick Wall which are far more exhaustive and extensive. No, we've set out to provide a guide, a map if you wish, that will take you through the maze that was – and always shall be – Led Zeppelin's formidable career.

While many see the band as heavy rock's satanic majesties, this was only a part of what they were about. As Robert Plant was fond of pointing out – and still does – they did so much more than create a heavy mythos. Funk, folk, soul, blues, prog, world music, jazz, even reggae found their way into the music they generated. And let's not forget that, such was their clever use of melodies, some songs were most certainly pop.

It's so true that Zeppelin's grasp on musical exploration was such a vast tapestry that many bands subsequently have carved out successful careers by reweaving mere threads. Their vision was enormous and the acclaim was deafening.

Jimmy Page, Robert Plant, John Paul Jones and John Bonham have left behind a unique legacy – one that will be talking about, analysed, discussed and written upon for decades to come.

It is our honour to be able to present to you this A-Z guide to the band, their works and associated subjects. For those who already know the intimate details, hopefully it'll serve as a reminder – and who knows, one or two entries might even surprise. For people only just beginning the journey through Zeppelin-mania, welcome to the musical ride of your lives. Strap in, hold on tight, and let's start up the band...

Malcolm Dome and Jerry Ewing
London, 2010

A&M STUDIOS

Were it not for Charlie Chaplin there may never have been an A&M Studios in Hollywood. Chaplin bought five acres of land in 1917 and turned it into a complex where he filmed no less than 17 films in just five years.

In the mid-Fifties, this location was where the *Superman* TV series was filmed. But it was in 1966 that it became a recording facility when Herb Alpert and Jerry Moss, who co-founded A&M Records bought the complex and set it up as a studio.

It was here – along with several other studios around the world – that Led Zeppelin recorded part of their iconic second album.

ARMS CONCERTS

ARMS stands for Action into Research for Multiple Sclerosis. The idea for these concerts came from former Small Faces and Faces bassist Ronnie Lane, who suffered from the disease (he subsequently died in 1997).

At first it was envisaged that

there would be just one show, at the Royal Albert Hall in London on 29 September 1983. Lane assembled a stellar group of musicians. This included: Eric Clapton, Jeff Beck, Steve Winwood, Andy Fairweather Low, Kenney Jones, Bill Wyman, Charlie Watts… and Jimmy Page and John Paul Jones.

It was the first time Clapton, Beck and Page (all former guitarists with the Yardbirds) had performed together on the same stage. Page also did his own set, featuring three instrumental tracks from the *Death Wish II* soundtrack, plus a well-received instrumental version of 'Stairway To Heaven'. After Page's four-song cameo, the whole ensemble got together for Clapton's 'Tulsa Time' and Derek and the Dominos' 'Layla'. The latter featured solos from Beck, Clapton and Page.

This proved such a successful night that there was a subsequent nine-date tour of America, again with Clapton, Beck and Page involved. This time the trio got

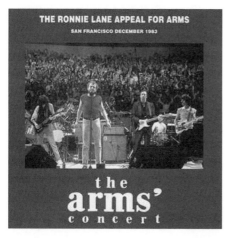

THE RONNIE LANE APPEAL FOR ARMS
SAN FRANCISCO DECEMBER 1983

the
arms'
concert

together on 'Stairway To Heaven'.

A video of the London show was released at the time, and is now on DVD.

ACHILLES LAST STAND

The opening song from the 1976 album 'Presence' is an epic, the third longest studio track recorded by Zeppelin. One of its standout features is a breathtaking, orchestral-style guitar solo from Jimmy Page.

In an interview with American magazine *Trouser Press* in 1977, Page had this to say about the solo: 'I'll tell you about doing all the guitar overdubs to "Achilles Last Stand". There were basically two sections to the song when we rehearsed it. I know John Paul Jones didn't think I could succeed in what I was attempting to do. He said I couldn't do a scale over a certain section, that it just wouldn't work. But it did.

'What I planned to do was to try and get that epic quality into it so it wouldn't just sound like two sections repeated. To give the piece a totally new identity by orchestrating the guitars, which is something I've been into for quite some time. I knew it had to be jolly good, because the number was so long it just couldn't afford to be half-baked. It was all down to me how to do this.

'I had a lot of it mapped out in my mind, anyway, but to make a long story short, I did all the overdubs in one night... I thought,

as far as I can value tying up that kind of emotion as a package and trying to convey it through two speakers, it was fairly successful.'

Some believe that the song was to be titled 'The Wheelchair Song' because at the time Robert Plant was still confined to a wheelchair following the road accident in Greece in 1975. However, this was probably no more than a waggish working title.

Lyrically, the song was inspired by the trip Page and Plant had made to Morocco in '75, following the band's run of shows at Earl's Court. There was also a nod or two towards William Blake's work, with reference to his engraving *The Dance Of Albion* in the lines: 'Albion rose from where he labour'd at the Mill with Slaves/Giving himself for the Nations he danc'd the dance of Eternal Death'.

There's also acknowledgement of a famous statue in St Mary, Jersey. It's called Devil's Hole, and the line 'The Devil is in his hole' is a direct reference this artwork.

Often described by Page as his favourite Zeppelin song, it put such a demand on his abilities that he is said to have even thought – albeit briefly – about using a second guitarist on it. 'But it wouldn't be right to the audience,' he once said.

'Achilles Last Stand' is one of the few Zeppelin numbers to be licensed for use in a film. In 2001, it was used in the skateboard documentary *Dogtown And Z-Boys*, which told the history of sport. Narrated by Sean Penn, it also included the Zeppelin song 'Hots On For Nowhere', again featured on 'Presence'.

AFRO CELT SOUND SYSTEM

A British conglomerate who combine modern dance styles such as trip hop with traditional Irish and African influences. The band's third album, 'Volume 3: Further In Time', features a guest appearance from Robert Plant – not surprising given the band's world music and Plant's fascination with this style.

Afro Celt Sound System started out in 1991, since which time they've released a total of six albums, the last of which – 'Volume 5: Anatomic' – came out in 2005. Occasionally known as Afrocelts, the band are signed to Peter Gabriel's Real World Records, being the biggest sellers bar Gabriel himself.

ALL MY LOVE

Song from the band's final studio album, 1979's 'In Through The Out Door'. Originally, to be titled 'The Hook', it was written by Robert Plant and John Paul Jones. Plant wrote the lyrics in tribute to his son Karac, who died in 1977 from stomach complications.

At the time, Plant and Jones were more heavily involved in the recording of the album than Page and Bonham. The latter pair would tend to come into the studio at night to do their parts, leaving Plant and Jones to piece together much of the record. Plant did the vocals in one take, although whether this was due to the emotional content of the song proving to be too much for him or just that it worked better that way remains open to question. There's also a synthesiser solo from Jones.

This is one of only two songs, the other being 'South Bound Saurez', in which Page had no writing input. It was released as a single in various South American countries, with different B-sides. In Brazil and Paraguay, a stereo version appeared on the flip (the A-side being in mono). In Peru it was a cover of Herb Alpert's 'Rise', and in Argentina it was 'Hot Dog'.

There's also an unreleased, extended studio rendering of the song which is an extra two minutes in length, with an additional verse added.

While Plant has always been proud of the song, Page regards it less favourably. In 1998, he told *Guitar World* magazine: 'I was a little worried about the chorus. I could just imagine people doing the wave and all of that. And I thought, that's not us. That's not us. In its place it was fine, but I wouldn't have wanted to pursue that direction in the future.'

ALMOST FAMOUS

The 2000 coming of age rock movie featured 'That's The Way',

'Misty Mountain Hop', 'The Rain Song', 'Bron-Y-Aur' and Tangerine'. Of these, only 'That's The Way' is on the official soundtrack CD. Robert Plant and Jimmy Page agreed to the use of these songs after seeing a preview screening.

In one scene, the character of Russell Hammonds from the band Stillwater proclaims, 'I am a golden god' while on acid at a party, This is meant to shadow something Plant is alleged to have said while totally sober and straight, on a hotel balcony (probably the Hyatt) overlooking Sunset Boulevard.

Other Zeppelin references in the movie are as follows:

There is a Led Zeppelin fan seen in one scene, wearing a T-shirt. This had the lyric 'To be a rock and not to roll' on the front (from 'Stairway To Heaven') and 'Have you seen the bridge?' (from 'The Crunge' on the back). The same fan, Vic, is seen in a different scene in New York with a T-shirt bearing the lyrics to 'The Rain Song'.

Finally, the band Stillwater are seen riding into New York in a limo in a recreation of the footage from *The Song Remains The Same*, when Zeppelin did the same thing.

ANGER, KENNETH

Controversial film-maker and author who gained notoriety with his book *Hollywood Babylon* which purported to lift the lid on many of Tinseltown's most infamous characters and scandals.

Born Kenneth Wilbur Anglemyer in 1927, in Santa Monica, California, he attended the same dancing school (Maurice Kosloff) as both Judy Garland and Shirley Temple. He quickly became fascinated with the supernatural and Aleister Crowley in particular, and it was this that led to his association and subsequent falling-out with Jimmy Page.

This was over the film *Lucifer Rising*. Anger had originally cast Bobby Beausoleil (who would become connected to the Manson family) as Lucifer in this short film, but when the pair fell out the latter walked out, taking much of the footage with him.

In an effort to revive the project, Anger started to re-shoot with Marianne Faithfull, although some of the original film did turn up in the movie *Invocation Of My Demon Brother*.

Anger commissioned Page to score the music for the film. The pair first met at an auction at Sotheby's in London of boots once owned by Crowley. In 1973, the guitarist agreed to do the music for a film that was to be about the Fallen Angel of Christian mythology,

Although work on the film was intermittent, there seemed to be a harmony. Anger was even using film-editing equipment at Page's London house in order to edit down the 17 hours of footage, while at the same time Page was working on *The Song Remains The*

Same. Things started to go wrong when Anger was seemingly caught in the middle of an argument between Page and his girlfriend, as a result of which the film-maker was asked to leave the house, having trouble getting back his footage.

Page was summarily fired, with Anger claiming that he'd only ever delivered 28 minutes of music, which was totally unusable. He claimed that Page was too heavily into drugs to come up with anything worthwhile. He told the *New Musical Express* at the time: 'The way he's been behaving is totally contradictory to the teachings of Aleister Crowley and totally contradictory to the ethos of the film. Lucifer is the angel of light and beauty. But the vibes that come off Jimmy are totally alien to that – and to human contact. It's like a bleak lunar landscape. By comparison, Lucifer is like a field full of beautiful flowers-although there may be a few bumble bees waiting to sting you if you are not careful.

'I'm beginning to think Jimmy's dried up as a musician. He's got no themes, no inspiration, no melodies to offer. I'm sure he doesn't have another "Stairway To Heaven", which is his most Luciferian song. "Presence" was very much a downer album. In the first place his commitment to Lucifer seemed to be totally serious, and he was very enthusiastic about the project. On the other hand he's very into

enterprise and hard work. But on the other hand he has this problem dragging him down. He's been acting like Jekyll & Hyde, and I have to have someone who's 100%. This film is my life's work.

'I really don't think he has the zing – the capabilities to do it. If he'd have said he was bored with the project I'd have understood, but he's just strung me along. Now he's no longer on the project, I'm no longer interested in having him.'

According to Anger, Page was never actually employed to do the soundtrack. 'There was never any discussion about money, the whole idea was that it should be an offering of love. The idea was to go 50/50 on the films profits and that Jimmy should have all the proceeds from any soundtrack album that came out of it. We never put anything down on paper. We had a gentleman's agreement, which to me is more serious than anything written down by lawyers.'

There were wild reports that Anger had cursed Page. Whatever the truth, the film eventually saw the light of day in 1980, with Beausoleil providing the music. It wasn't a major success on any level.

ARDENT STUDIOS
Based in Memphis, this was started by John Fry in his family's garage during 1966. This moved to National Street four years later, which is where it was located when Zeppelin dropped in to mix

the 'Led Zeppelin III' album in 1970, on a break during their sixth US tour.

Ardent is still going strong, and you can find out more about it at *www.ardentstudios.com.*

ATLANTIC RECORDS

The label that signed Led Zeppelin and oversaw some of their greatest triumphs. Started in 1947 by Ahmet Ertegun and Herb Abramson, it was originally a jazz and rhythm and blues company.

Zeppelin signed in 1968, a year after it became part of the Warner-Seven Arts Empire. The band remained directly on the roster until 1973, when they formed the Swan Song imprint, although this was still distributed by Atlantic.

Such was the respect and admiration the band had for Ahmet Ertegun that they readily agreed to reform on 10 December 2007 to play a special tribute show at the O_2 Arena in London. It was Plant's admiration for the man that persuaded him to put aside all doubts about ever playing with Zeppelin again.

ATLANTIC RECORDS 40TH ANNIVERSARY

Not one of the most auspicious occasions in Led Zeppelin's career. On 14 May 1988, Atlantic celebrated their 40th anniversary at Madison Square Garden with a 13-hour concert, dubbed 'It's Only Rock'n'Roll'.

Only artists who'd released records on Atlantic in America

performed, with LaVern Baker and Ruth Brown being the oldest survivors, while Debbie Gibson was the youngest The list of artists included the Rascals, Emerson, Lake and Palmer, Yes, Foreigner, Vanilla Fudge, Phil Collins, Paul Rodgers, Ben E King and Michael Douglas.

Plant did a three-song solo set featuring 'Heaven Knows', 'Ship Of Fools' and 'Tall Cool One', with Zeppelin closing the show with 'Kashmir', 'Heartbreaker', 'Whole Lotta Love', 'Misty Mountain Hop' and 'Stairway To Heaven'. But, with Jason Bonham filling in for his late father, there was little to commend the performance. It seemed out of tune, Page playing well below his best while Plant appeared to struggle with the vocals.

Oddly, though, the *New York Times* hailed it as something of a triumph:

'Led Zeppelin, unlike its many imitators who now clog rock radio, usually tempered its brute force with musicianly experiments, and the reunited band still does. In a streamlined half-hour set, the band turned around the beat of "Whole Lotta Love" and revelled in the spaces and Arab inflections of "Kashmir".' Mr Plant, who used to strut and preen self-importantly, now plays his role with a bit of mature amusement while still finding new ways to stretch and bend 15-year-old lyrics. Led Zeppelin ended a mixed concert with triumphant, explosive rock.'

The whole gig was broadcast live by HBO in America. In the UK, BBC2 showed four hour-long episodes on television. Atlantic also released this on video under the title of *Atlantic Records 40th Anniversary: It's Only Rock'n'Roll*.

Photo licensed from Getty Images

have received a substantial sum in back royalties.

Following on from the raucous opener 'Dazed And Confused', the song offered an early indication of the way Zeppelin would move through differing musical styles with consummate ease on most of their albums, had also been performed by the Plebs (1964), the Association (1965) and Quicksilver Messenger Service (1967). Later covers include those by Man, Paul Oakenfold, Doro and Pink.

BABE I'M GONNA LEAVE YOU

The second song from Led Zeppelin's 1968 debut album was a folk song written and performed by Anne Bredon in the Fifties. The song was covered by folk/protest singer Joan Baez on her 1962 album 'Joan Baez In Concert, Part 1'.

Both Jimmy Page and Robert Plant were fans of Baez, and it is widely believed that Page played this song to Plant during their first meeting at Page's Pangbourne residence. The Baez version that inspired the pair to re-work and record the song credited 'Babe I'm Gonna Leave You' as a traditional song, and Led Zeppelin originally credited the song to 'Trad, arr. Page'. However Bredon was made aware of the Zeppelin version in the Eighties (one wonders where the musician might have spent the ensuing decade-plus) and since then the song has been credited to 'Anne Bredon/Jimmy Page and Robert Plant'. Bredon is also believed to

The song was originally performed on early Led Zeppelin concerts, but after 1969 it disappeared from the band's live sets. A live performance from Gladsaxe in Denmark in 1969 can be seen on the *Led Zeppelin* DVD. Page and Plant took to performing the song during their 1998 reunion tour, and Plant has been performing the song with his Strange Sensation band. There are unsubstantiated rumours that Page also recorded a version with Steve Winwood in 1968.

The song was issued as a promotional single in the US in 1967, backed with 'Dazed And Confused', and in 1969 in Greece, backed with 'How Many More Times'.

BABY COME ON HOME

'Baby Come On Home' was a song recorded by Led Zeppelin for inclusion on their 1968 debut album but ultimately left off the record. It would later materialise on the 1993 compilation 'Boxed Set 2'.

It was recorded under a working title of 'Tribute To Bert Berns', a nod to the American songwriter and producer who wrote 'Here Comes The Night', 'Twist And Shout' and 'Hang On Sloopy' amongst others. 'Baby Come On Home' is loosely based on two different Berns songs, written for Hoagy Land and Solomon Burke.

'Baby Come On Home' began life as a song that was worked on by the New Yardbirds on a studio reel simply labelled 'Yardbirds'. The story goes that this reel went missing for many years and was only discovered in 1991 in a skip outside Olympic Studios in Barnes. It was then mixed by Mike Fraser for the 1993 box set.

The song was released as a single to promote 'Boxed Set 2' in September 1993 and reached Number 4 on the US *Billboard* chart.

BAD COMPANY

Bad Company were the Seventies hard-rock supergroup that featured ex-Free vocalist Paul Rodgers and drummer Simon Kirke, Mott the Hoople guitarist Mick Ralphs and King Crimson bassist Boz Burrell. The band were managed by Led Zeppelin manager Peter Grant and were the first band signed to Led Zeppelin's Swan Song label.

Named after the 1972 Robert Benton film of the same name, Bad Company were a hit from the off. Both their 1974 self-titled debut album and the 1975 follow-up 'Straight Shooter' were massive selling albums and the band's energetic live show proved equally popular. The two albums were released on the Swan Song label in America and on the Island label in the UK.

1979's 'Desolation Angels' was the first Bad Company album to be released solely on Swan Song, as was 1982 follow-up 'Rough Diamonds'. This would be the last Bad Company album to feature Rodgers, who left to go solo and would later form the Firm with Jimmy Page.

Ralphs and Kirke resurrected the band name in 1986, without Rodgers' involvement. Rodgers returned to the fold in 1998 for a short-lived reunion with the original line-up. Burrell died of a heart attack in 2006. In November 2009 the surviving members of Bad Company announced an eight-date UK tour for 2010.

BAND OF JOY

The Band of Joy were a Birmingham based blues and soul-based rock band in the Sixties, notable for featuring Robert Plant and John Bonham within their ranks.

The band were formed by Plant in 1966, although he subsequently left for a short period of time after a clash with management. Plant would then form another, short-lived version of the band,

seemingly settling on a solid line-up in 1967 with Plant and Bonham joined by guitarist Kevyn Gammond, bassist Paul Lockey and organist Chris Brown. At some point future Fairport Convention bassist Dave Pegg is believed to have played lead guitar.

Aside from Plant and Bonham, the Band of Joy were notable for featuring future Slade frontman Noddy Holder as a roadie. Both Plant and Bonham would go on to join Led Zeppelin whilst Lockey and Gammond would form the country rock band Bronco, who also featured Jess Roden and future Robert Plant guitarist Robbie Blunt. The pair would reform Band of Joy in 1977, but Plant and Bonham did not take up an invitation to appear on their 1978 debut album. The band released a second album before breaking up in 1983.

Gammond would appear in the short-lived Priory of Brion with Robert Plant during 1999 and 2001.

BATH FESTIVAL

The Bath Festival of Blues and Progressive Music took place at the Bath And West Showground in Shepton Mallet on 27-28 June 1970. The festival was headlined by Led Zeppelin on the Saturday night, and also featured performances from Pink Floyd, Fairport Convention, Santana, Frank Zappa, Canned Heat, Colosseum, John Mayall, the Byrds, Jefferson Airplane and many more.

Led Zeppelin had appeared at the Bath Festival of Blues in 1969, but it was the performance in 1970 which is widely regarded as helping to seriously launch the band in the UK; prior to this they had tended to concentrate on touring in America.

They were reportedly paid

£20,000 for their three-hour performance, taking the stage at 8.30pm and were called back for five encores. The event was filmed although the footage was lost for many years and, even when recovered, was deemed as not being good enough quality.

'Some people were trying to videotape the Bath festival and they'd already been told beforehand they couldn't, so I had no qualms about throwing a bucket of water on to the tape machine which blew the whole lot up,' Peter Grant was quoted as saying.

'Whoosh! It made a horrible smell and then it melted.'

The band's set list on the day was: *Immigrant Song/Heartbreaker/ Dazed And Confused/Bring It On Home/Since I've Been Loving You/ Organ Solo/Thank You/That's The Way/What Is And What Should Never Be/Moby Dick/How Many More Times (Medley: Long Distance Call/Honey Bee/Need Your Love Tonight/That's Alright Mama)/ Whole Lotta Love/Communication Breakdown/Medley: Long Tall Sally/Say Mama/Johnny B Goode/ That's Alright Mama.*

Photo courtesy Mike Wheeler

BATTLE OF EVERMORE

A delightful folk-rock song written by Jimmy Page and Robert Plant which is the third track on Led Zeppelin's fourth album, released in 1971. It is the only Led Zeppelin song to feature a guest vocalist, Plant being joined by then Fairport Convention singer Sandy Denny.

'"Battle Of Evermore" was made up on the spot by Robert and myself,' Page told *Trouser Press* in 1977. 'I just picked up John Paul Jones's mandolin, never having played a mandolin before, and just wrote up the chords and the whole thing in one sitting.'

Lyrically, the song presents some of the more fantasy-themed lyrics from Robert Plant, with references to Tolkien's works as well as Scottish folklore, which Plant was interested in at the time. From this, Plant felt the need for a second vocalist to be added, so Sandy Denny was invited to work with the band. The pairing proved so successful that Denny was even given her own symbol – three connecting pyramids – to go alongside the four symbols chosen by the member of Led Zeppelin. Plant takes the role of the narrator of the song, Denny the role of town crier.

'For me to sing with Sandy Denny was great,' Plant told *Uncut* in 2005. 'We were always good friends with that period of Fairport Convention. Richard Thompson is a superlative guitarist. Sandy and I were friends and it was the most obvious thing to ask her to sing on "Battle Of Evermore". If it suffered from naiveté and tweeness – I was only 23 – it makes up for it in the cohesion of the voices and the playing.'

'Battle Of Evermore' was performed by the band as part of their acoustic set on the 1977 US tour, with mostly John Paul Jones, but occasionally John Bonham, handling Denny's part. A version was also recorded by Page and Plant for 1994's 'Unledded' project. Fairport Convention performed the song with Plant at Cropredy in August 2008, and Plant sang the song with Alison Krauss on their 2008 US and European tour.

BBC SESSIONS

'BBC Sessions' was a live album released on the Atlantic label in November 1997. Produced and compiled by Jimmy Page, the double CD set features material taken from five different 1969

radio sessions recorded by the band and the bulk of a 1971 concert recorded at the BBC's Paris Theatre. There was some criticism that some of the session songs had been edited and others dropped, notably a previously unreleased song, 'Sunshine Woman'. The sessions from which the material was taken were John Peel's *Top Gear* (March 1969), Alexis Korner's *Rhythm And Blues* (April 1969), Chris Grant's *Tasty Pop Sundae* (June 1969), John Peel's *Top Gear* (June 1969) and *One Night Stand* (August 1969)

The album was the first official live Zeppelin material to be released since 1976's 'The Song Remains The Same'. The album reached Number 23 in the UK and Number 12 in the American charts.

TRACKLISTING:

Disc One: *You Shook Me/I Can't Quit You Baby/Communication Breakdown/Dazed And Confused/ The Girl I Love She Got Long Black Wavy Hair/What Is And What Should Never Be/Communication Breakdown/ Travelling Riverside Blues/Whole Lotta Love/Somethin' Else/ Communication Breakdown/I Can't Quit You Baby/You Shook Me/How Many More Times.*

Disc Two: *Immigrant Song/ Heartbreaker/Since I've Been Loving You/Black Dog/Dazed And Confused/ Stairway To Heaven/Going To California/That's The Way/Whole Lotta Love (inc. Boogie Chillen/ Fixin' To Die/That's Alright Mama/ A Mess Of Blues)/Thank You.*

BECK, JEFF

Alongside fellow Yardbirds guitarists Jimmy Page and Eric Clapton, Beck is widely regarded as one of the rock world's finest guitar players. All three conveyed differing traits which would help establish them as pioneers of the electric guitar, Beck's technical wizardry matching Clapton's feel for the blues and Page's way with a monster guitar riff.

Beck originally started working as a session musician, but ended up joining the Yardbirds following Eric Clapton's defection to John Mayall's Bluesbreakers in 1965. Clapton had suggested Page, also a session musician, replace him. Page however, was reluctant to give up his session career and, in turn, suggested Beck who joined the band. Within the year Page had been recruited as bass player for the Yardbirds, following Paul Samwell-Smith's decision to work as a record producer. Rhythm guitarist Chris Dreja opted to take up the four-stringed instrument but needed practice, so Page was drafted in. Soon the band featured the two hotshot guitar players, whose twin-guitarwork on the likes of 'Stroll On' and 'Happenings Ten Times Years Ago' (which actually featured John Paul Jones playing bass) gave a glimpse of what might have been. However Beck was fired in 1966, leaving Page as sole guitarist until the band morphed into the New Yardbirds and ultimately Led Zeppelin.

However before his departure Beck, along with Page, Who drummer Keith Moon and bassist John Paul Jones and pianist Nicky Hopkins recorded the Page-penned track 'Beck's Bolero', a song based around Ravel's classical piece 'Bolero' (Beck would claim he also had a hand in writing the song), which appeared as

The Jeff Beck Group

the B-side to Beck's 'Hi Ho Silver Lining' single in 1967 and would also appear on his solo debut album 'Truth' (1968). For some, it represents the point where the seeds for what would become Led Zeppelin were sown, not least when one considers original plans to form a band around Page, Beck, Moon and fellow Who bassist John Entwistle.

'Me and Jim Page arranged a session with Keith Moon in secret, just to see what would happen,' Beck told *Guitar Player* magazine in 1995. 'But we had to have something to play in the studio, because Keith only had a limited time – he could only give us like three hours before his roadies would start looking for him. So I went over to Jim's house a few days before the session, and he was strumming away on this 12-string Fender electric that had

a really big sound. It was the sound of that Fender 12-string that really inspired the melody. And I don't care what he says, I invented that melody, such as it is. I know I'm going to get screamed at because in some articles he says he invented it, he wrote it. I say I invented it. This is what it was. He hit these chords, and I just started playing over the top of it. We agreed that we would go in and get Moonie to play a bolero rhythm with it. That's where it came from, and in three or four takes it was down. John Paul Jones is on the bass. In fact, that group could have been a new Led Zeppelin.'

Having performed with fellow Yardbird Eric Clapton in 1981 for the Secret Policeman's Seventh Ball event, two years later the pair also appeared with Jimmy Page at the Royal Albert Hall for

ARMS benefit show to raise money for multiple sclerosis, the only time the three Yardbirds guitarists have ever performed together in public (they all turned down the chance to appear at subsequent Yardbirds reunions). They jammed together on Clapton's 'Tulsa Time' and 'Layla' before an encore of 'Goodnight Irene' saw them onstage with all the other performers, such as Steve Winwood, Charlie Watts, Bill Wyman, Kenney Jones, Andy Fairweather Low and John Paul Jones.

Both Beck and Page, along with Clapton and Chris Dreja, Paul Samwell Smith, Jim McCarty and the late Keith Relf were inducted into the Rock and Roll Hall of Fame in 1992, and in 2009 Jimmy Page inducted Beck into the same as a solo artist, the pair performing 'Beck's Bolero' and 'Immigrant Song' before being joined by members of Metallica, Red Hot Chili Peppers, Aerosmith and Ronnie Wood for a version of 'Train Kept A Rollin".

BELL, MAGGIE

Maggie Bell is a Scottish-born blues-rock vocalist who first came to prominence as the singer for Stone the Crows, an early-Seventies progressive blues outfit. She was managed as a member of Stone the Crows (originally known as Power) and as a solo artist by Led Zeppelin manager Peter Grant, and released records on the band's Swan Song label.

Bell, who had sung in a stage production of the Who's *Tommy* in 1972, released her first solo album, 'Queen Of The Night' on Swan Song in 1974. It was produced by Jerry Wexler, and, touring with Earth, Wind and Fire, Bell made some inroads into the UK market. She followed this in 1975 with the equally well received 'Suicide Sal' which featured contributions from Jimmy Page.

In 1980 Bell formed Midnight Flyer, who also featured ex-Whitesnake drummer Dave Dowle; they released a self-titled debut album on Swan Song in 1981, produced by Bad Company guitarist Mick Ralphs. Midnight Flyer's main claim to fame was supporting AC/DC on their 'Back In Black' and 'For Those About To Rock' tours in 1981 and 1982, but their progress was hampered following the death of John Bonham and manager Peter Grant's subsequent drift into depression.

Bell released a few singles on the label in the early Eighties, prior to Swan Song's own demise in October 1983, and has continued a solo career both in the UK and abroad ever since.

BINDON, JOHN

John Bindon was an actor and bodyguard who was briefly involved with Led Zeppelin during the band's 1977 US tour. He featured heavily in what is referred to as the Oakland Incident.

Bindon's acting career began when he was spotted by film director Ken Loach who cast him in his 1967 film *Poor Cow*. He would also appear in *Performance* alongside Mick Jagger, *Get Carter* alongside Michael Caine and would also feature in the Who's film *Quadrophenia* in 1979.

His career was not without controversy, however. There were alleged connections to both the notorious Richardson Gang and to the Krays, and he had been accused of running a protection racket. He was also reported to have fraternised with Princess Margaret, sister of Queen Elizabeth II, on the Caribbean island of Mustique. And when he was given a Queen's Award for bravery for rescuing a man from the River Thames, it was shrouded with allegations he himself had thrown the man in and only attempted a rescue when a policeman appeared in the scene.

Bindon was hired by Led Zeppelin on the recommendation of tour manager Richard Cole for the band's 1977 US tour – he had previously provided security for US actors Ryan and Tatum O'Neal. Although this was the first Led Zeppelin tour of America for two years, the band were not in the best frame of mind. With Plant recovering from a 1975 car accident and Jimmy Page in the throes of various substance addictions, the tour was somewhat fraught.

'There was an extraordinary amount of tension at the start of that tour,' said Jack Calmes of Showco, the company charged with Zeppelin's tour logistics since 1973. 'It just got off to a negative start. It was definitely much darker than any Zeppelin tour ever before that time... The kind of people they had around them had deepened into some really criminal types. I think Richard Cole and, perhaps, some of the band and everybody around the band was so far into drugs at that point, that the drugs turned on them. They still had their moments of greatness (but) some of the shows were grinding and not very inspired.'

With gigs on the tour being cut short for various reasons, ranging from violent thunderstorms to Page contracting stomach cramps, everything came to a head after the band's performance at the Day on the Green concert at Oakland-Almeda County Coliseum in Oakland, California. Bindon allegedly pushed a member of Graham's staff out the way when the band arrived at the Coliseum. Later, after an exchange between Bindon and Bill Graham's head of security Jim Downey, he floored Downey.

John Bonham then witnessed a member of promoter Bill Graham's own security staff admonish Grant's son, Warren, when he tried to remove a dressing-room sign. Bonham intervened, kicking the man. When Grant heard about the incident, he, Bindon and tour manager Richard Cole found the protagonist in a trailer and, with Cole guarding the door, administered a severe beating. Led Zeppelin would only perform at a gig the next day if Graham signed a letter of indemnification absolving the band and entourage for the incident the previous night.

However, Graham did not sign the letter (some reports say that he did and then went back on this written agreement) and charges were brought against Bonham, Grant, Cole and Bindon. Grant immediately filed a suit against Graham, who publicly announced he would never book Led Zeppelin again. Following the second performance the band received word that Plant's son Karac had died of a stomach virus and the remainder of the tour was cancelled. Led Zeppelin would not appear in America again until their 1985 appearance at Live Aid.

Bindon was dismissed by Grant, who would later recount that hiring him had been one of his biggest mistakes. Following his involvement in the 1978 murder trial of gangster John Drake, from which Bindon would later be acquitted, he never worked in the entertainment industry again, his reputation for being awkward and the allegations of gangland connections smearing his name.

He spent his final years as a recluse at his Belgravia home. He died aged 50, at the Chelsea and Westminster Hospital, allegedly of complications arising from an AIDS-related illness. He is believed to have been the inspiration behind the Vinnie Jones character Big Chris in the film *Lock, Stock And Two Smoking Barrels*.

BLACK CROWES

The Black Crowes are a Southern rock band from Atlanta, Georgia, who swiftly rose to prominence following their 'Shake Your Money Maker' debut album, released in 1990 on the American Recordings label and who went on to consolidate their success with 'The Southern Harmony And Musical Companion' album, released in 1992.

In 1999, the band performed two pairs of gigs with Jimmy Page in New York and Los Angeles, at which they played a selection of Led Zeppelin material, as well as their own songs and some blues rock standards. The results of the Los Angeles shows, at the Greek Theatre, were released as the double CD 'Live At The Greek' album on TVT Records in July 2000.

Contractual problems meant that the Black Crowes' own songs, including 'Remedy', 'Hard To Handle', 'She Talks To Angels' and 'Wiser Time' could not be featured on the album (which was initially released as a download only). Also, the Led Zeppelin songs 'Misty Mountain Hop' and 'In The Light' appeared only on the Japanese version.

TRACKLISTING:

Disc One: *Celebration Day/Custard Pie/Sick Again/What Is And What Should Never Be/Woke Up This Morning/Shapes Of Things/Sloppy Drunk/Ten Years Gone/In My Time Of Dying/Your Time Is Gonna Come.* **Disc Two:** *The Lemon Song/ Nobody's Fault But Mine/ Heartbreaker/Hey Hey What Can I Do/Mellow Down Easy/Oh Well/ Shake Your Money Maker/You Shook Me/Out On The Tiles/Whole Lotta Love.*

BLACK COUNTRY WOMAN

The 14th track from 1975's epic 'Physical Graffiti' album is an acoustic blues number originally entitled 'Never Ending Doubting Woman Blues'. As the title implies, it refers to the constant nagging of a woman which was part of a spoken outro by Robert Plant, although that never actually made it to the final version.

The song was originally recorded during 1972 sessions for 'Houses Of The Holy' at Mick Jagger's Stargroves home which hosted the Rolling Stones mobile studio; the songs were actually recorded in the garden. In fact, engineer Eddie Kramer can be heard mentioning a plane flying overheard at the beginning of the track. The only time Led Zeppelin performed 'Black Country Woman' in concert was on the 1977 US tour, merging the song with 'Bron-Yr-Aur Stomp'. It has been

performed in concert by Robert Plant and Allison Krauss.

BLACK DOG

The opening track from Led Zeppelin's fourth album, 'Black Dog' must surely rate as one of the band's most easily recognisable songs. It features the highest vocal note that Robert Plant has ever sung on a Led Zeppelin track.

The title was taken from a nameless black Labrador that used to wander around Headley Grange, where the band recorded several of their albums, although the dog has little to do with the lyrical content of the song which is more carnal in nature.

'Not all my stuff is meant to be scrutinised,' Plant told Cameron Crowe in an interview for *Rolling Stone* magazine in 1975. 'Things like "Black Dog" are blatant, let's-do-it-in-the-bath type things, but they make their point just the same.'

The main riff was written by bassist John Paul Jones (who is credited alongside Page and Plant), who was looking to come up with something that made it difficult for people to dance to. 'I wanted to try an electric blues with a rolling bass part but it couldn't be too simple,' Jones explained to Cameron Crowe. 'I wanted it to turn back on itself. I showed it to the guys, and we fell into it. We struggled with the turnaround, until Bonham figured out that you just four-time as if there's no turn-around. That was the secret.'

'Black Dog' was an immediate live favourite with the band, first performed on 5 March 1971 in Belfast, and, despite rarely being used on the band's 1977 US tour, was back in the set for 1979's Knebworth shows. It was also performed on the Page and Plant tour of 1995, and Plant has performed the song as a solo artist, it appears on his DVD *Soundstage: Robert Plant And The Strange Sensation*, whilst Page performed the song on his tour with David Coverdale alongside Whitesnake's 'Still Of The Night', a song heavily influenced by Led Zeppelin. Plant and Alison Krauss have also been performing the song live.

'Black Dog' was released as a single in territories around the world, aside from the UK, in 1971, backed with 'Misty Mountain Hop'.

BLACK MOUNTAIN SIDE

The sixth track from Led Zeppelin's 1968 debut album is an acoustic folk instrumental credited to Jimmy Page, which is influenced by both the traditional folk song 'Down By Black Waterside' and the Bert Jansch song 'Blackwaterside' from his 1966 album 'Jack Orion' (see JANSCH, BERT).

In the song, Page uses his guitar to simulate the sound of a sitar and is accompanied by Indian musician Viram Jasani on tabla. The overall affect is to lend the song an Eastern feel, which Led Zeppelin would further explore to more emphatic effect on 'Kashmir'.

The Led Zeppelin song has attracted some controversy, not least over the fact that Page himself took credit for the song despite its evident origins in the aforementioned traditional song. Despite claims by Jansch that Page ripped him off (folk-rocker Al Stewart laid claim to teaching Page the chord progression for the song), no legal action has ever been forthcoming.

'Black Mountain Side' was performed live as part of a medley with 'White Summer', both performed with Page sitting on a stool. The song was performed up until the band's fifth US tour in 1970, and was restored to the Zeppelin live set for the 1977 US tour. On the band's final 1980 European tour it was used as an intro to 'Kashmir'. Page would also perform the song with the Firm. It has been covered by the likes of Dread Zeppelin and Vanilla Fudge.

BLACK SABBATH

Heavy-metal pioneers Black Sabbath were contemporaries of Led Zeppelin and hailed from Birmingham, the same area of the country as Robert Plant and Jimmy Page.

The title track of Black Sabbath's second album, 1970's 'Paranoid' features a riff strikingly similar to Led Zeppelin's 1968 track 'Dazed And Confused'. It is the subject of a fan video posted on the YouTube website which can be viewed here: *www.youtube.com/watch?v=BO5thW2M2tk*

The two bands were close friends, and would visit each other in the studio. Bill Ward, drummer with Black Sabbath, has said: 'We used to jam together a lot, and some of these were recorded. Where are those tapes? I wish I knew!'

Sabbath bassist Geezer Butler expanded this relationship to *Classic Rock* magazine in 2010: 'It did happen, yes. When we did "Sabotage" in early 1975 at Morgan Studios in North West London. The Zeppelin guys came down, and both bands did get together for a jam. I have no clue if it was recorded, though. I suspect it was, but what happened to the tapes…who knows? They might even have been wiped. But in those days

everything was recorded, which is why you ended up with things like "The Troggs Tapes".

'But we were on very good terms socially with Zeppelin, especially with John Bonham. We spent many a night drinking with him and putting stuff up our noses. That's probably the thing which amazes me most – with everything we got up to back then, how am I still alive?'

BOLESKINE HOUSE

Boleskine House is a residence situated on the south shore of Loch Ness, near the village of Foyers in Scotland. It used to be owned by renowned occultist Aleister Crowley and, between the early Seventies and 1991, was owned by Jimmy Page. He has professed a keen interest in the work of Crowley, once referring to him as 'A misunderstood genius of the 20th century'.

Boleskine House was built by Archibald Fraser in the late 18th

century. It was owned by Crowley between 1899 and 1913. Crowley specifically sought out a residence like Boleskine in order to undertake a certain occult ritual found in *The Book Of Abramalin*, a 14th-century work by the magician of the same name. Popular myth has it that, although Crowley began his sacred ritual, raising the required entity, he never performed a banishing ritual, leaving the place open to much speculation.

'Yes, it was owned by Aleister Crowley,' Page acknowledged to *Rolling Stone* in 1975. 'But there were two or three owners before Crowley moved into it. It was also a church that was burned to the ground, with the congregation in it. And that's the site of the house. Strange things have happened in that house that had nothing to do with Crowley. The bad vibes were already there. A man was beheaded there and sometimes you can hear his head rolling down. I haven't actually heard it, but a friend of mine, who is extremely straight and doesn't know anything about anything like that at all, heard it. He thought it was the cats bungling around.

'I wasn't there at the time, but he told the help: "Why don't you let the cats out at night? They make a terrible racket, rolling about in the halls". And they said, 'The cats are locked in a room every night'. Then they told him the story of the house. So that sort of thing was there before Crowley got there. Of course, after Crowley there have been suicides, people carted off to mental hospitals...'

The rock face behind Boleskine House is where Page filmed his fantasy sequence for the film *The Song Remains The Same*. The house has remained a private residence since Page sold it in 1991.

BONHAM, DEBORAH

Deborah Bonham is the sister of late Led Zeppelin drummer John Bonham and the aunt of Bonham's son Jason. She is also a recording artist in her own right, with three critically applauded albums under her belt.

Bonham – who lived at John Bonham's Old Hyde residence in Cutnall Green, Worcestershire – began writing and recording material with Jason in her teens. She was mentored to a certain extent by Robert Plant, and recorded her initial demos at his house nearby. These were sent out anonymously, securing Bonham a deal with French label Carrere, for whom she recorded 1985's 'For You The Moon' album.

It would be nine years before a follow-up would appear, this time with an all-new band built around Bonham and her husband/guitarist Peter Bullick (ex-Paddy Goes To Holyhead). 'The Old Hyde' saw a more stylistic shift towards more hard rock and blues-based material and was released on the Track label. Bonham's next album, 'Duchess' was released through

Track in 2008, and featured a duet with Paul Rodgers.

Bonham has toured with the likes of Alannah Myles, Foreigner, Humble Pie, and Uli Jon Roth.

In 2009 she, along with Bonham's mother Joan accepted the Tommy Vance Inspiration Award on behalf of John at the *Classic Rock* Roll of Honour Awards in London.

BONHAM, JASON

Jason Bonham is the son of late Led Zeppelin drummer John Bonham. He performed with Zeppelin at the band's hugely popular 2007 reunion show at London's O$_2$ Arena.

Bonham was first seen as a young boy in the film *The Song Remains The Same*, drumming on a scaled-down kit. As a child he was a keen Motocross participant, encouraged by his father, but ultimately, and somewhat unsurprisingly, music proved to have a greater calling for him.

Aged 17 he joined the band Airrace, for whom he recorded the album 'Shaft Of Light' for Atlantic Records. He then joined hopeful UK AOR band Virginia Wolf, with whom he cut 'Virginia Wolf' (1985) and 'Push' (1987) and toured with the Firm in America.

In 1988 Bonham drummed on Jimmy Page's 'Outrider' album, and also appeared with the three surviving members of Led Zeppelin at the Atlantic Records 40th Anniversary Concert in New York.

Bonham formed his own quartet, Bonham, in 1988, with whom he released two records, 1989's Zeppelin-like 'The Disregard Of Timekeeping' and 1992's 'The Mad Hatter', although the lukewarm response to the more than worthy second album, in the face of the grunge onslaught, proved to be the band's undoing. In the interim Bonham made his second appearance with Led Zeppelin during an impromptu jam at his wedding to Jan Charteris in Kidderminster.

Having drummed with Paul Rodgers on the latter's 1994 album 'Muddy Waters Blues', Bonham then formed Motherland. A year later he appeared with sister Zoe, also a musician, when his father was inducted into the Rock and Roll Hall of Fame. In 1997 he paid tribute to John with 'In The Name Of My Father: The Zepset' and in 1999 joined the band the Healing Sixes.

Bonham also had a role in the 2001 Mark Wahlberg film *Rock Star* as a member of the fictional band Steel Dragon (loosely based on Judas Priest) and in 2006 he appeared in the US reality TV show *SuperGroup* alongside Ted Nugent, Anthrax's Scott Ian, Biohazard's Evan Seinfield and former Skid Row singer Sebastian Bach.

He has also toured and recorded with the Quireboys, UFO and Foreigner, and teamed up once again with the remaining members of Led Zeppelin for the 2007 reunion show at London's O$_2$ Arena.

He then put together a new line-up of Bonham featuring original guitarist Ian Hart and former Baton Rouge singer Kelly Keeling to tour in America.

BONHAM, JOHN

When John Bonham was still at school, his headmaster once wrote in his school report: 'He will either end up a dustman or a millionaire.'

As history now relates, John Bonham didn't just become a millionaire. He became a millionaire thanks to his drumming prowess. He became a millionaire because John Bonham was the drummer for Led Zeppelin. John Bonham became the greatest drummer the rock world has ever seen.

Back in May 1948 (May 31, to be precise), such thoughts were the furthest thing from the minds of his parents Joan and Jack (better known as Jacko). They were dealing with the fact that, after a 26-hour labour, John Henry Bonham had arrived in this world with an enlarged and bruised cranium, prompting John's grandmother Amy to return to the family home in Redditch to announce, 'Our Joan's had one of those funny babies!'

Not that any of this bothered the young Bonham. By the age of five he was creating a drum kit out of almost anything he could lay his hands on – biscuit tins, coffee jars, even younger brother Michael! Although he never had any formal drum lessons,

Bonham's percussive prowess carried on unabated. Whilst still at school he would occasionally stand in for local bands such as the Blue Star Trio and Gerry Levene and the Avengers.

Although Bonham would take up an apprenticeship with his father as a trainee carpenter (his enthusiasm for the family building trade would never leave him), he still indulged his passion for drums. He ended up in his first semi-pro outfit, Terry Webb and the Spiders, in 1964 after a variety of appearances with local bands. He moved on through the Nicky James Movement and then the Senators, with whom Bonham actually cut a single, 'She's A Mod', before he began drumming full-time.

Bonham ended up in a local blues band called the Crawling King Snakes, and formed a friendship with their singer, Robert Plant. Even though the drummer would quit the band, returning to A Way of Life (with whom he'd drummed before joining up with the Snakes), he remained in touch with Plant, and when the latter formed the Band of Joy he asked his old pal to join him. The band recorded several demos, although no recording contract was offered, but did end up supporting folk rocker Tim Rose when he ventured over to the UK. When Rose returned to tour in 1968 his usual drummer Aynsley Dunbar was unavailable. Impressed with Bonham, he tracked him down and offered the talented youngster the gig at £40 per week.

It was whilst drumming with Rose that Jimmy Page and Peter Grant first encountered Bonham, at a gig at the Hampstead Country Club in North London in July 1968. Plant was in tow as well, as he'd already been sounded out by Page with as view to joining his new band. Page's original vocal choice was fast-rising UK star Terry Reid, but he'd declined, having signed a contract to support the Rolling Stones in America. He did, however, recall seeing the Band of Joy and suggested that, if Page wanted a singer, he check out a man he called 'The wild man of the Black Country'. And he suggested Page check out the drummer too.

By the time Page tracked down Plant, the singer was fronting the blues band Hobbstweedle, who he would leave to join up with Page. They, in turn, tracked down this supposedly impressive tub-thumper, Procol Harum's BJ Wilson and sessionman Clem Cattini having declined Page's initial overtures.

Impressed with what they'd seen on the night with Tim Rose, Page and Grant offered Bonham the gig, though he appeared initially reluctant, allegedly entertaining other offers from both Joe Cocker and Chris Farlowe. History shows that Bonham eventually chose Led Zeppelin. 'I decided I liked their music better

than Cocker's or Farlowe's,' Bonham was quoted as saying in *Rolling Stone* magazine.

Probably due to the fact that his friend Robert Plant was on board, Bonham liked his new bandmates, settled relatively easily into life in Led Zeppelin. The band's tour, as the New Yardbirds, in 1968 to fulfil contractual obligations in Scandinavia, might have been a baptism of fire, but it allowed them to settle, learn their way around each other and develop what would become the trademark Led Zeppelin sound away from the glare of the media spotlight. What press coverage there was merely served to develop the mystique that would surround the band for time immemorial.

Bonham's sheer power as a drummer was aligned with undoubted groove. Phil Collins, who would drum with the surviving members of Led Zeppelin at Live Aid in 1985, recalled his first sighting of Bonham at London's Marquee Club thus: 'I was dumbstruck by the drummer. He was doing things with his bass drum that I'd never seen or heard before – the last two beats of a triplet, something I've stolen and do whenever possible. He played a solo, and again I'd never heard or seen a drummer play like that. He played with his hands on the drums – I later found out that as a bricklayer he had very hard hands, and it was obvious on seeing him solo that night.'

Photo licensed from Getty Images

Bonham's drumming prowess was matched by his love of a good time, and this tended to reach epic proportions when Led Zeppelin would undertake their lengthy world tours. Tales of excess are the stuff of legend, whether it be throwing television sets out of hotel windows, demolishing hotel rooms in Japan with Samurai swords, riding a motorbike around the Hyatt Hotel in Los Angeles, fist-fights with unruly promoters and even forcing a photographer to crawl naked down the corridor of the band's 1977 tour plane, by way of initiation into the Zeppelin enclave.

And yet John Bonham was a committed family man. He suffered from terrible depressions when touring with Zeppelin brought about by homesickness and alcohol, and later headier excess inspired by tour manager Richard Cole. He also suffered from terrible nerves prior to Zeppelin gigs. His commitment to his wife Pat and son Jason (daughter Zoe would arrive later) was highlighted in Bonham's own fantasy sequence in the 1976 film *The Song Remains The Same* which featured the drummer enjoying time with his family at his beloved Old Hyde home in Worcestershire, as well as indulging his passion for motor vehicles by racing at Santa Pod raceway in Northamptonshire. This love of cars and bikes also manifested itself through his son Jason, who shared his father's keenness for Motocross as a youngster. All to the tune of 'Moby Dick', obviously.

Descriptions of Bonham as something of a Jekyll and Hyde character are correct. Tour reports are many that suggest how he could turn following one drink too many. And yet Bonham's revelry and drinking had been a constant throughout Zeppelin's lifetime. There is little to suggest that it caused the kind of friction within the band that Page's own battle with substances seemed to in their later days. However the fact that Bonham had collapsed at a show in Nuremburg on 27 June 1980 might have indicated that the years of excess were taking their toll. However Bonham completed Zeppelin's European tour, and his younger brother Michael told co-author Ewing, 'He returned home on 9 August in good spirits. And he gave Jacko some news which was to make him a very happy man. On 31 July he was to make his home at the cottage in the grounds of the Old Hyde.'

In his book *My Brother John*, the late Michael recalls the day John Bonham was picked up by Led Zeppelin employee Rex King to be driven to rehearsals with Led Zeppelin at Bray Studios as the band prepared for their first tour of America since 1977.

'On a beautiful sunny morning, John arrived on site early and in a very cheerful mood and thought it would be a good idea to get all the cars washed and polished. It was Wednesday 24 September and he was eager to get them out of the way before setting off for Jimmy's house in Windsor to start rehearsals. At lunchtime John's personal assistant Rex King arrived at the farm to take him down to London. As they disappeared down the long driveway I waved "Our Kid" goodbye.'

Bonham allegedly drank heavily on the journey – four quadruple vodkas were consumed with a ham roll when they stopped for a bite to eat on the way down, according to one story. The drinking continued at rehearsals and the whole band repaired to Page's Old Mill house in Clewer, Windsor for the evening. Bonham fell asleep and was put to bed after midnight, being placed on his side. At 1.45pm the next day, both John Paul Jones and tour manager Benji Le Fevre went to wake Bonham. They found him dead.

An inquest was held at which it was stated that the 32-year old John Bonham had died from asphyxiation due to vomit and a verdict of accidental death was returned. No other drugs were found in his body. Following Bonham's death the rumour mill went into overdrive. Would Led Zeppelin continue? And if so, who could replace the powerhouse that was John Henry Bonham? Bad Company drummer Simon Kirke was one name mentioned. So was ELO's Bev Bevan. Bonham's own Vanilla Fudge friend Carmine Appice, Jethro Tull's Barriemore Barlow and Rainbow's Cozy Powell were other possibilities mooted.

In the end the remaining members of Led Zeppelin – Jimmy Page, Robert Plant and John Paul Jones – along with manager Peter Grant, laid to rest all the speculation paying tribute to their dead comrade in the process.

'We wish it to be known that the loss of our dear friend and the deep respect we have for his family, together with the sense of un-divided harmony felt by ourselves and our manager, have led us to decide that we could not continue as we were. Led Zeppelin.'

BONZO'S MONTREUX

'Bonzo's Montreux', the seventh track on the posthumous 'Coda' album of 1982, is ostensibly a drum solo from John Bonham following in the style of the celebrated 'Moby Dick' from 1969's 'Led Zeppelin II'.

The piece was recorded at Mountain Studios in Switzerland during sessions for the 'Presence' album, and although written by Bonham, also features contributions from Jimmy Page and John Paul Jones. When compiling the 'Coda' album, Page subsequently added electronic effects.

'Bonzo's Montreux' has also appeared on both Led Zeppelin box sets. On the 1990 'Led Zeppelin' set it featured as a medley with 'Moby Dick'. On 1993's 'Boxed Set 2' it featured as a single track in its own right.

'Bonzo's Montreux' was never performed live.

BOOGIE WITH STU

The 13th track on 1975's 'Physical Graffiti', 'Boogie With Stu' is credited to all four members of Led Zeppelin as well as Ian Stewart, the Rolling Stones tour manager who played piano on the recording session, and 'Mrs Valens', an attempt by the band to acknowledge the mother of the late Ritchie Valens, whose 'Ooh My Head' served as inspiration for the track (see VALENS, RITCHIE).

The track developed out of a jam session recorded at Headley Grange during sessions for Led Zeppelin's 1971 fourth album. The song began life with the working title 'Sloppy Drunk'. Allegedly

AN A-Z ENCYCLOPEDIA   **35**

Jimmy Page plays mandolin on the track and Robert Plant the guitar.

The song was never performed live by the band, but did feature on an EP released in Thailand in 1975 backed by 'Custard Pie', 'Night Flight' and 'Down By The Seaside'.

BOX OF FROGS

Box of Frogs were, to all intents and purposes, a reunion of the Yardbirds, featuring in their line-up ex-Yardbirds members Chris Dreja, Paul Samwell-Smith and Jim McCarty. The band formed in 1983 and also featured vocalist John Fiddler, previously with Medicine Head and British Lions.

Box of Frogs released their debut album on Epic Records in 1984 – a pretty good selection of bluesy hard rock that featured a guest appearance from Jeff Beck. The band performed at London's Marquee Club, instigating much press speculation that Beck, along with other Yardbirds guitar alumni Eric Clapton and Jimmy Page, might join them. However all three guitarists chose to let the opportunity pass them by.

When Dreja, Samwell-Smith and McCarty stalled over a proposed US tour on which Beck had allegedly been pencilled in as lead guitarist, the band fell apart. Beck refused to play on the band's second album, 'Strange Land', and Fiddler's input was lessened, with the likes of Ian Dury, Graham Parker and Roger Chapman all guesting as vocalists alongside him. However Jimmy

Page did guest on the track 'Asylum'. Box of Frogs disbanded soon after.

The track 'Back Where I Started', from the band's debut, which was a Top 10 hit in America, was regularly performed by a re-formed Yardbirds.

BRAY STUDIOS

Bray Studios are a film and television studios near Windsor, in Berkshire. They are famous for their association with Hammer Horror films. Though sold by Hammer in 1970, they remain an active film and television studio.

Bray Studios were used by Led Zeppelin for rehearsals for a US tour in 1980, which would have been the band's first since the ill-fated 1977 tour. It was at Bray Studios where Led Zeppelin assistant Rex King picked up John Bonham on 25 September 1980, driving him to Jimmy Page's Old Mill House in Clewer, Windsor, on the night of his fatal alcohol overdose.

BREDON, ANNE

Anne Bredon is an American folk singer, best known for writing the song 'Babe I'm Gonna Leave You' whilst a student at UC Berkeley in the Fifties. The song was covered by Led Zeppelin on their 1968 debut album, and subsequently underwent a change of writing credit.[See BABE I'M GONNA LEAVE YOU]

Today Bredon resides in California where she concentrates

on making jewellery. Her work can be viewed here: *www.galwestcom/jewelry/anne_bredon/index.htm*

BRING IT ON HOME

'Bring It On Home' is the ninth and final track from Led Zeppelin's second album, released in 1968. The song was written by bluesman Willie Dixon and originally recorded in 1963 by Sonny Boy Williamson.

The Zeppelin version of the song is ostensibly a new composition penned by Jimmy Page and Robert Plant, although inspired by the Willie Dixon song. As homage to Dixon, Zeppelin used small parts of his song in the intro and outro. This caused Chess Records, who had released the Sonny Boy Williamson version on the 1965 album 'The Real Folk Blues', to take action, winning an out-of-court settlement in the Seventies for copyright infringement. Willie Dixon, however, was in turn forced to sue Arc Music, the publishing arm of Chess Records, to benefit, reclaiming a writing credit and acquiring royalties he was due.

'There's only a tiny bit taken from Sonny Boy Williamson's version and we threw that in as a tribute to him,' Jimmy Page told *Trouser Press* magazine in 1977. 'People say, "Oh, 'Bring It On Home' is stolen." Well, there's only a little bit in the song that relates to anything that had gone before it, just the end.'

'Bring It On Home' was performed in concert between 1970 and 1973. Live versions appear on both the *Led Zeppelin* DVD and 'How The West Was Won' live album. It was also performed by the remaining members of Zeppelin at Jason Bonham's wedding reception in Kidderminster in May 1990.

It has also been covered by Hawkwind, the Edgar Broughton Band, Michael White and Dread Zeppelin.

BRON-Y-AUR STOMP

Mis-spelled on the album cover for 'Led Zeppelin III' from the original Bron-Yr-Aur, this is a country inspired piece that began life at writing sessions at the Gwynedd-based cottage used as a writing retreat by Jimmy Page and Robert Plant in 1970, but ultimately recorded at Headley Grange, Island Studios in London and Ardent Studios in Tennessee, with additional input from John Paul Jones. The song is credited to Page, Plant and Jones.

The song was performed live, with bassist Jones using an upright bass and drummer John Bonham adding harmony vocals to Plant's performance. A 1975 performance from Earls Court in London can be seen on the *Led Zeppelin* DVD.

BRON-YR-AUR

Bron-Yr-Aur (sometimes mispelled Bron-Y-Aur) is an 18th Century Welsh cottage in Gwynedd, in mid-

West Wales, famous for its connections with Led Zeppelin. Bron-Yr-Aur means 'golden breast' in Welsh.

It had been used as a holiday home by the family of Robert Plant in the Fifties, and became famous for being used as a retreat (despite the place having no running water or electricity) by Jimmy Page and Plant, as well as Plant's then wife and daughter and Page's then partner, and two Led Zeppelin roadies, Clive Coulson and Sandy MacGregor.

Aside from the obvious Zeppelin songs 'Bron-Yr-Aur' and 'Bron-Y-Aur-Stomp' (the house's name was mis-spelled on the album cover of 'Led Zeppelin III'), the likes of 'Over The Hills And Far Away', 'The Rover', 'The Crunge', 'Down

By The Seaside' and 'Poor Tom' all have their basis in writing sessions at the cottage.

Page has credited Bron-Yr-Aur as being hugely instrumental in his relationship with Plant, stating, 'It was the first time I really came to know Robert. Actually living together at Bron-Yr-Aur, as opposed to occupying nearby hotel rooms. The songs took us into areas that changed the band, and it established a standard of travelling for inspiration…which is the best thing a musician can do. We'd been working solidly right up to that point. Even recordings were done in the road. We had this time off and Robert suggested the cottage. I certainly hadn't been to that area of Wales. So we took

our guitars down there and played a few bits and pieces. This wonderful countryside, panoramic views and having the guitars…it was just an automatic thing to be playing.'

Page and Plant returned to Bron-Yr-Aur cottage to film some sequences for their 1994 'Unledded' project. The cottage is today a private residence. One assumes that it now features electricity and running water.

BRON-YR-AUR (SONG)

'Bron-Yr-Aur' is the eighth song on 1975's 'Physical Graffiti' album. It is an instrumental guitar piece written by Jimmy Page, and simply features Page on guitar.

The song was inspired by the cottage, Bron-Yr-Aur, at which Page spent time writing with Robert Plant in 1970. Indeed it was written and recorded during those 1970 writing sessions for 'Led Zeppelin III'.

Although rarely performed live by Zeppelin, a version does appear on the bootleg 'Live On Blueberry Hill', which is introduced thus by Robert Plant: 'This is a thing called "Bron-Yr-Aur". This is a name of the little cottage in the mountains of Snowdonia in Wales, and Bron-Yr-Aur is the Welsh equivalent of the phrase "Golden Breast". This is so because of its position every morning as the sun rises and it's a really remarkable place. And so after staying there for a while and deciding it was time to leave for various reasons,

we couldn't really just leave it and forget about it. You've probably all been to a place like that, only we can tell you about it and you can't tell us.'

'Bron-Yr-Aur' is used in the film *The Song Remains The Same* in a scene where the band members are driven through New York on a limousine, although the song does not feature on the actual soundtrack.

The song has been covered by, amongst others, Michael White and Coheed and Cambria, and also features in the Cameron Crowe film *Almost Famous*.

BUELL, BEBE

Buell, an American-born model, occasional musician and former *Playboy* Playmate, dated Jimmy Page during the Seventies. She is most famous for being the mother of actress Liv Tyler, the daughter she had with Aerosmith frontman Steven Tyler (although for years Buell allowed her then-partner Todd Rundgren to believe he was the father).

BUTTERFIELD COURT

Butterfield Court is the tower block that can be seen on the cover of Led Zeppelin's 1971 fourth album. Butterfield Court is in the Eve Hill area of Dudley which gave rise, probably in the wake of the allegations of backwards masking by right-wing religious groups that followed the release of the album, to ludicrous suggestions that it had been used by the band because of its approximation to 'Ev-il'!

Jimmy Page subsequently explained the cover, which featured a painting the guitarist supposedly acquired in a Reading junk shop (Page has since claimed it was Plant that bought the picture) hung on a partly demolished house wall, with the Butterfield Court tower block in the background, thus: 'It represented the change in the balance which was going on. There was the old countryman and the blocks of flats being knocked down. It was just a way of saying that we should look after the earth, not rape and pillage it.'

The tower is often wrongly believed to be the Prince of Wales Court, which has subsequently been demolished. On a clear day the 20-storey high Butterfield Court can allegedly be seen 45 miles away in Wales.

CADILLAC

For five years the Cadillac automobile brand used 'Rock And Roll' from Led Zeppelin IV as soundtrack to the 'Breakthrough' series of ads. These began airing at the start of 2002 in America, during the coverage for the *Super Bowl*, traditionally one of the programmes with the highest audience reach in the States.

This is how www.slate.com described the advert: 'It's a traffic jam, cars stuck on a city street, horns bleating. A handsome yuppie is stuck in it, until he points his vintage Caddy down a side street and simply leaves it all behind. Suddenly he's on the open highway, cutting through the desert, presumably driving as fast as he wants to, top down. There's a familiar crashing of drums and the music kicks in: Led Zeppelin's "Rock And Roll". "Been a long time..." etc, goes the Robert Plant warble over the Jimmy Page riff that you've heard a million times. Then, in the rear-view mirror: another car. It's the new Cadillac CTS. The music drops out and an announcer says, "A legend...reborn." The music cranks up again and the new CTS blows past the Zep-loving yuppie. "Cadillac CTS", the announcer says, sounding vaguely smug. "Break through".'

There were to be variations on this theme over the next few years. You can check out one here: *www.spike.com/video/led-zeppelin-2/2419272*

The first Zeppelin song ever to be used in a commercial, this seemed to have an impact. Sales rose by 16 per cent in the first 12 months of the band's involvement. While this can't be strictly put down to the music alone, the recognition factor must have played its role.

A lot of fans were upset that Zeppelin had seemingly tainted their reputation by getting into the commercial world. However, Plant stoutly defended the choice to www.launch.com: 'I think that's appropriate. I don't know how people view it, but as far as a young generation goes, if you hear that music in as many possible places as you can outside of the normal home for it, then it can only be a good thing.'

The run of ads came to a close in 2006 when Cadillac moved from the Leon Burnett ad agency to Modernista! The latter decided it was time for change in approach, and 'Rock And Roll' was dropped.

CANDY STORE ROCK

The fifth track from the 1976 album 'Presence', this was actually released as a single in America (with 'Royal Orleans' on the B-side), and amazingly failed to chart. Co-written by Robert Plant and Jimmy Page, some of the lyrics were inspired by Elvis Presley songs, and the whole feel is of a Fifties rock'n'roll number.

The band only took an hour to write the song recorded at Musicland Studios in Munich, with Plant singing from a wheelchair because he was recovering from a road accident in Greece.

This is one song the band never performed live, although Page did briefly play a riff from it during a show at the Riverfront Colosseum in Cincinnati, Ohio on 20 April 1977. And on July 26 1995, at Wembley Arena in London, Page and Plant worked this into a one-minute improvised intro to 'Black Dog'.

CAROUSELAMBRA

Fifth track from the band's final studio album, 1979's 'In Through The Out Door', the tongue-twisting title is supposed to be a nod to the fact that the style of the song was similar to carousel music.

In many ways, it's an unusual song for Zeppelin in that Page's guitar work is overshadowed by John Paul Jones on synthesiser. The song was developed during rehearsals at Clearwell Castle in May 1978. It's split into three distinct sections. The first is

rather fast, the second being more sedate and allows Page the chance to play his double neck Gibson EDS-1275 – the only time he used this in the studio. The last segment returns to the quicker timbre. The synth Page used on the track is a Yamaha GX-1 which he bought from Keith Emerson after Emerson Lake and Palmer split up.

Robert Plant has stated that the lyrics were about a particular person who would be shocked when they realised what he was talking about. It's also supposed to be a continuation of the theme on 'Battle Of Evermore' from the 'Led Zeppelin IV' album.

'Carouselambra' was never performed live by Zeppelin, although they were planning to put it in the set for their 1980 North American tour. They were said to have actually rehearsed it on the day that John Bonham died.

One fan insisted the band did this as an encore at the Forum in Los Angeles on 26 June 1977. But the song to which they're referring was actually 'It'll Be Me'. You can check this out for yourself at *www.ledzeppelin.com/video/los-angeles-6-26-77-itll-be-me*

CELEBRATION DAY

Third track from 1970's 'Led Zeppelin III', this was almost left off the album. An engineer inadvertently erased the first part of John Bonham's drum opening. In the end, the only way to overcome the problem was to take out the ending of the previous song on the album, 'Friends', and put it on the start of 'Celebration Day', this being a moog synthesiser from John Paul Jones.

Talking to *Guitar World* magazine in 1993, Page said of this song: 'There's about three or four riffs going down on that one, isn't there? Half was done with a guitar in standard tuning and the other half was done on slide guitar tuned to an open A, I think. We put that together at Headley Grange. Because we rented the Rolling Stones' mobile recording studio, we could relax and take our time and develop the songs in rehearsals. I do not remember too much about that song other than that and what I told you earlier about the opening being erased. I used to play the whole thing live on my electric 12-string.'

The lyrics were very evocative of New York, and on the band's 1971 tour of America Plant often referred to this as 'The New York Song'. 'Celebration Day' was filmed for *The Song Remains The Same*, but left off the final cut and accompanying album. However, it was restored to both when the movie was released on DVD in 2007 (being added to the second disc of extras) and the double CD.

'Celebration Day' was released as a single in Poland, with 'Paranoid' (the Black Sabbath song) on the B-side. In South Africa, it was released as a single the same year with 'Immigrant Song' on the flip.

CLEARWELL CASTLE

Originally known as Clearwell Court, this gothic-style mansion was built in 1728 by Thomas Wyndham.

Becoming Clearwell Castle in

1908, it was to be the setting for a few renowned bands, seeking inspiration. It was here that Deep Purple decamped in 1973 to write the 'Burn' album. Black Sabbath also came down to work on songs for their 'Sabbath Bloody Sabbath'. Led Zeppelin used the facilities to rehearse the 'In Through The Out Door' album in 1978.

These days, Clearwell Castle is primarily known as a wedding venue. Should you fancy getting married at a location associated with Zeppelin, then check out *www.stayattherock.com/#/clearwell-castle/4533488229*

CLIFTON, PETE

The Australian born director who helmed the movie *The Song Remains The Same*.

Born in 1947, Clifton got his first taste of working with a band when he followed the Easybeats on a UK tour in 1967, the resulting film being called *Somewhere Between Heaven And Woolworth's*. Subsequently, he worked with Jimi Hendrix, and was also behind *The London Rock And Roll Show*, documenting a Wembley Stadium gig in 1973, featuring the likes of Jerry Lee Lewis, Chuck Berry Bill Haley and the Comets, Little Richard and Screaming Lord Sutch.

In 1974, Clifton was asked to take over as director on *The Song Remains The Same* when original choice Joe Massot was fired. But things turned sour when Peter

Grant, suspicious that Clifton had stolen some negatives, had the Australian's house searched while he and his family were on holiday! All that was found was some footage, he had intended to give to the band as a gift.

Clifton has subsequently worked with a number of artists, including Frank Sinatra, America, the Rolling Stones and Eric Clapton. In 2010 he was working a movie called *The Bloody Ashes* about the infamous 'Bodyline' cricket test series between Australia and England in 1932-33 and developing a film based on the Peter Fitzsimons novel *Tobruk*.

CODA

To call this the last official Led Zeppelin album is to overstate the value of what is no more than a hotch-potch collection of outtakes released in 1982, and spanning the band's 12-year career. While it might have been of interest to diehards, it did little service to the legend of a band who always took such pride in presenting nothing but the highest quality work.

Said Jimmy Page of the decision to release this album: '"Coda" was released, basically, because there was so much bootleg stuff out. We thought, "Well, if there's that much interest, then we may as well put the rest of our studio stuff out".'

It's more likely that this was a contractual obligation, as the band still owed Atlantic Records one more album when they started up

Swan Song Records in 1974.

The album opens with 'We're Gonna Groove', which it's claimed came from a studio session at Morgan Studios in north-west London in 1969. In reality, it was taken from a live show at the Royal Albert Hall in London the following year, with the guitar parts overdubbed.

'Poor Tom' is taken from recording sessions for the 'Led Zeppelin III' album at Olympia Studios in London during 1970.

'I Can't Quit You Baby' is down as being from a rehearsal tape. However, like 'We're Gonna Groove' it's from a 1970 show at the Royal Albert Hall. For reasons best known to the band, all the crowd noises were either removed or muted as much as possible to give the impression of this being a rehearsal.

'Walter's Walk' was an outtake from the 1972 album 'Houses Of The Holy', although it's generally assumed the song was built from the basic recordings for the 'Coda' album.

There are then three songs from 'In Through The Out Door' sessions: 'Ozone Baby', 'Darlene' and 'Wearing And Tearing'. Even here, though, there's been some tampering, the drum sounds having added reverb.

'Bonzo's Montreux' is a John Bonham drum extravaganza recorded at Mountain Studios in Montreux in 1976 with added electronic effects.

The overall impression is of a record that really only has historical interest rather than genuine musical quality. And quite why the band felt obliged to mask the truth about the origins of some of the songs remains a mystery.

Still, with the cachet of being a Zeppelin album, 'Coda' did well. It reached Number 6 in the US charts, selling over a million copies. In the UK it made it to Number 4.

It was John Paul Jones who came up with the title of the album, as it meant the end of a musical piece. Rather appropriate.

TRACKLISTING:
We're Gonna Groove/Poor Tom/ I Can't Quit You Baby/Walter's Walk/Ozone Baby/Darlene/Bonzo's Montreux/Wearing And Tearing. The 1993 reissue added *Baby Come On Home/Travelling Riverside Blues/White Summer/Black Mountain Side/Hey Hey What Can I Do.*

COLE, RICHARD
The man who was Led Zeppelin's tour manager from 1968 to the Eighties (basically, their entire career), Richard Cole has rather

blotted his copybook with the members of the band in recent times, thanks to his contributions to Stephen Davis' infamous biography, *Hammer Of The Gods.*

Peter Grant claimed that Cole had been got at by Davis and others when he was still recovering from various problems and hadn't realised where these revelations would end up.

This seems highly unlikely as Cole himself has openly complained about his involvement in the book, but only because he was paid just $1,250. At no time has the man himself tried to suggest that he was coerced into the project through any devious means.

Cole got his start in the music business working as road manager in 1965 for Unit 4 + 2. From there, he went on to to work with the Who, the New Vaudeville Band (managed by Grant) and Vanilla Fudge.

Over his years with Zeppelin, Cole became a somewhat controversial yet effective figure. It has been claimed by some in the band that stories about them from *Hammer Of The Gods* actually happened to Cole, who then transposed them for effect.

In addition, he was suspected of stealing over $200,000 from a safe-deposit box at the Drake Hotel in New York during 1973. These were the band's takings – in cash! – for Zeppelin's last show at Madison Square Garden on that tour. He passed a lie-detector test, though, and was never charged.

However, nobody was arrested for the crime.

Cole was fired by the band in 1980 after their last European show as it was felt his substance dependence had become a major issue. He went to Italy to recover, but was detained for a while as a suspected terrorist involved in the 1980 bombing of Bologna Railway Station – one incident he was clearly innocent of!

Since then, he's worked with Black Sabbath, Eric Clapton, Ozzy Osbourne and Lita Ford.

In 1992, he published his own account of life with Zeppelin. Called *Stairway To Heaven: Led Zeppelin Uncensored*, it did not go down at all well with Jimmy Page. He said: 'There's a book written by our former road manager Richard Cole that has made me completely ill. I'm so mad about it that I can't even bring myself to read the whole thing. The two bits that I have read are so ridiculously false that I'm sure if I read the rest I'd be able to sue Cole and the publishers. But it would be so painful to read that it wouldn't be worth it.'

However, Cole remains a pivotal figure in the Zeppelin story. Now 63, he divides his time between London, California and Venice.

COLLINS, PHIL
The famed former child actor and Genesis drummer played with Zeppelin for their Live Aid performance on 13 July 1985 in Philadelphia. Jimmy Page, though,

blames the hapless star for ruining Zeppelin's set: 'I don't want to blame anyone but the two drummers (Phil Collins and Tony Thompson of Chic) hadn't learned their parts. You can get away with that in a pop band but not with Led Zeppelin.'

In his defence, Collins told *Playboy* magazine: 'They wanted me there early to rehearse the old Zeppelin songs, but I couldn't make it and I told them, "Listen, I know the songs. I know them backward and forward." Well, that day the tempos were all over the place, and it may have seemed like it was my fault, because I was the one who hadn't rehearsed, but I would pledge to my dying day that it wasn't me. In fact, it was Tony Thompson who was racing a bit; he was a bit nervous, I guess. It came off because of the magic of being Zeppelin; but I remember in the middle of the thing, I actually thought, "How do I get out of here?"'

Perhaps Collins was fatigued? He did a set at Wembley Stadium, then got on Concorde to fly to Philadelphia to join Zeppelin. Whatever, it was neither Zeppelin nor Collins' greatest moment.

COMMUNICATION BREAKDOWN

The seventh song on the first Zeppelin album, this has the distinction of being one of the first on which both Jimmy Page and Robert Plant worked together.

And Page does backing vocals, which was rare.

There's also one unique distinction about 'Communication Breakdown' – it's the only song the band played live on every tour they did. It was also the B-side of the single 'Good Times, Bad Times' in Mexico, France, New Zealand, Australia, Canada, Germany, Greece, Italy, the Philippines, Sweden, Japan, South Africa and Argentina.

You'll also find it in the 1998 movie *Small Soldiers*.

COMPLETE STUDIO RECORDINGS

Does what it says on the tin. Or, in this case, on the box. This is a ten-CD box set released in 1993, featuring all of the band's albums, plus an expanded edition of 'Coda'.

Oddly, it sticks to chronological sequence, apart from inserting 'Presence', before 'Physical Graffiti'. The latter, by the way, takes up two discs.

'The Complete Recordings', with all tracks remastered, and a booklet written by Cameron Crowe, sold over two million copies in America, although it peaked at a comparatively lowly Number 22.

CORRISTON, PETER

Based in Greenwich Village, New York, Peter Corriston is the man who designed the sleeve for 'Physical Graffiti'.

Corriston created the remarkable

tenement-block cover art, based on 96 and 98 Avenue A in New York. Says the designer: 'We walked around the city for a few weeks looking for the right building. I had come up a concept for the band based on the tenement, people living there and moving in and out. The original album featured the building with the windows cut out on the cover and various sleeves that could be placed under the cover, filling the windows with the album title, track information or liner notes.'

The front cover shows the building in daylight, while the back has the same shot at night. A number of different items were included which could be seen in each window. These included both Robert Plant and Richard Cole in drag. 'Physical Graffiti' was nominated for a Grammy in 1975, in the 'Best Album Package' category, one of Corriston's five nominations over the years. He only won a solitary award, though, for the Rolling Stones' 'Tattoo You' album in 1981.

Corriston, who also worked with Andy Warhol, currently lives in Pennsylvania.

COVERDALE PAGE

In theory this was a relationship that could have been an utter disaster. Equally, it could have been one of the most thriving collaborations of the era. The prospect of Whitesnake's David Coverdale teaming up with Jimmy Page confused a lot of people. But

it happened in 1991. Now, at the time there was friction between Coverdale and Plant, mainly due to the fact that the latter felt the former was trading off his own style. This was based mostly on 'Still Of The Night', the Zeppelin-esque epic from the '1987' album by Whitesnake.

Plant's attitude seemed to suggest that he felt Coverdale had become a clone of himself, although at the point when '1987' was released the latter was a well-established and successful singer, having also found fame with Deep Purple prior to forming Whitesnake.

'Let's not pull any punches,' Coverdale said at the time. 'There has been something of a hate campaign conducted by Robert. A lot of the things discussed by Jimmy and myself are, I'm afraid, very personal, but there's never, ever been a problem between Mr Page and myself.

'The thing that hurt me most of all is Robert saying that we didn't know each other. When you asked before if Jimmy and I knew each other, we'd crossed paths, had maybe three chance meetings through the Seventies; whereas Robert had brought his daughter to Whitesnake shows when we played in his neck of the woods and he'd been given the whole royal treatment and all that. I knew Robert back in the Purple days, him and Bonzo. I never knew John Paul Jones. So that was a weird thing for me. But I'd

rather stay out of all that and let the music do the talking, really I admire Robert immensely – I'll leave it at that.

'That's what it was about. It wasn't anything to do with the rest of the song – it was purely the reference to the bow, which wasn't used on the record, as far as I know.' [Read more: *www.led-zeppelin.org/reference/index.php?m=assorted3#ixzz0YAHmgZGO*]

There was also a theory that, knowing Plant's antipathy towards Coverdale, Page set out to irritate his old bandmate as much as possible by working with his nemesis. At this stage, Plant had rejected Page's idea of the pair working together again. But whether someone as celebrated as Jimmy Page would take such a childish approach remains open to question.

The Coverdale-Page axis only lasted long enough to record and release one album, 1993's self-titled affair. In all honesty, it got short critical shrift at the time, but deserved better. The record is far from a disaster, and did allow the two main protagonists the chance to gel and create some interesting music.

Perhaps it was all just a little too studio-based, however. The record utilised the services of a number of different musicians that there's no cohesion. Those involved are Jorg Casas (bass), Ricky Phillips (bass), Denny Carmassi (drums), Lester Mendell (keyboards), John Harris (harmonica), Tommy Funderburk (backing vocals) and John Sambataro (backing vocals).

They also used four studios: Little Mountain (Vancouver), Criteria (Miamia), High Brow (Las Vegas) and Abbey Road (London), with Mike Fraser co-producing alongside Coverdale and Page.

Still, the album made it to Number 4 in the UK and only a slot below this in America, with four singles actually being released: 'Pride And Joy', 'Shake My Tree', 'Take Me For A Little While' and 'Take A Look At Yourself'. Sadly, this project quickly disbanded, propelled by slow ticket sales for a world tour.

One of the best rumours about this was that Page had plans to bring in John Paul Jones and Jason Bonham, and change the name of the band to...Led Zeppelin. Thankfully, this never happened.

So, is Coverdale Page an embarrassment? Not at all. Just an idea that was never able to take root. But there are said to be six still unreleased songs. Who knows, we might yet hear more.

TRACKLISTING:
Shake My Tree/Waiting On You/Take Me For A Little While/Pride And Joy/ *Over Now/Feeling Hot/Easy Does It/ Take A Look At Yourself/Don't Leave Me This Way/Absolution Blues/ Whisper A Prayer For The Dying.*

CRAWLING KING SNAKES

One of the earliest bands to feature Robert Plant on vocals. This was the one he joined after leaving home, at the age of 16. He didn't last long with them, though: 'The group was into a bit more of a commercial sound than the other bands I'd played with. I'd be hopping around the stage with the mike stand in the air. A lot of incredible things happened to us and I met a lot of people who made sure that I'd carry on in the way I was going.'

However, it was during his tenure with the Crawling King Snakes that Plant first met John Bonham. While the band were playing at the Old Hill Plaza. Bonham is said to have gone up to Plant and suggested the King Snakes needed a new drummer – him!

They rehearsed and played locally, but soon split up. Plant and Bonham subsequently did quite well. The rest of the band – lead guitarist 'Maverick', rhythm guitarist Roy Price and bassist Terry Edwards – didn't.

CROWE, CAMERON

Director and screenwriter, Cameron Crowe was the journalist who did the very first Led Zeppelin interview for

Rolling Stone magazine and wrote the booklet that accompanied 'The Complete Recordings Box Set'. He used the band as partial inspiration for his 2000 movie *Almost Famous*, which features the fictitious band Stillwater but is based at least in part on his experiences on the road with Zeppelin.

Back at that famous *Rolling Stone* feature in '75, Crowe (who was then 18) recalled 25 years later: 'Very, very proud of this one. The quest to land *Rolling Stone*'s first interview with Led Zeppelin was a rough one. The magazine had been tough on the band. Guitarist Jimmy Page vowed never to talk with them. While touring with the band for the Los Angeles Times, I attempted to talk them into speaking with me for *Rolling Stone* too. One by one they agreed, except for Page. I stayed on the road for three weeks, red-eyed from no sleep, until he finally relented...out of sympathy. I think my mother was about ready to call the police to drag me home. Needless to say, the incident shows up in a slightly different form in *Almost Famous*.'

Crowe first used a Zeppelin song in his 1981 movie *Fast Times At Ridgemont High* (this being 'Kashmir'). He then persuaded them to allow the use of 'That's The Way' in *Almost Famous*, although he was turned down for 'Stairway To Heaven' in the same film.

Now 52, Crowe has been married to Heart guitarist Nancy Wilson since 1986.

CROWLEY, ALEISTER

One dubbed 'The Wickedest Man In The World', Crowley was an occultist, writer, mountaineer and, some say, a spy. These days, he's renowned for his occult writings, especially *The Book Of The Law, The Book Of Lies* and *Magick (Book 4)*.

He was an influential member of the occult organisations the Golden Dawn and Ordo Templi Orientis, and is said to have used his position to experiment both sexually and with drugs. Often referred to as the Beast 666, Crowley was alleged to have been a 33rd and 97th degree Freemason, and some have proclaimed him to be the Master Satanist of the 20th Century.

Crowley's life and death have been couched in so many lurid, sensational and otherwise unsubstantiated tales that it is hard to separate myth from reality. Was he truly a British spy, as has been claimed? Did he make human sacrifices, another allegation?

Jimmy Page had already collected a lot of Crowley works by 1970 when he acquired the man's one-time house, Boleskine, on the shores of Loch Ness. This was said to have been built on the site of a church that burned down with all the parishioners inside. Crowley bought the house at the start of the 20th Century, styling himself the laird of Boleskine, and immediately rumours ran riot that he was summoning demons, the house awash with dark shapes and figures.

The lodgekeeper there is said to have gone crazy and tried to murder his family, and there were constant local reports of hauntings. Page thought it was perfect for his needs, and owned it until 1991.

Never inducted into any of Crowley's societies, Page said of Crowley in 1978: 'I feel Aleister Crowley is a misunderstood genius of the 20th century. Because his whole thing was liberation of the person, of the entity, and that restrictions would foul you up, lead to frustration which leads to violence, crime, mental breakdown, depending on what sort of makeup you have underneath. The further this age

we're in now gets into technology and alienation, a lot of the points he's made seem to manifest themselves all down the line.'

Much more can – and has – been written about the relationship between Crowley's teachings and Page. There have been those who've used the latter's interest to claim that he was practising occult arts and this had left directly to tragedies in the career of Led Zeppelin and the lives of those involved with him. However, the fact remains that there is no evidence to suggest any of this is true. As for Crowley's influence on the malevolence of Boleskine, this is what Page said in 1975: 'Strange things have happened in that house which have nothing to do with Crowley. The bad vibes were already there.'

CRUNGE, THE
If you've ever heard this song (the fourth on the tracklisting) from the 1973 album 'Houses Of The Holy', then it will come as no surprise that it started out as a jam, based around a James Brown style funk number.

In fact, so determined were the band to pay tribute to the way that Brown recorded that you can hear Robert Plant at one point asking 'Where's that confounded bridge?' This was because usually Brown used to record live with virtually no rehearsal and bark out instructions as he went along; for instance he'd say 'Take it to the bridge'. For trivia fiends, right at the start, there are voices which are just audible. These belong to Jimmy Page and engineer George Chkiantz.

This was the B-side to the 1973 single 'D'yer Mak'er', which was released in South Africa, Australia, New Zealand, Austria, Germany, Canada, France, Greece, Japan, Mexico, Peru, Yugoslavia, Spain, Venezuela and Argentina.

It was also the title of an episode of TV's *That 70s Show*; each episode in Season Five was named after a Zeppelin song.

CUSTARD PIE

A song full of sexual innuendo, and the opening track from the 1975 album 'Physical Graffiti'. Once you realise that 'Custard Pie' is a term here used to describe female sex organs, everything else fits into gear. Lines like 'Chewin' a piece of your custard pie' no longer appear to be culinary in origin.

Inspired by songs such as 'I Want Some Of Your Pie' by Blind Boy Fuller, 'Shake 'Em On Down' from Bukka White and 'Drop Down Mama' (Sleepy John Estes), this is a riff-laden tribute to the great blues era of the Thirties. During the song, John Paul Jones plays the electric clavinet, while Robert Plant hits on the mouth organ.

This was never played in its entirety live by Zeppelin, although it does crop up on the Jimmy Page and the Black Crowes album 'Live At The Greek', released in 2000. Plant

has also used part of the song during his own 'Tall Cool One'.

'Custard Pie' was released as a single in 1975 in Thailand, backed with the songs 'Boogie With Stu' and 'Trampled Underfoot'.

DANCING DAYS

The hard-rocking 'Dancing Days' was the fifth track on Led Zeppelin's fifth studio album, 'Houses Of The Holy'. The song was written by Jimmy Page and Robert Plant and allegedly inspired by a trip to India.

Recorded during the Stargroves recording sessions of 1972 for 'Houses Of The Holy', 'Dancing Days' had already been performed live in concert by Led Zeppelin prior to the recording. The first known performance was at a Seattle show in June 1972. Strangely, however, the song was dropped from the band's set following the release of 'Houses Of The Holy', but a live version can be heard on 'How The West Was Won'.

'Dancing Days' was released as a French single, backed with 'Over The Hills And Far Away' in 1973. A double-sided radio edit appeared in the same year in South Africa as did an American EP, that also featured the tracks 'D'yer Mak'er', 'The Crunge' and 'The Song

Remains The Same'.

'Dancing Days' has been covered by HP Zinker, Stone Temple Pilots, Vanilla Fudge, Gov't Mule and Asia's Geoff Downes and John Wetton.

DARLENE

'Darlene', a song written by all four members of Led Zeppelin, appears as the sixth track on 1982's 'Coda' album. The song, which was never performed live, was originally recorded during sessions for 1979's 'In Through The Out Door'. It was recorded at Abba's Polar Studios in Sweden. Two other songs from the same sessions, 'Ozone Baby' and 'Wearing And Tearing', also did not make the final cut of 'In Through The Out Door' but also appeared on 'Coda'.

DAVIS, STEPHEN

Stephen Davis is the author of the 1985 book *Hammer Of The Gods*, sometimes subtitled 'The Led Zeppelin Saga' and 'Led Zeppelin Unauthorised'.

Davis has been called 'America's best-known rock biographer' and has written for *Rolling Stone*, the *Boston Globe* and the *New York Times* amongst others. He has also written biographies on Guns N' Roses, Aerosmith (with the band), Fleetwood Mac, Jim Morrison and Bob Marley.

Davis ran into some controversy over *Hammer Of The Gods*, not least for its lurid descriptions of alleged activities by the band and their entourage, the first time such activities had been open to such scrutiny. The book was pilloried by members of Led Zeppelin, with Jimmy Page stating: 'I think I opened (the book) up in the middle somewhere and started to read it, and I just threw it out the window. I was living by a river then, so it actually found its way to the bottom of the sea.'

Davis retorted by claiming that the book 'outed members of Led Zeppelin as heroin addicts, and as people that brutalised other people.'

DAY ON THE GREEN

Day on the Green is the name of a series of concerts that were held at the Oakland Coliseum Stadium from 1973 to 1992, and promoted by legendary impresario Bill Graham. Over the years they featured the likes of the Beach Boys, the Grateful Dead, Lynyrd Skynyrd, Chicago, the Doobie Brothers, Peter Frampton, Rolling Stones, AC/DC, the Police, Pink Floyd, the Who, Journey – and even Wham!

Led Zeppelin performed only once, in 1977, although they had been booked to appear in 1975 along with Joe Walsh and Swan Song labelmates the Pretty Things. They had to cancel this show after Plant was seriously injured in a car accident in Greece.

The band did appear, on 23-24 July 1977 as part of a North American tour. However their appearance was not without controversy when, following the band's appearance on the first night, John Bonham, Peter Grant, Richard Cole and John Bindon were all involved in a fracas with a members of Graham entourage, which led to all four members being arrested and later bailed. This almost led to the cancellation of the date the next day [see BINDON, JOHN].

The band's set list on 23 July was: *The Song Remains The Same/ The Rover intro/Sick Again/ Nobody's Fault But Mine/Over the Hills And Far Away/Since I've Been Loving You/No Quarter/Ten Years Gone/Battle Of Evermore/Going To California/Black Country Woman/ Bron-Yr-Aur Stomp/Trampled Underfoot/White Summer – Black Mountainside/Kashmir/Jimmy Page solo/Achilles Last Stand/Stairway To Heaven/Whole Lotta Love – Rock And Roll/Black Dog.*

At the July 24 show, the band included the song 'Mystery Train' between 'Going To California' and 'Black Country Woman' and did not play 'Black Dog' at the end of the set.

Led Zeppelin's 1977 US tour was cut short directly after the second of the two Oakland shows, when the band received news that Plant's son Karac had passed away.

DAZED AND CONFUSED

'Dazed And Confused' is the fourth song from the 1969 debut album 'Led Zeppelin'. It was written by American folk musician Jake Holmes, although the Zeppelin version is credited to Jimmy Page.

The towering rock epic was one of the main songs that signalled the arrival of Led Zeppelin as a major force to be reckoned with on the world stage and laid down the blueprint for the band's towering riffs, powerful, proto-heavy metal sound and all-round enigmatic performance.

The Led Zeppelin version of 'Dazed And Confused' was recorded at Olympic Studios in October 1968 and features Page using a bowed guitar. The song's tempo switches between an opening slow blues, with some descending bass lines from John Paul Jones, before exploding into life with frenetic drums from John Bonham and a terrific riff from Page (one similar to that which would be used by Black Sabbath on their own signature track, 'Paranoid'), before Page eventually ripped into an electrifying guitar solo that would rapidly become one of the highlights of live shows.

The song originally featured on Jake Holmes' debut album 'The Above Ground Sound Of Jake Holmes' (1967) and came to the attention of Page and the Yardbirds when Holmes supported them on a 1967 US tour. The band heard Holmes perform the song at a gig in Greenwich Village and were supposedly so impressed that both drummer Jim McCarty and Jimmy Page went out immediately and purchased a copy of Holmes' album. The Yardbirds would then rework the song, with Page adding the bowed guitar sound he'd begun using at the suggestion of David McCallum Sr [see McCALLUM, DAVID] and extra, Eastern-tinged instrumental sections. The song immediately became the central point of the band's live set and was played during their last six months as a touring band.

The Yardbirds never recorded a studio version of 'Dazed And Confused', although a live version did appear on a 1971 American release on Epic Records, 'Live Yardbirds Featuring Jimmy Page', a recording of a 1968 show from New York's Anderson Theatre during the Yardbirds' final US tour. On the album 'Dazed And Confused' is wrongly credited as 'I'm Confused'. Page gained a court injunction that got the album withdrawn, stating that Epic had overdubbed crowd noises. The album has since appeared as a bootleg.

Page altered the lyrics considerably and also changed the melody sufficiently, although the Zeppelin version still sounds similar to the Holmes original. However Page claimed sole credit for songwriting and, despite being written to by Holmes, who never opted to undertake legal action, has allegedly never replied. However he was quizzed by *Musician* magazine in 1990. The exchange ran thus:

MUSICIAN: I understand 'Dazed and Confused' was

originally a song by Jake Holmes. Is that true?

PAGE: (Sourly) I don't know. I don't know. (Inhaling) I don't know about all that.

MUSICIAN: Do you remember the process of writing that song?

PAGE: Well, I did that with the Yardbirds originally… The Yardbirds were such a good band for a guitarist to play in that I came up with a lot of riffs and ideas out of that, and I employed quite a lot of those in the early Zeppelin stuff.

MUSICIAN: But Jake Holmes, a successful jingle writer in New York, claims on his 1967 record that he wrote the original song.

PAGE: Hmm. Well, I don't know. I don't know about that. I'd rather not get into it because I don't know all the circumstances. What's he got, the riff or whatever? Because Robert wrote some of the lyrics for that on the album. But he was only listening to…we extended it from the one that we were playing with the Yardbirds.

MUSICIAN: Did you bring it into the Yardbirds?

PAGE: No, I think we played it 'round a sort of melody line or something that Keith (Relf) had. So I don't know. I haven't heard Jake Holmes, so I don't know what it's all about anyway. Usually my riffs are pretty damn original (laughs) What can I say?

'Dazed And Confused' has been an enduring live favourite at Led Zeppelin concerts, and would often form the basis of an improvised jam that could become so lengthy that it reached near 45 minutes in 1975. Live versions of 'Dazed And Confused' feature on the soundtrack to the 1976 film *The Song Remains The Same*, where it formed part of Page's own fantasy sequence. It also appears on 'BBC Sessions', the *Led Zeppelin* DVD and 'How The West Was Won'. It was dropped from the Zeppelin set after the 1975 tour, although Page would perform parts of the bowed guitar section on the 1977 and 1979 tours. Led Zeppelin performed the song at their 2007 reunion show at the O_2 Arena. Page also performed the song on his own 1988-89 solo tour.

The song formed the basis of Richard Linklater's coming-of-age film *Dazed And Confused* (1993), although the band refused Linklater permission to use any of their music in the film.

DEATH WISH II

Death Wish II is the title of a 1982 film directed by Michael Winner, the second instalment of his vigilante franchise, for which Jimmy Page wrote and recorded the soundtrack.

'I'd lived next door to Jimmy for many years,' director Winner told *Uncut* magazine in 2009. 'It was a very bad time for him – the drummer had died, and he was in a very inactive period. Peter Grant and I made arrangements for Jimmy to do the *Death Wish II* score, for which he wasn't actually paid, because Grant wanted to restore Jimmy back to creativity. Jimmy rang the doorbell, and I thought if the wind blew he'd fall over. He saw the film, we spotted where the music was to go, and then he said to me, "I'm going to my studio. I don't want you anywhere near me, I'm going to do it all on my own." My editing staff said this is bloody dangerous! Anyway, we gave him the film, we gave him the timings, and he did it all on his own. Everything hit the button totally! I've never seen a more professional score in my life.'

Page recorded the bulk of the music at his Sol Studios in Cookham, Berkshire, and some in Los Angeles with Winner. He also enlisted the help of singer Chris Farlowe (who would later work on Page's 'Outrider' album), Fairport Convention's Dave Mattacks, the Pretty Things' Gordon Edwards and David Paton of the Alan Parsons Project.

The album was released on the Swan Song label in February 1982, Page's only solo release on the label. A CD version was released in 1999, but is now out of print. The album reached Number 40 in the UK charts and Number 50 in America.

The song title, 'Prelude', is credited to Page, but is in fact based on Chopin's 'Prelude in E Minor (Op. 28)'. Winner would re-use some of Page's material in the ensuing *Death Wish 3* (1985).

TRACKLISTING:
Who's To Blame/The Chase/City Sirens/Jam Sandwich/Carole's Theme/ The Release/Hotel Rats And Photostats/A Shadow In The City Jill's Theme/Prelude/Big Band, Sax And Violence/Hypnotizing Ways (Oh Mamma).

DEFINITIVE COLLECTION

'Definitive Collection' is a 12-disc mini replica box set released through Atlantic Records and Rhino Entertainment in November 2008. The set features every Led Zeppelin studio album, as well as a two-disc version of 'The Song Remains The Same' and a single-disc version of 1982's 'Coda'.

Only 'The Song Remains The Same' and 'Coda' feature bonus tracks. Disc one of 'The Song Remains The Same' features 'Black Dog' with 'The Rover' intro, 'Over The Hills And Far Away', 'Misty Mountain Hop', 'Since I've Been Loving You' and 'The Ocean', whilst disc two features 'Heartbreaker'. 'Coda' features 'Baby Come On', 'Travelling Riverside Blues', 'White Summer' – 'Black Mountain Side' and 'Hey Hey What Can I Do'.

The set only charted in Japan, reaching Number 23.

DELTAS

The Deltas were the very first band joined by John Paul Jones. He joined them, aged 15, in 1961 before moving on to the jazz-based Jett Blacks.

DENNY, SANDY

Sandy Denny was a female UK folk singer, best known for her performances as lead singer of Fairport Convention. She also duetted with Robert Plant on 'Battle Of Evermore', the only time an outside singer was used in such a capacity.

Denny rose to prominence as a teenager on the early-Sixties folk revival circuit, noted for her

interpretational skills and mastery of traditional singing. She joined a very early version of the Strawbs, with whom she recorded 'Who Knows Where The Time Goes', her best-known song, in 1967. It was covered by Judy Collins, which helped bring Denny to a wider audience.

Denny joined Fairport Convention in 1968 and appeared on the albums 'What We Did On Our Holidays', 'Unhalfbricking' (which featured an excellent version of 'Who Knows Where The Time Goes') and 'Liege And Lief', all remarkably released in 1969. She then left to form Fotheringay, releasing just one album before going solo and releasing 'The North Star Grassmen And The Ravens' (1971), 'Sandy' (1972) and 'Like An Old Fashioned Waltz' (1973). She rejoined Fairport for 'Live Convention' (1974) and 'Rising For The Moon' (1975), releasing a final solo album, 'Rendezvous', in 1977.

Denny died of a traumatic mid-brain haemorrhage in 1978, a month after falling down a straircase whilst on holiday with her parents. She is buried in Putney Vale Cemetery.

Denny was chosen by Led Zeppelin to perform with Plant on 'Battle Of Evermore', after the latter felt he needed a second voice to enable him to tell the fantasy-based tale of the lyrics. Zeppelin had appeared with Fairport Convention at the Bath Festival in 1970.

'(The song) sounded like an old English instrumental first off,' Jimmy Page said in a 1977 interview with *Trouser Press*. 'Then it became a vocal and Robert did his bit. Finally we figured we'd bring Sandy by and do a question-and-answer-type thing.'

As a thank you, Denny was given her own symbol of three connected pyramids to go along with the four symbols chosen by the different members of Zeppelin.

DES BARRES, PAMELA

Pamela Des Barres (née Pamela Ann Miller) is a former groupie and member of the GTOs (Girls Together Outrageously), the all-female singing group of groupies formed by Frank Zappa. An

actress and author, Des Barres was involved for a time with Led Zeppelin guitarist Jimmy Page.

Of Page, Des Barres told *Uncut* magazine: 'Some people just have it. Jimmy obviously has insane charisma and his talent is unsurpassed, innovative and majestic. Not to mention he was the epitome of what a British Rock God should look like: delicate, mysterious, androgynous, sensuous. And he made sure you never really knew what was on his mind. He loved being in control of every situation, still somehow remaining an elegant, intense gentleman. One wild night, he gave me a dose of mescaline and didn't take any himself. He enjoyed being my provider, lover, teacher. It went on for hours, all night long. And I was a joyous, blissed-out basket-case when the sun came up.'

Des Barres wrote two books about her experiences as a groupie, namely 1987's *I'm With The Band* and 2003's *Take Another Little Piece Of My Heart: A Groupie Grows Up*. She was married for a time to Michael Des Barres, who sang for Detective, a band signed to the Swan Song label.

DETECTIVE

Detective were a five-piece American-based hard rock band who were signed to Led Zeppelin's Swan Song label.

The band were fronted by English singer Michael Des Barres who had also been the vocalist for UK glam rock band Silverhead and who would subsequently marry groupie/actress Pamela Ann Miller, who also had a relationship with Jimmy Page. Detective featured ex-Yes keyboard player Tony Kaye and Steppenwolf guitarist Michael Monarch.

Detective released two albums on Swan Song, 1975's self-titled debut produced by Jimmy Page under the pseudonym of Jimmy Robinson and 1978's 'It Takes One To Know One' as well as a radio-only promo album 'Live From The Atlantic Studios' (1978). They featured in one episode of the US sitcom *WKRP In Cincinnati*.

Des Barres then began a solo career before forming Chequered Past with Sex Pistols guitarist Steve Jones and Blondie's Clem Burke and Nigel Harrison. He would later front the Power Station in a live capacity only. Kaye rejoined Yes in 1983.

DIXON, WILLIE

Willie Dixon is a legendary bluesman from Mississippi who penned such evergreen blues standards as 'Little Red Rooster', 'Hoochie Coochie Man', 'Spoonful', 'Evil', 'I Ain't Superstitious', 'Bring It On Home', 'I Can't Quit You Baby', 'You Shook Me' and 'You Need Love'. The last four songs were all covered or adapted by Led Zeppelin.

Although the Zeppelin version of 'You Shook Me' on their debut album was correctly credited to Willie Dixon, both 'Bring It One

WILLIE DIXON

Home' and 'You Need Love', the latter of which Zeppelin appropriated for 'Whole Lotta Love' on 'Led Zeppelin II', were both the subject of lawsuits that were eventually settled out of court. The songs were originally credited on Zeppelin albums as being written by Jimmy Page and Page/Plant/Jones/Bonham respectively, but now feature the added credit of Dixon.

Speaking of the closeness between Dixon's 'You Need Love' and Zeppelin's own 'Whole Lotta Love' on Australian radio station Triple J in 2000, Plant offered, 'Page's riff was Page's riff. It was there before anything else. I just thought, "Well, what am I going to sing?" That was it, a nick. Now happily paid for. At the time, there was a lot of conversation about what to do. It was decided that it was so far away in time (it was in fact seven years) and influence that... Well, you only get caught when you're successful. That's the game.'

Dixon's material has also been covered by the likes of the Rolling Stones, Bob Dylan, Cream, Queen, the Doors, the Grateful Dead and the Allman Brothers Band.

Dixon, who died of heart failure, aged 76, in 1992, is today recognised as one of the pioneers of the Chicago blues movement.

DOWN BY THE SEASIDE

'Down By The Seaside' is the ninth song from 'Physical Graffiti', Led Zeppelin's sixth studio album 'Physical Graffiti'.

The song began life as an acoustic piece written by Jimmy Page and Robert Plant in 1970 during their time at Bron-Yr-Aur cottage in Gwynedd, Wales and was inspired by Neil Young's 'Down By The River'. The song was recorded for inclusion on Led Zeppelin's fourth album, but was ultimately held over until 'Physical Graffiti'.

Although never performed live by Zeppelin, Robert Plant recorded a duet of the song with Tori Amos for the 1995 Led Zeppelin tribute album 'Encomium'.

DRAKE HOTEL

The Drake Hotel in New York was a popular destination for touring rock bands in America and was frequented by the likes of the Who and Led Zeppelin.

There was controversy during Zeppelin's stay on their 1973 tour, which included three sell-out nights at Madison Square Garden (filmed for what would become *The Song Remains The Same* movie). On the final night, the receipts, reportedly variously at $180,000 and $203,000, were stolen from the band's safety deposit box at the hotel. The money was never recovered, although police suspicion fell upon the shoulders of Led Zeppelin tour manager Richard Cole who had the key to the box and was the first person to discover the money missing. Cole took a lie-detector test to prove his innocence and no-one from Led Zeppelin was ever charged. The band later sued the hotel.

DREAD ZEPPELIN

Dread Zeppelin were a group of American musicians who, having failed in their earlier incarnation as the Prime Movers, decided it would be funny to re-present themselves to the world as a band who covered Led Zeppelin songs in a reggae style, but sung with a 300lb Elvis impersonator, known as Tortelvis (better known to his parents as Greg Tortell).

Their first single was their own take on Zeppelin's 1973 single

'Immigrant Song' backed, like the original, with 'Hey Hey What Can I Do', released in 1989 on the band's own Birdcage label. The single sold well, prompting a repress. Further singles followed, all recorded at the home studio of Eurythmics man Dave Stewart where a member of Dread Zeppelin worked.

The band signed to the IRS label and released their debut album 'Un-Led-Ed' in 1990, which was surprisingly successful, and ventured to the UK to tour. A second album, '5,000,000 Tortelvis Fans Can't Be Wrong', followed in 1991, but the 'joke' was wearing somewhat thin, not least with the band expanding their repertoire to include Bob Marley covers and originals.

Dread Zeppelin still tour and release albums, but their attention has turned towards bands like the Yardbirds and Queen in later years. Astonishingly they were around to celebrate their 20th Anniversary in 1989.

DREAMLAND

'Dreamland', the seventh solo album from Robert Plant, released on the Mercury label in July 2002, was his first new album for nine years. It was the first he recorded with his new band Strange Sensation and featured a mix of original material and cover versions from bands like Bob Dylan, Skip Spence, Tim Rose and Jesse Colin Young.

Following on from 1993's 'Fate Of Nations' Plant continued to seek inspiration from the music that inspired him when he was in Led Zeppelin. The album was nominated for two Grammys, in the categories of Best Rock Album and Best Male Rock Vocal Performance.

TRACKLISTING:

Funny In My Mind (I Believe I'm Fixin' To Die)/Morning Dew/One More Cup Of Coffee/The Last Time I Saw Her/Song To The Siren/Win My Train Fare Home/Darkness Darkness/ Red Dress/Hey Joe/Skip's Song/Dirt In A Hole.

DREJA, CHRIS

Chris Dreja was the rhythm guitarist and bass player with the Yardbirds for the band's initial career, and he was also the first bassist approached by Jimmy Page to join the band that would become Led Zeppelin. However, Dreja was keen to explore a new career in photography and declined the offer, although one of his photographs was used on the back cover of 'Led Zeppelin'.

He says of turning down the chance to join the band: 'Do I regret it? No. While it might have led to riches and fame, I was done with trying to be a rock star at the time. I wanted something new. If I had joined the band, then I would now be locked in an asylum.'

Ironically it was Dreja who opted to learn bass guitar when Jeff Beck left the band, allowing then bassist Page to move over to lead guitar. Dreja was also a

member of Box of Frogs with other members of the Yardbirds (Page plays on the band's second album 'Strange Land'). He became a member of the re-formed Yardbirds.

DUNLUCE CASTLE

Dunluce Castle is a now-ruined medieval castle in Country Antrim, Northern Ireland. It was used as the setting for the inside gatefold sleeve in the 1973 Led album 'Houses Of The Holy'.

The setting was used by Hipgnosis's Aubrey Powell, who worked on the sleeve due to its close proximity to the Giant's Causeway, which was the setting for the front cover photography.

DVD

The much-anticipated double DVD, simply titled *DVD* (although sometimes called *Led Zeppelin*), was released on the Atlantic label in May 2003. It was the first officially released live footage of the band since the 1976 film *The Song Remains The Same*.

This spans the years 1969-79 and features footage from a variety of Led Zeppelin concerts including Royal Albert Hall, 9 January 1970, Madison Square Garden 27-29 July 1973, Earl's Court 24-25 May 1975 and Knebworth Park 4 August 1979, plus a variety of other footage.

The entire project was overseen by Jimmy Page, who requested bootleg footage from fans which he went through to find the perfect representation of Zeppelin material. Some of the film stock had to be baked and worked on for a year to bring the quality up to the required standard.

Unsurprisingly, this reached the Number 1 spot in the UK, US, Australia and Norway.

TRACKLISTING:

Disc One: (Royal Albert Hall, 9 January 1970) *We're Gonna Groove/ I Can't Quit You Baby/Dazed And Confused/White Summer/What Is And What Should Never Be/How Many More Times/Moby Dick/Whole Lotta Love/Communication Breakdown/C'mon Everybody/ Something Else/Bring It On Home.* (Atlantic Records February 1969) *Communication Breakdown.* (Denmark Radio, Gladsaxe Teen Club, 17 March 1969) *Communication Breakdown/Dazed And Confused/Babe I'm Gonna Leave You/How Many More Times.* (Supershow, Staines Studio, 25 March 1969) *Dazed And Confused.* (Tous En Scene, Olympia Theatre Paris June 19 1969)

Communication Breakdown/Dazed And Confused.
Disc Two: (Sydney Showground, 27 February 1972) *Immigrant Song.* (Madison Square Garden, 27-29 July 1973) *Black Dog/Misty Mountain Hop/Since I've Been Loving You/The Ocean.*
(Earls Court, 24/25 May 1975) *Going To California/That's The Way/Bron-Yr-Aur Stomp/In My Time Of Dying/Trampled Underfoot/Stairway To Heaven.* (Knebworth, 4 August 1979) *Rock And Roll/Nobody's Fault But Mine/Sick Again/Achilles Last Stand/In The Evening/Kashmir/Whole Lotta Love/You'll Never Walk Alone.*
(NBC Studio, New York, 19 September 1970) Press Conference. (Sydney Showground, 27 February 1972) *Rock And Roll.*
(ABC Get To Know, 27 February 1972) Robert Plant and Jimmy Page aftershow interviews. (BBC2 Old Grey Whistle Test, 12 January 1975) Robert Plant interview. (Remasters Promo) *Over The Hills And Far Away/Travelling Riverside Blues.*

D'YER MAK'ER

'D'yer Mak'er' is the sixth track from Led Zeppelin's 1973 album 'Houses Of The Holy', their only song ever to display a reggae feel. It wasn't only reggae, but also doo-wop, another early influence for the band which can be seen from the reference to Sixties doo-wop band Rosie and the Originals on the inner sleeve of the album.

The song developed out of 1972 rehearsals at Stargroves, beginning with a John Bonham drumbeat that soon shifted to a reggae style, enhanced by placing the microphones away from Bonham's drum kit. The song is credited to all four members of Led Zeppelin.

The song title came from an old joke that went 'My wife's gone on holiday' 'Jamaica?' 'No, she went of her own accord!' In 2005 Robert Plant told an American radio station the song's title came because the band felt it reflected the reggae style of the song; he found it amusing that some fans would ignore the apostrophes, pronouncing the song Dire Maker. This has been reflected in the lyrics to rock band the Hold Steady's 'Joke About Jamaica'.

'D'yer Mak'er' was released as a single in 1973, backed by 'The Crunge' (ironically pairing the two tracks that came in for criticism upon the release of 'Houses Of The Holy'). It reached Number 20 in the US charts. Plant was keen for the song to be released in the UK and promo versions of the song were released to radio, but the single never came out. A Dutch version, backed with 'Gallows Pole' was released in 1973, and a Mexican EP with 'Over The Hills And Far Away', 'Black Dog' and 'Misty Mountain Hop', and an Argentinean EP with 'The Crunge', 'The Ocean' and 'No

Quarter', were also released.

'D'yer Mak'er' was never performed live by Led Zeppelin in its entirety, although snippets of the song did feature on the band's 1975 tour. The song has been covered by Eek-A-Mouse, Lady GaGa and 311.

EARLS COURT

Led Zeppelin played a series of legendary shows at this cavernous west London venue in 1975. In all, the band performed five nights there: 17, 18, 23, 24 and 25 May. Initially, they were due to do only three nights, but these sold out in four hours, with the extra two (on 17-18 May) being hastily added.

Zeppelin went out of their way to make these shows memorable for the 85,000 fans who'd bought tickets, which were priced from £1 to £2.50(!). They airlifted in the whole of their American stage set and erected a video screen so fans further back could see what was going on – the first time such a device had been used.

Zeppelin were introduced onstage by a different radio DJ each night – in sequence: Bob Harris, Johnnie Walker, Kid Jensen, Nicky Horne and Alan Freeman – and played for over three hours each night. The final show clocked in at an astonishing three hours, 43 minutes and 50 seconds.

Co-author Dome, who was at that final night, recalls: 'It was simply the most evocative, powerful and moving rock experience of a lifetime. This was a band playing at the peak of their considerable powers. But they were also more than remote rock gods. They had a rapport with the fans that veered from the bonhomie of a bunch of nice guys just jamming for some mates in the local boozer, to the most extraordinarily extravagant musical gestures – it was here that we all began to appreciate why America worshipped them. Anyway, it was here that they moved away from being a damn fine rock band and became historic, mythic.'

Respected author/journalist Chris Welch wrote in his book *Led Zeppelin* (1994): 'The band played with tremendous fire, possessed by an almost demonic power, amidst clouds of smoke pierced by green laser beams. Jimmy Page flailed his violin bow against the guitar strings, producing eerie, echoing gothic howls. At the time, I wrote in a review that, "Robert Plant maintains an essentially human, chatty approach to audiences, almost like a guide taking us through the story of the band, a jester at the wheel of some fearsome juggernaut, offering sly asides and poetic ruminations between moments of terrible power..." The band enjoyed the "Physical Graffiti" material far more than the old war horses, and the best moments from the previous albums came in the shape of ballads and acoustic songs.'

The set list, which wasn't varied on any night, is:
Rock And Roll//Sick Again/Over The Hills And Far Away/In My Time Of Dying/The Song Remains The Same/ The Rain Song/Kashmir/No Quarter/ Tangerine/Going To California/That's The Way/Bron-Yr-Aur Stomp/ Trampled Underfoot/Moby Dick/ Dazed And Confused/Stairway To Heaven.

The encores for the first four nights were 'Whole Lotta Love' and 'Black Dog'. For the final night, 'Heartbreaker' and 'Communication Breakdown' were added.

Although the concerts were filmed, nothing was officially released until 2003, when some footage was incorporated into the *Led Zeppelin* DVD. There have been numerous bootlegs over the years which capture some, but not all, of the magic of these shows.

EARLY DAYS: BEST OF LED ZEPPELIN

A compilation of tracks spanning the band's career from 1968 to 1971. Released in 1999, it was no

more than a collection of already available songs, and also something of a quick cash-in. Still, the enhanced CD did contain a promo video for 'Communication Breakdown' which made its appearance a little more credible.

The sleeve – showing the heads of the four members of the band superimposed onto the bodies of NASA astronauts – was as poorly realised as this whole project.

This was also part of a double CD released in 2002, featuring both 'The Early Days' and the subsequent 'The Latter Days' compilations.

TRACKLISTING:
Good Times, Bad Times/Babe I'm Gonna Leave You/Dazed And Confused/Communication Breakdown/Whole Lotta Love/What Is And What Should Never Be/Immigrant Song/Since I've Been Loving You/Black Dog/Rock And Roll/The Battle Of Evermore/When The Levee Breaks/Stairway To Heaven.

EDGEWATER INN, SEATTLE

Most people believe that Led Zeppelin were banned from this hotel for indulging in sexual activities with sharks and a groupie. The whole incident has become confused and confusing over the decades.

What appears to have happened is that the band stayed there in July. 1969. Now, at the time guests could fish out of the hotel windows (the hotel itself overlooking Puget Sound). What happened next is disputed.

Stephen Davis, in *Hammer Of The Gods*, wrote: 'One girl, a pretty young groupie with red hair, was disrobed and tied to the bed. According to the legend of the Shark Episode, Led Zeppelin then proceeded to stuff pieces of shark into her vagina and rectum.'

Richard Cole responded to this as follows: 'It wasn't Bonzo (as was alleged), it was me. It wasn't shark parts anyway: It was the nose that got put in. We caught a lot of big sharks, at least two dozen, stuck coat hangers through the gills and left 'em in the closet... But the true shark story was that it wasn't even a shark. It was a red snapper and the chick happened to be a fucking redheaded broad with a ginger pussy. And that is the truth. Bonzo was in the room, but I did it. Mark Stein (of Vanilla Fudge, who were also in the hotel) filmed the whole thing. And she loved it. It was like, "You'd like a bit of fucking, eh? Let's see how your red snapper likes this red snapper!" That was it. It was the nose of the fish, and that girl must have cum 20 times. But it was nothing malicious or harmful, no way! No-one was ever hurt.'

In his own book, *Stairway To Heaven: Led Zeppelin Uncensored*, Cole appears to dispute some of the 'facts': 'Word about the escapade spread quickly. Rumours circulated that the girl had been raped...that she had been crying hysterically...that she had pleaded for me to stop...that she had struggled to escape...that a shark had been used to penetrate her. None of the stories was true.'

The reality is that nobody has ever seen footage of this, and that Zeppelin were only banned from the hotel in 1973 for leaving 30 mudsharks in all sorts of locations and for throwing TV sets, beds and all manner of furniture into the bay below.

When asked about the story, all Peter Grant would enigmatically reply was: 'I'm surprised they never asked me about the octopus!' Needless to say, fishing has now been outlawed by the hotel!

EDMUNDS, DAVE

Welsh singer, guitarist and producer who first made his name with late-Sixties band Love Sculpture. They had a Top 5 hit in the UK with a reworking of Khachaturian's classical piece 'Sabre Dance' in 1968.

After the band split up, Edmunds had an Xmas Number 1 hit in Britain with 'I Hear You Knocking' in 1970. This Smiley Lewis cover also got to Number 4 in America, and Edmunds has been continuously busy ever since. He recorded solo albums, and was also a member of rockabilly/power-pop band Rockpile, who recorded one album in 1980 ('Seconds Of Pleasure'). He also produced and collaborated with the likes of the Flamin' Groovies, Ducks Deluxe, Paul McCartney, Man, Status Quo, the Fabulous Thunderbirds, Elvis Costello, Graham Parker and the Stray Cats.

In all, Edmunds recorded the following albums for the Swan Song label: 'Get It' (1977), 'Tracks On Wax 4' (1978), 'Repeat When Necessary' (1979) and 'Twangin...' (1981). Of these, only the last two made any commercial headway. 'Repeat When Necessary' made it to Number 39 in the UK and Number 54 in America, while 'Twangin....' got to Number 37 in Britain. However, he did have three hit singles in the UK during this period. In 1977 'I Knew The Bride' (written by Nick Lowe) made it to Number 26. Then 'Girls Talk' (written by Elvis Costello) and 'Queen Of Hearts' (written by country star Hank DeVito) got to Numbers 4 and 11, respectively, both in 1979.

Including a 1981 compilation called 'The Best Of Dave Edmunds', the man released five albums on the label, as many as Led Zeppelin!

EISSPORTHALLE, GERMANY

The venue for the last ever Led Zeppelin show with John Bonham which took place on 7 July 1980. A second night at the venue appears to have been contemplated (posters were even printed), but wasnever announced, let alone played.

This has been available as a bootleg for years, and also part of a 26-disc bootleg box set, featuring all 14 shows on this tour, which was dubbed 'Tour Over Europe 1980'.

The final gig with John Bonham had this set list:
Train Kept A-Rollin', Nobody's Fault But Mine/Black Dog/In The Evening/ The Rain Song/Hot Dog/All My Love/Trampled Underfoot/Since I've Been Loving You/Achilles Last Stand/White Summer/Black Mountain Song/Kashmir/Stairway To Heaven/Rock And Roll/Whole Lotta Love.

ENCOMIUM

This was a 1995 tribute album, put out by Atlantic Records, with the full title of 'Encomium: A Tribute To Led Zeppelin'. Most of the artists on the record were either directly signed to the label, or affiliated in some shape or form.
TRACKLISTING:
4 Non Blondes
Misty Mountain Hop
Hootie and the Blowfish
Hey Hey, What Can I Do
Sheryl Crow
D'Yer Mak'er
Stone Temple Pilots
Dancing Days
Big Head Todd And The Monsters
Tangerine
Duran Duran
Thank You
Blind Melon
Out On The Tiles
Cracker
Good Times, Bad Times
Helmet with David Yow
Custard Pie

The Rollins Band
Four Sticks
Never The Bride
Going To California
Tori Amos and Robert Plant
Down By The Seaside.
Mexican band Mana were added to the album for the LaserDisc version, with a Spanish rendition of *Fool in The Rain.*

Incidentally, the word 'encomium' is Latin for 'in praise of a person or thing'. Hence its use here.

ENTWISTLE, JOHN

While perceived wisdom has it the late Who drummer Keith Moon gave Led Zeppelin their name, the late Who bassist once claimed it was him! The man himself once said:

'Led Zeppelin is a good name, isn't it? I made it up. Everybody says Keith Moon made it up, but he didn't. About four years ago I was really getting fed up with the Who. And I was talking with a fellow who is the production manager for Led Zeppelin now (presumably Richard Cole). I was talking to him down in a club in New York. And I said, "Yeah, I'm thinking of leaving the group and forming my own group. I'm going to call the group Led Zeppelin. And I'm going to have an LP cover with, like, the Hindenburg going down in flames, and, you know, this whole business." And like two months later he was working for Jimmy Page and, like, they were looking for a name, and so he suggested Led Zeppelin, and Page liked it, and they came out with the same LP cover that I'd planned.'

How true this actually is remains open to conjecture. However, there have always been major rumours that Moon and Entwistle were fed up with the infighting in the Who and, in 1968, were considering starting a band with Jimmy Page and Jeff Beck. This, of course, never led anywhere.

EQUINIOX BOOKSELLERS AND PUBLISHERS

The name of a store opened by Jimmy Page in Kensington High Street, London. It specialised in occult works, with particular connections to Aleister Crowley. Not only did the company publish a facsimile of Crowley's 1904 work *The Goetia*, but also sold Crowley paraphernalia, and even had a tapestry of *The Stele Of Revealing* hanging in the window.

This was an ancient Egyptian funerary artefact connected to Ankhefenkhons 1, who is said to have founded the Thelema religion, which was developed by Crowley in The *Book Of The Law*.

Page sold off the shop and publishing house in the early Eighties.

ERTEGUN, AHMET

The co-founder of Atlantic Records alongside Herb Abramson, Turkish-born Ertegun was one of the most significant music-business figures of the 20th Century. The pair started the label in 1947, eventually having their first success with the Stick McGhee single 'Drinkin' Wine Spo-Dee-O-Dee'. From here onwards, the label's level of success was consistent and impressive. Starting out rooted in the blues, the company expanded its portfolio, signing some of the biggest names in rock history. The Rolling Stones, Cream, Vanilla Fudge, Iron Butterfly, Emerson Lake and Palmer, Foreigner, Crosby Stills & Nash and...Led Zeppelin.

Such was the band's respect for Ertegun that, when Zeppelin were being inducted into the UK Music Hall of Fame in 2006, Jimmy Page dedicated the award to the man, who was seriously ill at the time and would die shortly thereafter.

Zeppelin even agreed to reform for the Ahmet Ertegun Tribute

Concert held on 10 December 2007 at the O_2 Arena in London. The bill featured Foreigner, Bill Wyman's Rhythm Kings, Paolo Nutini, Paul Rodgers and a supergroup featuring Keith Emerson, Chris Squire, Alan White and Simon Kirke. But it was Zeppelin who were the main attraction.

Over a million people applied for tickets to the event, almost all because they wanted to see Robert Plant, Jimmy Page, John Paul Jones and Jason Bonham. However, Plant made it abundantly clear the only reason he did this was out of respect for Ertegun.

The band's set list that night was:
Good Times, Bad Times/Ramble On/ Black Dog/In My Time Of Dying/ Honey Bee/For Your Life/Trampled Underfoot/Nobody's Fault But Mine/ No Quarter/Since I've Been Loving You/Dazed And Confused/Stairway To Heaven/The Song Remains The Same/Misty Mountain Hop/Kashmir/ Whole Lotta Love/Rock And Roll.

ES PARANZA

The label started by Robert Plant when Swan Song finally closed. The first release was the second Plant solo album 'The Principle Of Moments' in 1983. Every Plant record over the next decade, up to and including 'Fate Of Nations' in 1993, came out under this imprint.

FALLON, BP

BP Fallon is an Irish DJ, photographer, writer and broadcaster who, from 1972-79, acted as publicist for Led Zeppelin.

Fallon initially worked for the Beatles' Apple Records with Derek Taylor when he first came to London from Dublin. From there he moved on to working as a publicist for T Rex (he allegedly came up with the phrase 'T Rextasy') and Irish rockers Thin Lizzy. He began working with Led Zeppelin as a publicist around 1972 and carried on working with the band, on and off, until their massive shows at Knebworth in 1979.

His job would have been ensuring that Zeppelin's image was portrayed in the press according to the way the band and/or manager Peter Grant wished it to be so. One example of Fallon's manipulation of the media came in 1977 when Roy Harper, the folk musician who worked with Zeppelin, was hospitalised with toxoplasmosis – the result of attempting to give an ailing sheep on his farm mouth-to-mouth resuscitation. The news as widely reported, that he'd almost died from kissing a sheep, was a result of some subtle spin placed on the story by Fallon to gain maximum column inches.

Fallon went on to work with Ian Dury and Johnny Thunders. He toured with U2 as a DJ during their 1992-93 'Zoo TV' tour and has also acted as touring DJ for bands like My Bloody Valentine and the Kills.

He was reunited with Robert Plant in 2006 when the pair worked on a tribute concert in New York to raise money to pay for hospital bills for Love frontman Arthur Lee. In 2009 he released a solo record, on which he worked with Jack White of the White Stripes.

www.bpfallon.com

FAMILY DOGG, THE

The Family Dogg were a British Sixties vocal group specialising in vocal harmonies.

They included amongst their number Albert Hammond (author of the hit 'It Never Rains In California' and father of Albert Hammond Jr of the Strokes), Mike Hazelwood (songwriter and DJ, credited as co-writing 'Creep' with Radiohead) and Steve Rowland (producer of Dave, Dee, Dozy, Beaky, Mick and Tich, and the man credited with discovering Peter Frampton).

Jimmy Page, John Bonham and

John Paul Jones all appear on the Family Dogg's 1969 debut album 'A Way Of Life'.

FATE OF NATIONS

Released in May 1993, 'Fate Of Nations' was Robert Plant's sixth solo album, following 1990's 'Manic Nirvana'.

The album found Plant in reflective mode, following on from the post Zeppelin bombast of 'Manic Nirvana' and 1987's 'Now And Zen'. It finds Plant looking back to the music that inspired him as a member of Zeppelin, although not as the aspiring musician who would become a member of Led Zeppelin. Thus he looks back to the likes of Moby Grape, Jefferson Airplane and Quicksilver Messenger Service. One of the highlights of the album is a cover of Tim Hardin's 'If I Were A Carpenter'.

'These people were trying to tell the listener something, joining various traditions, with the sense of a quest being insinuated and bandied in their acoustic and electronic themes,' Plant said of the album. 'I'm also proud of what I've attempted to do lyrically (on the album), trying to tell vivid tales that come from a hearty tradition of prose.'

From name-checking Jimmy Page on opening track and first single 'Calling To You', through the more folk-laden strains of the brilliant '29 Palms' to the poignant 'I Believe' which tackled the issue of his late son Karac, Plant

unveiled what possibly rates as his finest solo work – perhaps the best set of solo material there has been from a member of Led Zeppelin.

One can certainly see a direct link between the folkier, more introspective material on 'Fate Of Nations' and Plant's subsequent solo albums, 2002's 'Dreamland' and 2005's 'Mighty ReArranger'.

Plant was joined on 'Fate Of Nations' by such musicians as Maire Brennan of Clannad, Francis Dunnery (It Bites), violinist Nigel Kennedy and ex-Fairport Convention member Richard Thompson. The album reached Number 6 in the UK charts upon release.

TRACKLISTING:

Calling To You/Down To The Sea/ Come Into My Life/I Believe/29 Palms/Memory Song (Hello Hello)/ If I Were A Carpenter/Memories Of A Shade/Promised Land/The Greatest Gift/Great Spirit/Network News.

FIRM, THE

On paper, the pairing of one of the world's finest guitarists with one of the rock world's leading vocalists looked like it simply could not fail, yet somehow the work Jimmy Page and Paul Rodgers conjured up with the short-lived Firm failed to truly capture the imagination of the rock loving public.

For Page, still perhaps in something of a malaise following the demise of his beloved Led Zeppelin, this was the first true chance, aside from an appearance at the Royal Albert Hall in 1983 for the ARMS charity concerts, to make his first public stand. Paul Rodgers, who had left Bad Company (themselves signed to Led Zeppelin's Swan Song label) in 1982, was coming off the back of a 1983 solo album 'Cut Loose', and again the Firm seemed to present a chance to reclaim the spotlight.

Things didn't exactly get off to a great start when Page and Rodgers' preferred rhythm section, ex-Yes drummer Bill Bruford and renowned fretless bassist Pino Palladino, could not make the line-up, the former being contracted to another label, the latter touring with pop singer Paul Young. In their place came ex-Uriah Heep/Manfred Mann's Earth Band drummer Chris Slade and Roy Harper's bassist Tony Franklin, also known for his fretless work.

The band's debut album, 1982's 'The Firm', was released on Geffen Records and, although it met with critical indifference, remains a worthy set of soulful hard rock, ranging from a cover of the Righteous Brothers' 'You've Lost That Lovin' Feelin'' through the US hit single 'Radioactive' to the spellbinding album closer 'Midnight Moonlight', itself a song derived from an unrecorded Led Zeppelin track 'The Swan Song'. The band toured the UK and the US but resolutely refused to perform any Led Zeppelin, Free or Bad Company material, performing only their own album and songs from Rodgers 'Cut Loose' and Page's *Death Wish II* soundtrack. Despite this, the US and European tours were a resounding success.

The band released a second, less well received album, 'Mean Business', on Geffen Records in 1986, which was musically more robust but seemed to lack the finesse of the debut album. With no tour forthcoming the group soon went their separate ways, with Slade joining AC/DC, Franklin hooking up with Whitesnake guitarist John Sykes in the equally short-lived Blue Murder and both Page and Rodgers returning to solo work.

FOOL IN THE RAIN

The third song from Zeppelin's final studio album 'In Through The Out Door' was also their final ever single in America, where it reached Number 21 in 1979 (backed by the country romp 'Hot Dog').

The song tells the tale of a man who has arranged to meet a woman on a specific street corner, only to arrive and feel he's been stood up. The song ends with the realisation that he is actually standing at the wrong street corner.

In keeping with many of the more varied musical ideas Zeppelin displayed on 'In Through The Out Door', 'Fool In The Rain' features a Latino feel, allegedly inspired by Robert Plant watching coverage of the 1978 World Cup Finals which took place in Argentina.

The song was never performed live by the band, but Plant did perform it in concert with Pearl Jam in 2005 at a benefit show for victims of Hurricane Katrina.

FOR YOUR LIFE

The second track from Led Zeppelin's 1976 album 'Presence' is a sturdy rocker which warns against the perils of drug usage, which Robert Plant had noted seemed to have become endemic throughout the music industry, especially in Los Angeles. Hence lines (sic) such as 'With the fine lines of the crystal payin' through your nose.'

Plant's vocals were recorded whilst he was confined to a wheelchair following the car accident he'd been involved in on a Greek Island in 1975 during which both he and his wife Maureen were seriously injured.

Although Led Zeppelin never performed 'For Your Life' live during their original incarnation, the song did form part of their set at the O_2 arena in 2007. It is also alleged that the song was rehearsed for the Coverdale/Page tour but never performed live.

FOUR STICKS

If you were to take the reason behind the title of the sixth track of Led Zeppelin's legendary fourth album literally, you might be tempted to believe that the straightahead rocker was less spectacular than some of the songs it accompanies.

'Four Sticks' refers to the fact that drummer John Bonham, frustrated at not being able to lay down the perfect beat required of the track, angrily picked up four drum sticks instead of his usual two and, pounding his drum kit as hard as he could, blasted out the required rhythm in one perfect take.

Yet that story belies the fact that 'Four Sticks' is far more complex than it might appear, with guitar riffs jumping between 5/8 and 6/8 time. It was also during the recording of 'Four Sticks' that the band took a break and ended up with the song 'Rock And Roll', to which 'Four Sticks' would end up as the B-side when released as a single.

There is only one known live performance of the song, from a 1971 Copenhagen show. 'Four Sticks' was also covered by Page and Plant's 1994 'Unledded' project and was performed on subsequent world tours by the pair, drummer Michael Lee also using four drum sticks. Robert Plant has also performed the song live as a solo artist in recent years.

'Four Sticks' was also one track (the other being 'Friends'), which Page and Plant re-recorded with the Bombay Symphony Orchestra during a 1972 trip to India. Although neither recording has ever been officially released, they have surfaced on various Led Zeppelin bootlegs.

FRIENDS

The second track from Led Zeppelin's 1970 third album and the first indication that, following the expected bombast of opening track 'Immigrant Song', the band had opted to take a more reflective, folky approach on the album.

Led Zeppelin manager Peter Grant can be heard at the beginning of the track amongst some studio chatter before the music kicks in. 'Friends' also features a rare, Eastern-themed string arrangement from John Paul Jones. The song was written by Jimmy Page and Robert Plant during the band's 1970 retreat at Welsh cottage Bron-Yr-Aur.

Released as a 1970 single in Poland and Brazil only, "Friends' was only ever performed live once, in Osaka in September 1971 – it is alleged that on bootlegs of the show Page can be heard asking Plant whether he wants to perform the song. 'Friends' was recorded for the 1994 album 'No Quarter: Jimmy Page And Robert Plant Unledded' and has also been covered by Jaz Coleman and Elliott Smith, amongst others.

time was working at a studio, SIR, with a Hammond organ.'

Jones co-wrote all the songs, apart from the cover of 1967 soul song 'The Dark End Of The Street', plus 'You're Mine', 'Tony' and 'Baby's Insane'. He also produced the album.

The full tracklisting of 'The Sporting Life' is:
Skotoseme/Do You Take This Man/ Dark End Of The Street/You're Mine/ Tony/Devil's Rodeo/The Sporting Life/ Baby's Insane/Last Man Down/Hex.

GALAS, DIAMANDA

The extraordinarily talented and unique singer collaborated with John Paul Jones on the 1994 album 'The Sporting Life', released by Mute. Talking to *Bomb* magazine at the time, Jones said of this union:

'Well, it's not as if Zeppelin was exactly a rock band. We were a blues band…and there were a lot of excursions and journeys into unusual areas. So anybody familiar with that shouldn't be surprised by anything we do. With this record, there's still definitely the energy that is found in the best of rock'n'roll, and there's a lot of stuff that hasn't been heard before. Nobody else is doing anything like this.

'We met once in London for an evening and talked about music and our backgrounds and what we liked. Then we went away. Diamanda went back on tour and then to New York, and I went back home and started thinking about this. And I put down some riffs with a drum machine and sent them to Diamanda, who by that

GALLOWS POLE

Recorded by Led Zeppelin for 'Led Zeppelin III', this is a traditional folk song with a long and varied history, and is the sixth song on that album.

The storyline is about a girl pleading to be freed from impending execution. What her crime is supposed to be is never explained, but it would appear that a bribe is involved in the situation, one that is eventually brought along by her lover right at the end of the song. Others, including her own family, come beforehand, but only to witness her death, not to save the maid. There are some interpretations which believe the 'bribe' is actually proof of innocence rather than a financial exchange.

It's thought unlikely that this song originated in England, with may variations throughout Scandinavia. It was 19th Century scholar Francis James Childs who first noted this song in his collection called *Childs Ballads*. Titled 'The Maid Freed From The Gallows', it was one of 305 such traditional tunes he collated, although Childs did note that the English version appeared to have lost much of the meaning inherent in the story itself.

It was a cover by Huddie 'Leadbelly' Ledbetter in the 1930s that really gave this song a modern context. Calling it 'The Gallis Pole', the legendary bluesman introduced both an acoustic sensibility and high-pitched tenor notation.

Zeppelin made a few changes of their own. The song became 'Gallows Pole', the protagonist was now male and the execution was carried out, despite the bribe being paid. This version includes banjo and mandolin. About playing the banjo, Page told *Trouser Press* magazine in 1977: 'I just picked it up and started moving my fingers around until the chords sounded right, which is the same way I work on compositions when the guitar's in different tunings.'

Credited as a traditional song on, 'Gallows Pole' remains a standout song on the third album, and something Zeppelin made their own. Plant and Page were to revisit it on the 1994 album 'No Quarter: Jimmy Page And Robert Plant Unledded'.

GATES, STEFAN AND SAMANTHA

The brother and sister who were used as models on the cover for 'Houses Of The Holy'. At the time, Stefan was five and his sister two years older. Both had already done modelling, mostly for knitwear patterns, and also appeared in the Seventies BBC-TV series *Poldark*.

Said Stefan in 2007 about this assignment: 'We only got a few quid for the modelling and the chance to travel to places we had never been before. Our family wasn't well off, we certainly couldn't afford holidays, so it worked out great for us.

'For the Zeppelin cover we went to Ireland during the Troubles. I remember arriving at the airport and seeing all these people with guns. We stayed in this little guesthouse near the Giant's Causeway and to capture the so-called magic light of dawn and dusk we'd shoot first thing in the morning and at night.

'I used to love being naked when I was that age so I didn't mind. I'd whip off my clothes at the drop of a hat and run around having a great time, so I was in my element. My sister was older so she was probably a bit more self-conscious.'

The idea for the cover was developed by Aubrey Powell and Storm Thorgerson of Hipgnosis, who took multiple-exposure shots of the two children in order to create the illusion of several others being involved.

Today, Stefan is a TV presenter, while Samantha is a scriptwriter living in Cape Town.

It's hard to imagine a cover like

this being allowed in today's politically correct society.

GIANT'S CAUSEWAY
This strangely surreal, almost alien environment was the setting for the cover of 'Houses Of The Holy'.

Situated in County Antrim, Northern Ireland, it features 40,000 interlocking basalt columns, the result of a volcanic eruption. It was declared a World Heritage Site by UNESCO in 1986, and a National Nature Reserve a year later by the Department of the Environment for Northern Ireland.

The Causeway is featured in the Marillion video for 'Easter', as well as in the movie *Hellboy II: The Golden Army* and in the Simpsons' episode In *The Name Of The Grandfather*.

In legend, Irish warrior Fionn mac Cumhaill (Finn McCool) is said to have built the causeway so that he could walk to Scotland to fight his Scottish counterpart Benandonner.

GIRL I LOVE SHE GOT LONG BLACK WAVY HAIR, THE
A song you won't find on any Zeppelin studio album. It was recorded on 16 June 1969 for the *Chris Grant's tasty pop Sundae* show, and broadcast six days later. This is the only known performance of the song, which was eventually released on the 'BBC Sessions' album and as a single in 1997.

It's credited to the band and to Sleepy John Estes. The latter's name is there because the first verse was strongly influenced by his 1929 blues number 'The Girl I Love She Got Long Curly Hair'.

GLADSAXE
This Danish town is where the band played their first ever gig together, albeit billed as the Yardbirds and not Led Zeppelin, on 7 September 1968. 'They don't cheer too madly there, you know?' Jimmy Page recalled later that year. 'We were really scared, because we only had about fifteen hours to practice together. It was sort of an experimental concert to see if we were any good, I guess.'

The band played an early-evening set, supported by Fourways and Bodies, before playing another show later that night at Brondby Pop Club. Their set was a mixture of old Yardbirds songs plus material they were then working on. The former included 'Train Kept A-Rollin'', 'Dazed And Confused', 'White Summer' and 'For Your Love'. The later boasted the likes of 'Communication Breakdown', 'I Can't Quit You Baby', 'You Shook Me', 'Babe I'm Gonna Leave You', 'How Many More Times' and a cover of the Garnet Mimms song 'As Long As I Have You'.

GOING TO CALIFORNIA
Featured as the seventh song on the 'Led Zeppelin IV' album, its a

wistful folk style is said to have been inspired by Joni Mitchell, with whom both Robert Plant and Jimmy Page were entranced at the time. In fact, Plant would often intone the name 'Joni' during this song live.

Originally called 'Guide To California', it started out being about earthquakes in the area. Oddly, and ironically, when Page, manager Peter Grant and engineer Andy Johns mixed the album in Los Angeles, they did experience a minor earthquake!

A live version from the Earl's Court concert on 25 May 1975 is included on the DVD *Led Zeppelin*.

GOLDBERG, DANNY

Now president of Gold Village Entertainment, Danny Goldberg has been involved in the music business for over 40 years. Prior to being vice-president of Swan Song Records from 1974-76 he was the band's US publicist

'I was the kid who went to school, graduated in the late Sixties and loved rock'n'roll. I thought those bands were speaking for me,' Goldberg said in a radio interview with *Music Radar* in 2009. Originally, he wanted to be a writer and critic, but eventually moved into the record label and management side of things with a huge impact.

Over the years, Goldberg haws worked with, or managed, giants such as Nirvana, Steve Earle, the Allman Brothers, Sonic Youth, the Pretenders and Stevie Nicks. He also was a major player at Mercury Records, Atlantic Records and Warner Brothers Records – quite a CV!

Oddly, Peter Grant blames Goldberg for the *Hammer Of The Gods* biography on Led Zeppelin. Rightly or wrongly, he cited Goldberg's alleged involvement with the controversial book as being a 'betrayal for which I will never forgive him'.

GOOD TIMES BAD TIMES

The opening song of the first Led Zeppelin album, and a track with a genuinely live feel to it.

Page told *Guitar World* magazine: 'The most stunning thing about the track, of course, is Bonzo's amazing kick drum. It's superhuman when you realise he was not playing with a double kick. That's one kick drum! That's when people started understanding what he was all about.'

Rarely played live by the band, it was the song with which they chose to open their 2007 reunion show at the O_2 Arena in London – possibly because it is the very first Zeppelin most people ever heard on record.

It was also released as a single in various countries in 1969, these being America, New Zealand, Australia, Canada, France, Argentina, Mexico, Germany, Greece, Japan, Philippines, Sweden, South Africa and Holland. Only in Holland, though, did it break into the Top 20.

GRAHAM, BILL

The famed American promoter who was responsible for putting on some of the greatest shows in Led Zeppelin's history, However, the story that will forever link Graham and Zeppelin was an incident on 23 July 1977 at the Oakland Coliseum. (See BINDON, JOHN) It was sad ending to what had been a fruitful relationship between Bill Graham and Led Zeppelin.

Graham himself had made a name as a shrewd promoter during the late Sixties, working with counter-culture artists such as Jefferson Airplane, Country Joe and the Fish, the Fugs, the Grateful Dead and Janis Joplin. He opened the Fillmore West (San Francisco) and Fillmore East (New York) venues. He was also to promote the Rolling Stones on a number of tours, and founded the annual Day on the Green festivals at various Bay Area stadia.

Involved in the American portion of Live Aid (at JFK Stadium in Philadelphia), he had a reputation for being both brilliant and difficult.

He died in 1991, aged 60.

GRAMMY

It's incredible to think that, despite their enormous success and influence, Led Zeppelin just have one Grammy to show for it all – a Lifetime Achievement award given out in 2005. During their 12 years together, the band were nominated, but never won anything.

Robert Plant walked off with five of his own in 2009 for 'Raising Sand', his collaboration with Alison Krauss, including Album of the Year. As he didn't even turn up for the 2005 ceremony (Page and Jones were there, together with Bonham's children, Jason and Zoe), one can infer what meant more to him.

GRANT, PETER

The fifth member of Led Zeppelin, the man who masterminded their career and plotted some of the most innovative and far-reaching managerial breakthroughs, it's fair to say that, without Peter Grant, the band would have never achieved such success.

He was passionate, ruthless, focused and also a visionary. Grant strode like a colossus through the music industry, bending people and events to his will, and that of his charges, He was a man who would deliver to the letter on a contract, and would expect nothing less from anybody else. If someone let him down, then they'd know about it – and in no uncertain terms.

He was harsh with promoters, record label executives and bootleggers. The last-named felt his wrath on more than one occasion.

'My view on these people was this: they were taking money out of my artists' pockets – and I wasn't prepared to accept this. If the authorities were powerless, then I took my own action.'

That's what Grant told *Raw* magazine in 1989, and there are so many legendary stories of raids on record shops, broken records and, sometimes, an equal number of shattered limbs.

Born in South Norwood, Surrey on 5 April 1935, Grant had a number of jobs, before getting into wrestling under the names of 'Count Massimo' and 'Count Bruno Alassio of Milan'. This led to an acting career, albeit on the fringes. In the ten years from 1953, he appeared in films such as *A Night To Remember, The Guns Of Navarone* and *Cleopatra*, as well as TV shows like *The Benny Hill Show* and *Dixon Of Dock Green*. He was also actor Robert Morley's stunt double.

In 1963 Don Arden hired him as tour manager for American artists like Bo Diddley, Little Richard, the Everly Brothers and Chuck Berry. Within a year, he was managing in

his own right, working with the likes of Terry Reid, Jeff Beck, the New Vaudeville Band, Stone the Crows and the Nashville Teens.

Two years later, he took over the Yardbirds, developing a penchant for persuading promoters to pay up. It's said this was the only time in their career that the Yardbirds actually made money!

When the band fell apart, he helped to mastermind the rise of Led Zeppelin. He negotiated a huge contract with Atlantic, sidestepped singles and TV appearances, and thereby made Zeppelin a little more unattainable. It was the sort of business acumen that not only propelled Zeppelin to great success, but also earned Grant the adulation and respect of his peers, and of subsequent managerial generations.

Grant virtually became a recluse after the death of John Bonham, whom he almost regarded as a surrogate son, in 1980. This blow, together with a crippling battle against diabetes and addictions, led to him retiring to his estate in Hellingly, East Sussex. But, after losing a considerable amount of weight, Grant re-emerged at the end of the decade, moving to Eastbourne and getting his life back on track. He appeared as a Cardinal in the 1992 movie *Carry On Columbus* and also was a keynote speaker at many music-business conferences. He was also planning his autobiography when he suffered a fatal heart attack on

21 November 1995.

Grant's legacy is truly impressive and inspirational. And, at no point has any member of Led Zeppelin said he was anything but straightforward in his dealings with them. He was a hard negotiator, but one who was also fair. He wanted what was best for the four members of the band – and, more often than not, got it.

Even in his latter years, Grant was a charismatic, imposing figure, but one who spoke passionately about the music and the musicians he loved.

A family man, he had two children (Warren and Helen) and it

says much of his standing that he was actually asked to become a magistrate in the early Nineties – an honour he turned down.

'I don't know how I'd like to be remembered,' he told *Raw* magazine in 1989. 'Perhaps as someone who was privileged to be able to work with such talented people, and was in a position to help facilitate their genius coming through. Not bad for a one-time sheet metal worker, eh?'

GROHL, DAVE

The Foo Fighters leader and former Nirvana drummer is a massive Zeppelin fan, to the point of having three tattoos of John Bonham's famed three-circle emblem.

'I did the first one myself when I was 16,' he told *Rolling Stone* in 2009. 'I tried to get different coloured ink to make it seem pro, but now it looks like someone put a cigarette out on my fucking arm.'

The second was done in an illegal squat in Amsterdam 'by an Italian guy named Andrea whose tattoo gun was made out of a doorbell machine. When my mother saw it, she was like, "David!". I was like, "Mom, I've done a lot worse shit than this, believe me. Look at my other arm".'

The third one he paid for out of his first cheque from Nirvana: 'Kurt (Cobain) and I were living with each other in Olympia. The place was so depressing, I took the $400 and bought a Nintendo, a BB gun – mind you, I was 21, not

12 – and got that tattoo. One of my fondest memories of living in that rat-shit-hole apartment was buying a dozen eggs at the A&P, bringing them to Kurt's backyard, and me and Kurt and Buzz (Osborne) from the Melvins shooting at the eggs. Those were the days.'

Grohl actually offered his services to Zeppelin for their 2007 reunion show at the O$_2$ Arena. Two years later he was working with John Paul Jones in Them Crooked Vultures.

'Heavy metal would not exist without Led Zeppelin,' he wrote for *Rolling Stone* in 2004, 'and if it did, it would suck. Led Zeppelin were more than just a band – they were the perfect combination of the most intense elements: passion and mystery and expertise. It always seemed like Led Zeppelin were searching for something. They weren't content being in one place, and they were always trying something new. They could do anything, and I believe they would have done everything if they hadn't been cut short by John Bonham's death. Zeppelin served as a great escape from a lot of things. There was a fantasy element to everything they did, and it was such a major part of what made them important. Who knows if we'd all be watching *Lord of the Rings* movies right now if it weren't for Zeppelin?

'They were never critically acclaimed in their day, because

they were too experimental and they were too fringe. In 1968 and '69, there was some freaky shit going on, but Zeppelin were the freakiest – I consider Jimmy Page freakier than Jimi Hendrix. Hendrix was a genius on fire, whereas Page was a genius possessed. Zeppelin concerts and albums were like exorcisms for them. People had their asses blown out by Hendrix and Jeff Beck and Eric Clapton, but Page took it to a whole new level, and he did it in such a beautifully human and imperfect way. He plays the guitar like an old bluesman on acid. When I listen to Zeppelin bootlegs, his solos can make me laugh or they can make me tear up. Any live version of "Since I've Been Loving You" will bring you to tears and fill you with joy all at once. Page doesn't just use his guitar as an instrument. For him, it's like some sort of emotional translator.

'John Bonham played the drums like someone who didn't know what was going to happen next – like he was teetering on the edge of a cliff. No-one has come close to that since, and I don't think anybody ever will. I think he will forever be the greatest drummer of all time. You have no idea how much he influenced me. I spent years in my bedroom – literally fucking years – listening to Bonham's drums and trying to emulate his swing or his behind-the-beat swagger or his speed or power. Not just memorizing what

he did on those albums but getting myself into a place where I would have the same instinctual direction as he had. I have John Bonham tattoos all over my body – on my wrists, my arms, my shoulders.

'"Black Dog", from "Zeppelin IV", is what Led Zeppelin were all about in their most rocking moments, a perfect example of their true might. It didn't have to be really distorted or really fast, it just had to be Zeppelin and it was really heavy. Then there's Zeppelin's sensitive side – something people overlook, because we think of them as rock beasts, but "Zeppelin III" was full of gentle beauty. That was the soundtrack to me dropping out of high school. I listened to it every single day in my VW bug, while I contemplated my direction in life. That album, for whatever reason, saved some light in me that I still have.

'I heard them for the first time on AM radio in the Seventies, right around the time that "Stairway To Heaven" was so popular. I was six or seven years old, which is when I'd just started discovering music. But it wasn't until I was a teenager that I discovered the first two Zeppelin records, which were handed down to me from the real stoners. We had a lot of those in the suburbs of Virginia, and a lot of muscle cars and keggers and Zeppelin and acid and weed. Somehow they all went hand in hand. To me, Zeppelin were spiritually inspirational. I was going to Catholic school and questioning God, but I believed in Led Zeppelin. I wasn't really buying into this Christianity thing, but I had faith in Led Zeppelin as a spiritual entity. They showed me that human beings could channel this music somehow and that it was coming from somewhere. It wasn't coming from a songbook. It wasn't coming from a producer. It wasn't coming from an instructor. It was coming from somewhere else.

'I believe Zeppelin will come back and prove themselves to once again be the greatest rock band of all time. It will happen. They'll find someone to play the drums and I'll be right there, front row at every goddamn show. Then I could finally die a happy man.'

HAMMER OF THE GODS

Hammer Of The Gods is the title of a 1985 biography of Led Zeppelin written by Stephen Davis, who has also penned works on Bob Marley, Fleetwood Mac, Aerosmith and Guns N' Roses. The book takes its title from a line in the band's 'Immigrant Song'.

Hammer Of The Gods became widely known due to its sensationalist tone and lurid descriptions concerning the band's alleged activities, or those surrounding them. Davis had only spent two weeks on tour with Led Zeppelin, covering the band for *Rolling Stone* magazine, of which he was an editor at the time. However, he based a lot of his material in *Hammer Of The Gods* on interviews with ex-Led Zeppelin tour manager Richard Cole, who had been fired by the band prior to their 1980 European tour because of substance issues.

Given the insular nature of Led Zeppelin, and the fact that the band operated at a time when the prying eyes of the media could easily be kept at bay (a far cry from today's Internet-fuelled instant news coverage), *Hammer*

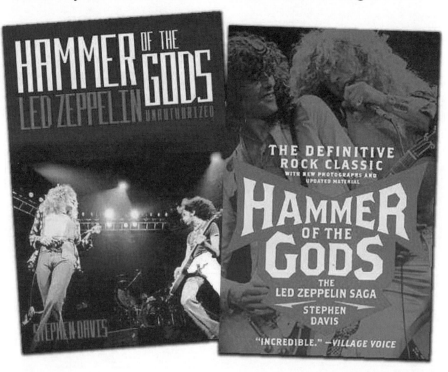

Of The Gods was an immediate best-seller. Equally unsurprisingly, the surviving members of Led Zeppelin were less than pleased, to put it mildly.

'The guy who wrote that book knew nothing about the band,' Robert Plant told *Spin* magazine. 'I think he'd hung around us once. He got all his information from a guy who had a heroin problem who happened to be associated with us. The only thing I read was the "After Zeppelin" part, because I was eager to get on with the music and stop living in a dream state.'

Plant continued this theme when he spoke to *New Musical Express* in 2008: 'He did a lot of investigations with a guy who used to work with Led Zeppelin, Richard Cole, who, over the years, had shown deep frustration at not being in a position to have any authority at all. He was tour manager, and he had a problem which could have been easily solved if he'd been given something intelligent to do rather than check the hotels, and I think it embittered him greatly. He became progressively unreliable and, sadly, became a millstone around the neck of the group.

'These stories would filter out from girls who'd supposedly been in my room when, in fact, they'd been in his. That sort of atmosphere was being created, and we were quite tired of it. So eventually we relieved him of his position. And in the meantime he got paid a lot of money for talking crap. A lot of the time he wasn't completely…well. And so his view of things was permanently distorted one way or another.'

Hammer Of The Gods has been updated since its publication, with the added title 'The Led Zeppelin Saga' and 'Led Zeppelin Unauthorised'.

HARDIE, GEORGE

George Hardie is an artist and illustrator who worked on the cover for Led Zeppelin's debut album, released in 1968. He would later collaborate with Storm Thorgerson and Hipgnosis on the covers for Pink Floyd's 'Dark Side Of The Moon' and 'Wish You Were Here' albums. He also worked on Led Zeppelin's 1976 album 'Presence' for which he was nominated for a Grammy in 1977. Most recently he has been lecturer at the University of Brighton.

HARPER, ROY

Roy Harper is an English folk musician who has toured and recorded with Led Zeppelin and Jimmy Page over the years. He was the subject of the 'Led Zeppelin III' song 'Hats Off To (Roy) Harper'.

Harper met Jimmy Page and Led Zeppelin at the 1970 Bath Festival, by which time he'd already established himself as a unique solo artist in his own right with albums such as 'Folkjokeopus' (1969) and 'Flat Baroque And Berserk' (1969).

Impressed with Harper's bullish insistence in doing things his own way and refusing to adhere to record-company interference, Page and Harper became friends. Harper was invited to tour with Led Zeppelin in 1971, further cementing his friendship with the band, one that would endure throughout the remainder of Zeppelin's career.

Page appeared on Harper's legendary 1971 epic 'Stormcock', although contractual issues meant he appeared under the pseudonym S Flavius Mercurius (which was bound to have conspiracy theorists frothing at the mouth). He also appeared on 1972's 'Lifemask' and 1974's 'Valentine'. John Paul Jones featured on Harper's 1975 album 'HQ'. There is even a rumour that, with Robert Plant sidelined after the death of his son Karac, Harper had been drafted in by Page to help write lyrics for a new Led Zeppelin album, but a returned Plant meant that Harper

ultimately wasn't needed. Harper also supplied photography that was used on the inner sleeve of 'Physical Graffiti'.

Post-Zeppelin, Page made one of his first public forays with Harper, appearing with him for an acoustic performance at the Cambridge Folk Festival in July 1984. The pair also toured together and in 1985 released the album 'Whatever Happened To Jugula?'. In 2005, Page presented Harper with *Mojo* magazine's Hero Award at London's Porchester Hall.

HARRISON, GEORGE

Of all the Beatles, guitarist George Harrison was closest to Led Zeppelin, and is credited with being the inspiration behind 'The Rain Song', having mentioned to Jimmy Page that the problem with the band was that they didn't have enough ballads. In honour of Harrison, Page included two recognisable chords from Harrison's own Beatles song 'Something' as the opening of

'The Rain Song'.

Another story emanates from John Bonham's 25th birthday party, attended by Harrison. Rumours suggest that it was Harrison who instigated the expected tomfoolery by taking the top tier of Bonham's birthday cake and depositing it on Bonham's head. It didn't take long for most guests to end up in the swimming pool. So legend has it, the expensively suited Jimmy Page, who couldn't swim, sidestepped the inevitable dunking by gallantly walking into the pool himself.

HATS OFF TO (ROY) HARPER

'Hats Off To (Roy) Harper' is the tenth and final track on Led Zeppelin's 1970 third album. The title is a nod to British folk musician Roy Harper, Zeppelin's good friend and sometime collaborator.

The song also pays tribute to the many American bluesmen who inspired the band by essentially being a series of segments of traditional blues songs, such as Bukka White's 'Shake 'Em On Down'. The song came about during a medley of different styles of blues songs that the band recorded at Robert Plant's suggestion, while in the throes of recording 'Led Zeppelin III'. However the only one to make the album's final cut was 'Hats Off To (Roy) Harper'.

Other songs that appear to have been recorded during these sessions, as has been suggested by various bootlegs, were many of the songs Led Zeppelin would cover in live medleys which they would perform during 'Whole Lotta Love' and 'How Many More Times', such as Elvis Presley's 'That's Alright Mama'. Ironically Zeppelin never performed 'Hats Off To (Roy) Harper' live. It was, however, released as a single in Poland in 1970, with 'Out On The Tiles' as a B-side.

HEADLEY GRANGE

Headley Grange is a house situated in Headley, North-East Hampshire, which was used by Led Zeppelin. The band wrote and recorded parts of the 'Led Zeppelin III', 'Led Zeppelin IV', 'Houses Of The Holy' and 'Physical Graffiti' albums there.

Originally built as a poorhouse in 1795, it was the scene of a legendary riot in 1830, which was later publicised in the book *One Monday In November – The Story Of The Selborne And Headley Workhouse Riots Of 1830*. Purchased by local builder Thomas Kemp in 1850, it was renamed Headley Grange and became a private residence.

Headley Grange began being let out for various uses in the early Sixties, and before long began to become popular with rock bands.

'Headley Grange was somewhat rundown, the heating didn't work,' Jimmy Page recalled for *Uncut* in 2009. 'But it had one major advantage. Other bands had

rehearsed there and hadn't had any complaints. That's a major issue, because you don't want to go somewhere and start locking into the work process and then have to pull out.'

The drawing room, in particular, proved to have some fine acoustics for recording. Zeppelin wrote much of 'Stairway To Heaven' at Headley Grange, as well as naming the song 'Black Dog' after an unnamed black Labrador that used to roam around the grounds.

Headley Grange was also used by Genesis, Peter Frampton, Fleetwood Mac, Bad Company and Ian Dury. Today, the building is once more a private residence.

HEARTBREAKER

'Heartbreaker' is the fifth track on 1969's 'Led Zeppelin II'. The song opened the original side two of the vinyl version of the album and features one of Jimmy Page's most recognisable riffs, and an incendiary solo that Page is rumoured to have improvised on the spot; this solo is said to have been the inspiration behind Eddie Van Halen's own tapping technique.

Page would continue his improvisation during the song's solo when performing 'Heartbreaker' live, and would lengthen out the solo to include such pieces as the traditional 'Greensleeves', Simon and Garfunkel's '59th Street Bridge Song (Feelin' Groovy)' and Bach's 'Bourrée In E Minor'.

'Heartbreaker' proved to be a huge live favourite for Zeppelin. On 1971-72 tours the band would open their shows with a lethal one-two of 'Immigrant Song', segueing straight into 'Heartbreaker'. On later tours 'Heartbreaker' would be performed as an encore.

Although sections of 'Heartbreaker' appear in the 1976 film *The Song Remains The Same*, it did not feature on the soundtrack album of the same name until a 2007 remastered version appeared.

'Heartbreaker' was released as a 1969 single in Italy (backed with 'Bring It On Home'), in the Philippines (backed with 'Ramble On') and in South Africa (backed with 'Living Loving Maid (She's Just A Woman)'. The song, which was co-written by all four members of the band, has been covered by Nirvana, Sly and Robbie, Michael White, Steve Morse and George Clinton.

HEY HEY WHAT CAN I DO

'Hey Hey What Can I Do' is the only non-album track to have appeared during Led Zeppelin's existence, which appeared as the B-side to the 1970 'Immigrant Song' single.

The song, which was written by all four members of Led Zeppelin, and deals with love and infidelity, subsequently appeared on a 1972 compilation entitled 'The Golden Age Of Atlantic' (which can occasionally be found in second-hand record shops), and also featured on the four-disc 'Led Zeppelin' box set that appeared in 1990. It also featured in the 10-CD set 'The Complete Recordings' as one of four extra tracks added to 'Coda' and was also the B-side to a vinyl replica single of 'Immigrant Song' in 1993.

Robert Plant performed the song in concert with Alison Krauss.

HILTON, TOKYO

Led Zeppelin were banned from the Tokyo Hilton for life during the band's first Japanese tour, which began in September 1971. Already no strangers to offstage tomfoolery and excess, it is widely alleged that, whilst staying at the Tokyo Hilton, drummer John Bonham and tour manager Richard Cole proceeded to destroy a hotel room with recently acquired Samurai swords.

HIP YOUNG GUITAR SLINGER

Another compilation gathering together many of the recording sessions Jimmy Page worked on between 1962 and 1966. It was released on the Sanctuary label in 2000. Fans should note that there are tracks that Page did not play on. For example the Lancastrians' 'We'll Walk In The Sunshine' is featured, although Page only appeared on the B-side, 'Was She Tall'.

TRACKLISTING:

Disc One:
Carter Lewis and the Southerners
Who Told You?
Gregory Phillips
Angie/Please Believe Me
Carter Lewis and the Southerners
Somebody Told My Girl/
Skinny Minnie
Wayne Gibson and Dynamic Sounds
– Kelly/See You Later, Alligator
The Kinks
Revenge/Bald Headed Woman
The First Gear
A Certain Girl/Leave My Kitten Alone

The Primitives
Help Me/Let Them Talk
The Lancastrians
*We'll Sing In The Sunshine/Was
She Tall*
The Primitives
You Said/How Do You Feel
The First Gear
*The 'In' Crowd/Gotta Make Their
Future Bright*
The Fifth Avenue
*The Bells Of Rhymney/ Just Like
Anyone Would Do*
Nico
I'm Not Sayin'/The Last Mile
Gregory Phillips
*Down In The Boondocks/That's
The One*
The Masterminds
She Belongs To Me/Taken My Love.
Disc Two:
John Mayall's Bluesbreakers
I'm Your Witchdoctor/Telephone Blues
John Mayall and the
Bluesbreakers with Eric Clapton
On Top Of The World
Les Fleur De Lys
Moondreams/Wait For Me
The Lancastrians
*The World Keeps Going Round/Not
The Same Anymore*
The Factotums
Can't Go Home Anymore My Love
Les Fleur De Lys
Circles/So Come On
Twice As Much
Sittin' On A Fence/Step Out Of Line
Chris Farlowe
Moanin'
Eric Clapton and Jimmy Page
*Choker/Freight Loader/Miles Road/
Draggin' My Tail*
All Stars featuring Jimmy Page

LA Breakdown/Down In The Boots
Eric Clapton
*Snake Drive/West Coast Idea/Tribute
To Elmore*
The All Stars With Jeff Beck
Chuckles/Steelin'
The All Stars with Nicky Hopkins
Piano Shuffle
Cyril Davies and the All Stars
Not Fade Away.

HOBBSTWEEDLE

Hobbstweedle were a Midlands blues band that featured Robert Plant on vocals. They were the band Plant was fronting when Jimmy Page travelled to check out the singer who had been suggested by Page's original choice, Terry Reid.

'I had nowhere to live and the keyboards player's dad had a pub in Wolverhampton with a spare room,' Plant told *Q* magazine in 1990 of his 'Tweedling days. 'The pub was right over the road from Noddy Holder's father's window-cleaning business, and Noddy used to be our roadie. We used to go to gigs with Noddy Holder's dad's buckets crashing around on top of the van! And that is when I met Pagey.'

HOLMES, JAKE

Jake Holmes is an American folk singer and jingle writer who originally wrote 'Dazed And Confused', a song Led Zeppelin featured on their 1968 debut album and which is credited to Jimmy Page.

Holmes started out in a folk band with Tim Rose, whose version of 'Hey Joe' inspired Jimi Hendrix's. Holmes went solo with 1967's 'The Above Ground Sound Of Jake Holmes', which included his version of 'Dazed And Confused'. It was around this time that Holmes supported the Yardbirds who were on tour in America. The band heard him perform 'Dazed And Confused' at Greenwich Village, which inspired them to seek out Holmes' debut album and rework 'Dazed And Confused' themselves; this swiftly became a highpoint of the band's live set.

When the Yardbirds dissolved, Page took 'Dazed And Confused' with him to his new band, with Robert Plant re-writing many of the lyrics and the song ending up being credited to Jimmy Page. Holmes is said to have written to Page about the incorrect crediting of the song, but never received a reply. He declined to proceed with legal action.

Holmes' second solo album, 'A Letter To Katherine December', also appeared in 1967, and Holmes has continued to write and record ever since. He hit paydirt in America with a famous jingle written for the US Army, and also one co-penned with Randy Newman, for the soft drink Dr. Pepper.

He can be found on MySpace at: *www.myspace.com/jakeholmes*

HONEYDRIPPERS

The Honeydrippers was a Robert Plant side project that in turn developed into Plant's first solo album, 'Pictures At Eleven', and a successful superstar project that found chart success in America in the mid Eighties.

The Honeydrippers, who took their name from the nickname of blues pianist Roosevelt Sykes, was originally intended as an outlet to allow Plant to take tentative musical steps after the demise of Led Zeppelin, and indulge his pre-Zeppelin fondness for R&B. The original line-up featured Robbie Blunt and Andy Sylvester (guitar), Kevin O'Neil (drums), Jim Hickman (bass), Keith Evans (saxophone) and Ricky Cool (harmonica). The line-up played a gig in 1981 at Keele University, but eventually the material that Plant was writing with Blunt was deemed more appropriate for Plant's return to the rock scene and became the basis for his first solo band and album.

Following 1983's Principle Of Moments' album, Plant returned to the idea of the Honeydrippers, only this time they featured both Jimmy Page and Jeff Beck on guitar, Chic bassist Nile Rodgers, Paul Shaffer (keyboards) and Dave Weckl (drums). This new line-up recorded the five-track 'The Honeydrippers Volume One' on the Es Paranza label. The album, proved popular in America, where the band's refreshing takes on Fifties and Sixties R&B material found favour – the single 'Sea Of Love' even charted one place higher than Led Zeppelin's 'Whole Lotta Love' had done.

Robert Plant performed as the

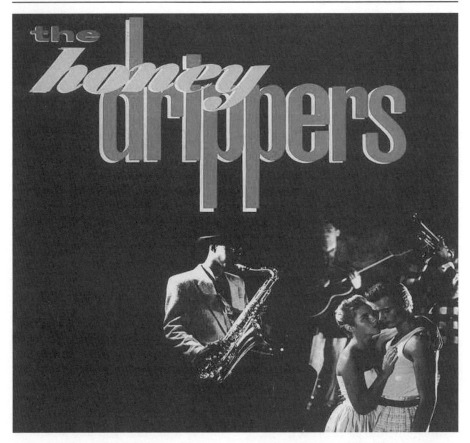

Return of the Honeydrippers in Kidderminster in December 2006 to raise money for a neighbour suffering from a brain tumour. A new Honeydrippers album was allegedly discussed by Plant and Atlantic boss, the late Ahmet Ertegun, following Plant's appearance at the 2006 Montreux Jazz Festival, though this would now seem unlikely.

THE HONEYDRIPPERS: VOLUME ONE

'The Honeydrippers: Volume One' was a 1984 five-track EP released on the Es Paranza label that saw Robert Plant and Jimmy Page unite for the first time since the demise of Led Zeppelin in 1980.

The album approximated a pre-Beatles R&B sound, awash with horns and strings, and reached Number 4 in the US album charts. That it reached a lowly 56 in the UK charts gives some indication of the manner in which Zeppelin were viewed for a while in their home country.

However, in America the band continued to reap rewards. The band's cover of Phil Phillips' 'Sea Of Love' reached Number 3 in the US singles chart. The Honeydrippers did not tour, but did appear on the TV show *Late Night Live*, performing 'Rockin' At Midnight' and 'Santa Claus Is

Back In Town', featuring Stray Cat Brian Setzer on guitar.

TRACKLISTING:

I Get A Thrill/Sea Of Love/I Got A Woman/Young Boy Blues/Rockin' At Midnight.

HOT DOG

'Hot Dog' is the fourth song on Led Zeppelin's eighth studio album 'In Through The Out Door'. The country-inspired song, which seems to be a light-hearted celebration of all things American, was written by Robert Plant and Jimmy Page.

The song developed out of the band's fondness for jamming rockabilly tunes at pre-production rehearsals. The song was performed live by Led Zeppelin at both Knebworth shows in August, and also on the band's 1980 European tour. Footage from Knebworth was not included on the *Led Zeppelin* DVD release, possibly because Plant forgot the lyrics.

HOTS ON FOR NOWHERE

A song of frustration that appeared as track number six on Led Zeppelin's 1976 album 'Presence', 'Hots On For Nowhere' was written by Robert Plant and Jimmy Page.

Lyrically, 'Hots On For Nowhere' deals with frustrations Plant had at the time with Page and Led Zeppelin manager Peter Grant. It is also one of the rare times the word 'fuck' is almost used in the lyrics, Plant opting for 'fluck' by way of replacement (the only other occasion was Jimmy Page muttering 'fuck' before 'Friends').

'Hots On For Nowhere' was never performed live by Led Zeppelin. It was covered by Van Halen and Stevie Salas, and also featured in the 2001 skateboard movie *Dogtown And Z-Boys*.

HOUSES OF THE HOLY (SONG)

'Houses Of The Holy' is the fourth song from Led Zeppelin's sixth studio album 'Physical Graffiti'. Written by Jimmy Page and Robert Plant, the song shares its title with the preceding Led Zeppelin album, for which it was intended for inclusion but was removed when it was decided it did not fit in with the remainder of the material.

The song title and lyrics refer to Led Zeppelin's own concerts – the houses being the massive arenas that the band would perform in. Ironically the band never performed the song live. It was released as an Italian single, reaching Number 27 in 1975.

HOUSES OF THE HOLY (ALBUM)

'Houses Of The Holy' is Led Zeppelin's fifth studio album, released on 28 March 1973. It was the first album not to feature the band's name in the title and also the first to feature entirely original material written by the band. It is also one of the most diverse of all their albums, adding funk and reggae to the band's strident hard rock and folk influences.

Kicking off with the swirling hard rock of 'The Song Remains The Same' (which would lend its name to the soundtrack for the band's 1976 film), it was a slightly different Led Zeppelin that faced record listeners in 1973. Having created the desired impression with the bombastic new rock sound of 'Led Zeppelin' and 'Led Zeppelin II', they proved adept at diversity with the delightfully folk and even country-infused 'Led Zeppelin III' and finally seemingly drawing it altogether in emphatic style with their fourth album. 'Houses Of The Holy', however, found Led Zeppelin taking stock and trying some new tricks. The guitars were far more layered than on previous albums, the production again handled by Jimmy Page but with help from engineers Andy Johns and Eddie Kramer, and with John Paul Jones truly coming into his own as an arranger.

The first surprise was the grandiose 'The Rain Song', inspired by a George Harrison comment about the band never recording ballads (he'd obviously not heard 'Stairway To Heaven'). With a hauntingly effective melody line that Mancunian indie sensations the Smiths would appropriate for 'How Soon Is Now', the song builds effectively to its climax, and displays further evolution in the songwriting stakes. And if 'Over The Hills And Far Away' was a more traditional Zep mix of folk music and bombastic rock'n'roll, then the James Brown-like yelps of 'The Crunge' showed that there was no fear in mixing musical styles deemed previously ill-matched. The funk would also rear its head on the impressive 'The Ocean', with its jagged riffing (which in turn would inspire AC/DC's own 'Back In Black').

And even if the staccato hard rock of 'Dancing Days' and the cod-reggae of 'D'yer Mak'er' (the title a supposed joke on the pronunciation of 'Jamaica' that one can't imagine any band trying to get away with today) seem slightly ill-fitting, then the majesty and pomp of the enigmatic 'No Quarter' saw the whole band gel as one tightly bound, cohesive unit. Highlighting the musical skills of John Paul Jones and proving how important he was to the Zeppelin mix, the quasi-mystical sounding 'No Quarter', literally meaning show no mercy to your opponents, pointed the way ahead for Led Zeppelin. It would be sweeping musical epics from here on in.

Much of 'Houses Of The Holy' was recorded in spring 1972 at Mick Jagger's Berkshire residence Stargroves, which housed the Rolling Stones mobile and meant the band could record anywhere, even outside. Both John Paul Jones and Jimmy Page had recently had home studios built, so they came to sessions with some song arrangements almost complete. This was certainly the case with 'The Rain Song', and even Jones' 'No Quarter', which had previously been worked on at Headley Grange. The band also took some of the material on the road with them during their 1972 US tour and worked on it at New York's Electric Lady Studios. Other material was worked on at London's Olympic Studios.

Some songs from the sessions did not make the final cut of 'Houses Of The Holy' but would crop up on later Zeppelin albums, namely 'Black Country Woman', 'The Rover', 'Walter's Walk' and the title track.

The band drafted album-art specialists Hipgnosis to work on the sleeve concept – the first time the two parties would work together. Aubrey Powell took the cover photo which featured a young British brother and sister, Stefan and Samantha Gates, on the Giant's Causeway in Northern Ireland, which won out over on proposed location in Peru! The inside shot was taken at Dunluce Castle, near to the Causeway. The shoot lasted ten days and could only be undertaken in the morning and evening in order to attain the desired lighting effect. Although Hipgnosis were initially unhappy with the results of the photo-shoot, which was inspired by the Arthur C Clarke novel *Childhood's End*, the startling coloured effect came about through some accidental tinting work.

Like its predecessor, the band's name and album title did not appear anywhere on the album sleeve. Also, the fact that naked child buttocks could be viewed suggested the every pious and overtly prudent US market would kick up a fuss (needless to say the album was banned in certain Southern states), so manager Peter Grant allowed a paper band to be wrapped around the album which served to hide the offending buttocks.

Famously, this version of the sleeve was the second to be presented by Hipgnosis. Storm Thorgerson had presented a sleeve that featured an electric green tennis court with a tennis racquet on it but this was dismissed by a furious Page, who thought the designer was implying the music was simply a racket. The new sleeve is certainly far more in keeping with the idea behind the title, a thank-you from the band to the 'oceans' of fans who flocked to the venues, the 'houses of the holy' to see them. The sleeve was nominated for a Grammy for Best Album Package.

With of the album's songs already aired on the 1972 and 1973 tours, the album was a commercial success, reaching Number 1 in the UK, US, Australia and Canada, and charting highly elsewhere. Critically, some reviewers sniffed at the inclusion of 'D'yer Mak'er' (which was released as a single in America, as was 'Over The Hills

And Far Away') and even 'The Crunge', but 'Houses Of The Holy' is a splendid documentation of mid-period Led Zeppelin – the pivotal point between the fledgling young band and the giant behemoth to come.

TRACKLISTING:

The Song Remains The Same/The Rain Song/Over The Hills And Far Away/The Crunge/Dancing Days/ D'yer Mak'er/No Quarter/The Ocean.

HOW MANY MORE TIMES

'How Many More Times' is the epic final track on the band's 1969 debut album 'Led Zeppelin'. The song was written by Jimmy Page, John Paul Jones and John Bonham.

Not dissimilar to the Yardbirds', and ultimately Jeff Beck's, 'Beck's Bolero', which had been written by Page (who used a bowed guitar on the track), 'How Many More Times' is a collection of smaller blues pieces held together by a bolero-style rhythm. In 1951, the late Howlin' Wolf had penned a blues song entitled 'How Many More Times', and eventually Chester Burnett (Wolf's real name) was added to the song-writing credit by arrangement after 1990.

While Plant received no songwriting credit on 'Led Zeppelin' owing to an ongoing contractual problem, his influence on the likes of 'How Many More Times' is especially strong, given his previous experience adapting old blues tunes with previous band Hobbstweedle.

Although clocking in at eight-and-a-half minutes, the sleeve lists the track as only three-and-a-half – a deliberate move on behalf of Jimmy Page, who realised no radio station would play a song over eight minutes in length and was an attempt to hoodwink them into playing the song on the radio.

'How Many More Times' was performed live by the band on early tours, usually as an encore on which they would include the likes of Elvis Presley's 'That's Alright Mama' and John Lee Hooker's 'Boogie Chillen'. These would move to a medley in 'Whole Lotta Love' when the band dropped 'How Many More Times', although it did return to the set in 1975 when Page had injured a finger and couldn't perform 'Dazed And Confused'.

The song features on the DVD *Led Zeppelin* (featuring both a 1969 Danish performance and one from the Royal Albert Hall), and was also performed by Jimmy Page and Robert Plant on their 1998 tour. The duo even released a live version of the song recorded at the Shepherd's Bush Empire in London.

'How Many More Times' has been covered by LA Guns, Loudness, Dread Zeppelin, Pat Travers and Liquid Tension Experiment.

HOW THE WEST WAS WON

'How The West Was Won' is a triple live album that was released on the Atlantic label in May 2003.

The title alludes to the West Coast of America and the album showcases material recorded at two 1972 Los Angeles concerts, one at the LA Forum on 25 June and one at Long Beach Arena on 27 June.

Although many of these recordings had been widely available in bootleg form, 'How The West Was Won' answered the specific call from Led Zeppelin fans for a worthy live album. The soundtrack to *The Song Remains The Same* had long been the sole live document available for many years, and considered not to be the band at their most effective. 1997's 'BBC Sessions' had gone some way to answering the fan's call, but they still hankered for official recordings made in front of an audience – the arena in which Led Zeppelin excelled.

These two concerts were recorded during a period where Jimmy Page, who produced the album, believed the band to be at their creative peak. The original tapes underwent a period of editing and engineering at London's Sarm West Studios. To the ire of some fans, performance of 'Communication Breakdown', 'Thank You' and a rare cover of 'Louie Louie' were left off the finished running order.

The album hit the Number 1 spot in America and reached Number 5 in the UK.

TRACKLISTING:

Disc One: *LA Drone/Immigrant Song/Heartbreaker/Black Dog/Over The Hills And Far Away/Since I've Been Loving You/Stairway To Heaven/Going To California/That's The Way/Bron-Yr-Aur Stomp.*
Disc Two: *Dazed And Confused/ What Is And What Should Never Be/ Dancing Days/Moby Dick.*
Disc Three: *Whole Lotta Love/ Rock And Roll/The Ocean/Bring It On Home.*

HYATT HOUSE

The Hyatt House is a hotel on Los Angeles's Sunset Boulevard much loved by Led Zeppelin throughout the Seventies – and the scene, if rumours are to be believed, of much revelry and partying.

It was affectionately known as the Riot House, thanks to the salaciously revelatory nature of books like Stephen Davis' *Hammer Of The Gods* and Richard Cole's *Stairway To Heaven: Led Zeppelin Uncensored*, while stories such as John Bonham allegedly riding a motorbike around floors of the Hyatt House are the stuff of legend. As are rumours that Zeppelin would hire out six floors of the hotel whenever they were in town during the mid to late Seventies. Robert Plant is credited with uttering the phrase 'I am a golden god' whilst stood surveying LA from a hotel balcony (the scene was replicated in Cameron Crowe's film *Almost Famous*).

Certainly the Hyatt's position on Sunset Boulevard made it popular with visiting rock bands. Its close proximity to popular rock star haunts such as the Rainbow and

the Whisky A Go Go, the Roxy and
the Key Club. Other stories include
tales of Keiths Richards and Moon
hurling TV sets off balconies,
Motörhead's Lemmy writing the
band's titular song on a balcony
one night and the likes of Jim
Morrison and Little Richard living
in residence.

In January 2009 the 257-roomed
hotel was renovated and reopened
as the Andaz West Hollywood.

I CAN'T QUIT YOU BABY

The eighth track from the debut Led Zeppelin album, this was written by Willie Dixon and first recorded by Otis Rush in 1956. It was something of a hit for Rush back then, reaching Number 6 on the *Billboard* R&B charts.

Produced and arranged by Dixon, the song was a slow 12-bar blues, with lyrics inspired by a relationship Rush was in at the time. In 1967, John Mayall's Bluesbreakers covered it, and two years later Little Milton teamed up with Dixon himself for yet another version.

However, what interests us here is, of course, the Zeppelin rendition, which is based on a revamped version of the song done by Rush himself in 1966. It very much gets to the heart of Zeppelin's dedication to authentic blues as this time in their young career.

This song was regularly played by the band from 1968 until 1970. You can hear a 1969 version on the 1997 'BBC Sessions' album, and an edited version of a live performance from January 1970 at the Royal Albert Hall is on the 1982 'Coda' album. The full version of this was included in the 2003 DVD *Led Zeppelin*.

Replaced by 'Since I've Been Loving You' from 1970 onwards, the song was never again played in its entirety, although it was briefly part of the 'Whole Lotta Love' medley for some gigs in 1972-73.

The band did rehearse it for inclusion in their set for the 1988 Atlantic 40th Anniversary concert, but it wasn't played in the end.

I'M GONNA CRAWL

This was featured on the band's last studio album, 1979's 'In Through The Out Door'; it was the seventh track on the record. Most of the music was written by John Paul Jones, emulating the soul-blues style of legends such as Otis Redding and Wilson Pickett. Some of the lyrics are a tribute to Robert Plant's son Karac, who'd died in 1977 from a stomach infection.

This song was never performed live by Zeppelin.

IMMIGRANT SONG

Opening song on the 1970 album 'Led Zeppelin III'. This is regarded by many people as the first ever Battle Metal anthem!

It opens with a wailing Robert Plant, soaring over a staccato pulse. It was inspired by the band's trip to Iceland, as Robert Plant explained to journalist Chris Welch: 'We weren't being pompous... We did come from the land of the ice and snow. We were guests of the Icelandic Government on a cultural mission. We were invited to play a concert in Reykjavik and the day before we arrived all the civil servants went on strike and the gig was going to be cancelled. The university prepared a concert hall for us and it was phenomenal. The response from the kids was remarkable and we had a great time. "Immigrant Song" was about that trip and it was the opening track on the album that was intended to be incredibly different.'

What's remarkable is that, six days after playing in Reykjavik, the band performed it during the Bath Festival – now that's speed! Dedicated to tenth-century Norse explorer Leif Ericson, this has a lot of references to Viking conquests and celebrates that way of life.

The song was actually released in America as a single in 1970, despite the band's objections. Backed with the non-album song 'Hey Hey What Can I Do', it reached Number 16 in the charts. It also came out in Japan, with 'Out On The Tiles' on the B-side.

The band played this live on a regular basis from 1970 to 1972 before it became an occasional encore song and was finally dropped from the set. But it has taken on a cultural life of its own. You can hear it in the films *School Of Rock* and *Shrek The Third* (slightly altered in the latter case). Both Brentford Football Club and NFL team the Minnesota Vikings have used it as their music to run out to.

Finally, the title of the Stephen Davis book *Hammer Of The Gods* comes from this song: 'The hammer of the gods/will drive our ships to new lands.'

IN MY TIME OF DYING

The third song from the 1975 album 'Physical Graffiti', this started out as a gospel blues number, first recorded in the late Twenties by Blind Willie Johnson under the title 'Jesus Make Up My Dying Bed'. However, the song 'Jesus Goin' A-Make Up My Dyin' Bed' is actually mentioned as early as 1924. Johnson's version is not actually registered for copyright, so remains in the public domain.

Bob Dylan included a song called 'In My Time Of Dyin'' on his 1962 self-titled debut album (based on a Joshua White recording from 1933). White's version was also the inspiration for John Sebastian's 1971 song 'Well, Well, Well', from his album 'The Four Of Us'.

Zeppelin's rendition is based on the Willie Johnson recording, although he gets no songwriting credit; presumably, this is because (as said earlier) Johnson's song was in the public domain.

Jimmy Page plays slide guitar here, with John Paul Jones on

fretless bass. There's a real improvisational feel to the song, heightened by the clearly unrehearsed ending. You hear a cough (said to be from John Bonham), Page then says, 'Cough'. There then follows a moment when engineer Andy Johns invites the band to, 'Come and have a listen, then', and Bonham recants, 'Oh yes, thank you.'

Page told *Uncut* magazine in 2008: 'We were just having such a wonderful time. Look, we had a framework for "In My Time Of Dying", okay, but then it just takes off and we're just doing what Led Zeppelin do. We're jamming. We're having a ball. We. Are. Playing.'

The longest song the band ever recorded, this was part of their live set form 1975 to 1977, with Robert Plant regularly dedicating it to Chancellor of the Exchequer Denis Healey on UK tours! A version from Earls Court on 24 May 1975 is featured on the 2003 DVD *Led Zeppelin*, while the first episode in Season Two of the US TV series *Supernatural* is called 'In My Time Of Dying'.

Page performed this with the Black Crowes on tour in 1999, and it featured on the 2000 album 'Live At The Greek'.

IN THE EVENING

A synthesiser-driven song with a huge repetitive guitar part, this is the opening song on the 1979 album 'In Through The Out Door'.

Created by John Paul Jones in the main, one of the reasons that he worked on this alone is that both Jimmy Page and John Bonham tended to turn up very late to the studio, so the musical composition of this song was left to Jones. He initially pieced it together using keyboards and a new drum machine.

The band played the song live in 1979 and 1980 on tour, with footage from Knebworth Park in 1979 turning up on the *Led Zeppelin* DVD, released in 2003.

The song was revived by Robert Plant for his 1988 tour and was also played occasionally by Page and Plant in 1996. It has been covered by reggae rhythm masters Sly and Robbie, and also by rapper Tracy G.

IN THE LIGHT

The seventh song from the 1975 album 'Physical Graffiti', this was based on an earlier Zeppelin song called 'In The Morning', which is also known as 'Take Me Home'.

It was written by John Paul Jones using a synthesiser. One of the reasons it always creates interest is that it's one of only three songs on which Jimmy Page used a violin bow, the others being 'Dazed And Confused' and 'How Many More Times'. However, this is the sole occasion when he used an acoustic guitar.

This was never played live by the band because Jones couldn't reproduce the synthesiser sound outside the studio. By contrast, Robert Plant was always keen to perform it. Page, though, did play it live with the Black Crowes on their 1999 tour. This turned up as a Japanese bonus track on the 2000 album 'Live At The Greek'.

IN THROUGH THE OUT DOOR

The final studio album from Led Zeppelin is regarded by some as something of an inconsistent disappointment. The reality is that, despite the circumstances under which it was recorded, there are some quite breathtaking and beautiful moments here. And perhaps it does give a hint as to where the band were headed.

This was recorded in a three-week period at Abba's Polar Studios in Stockholm during November and December 1978. But it was done with a lot of problems hanging over them. For a start, the band were now tax exiles, driven out of their home country by punitive financial measures brought in by the Labour Government of the day. They were also still dealing with the fallout from the death of Robert Plant's son Karac in 1977.

Added to this was the fact that, while Plant and John Paul Jones worked steadily during the day, Jimmy Page and John Bonham came in only during the night. Jones told *Uncut* magazine: 'There were two distinct camps by then, and we (myself and Plant) were in the relatively clean one... I had this big new keyboard. And Robert and I just got to rehearsals early, basically... So Robert and I, by

the time everybody turned up for rehearsals, we'd written three or four songs. So we started rehearsing those immediately, because they were something to be getting on with.'

The album opens with the haunting yet slightly oddball 'In The Evening', setting the tone for what is a somewhat laid-back and relaxing atmosphere. When Page subsequently complained that the album was a little too comfortable and lacking in riffs, he might have had a point. But it works really well.

Thanks to Jones and Plant, there's a real cohesion to the record, which features the only two songs not to feature Page on the songwriting credits: 'All My Love' and 'Southbound Suarez'. 'Carouselambra' has a lilting synthesiser-led glint that has a certain carousel pace and pattern. And 'Fool In The Rain' is steeped in Latin rhythms. The impression is of a band still taking risks, and most of them work. And if neither Page nor Bonham were as directly involved as they should have been, then the overall album doesn't suffer.

The cover concept was cunning, to say the least. The record came in plain brown wrapper. Inside was a bar scene, with someone burning a 'Dear John' letter. There were actually six different sleeves, each depicting the same scene from a different angle. There was no way of knowing which one you had until the brown wrapper was removed.

Storm Thorgerson, of Hipgnosis (who designed this) said of the idea: 'The sepia quality was meant to evoke a non-specific past and to allow the brushstroke across the middle to be better rendered in colour and so make a contrast This self-same brushstroke was like the swish of a wiper across a wet windscreen, like a lick of fresh paint across a faded surface, a new look to an old scene, which was what Led Zeppelin told us about their album. A lick of fresh paint, as per Led Zeppelin, and the music on this album… It somehow grew in proportion and became six viewpoints of the same man in the bar, seen by the six other characters. Six different versions of the same image and six different covers.'

Little wonder 'In Through The Out Door' received a Grammy nomination in 1980 for Best Album Package (they lost to 'Breakfast In America' by Supertramp).

The album was released on 15 August 1979. It had been due out to coincide with the band's earlier shows at Knebworth Park, but there were production delays. The critical reception might have been lukewarm – *Sounds* music paper, for instance, used the headline 'Close The Door, Put Out The Lights', a line from 'No Quarter', to illustrate a downbeat two-star review from an unimpressed Geoff Barton – but commercially it held up well. It topped both the UK and American charts, reaching the pinnacle in six countries. Only in Germany did it fail to make the Top 20.

Whether this marked a fresh direction for Zeppelin one can only speculate over. Page himself strongly suggested to *Guitar World* that both he and Bonham felt 'In Through The Out Door' 'was a little soft. I wasn't really keen on "All My Love"…I wouldn't have wanted to pursue that direction in the future.'

In 2004, he told *Mojo* that his plan was get back to a riff-heavy album for the next release, which would never happen. No-one expected this to be the band's last album, but as such it's an intriguing glimpse at one possible future. A definite case of out through the last door.

Incidentally, the album title came from the fact that the band felt they'd been away from the UK for so long they'd almost have to sneak back in throughl the out door.

TRACKLISTING:
In The Evening/South Bound Saurez/ Fool In The Rain/Hot Dog/ Carouselambra/All My Love/I'm Gonna Crawl.

In addition, the songs 'Darlene', 'Wearing And Tearing' and 'Ozone Baby' were recorded during these sessions but were left out due to space constrictions. They eventually turned up on the 'Coda' album in 1982.

ISLAND STUDIOS
The studio in London's Notting Hill district where the band

recorded parts of 'Led Zeppelin III' and 'Led Zeppelin IV'. The latter was also mixed there, while 'Down By The Seaside', which appeared on 'Physical Graffiti', was also recorded there during the sessions for the fourth record.

Altogether the following songs from 'Led Zeppelin III' were also mixed there: 'Immigrant Song', 'Friends', 'Celebration Day', 'Since I've Been Loving You', 'Tangerine' and 'Bron-Y-Aur Stomp'. All were mixed by Andy Johns. As for 'Led Zeppelin IV', the following were mixed there: 'Black Dog', 'Rock And Roll' and 'Stairway To Heaven'. Again, it was Andy Johns who oversaw the mixing.

Established by Island Records founder Chris Blackwell, Island Studios was based in a deconsecrated church and was originally used to record Island acts such as Bob Marley, Free Nick Drake, Quintessence and Roxy Music.

During 1970, not only did Zeppelin record their third album, but Jethro Tull were among a number of other top acts booked in, recording 'Aqualung'. Now known as Sarm West, this is where the Band Aid single 'Do They Know It's Christmas?' was recorded in 1984.

The studio is now owned by the SPZ Group, run by Trevor Horn and Jill Sinclair.

IT MIGHT GET LOUD
A 2009 documentary, made by Davis Guggenheim, which follows the history of the electric guitar by focusing specifically on three musicians: Jimmy Page, the Edge (U2) and Jack White (White Stripes).

Page discusses his formative years as a guitarist, mentioning the blues and skiffle. Many of his scenes were filmed at Headley Grange, where parts of 'Led Zeppelin IV' was recorded.

The highpoint in the film comes when the three are brought together, not just to chat about guitars but to play each other's songs. Page teaches the others 'In My Time Of Dying', while the Edge presents 'I Will Follow' and White does 'Dead Leaves And The Dirty Ground'. The movie ends with the trio performing 'The Weight' by the Band...on acoustic guitars.

It Might Get Loud premiered at the Toronto Film Festival in 2008.

ITUNES

On 13 November 2007, Led Zeppelin finally embraced Apple's iTunes music file format. The band's first official venture into the world of downloading offered all of their albums individually, plus a special digital box set with every album included.

JOHN F KENNEDY STADIUM

More widely know as the JFK Stadium, this Philadelphia arena was a sports arena in Philadelphia which played home to the Philadelphia Quakers and Philadelphia Eagles.

It was built in 1936 as part of the Sesquicentennial International Exposition and was originally known as the Sesquicentennial Stadium, changing its name to the Philadelphia Municipal Stadium immediately following the Exposition. It was re-named the John F Kennedy Stadium in 1964, a year after the assassination of the US president.

The Stadium is best known outside American sport as the US venue for the Live Aid concert on 13 July 1985, to raise awareness and aid for the plight of famine-hit Ethiopia. And on paper at least, the jewel in the crown of the US line-up was the appearance on the bill of the surviving members of Led Zeppelin.

The Stadium had some history

of putting on rock concerts – the Beatles had performed there in 1966, and it had also been used by acts such as The Rolling Stones, Pink Floyd, Yes, Van Halen, the Grateful Dead, the Police, Genesis, Aerosmith and Journey.

Led Zeppelin had been slated to appear in 1977 on the Presence tour, but it was one of seven final dates of the US tour that were cancelled in the wake of the death of Robert Plant's son Karac. Led Zeppelin never played in America again prior to their Live Aid appearance.

The stadium was demolished following a Grateful Dead show in 1992 and was replaced by the Wachovia Centre, an indoor arena that would be home to hockey team the Philadelphia Flyers and basketball team the Philadelphia 76ers.

JAMES PATRICK PAGE: SESSION MAN

This was a two-volume release on the Archive International Productions label in 1989 and 1990 which concentrated on Page's career as a session musician prior to joining the Yardbirds. The bulk of material on both volumes were recorded between the period between 1963 and 1965, from sessions involving the likes of Mickie Most, Lulu, Brenda Lee and Mickey Finn.

Of most interest are the inclusion of both sides of a 1965 Jimmy Page solo single, 'She Just Satisfies' and 'Keep Moving', the

A-side featuring a rare vocal performance from Page over a Bo Diddley-style slice of garage rock; the B-side is a powerful instrumental track. There is also Jake Holmes' original version of 'Dazed And Confused' on which Page didn't actually perform, included by the compilers for reasons best known to themselves. There are also three Yardbirds tracks, a live version of 'White Summer' and BBC recordings of 'Little Games' and Dylan's 'Most Likely You'll Go Your Way (And I'll Go Mine)'.

The bulk of the remainders of the material is a mixture of beat music of the time and more balladic material of which Page's distinct lead breaks are likely to be of most interest to the committed Zeppelin acolyte.

TRACKLISTING:

Volume One:
Chris Ravel and the Ravers
Don't You Dig This Kinda Beat
The Zephyrs
Sweet Little Baby
Pat Wayne with the Beachcombers
Roll Over Beethoven
Carter Lewis and the Southerners
Somebody Told My Girl
Dave Berry and the Cruisers
My Baby Left Me
The Brooks
Once In A While
Mickie Most and the Gear
Money Honey/That's Alright
The Sneekers
I Just Can't Go To Sleep
The First Gear
A Certain Girl/Leave My Kitten Alone

The Primitives
How Do You Feel
Bobby Graham
Zoom, Widge And Wag
Jimmy Page (solo)
She Just Satisfies/Keep Moving
The Mickey Finn
Night Comes Down
The Pickwicks
Little By Little
Lulu and the Luvvers
Surprise, Surprise
The Yardbirds
Little Games/Most Likely You'll Go Your Way (And I'll Go Mine)
Jake Holmes
Dazed And Confused

Volume Two:
The Sneekers
Bald Headed Woman
Wayne Gibson and the Dynamic Sounds
See You Later Alligator
The Zephyrs
I Can Tell
 The Talismen
Castin' My Spell
Mickie Most
The Feminine Look
The Untamed
I'll Go Crazy
The Redcaps
Talkin' Bout You
Neil Christian and the Crusaders –
Honey Hush/I Like It
Mickey Finn
This Sporting Life
The Blue Rondos
Baby I Go For You
Lulu and the Luvvers
I'll Come Running
Brenda Lee
Is It True

The Pickwicks
I Took My Baby Home
The Lancastrians
The World Keeps Going Round
The Talismen
Masters Of War
The Primitives
You Said
Scotty McKay Quintet
Train Kept A-Rollin'
Sean Buckley and the Breadcrumbs
Everybody Knows
Billy Fury
Nothin' Shakin'
The Yardbirds
White Summer

JANSCH, BERT

Bert Jansch is a Scottish folk musician and founding member of folk supergroup Pentangle who has wielded tremendous influence over Jimmy Page as far as acoustic guitar-playing is concerned.

A fan of the music of Big Bill Broonzy, Woody Guthrie, Brownie McGhee and Pete Seeger, Jansch's own stunning 1965 debut album 'Bert Jansch' was recorded on a simple reel-to-reel tape recorder and sold to the Transatlantic label (a hotbed for British folk talent in the mid Sixties) for a mere £100, before going on to shift over 150,000 copies.

Jansch's third album, 1966's 'Jack Orion', featured the track 'Blackwaterside'. It is this track that Jimmy Page utilised when writing Led Zeppelin's own 'Black Mountain Side', which has proved to be something of a thorny issue

over songwriting credits. Jansch's song was inspired by the traditional tune 'Down By Blackwaterside', and is credited as a traditional arrangement. Page takes sole credit for 'Black Mountain Side'.

'I wasn't totally original on that,' Page told *Guitarist* magazine in 1977. 'It had been done in the folk clubs a lot; Annie Briggs was the first one that I heard do that riff. I was playing it as well, and then there was Bert Jansch's version. He's the one who crystallised all the acoustic playing, as far as I'm concerned.'

Jansch himself was a little more frank on the issue when interviewed by *Classic Rock* magazine. 'The thing I've noticed about Jimmy (Page) whenever we meet is that he can't look me in the eye. Well, he ripped me off, didn't he? Or let's just say he learned from me. I wouldn't want to sound impolite.'

Jansch, also an influence on the likes of Neil Young, Donovan, Jethro Tull, Johnny Marr and Bernard Butler amongst others, continued a hugely successful solo career and also occasionally tours with Pentangle.

JASANI, VIRAM
Viram Jasani is a Kenyan-born, Indian sitar and table player who featured on Led Zeppelin's 'Black Mountain Side' from their 1969 debut album 'Led Zeppelin'.

Jasani has released two solo

albums, 1972's 'Ragas: Streams Of Light' and 1995's 'Tags, Malkauns And Megs'.

JETT BLACKS

Jett Blacks were a jazz-influenced rock band of whom John Paul Jones was a member. They also included noted jazz-fusion guitarist and future Mahavishnu Orchestra leader John McLaughlin.

JOHNS, ANDY

Andy Johns is a noted producer and engineer who worked as an engineer on most of Led Zeppelin's album releases.

He first engineered 'Led Zeppelin' in 1969, and went on to work with the band on 'Led Zeppelin II' (1969), 'Led Zeppelin IV' (1971), 'Houses Of The Holy' (1973), 'Physical Graffiti' (1975) and 'Coda' (1982).

Amongst his prolific production work are Free's 'Highway' (1970), 'Live!' (1971) and 'Heartbreaker' (1972), Television's groundbreaking 'Marquee Moon' (1977), 'Hughes/Thrall' (1982), Van Halen's 'For Unlawful Carnal Knowledge' (1991) and Chickenfoot's 2009 self-titled debut.

He has also engineered 'Sticky Fingers' (1971), 'Exile On Main Street' (1972),'Goats Head Soup' (1973) and 'It's Only Rock'n'Roll' (1974) by the Rolling Stones.

JOHNS, GLYN

Glyn Johns is the older brother of producer and engineer Andy Johns, and was director of engineering on Led Zeppelin's 1969 debut album 'Led Zeppelin'.

Johns worked on the Beatles; notorious 'Get Back' sessions (ultimately produced by Phil Spector as 'Let It Be', although re-worked by Paul McCartney as 'Let It Be...Naked' in 2003).

Johns, who is best known for his work with the Eagles, has also worked with Bob Dylan, Eric Clapton, the Rolling Stones, the Who, Rod Stewart, Emmylou Harris and Blue Oyster Cult.

JOHNS, GLYNIS

Glynis Johns, an actress best known for her role in the hit Walt Disney film *Mary Poppins*, is the female who appears with Zeppelin on the front cover of 1969 second album 'Led Zeppelin II'. Her appearance, alongside bluesman Blind Willie Johnson is clearly a tongue-in-cheek reference to the name of engineer Glyn Johns.

JOHNSON, BLIND WILLIE

Blind Willie Johnson was an American bluesman who, like other notables such as Willie Dixon, Otis Rush and Leadbelly, exerted an influence over the music of Led Zeppelin.

His photograph appears on the cover for 'Led Zeppelin II' alongside the band and actress Glynis Johns, no doubt a nod to the influence of his music. [See 'IN MY TIME OF DYING' entry.]

Some have pointed to the fact that Led Zeppelin's 'Nobody's Fault But Mine' could be construed as similar to Johnson's own 1927 song 'It's Nobody's Fault But Mine'. However, aside from the title, Johnson's overtly religious blues number seems to have little in common with Zeppelin's chugging prog-rock tale of giving in to pleasures of the flesh.

JOHNSTONE, PHIL

Johnstone was the keyboard player and producer who worked with Robert Plant on the albums 'Now And Zen' (1988), 'Manic Nirvana' (1990) and 'Fate Of Nations' (1993).

He is also widely credited as the musician who coerced Plant into including Led Zeppelin material in his live sets again. Plant steadfastly refused to perform anything from the repertoire during the early days of his solo career, not wanting to be labelled as the former Led Zeppelin singer.

JONES, CHARLIE

Jones is the bass player who worked with Robert Plant on 'Manic Nirvana' (1990), 'Fate Of Nations' (1993) and 'Dreamland' (2002) and who is married to Plant's daughter Carmen.

Jones also worked with Jimmy Page and Robert Plant on 1994's 'No Quarter: Jimmy Page And Robert Plant Unledded' and 1996's 'Walking Into Clarksdale' and who toured with the band.

In 2010 he was the bassist for quirky dance-pop act Goldfrapp.

JONES, JOHN PAUL

'I once read the Beatles did a whole tour of America and never left their hotel rooms. And I thought, "I can't see the point of travelling around the world and not seeing anything."'

This quote from Led Zeppelin bassist John Paul Jones gives a good indication as to why he was often viewed as 'the quiet one'. Another was the quote from a French Atlantic Records company employee, who simply stated: 'The wisest guy in Led Zeppelin was John Paul Jones. Why? He never got caught in an embarrassing situation!'

Jones was without a doubt the quietest member of Led Zeppelin, as far as the public were concerned. Yet he was also a fiercely loyal member of the tight-knit unit, a musical force whose prodigious talent would push him to the fore in Zeppelin's later years as being a musician whose almost studious intellect matched that of his illustrious bandmates. And yet he still managed to enjoy the fruits of Led Zeppelin's success.

Born John Baldwin on 3 January 1946 in Sidcup, Kent, he began playing piano at six years old, although it perhaps should come as no surprise that the young Baldwin (as was) took to music. His parents were professionally connected to music; his father was pianist and arranger for the Ambrose Orchestra Big Band, and his mother was also involved. The family would often perform together. Jones was schooled at Christ's College in London's Blackheath, where his impressive talent became more than evident when, aged just 14, he became a choirmaster and organist at his local church.

Early musical influences aside from classical music were blues and jazz, and it was the Chicago jazz and R&B bassist Phil Upchurch, especially his 'You Can't Sit Down' album, that inspired the young Jones to pick up a bass. At 15 he bought a Dallas solid-body electric bass, and thus began his foray into popular music.

Jones' first band were the Deltas, whom he joined when he was just 15 years old. He went on to jazz-rock outfit the Jett Blacks, a band which also featured the young John McLaughlin. He was then picked out by Jet Harris and Tony Meehan of the Shadows for

a stint in the early Sixties (ironically just prior to Jones hooking up with the Shadows, Jimmy Page had played on a session for the band's Number 1 hit 'Diamonds'). Jones remained with the former Shadows duo for two years, never becoming an official member, and in 1964, on the advice of Meehan, he turned his hand to session work.

Like his future bandmate Jimmy Page, Jones became a prolific sessioneer, and worked on over 100 sessions between 1964 and 1968, when he would join Zeppelin. Some of the more notable sessions Jones worked on were for the Rolling Stones on the album 'Their Satanic Majesties Request' (he arranged the strings on 'She's An Angel'), Donovan (the hit singles 'Mellow Yellow' and 'Sunshine Superman'), Dusty Springfield (as well as recording sessions, Jones played bass on her Talk of the Town shows), as well as working with the likes of Cat Stevens, Jeff Beck, Rod Stewart, Lulu, Shirley Bassey, Tom Jones, Nico and the Walker Brothers.

He also changed his name, at the suggestion of Rolling Stones manager and Immediate Records boss Andrew Loog Oldham, to John Paul Jones (Oldham had seen the name on a film poster). It was inevitable that Jones and Page's paths would cross, so prolific were they in the session world, and Jones performed on the Yardbirds' 'Little Games' album. And during sessions for Donovan's 'Hurdy

Photo licensed from Getty Images

Gurdy Man', both Page and Jones, each tiring of the session world, discussed the idea of forming a band. When Page finally made his move following the disbandment of the Yardbirds, Jones got in touch at the suggestion of his wife Maureen to see if a position was available. After Yardbirds bassist Chris Dreja opted out for a career in photography. Page was more than happy to welcome Jones into the fold.

His impact on Led Zeppelin's music was instant, although perhaps not as evident as Page's ferocious guitar work and Plant's heroic blues howl. But he quickly locked into a sold rhythm groove with John Bonham. 'As soon as I heard John Bonham play,' Jones told *Rolling Stone* magazine, 'I knew this was going to be great. We locked together as a team immediately.'

Equally Jones and Bonham shared a love of funk and soul music, whilst Page and Plant were big fans of the Fifties and Sixties blues and R&B sound. Between them, all this helped to add a vital ingredient to Zeppelin's music that allowed it to transcend mere blues-rock power or folk-rock whimsy.

'We were huge Motown and Stax fans and general soul-music fans, James Brown fans,' Jones told the online website *Global Bass Online*. 'Which is one of the reasons why I've always said that Zeppelin were one of the few bands to "swing". We actually had a groove in those days. People used to come to our shows and dance, which was great. To see all the women dancing, it was really brilliant. You didn't necessarily see that at a Black Sabbath show or whatever. So we were different in that way. We were a groovy band. We used all our black pop music influences as a key to the rock that went over the top.'

Jones' talent as an arranger of music and multi-instrumentalist came to the fore on 1973's 'Houses Of The Holy'. Over their first four albums, Led Zeppelin had displayed an increased mastery of their craft, shifting from a raw bluesy powerhouse to adding folkier textures and exploring deeper acoustic musical avenues, as both Jimmy Page and Robert Plant, and to a lesser extent John Paul Jones and John Bonham, would combine as writers of the band's music. If everything Zeppelin had been striving for musically came together on 1971's 'Led Zeppelin IV', then from there the band sought to elevate themselves even further.

'No Quarter', from 'Houses Of The Holy', was an epic overture courtesy of Jones, who also highlighted his talent as an organist and pianist (this avenue of Jones' talents would now become increasingly evident in live performance), and as Zeppelin's sound became ever more complex and far reaching, so Jones' contribution to the band increased. By the time of 1979's 'In Through The Out Door', it was Jones, along with Plant, who was very much the driving force behind the music that made it onto the record. One can only marvel at what the band might have continued to create had Bonham not sadly passed away in 1980.

Away from the spotlight, Jones was perceived as 'the quiet one'. Still, if one considers a similar epithet was bestowed upon the Who's John Entwistle, a hardened party man offstage, then this may be somewhat off the mark with the Zeppelin man as well. As he himself told the website *CelebrityCafe.com*; 'I did more drugs than I care to remember. I just did it quietly.'

In 1973 it did seem apparent that the incessant touring and crazy adventures of Led Zeppelin were taking their toll on Jones. A rumour suggests that he was contemplating leaving the band to spend more time with his family, although one report suggests he'd been offered and was considering the job as choirmaster or organist at Winchester Cathedral.

'I didn't want to harm the

group, but I didn't want my family to fall apart either,' Jones explained to *Mojo* in 2007. 'We toured a huge amount in those early days. We were all very tired and under pressure and it just came to a head. When I first joined the band, I didn't think it would go on for that long, two or three years perhaps, and then I'd carry on with my career as a musician and doing movie music.'

Manager Peter Grant was aware of the discontent, although unsure of whether the cathedral job rumours were truly behind it. But as it was, Jones remained in Led Zeppelin. He continued to work with other musicians, such as the Family Dogg, Maggie Bell, Paul McCartney and Roy Harper during his tenure as Zeppelin bass player.

However Jones' dedication to the cause really could not be faulted, as Cameron Crowe made clear in the intro to his now-legendary 1975 *Rolling Stone* interview: 'John Paul Jones, Led Zeppelin's bassist and keyboard player, was quietly playing backgammon and half listening to a phone-in radio talk show on New York FM.

'"I was in a club last night when someone asked me if I wanted to meet Jimmy Page," the show's host suddenly offered between calls. "You know, when I think about it, there's no one I'd rather meet less than someone as disgusting as Jimmy Page."

'Jones bolted up from his game. "Let me just say that Led Slime can't play their way out of a paper bag and if you plan on seeing them tomorrow night at the Garden, those goons are ripping you off. Now don't start wasting my time defending Led Slime. If you're thinking about calling up to do that, stick your head in the toilet and flush."

'Jones, normally a man of quiet reserve, strode furiously across the room. He snapped up a phone and dialled the station. After a short wait, the talk-show host picked up the phone.

'"What would you like to talk about?"

'"Led Zeppelin," Jones answered coolly in his clipped British accent. The line went dead. Victim of an eight-second delay button, the exchange was never given any airtime.

'It was a familiar battle, as Jones saw it. Although Led Zeppelin has managed to sell more than a million units apiece of all five of its albums and is currently working a US tour that is expected to be the largest-grossing undertaking in rock history, the band has been continually kicked, shoved, pummelled and kneed in the groin by critics of all stripes. "I know it's unnecessary to fight back," Jones said. True enough: Zep's overwhelming popularity speaks for itself. "I just thought I'd defend myself one last time."'

Jones' work with other musicians continued after Led Zeppelin called a halt in December 1980. His esteemed prowess as a musician and arranger saw him in demand, and he collaborated with performance artist Diamanda Galas, produced Zeppelin-lite goth-rockers the Mission and has also worked with the likes of Paul McCartney, REM, Heart, Peter Gabriel, Foo Fighters, Cinderella, Ben E King, Butthole Surfers and Brian Eno amongst others.

As an artist in his own right Jones recorded the soundtrack for the 1985 Michael Winner film *Scream For Help*, on which he worked with Jimmy Page and his own daughter Jacinda, and composed the soundtrack to the 1993 film *Tom Thumb*. He also released two more than worthy solo albums, the instrumental 'Zooma' in 1999 and 'The Thunderthief' in 2001, touring to support both.

Jones was involved in both reunions of remaining members as Led Zeppelin, at Live Aid in 1985, and also at the Atlantic Records 40th Anniversary show in New York in 1988. He also played with them at Jason Bonham's 1990 wedding reception. However Jones was notably absent from the 1994 reunion between Jimmy Page and Robert Plant for the 'No Quarter: Jimmy Page And Led Zeppelin Unledded' and subsequent work between the pair throughout the remainder of the decade. Whether this was due to existing tension between Plant and Jones, or merely whether Plant was intent on making the whole scenario appear as unlike a Led Zeppelin

reunion as he could we'll probably never know. However, when Zeppelin were inducted into the Rock and Roll Hall of Fame in 1995, there were some embarrassed looks when Jones declared: 'Thank you, my friends, for finally remembering my phone number.'

However Jones was very much involved in the band's most recent performance at London's O_2 Arena in 2007 at the Ahmet Ertegun tribute concert, at which the band clearly buried the memories of past performances in a vibrantly enjoyable performance with the late John Bonham's son Jason on drums. Indeed it seems Jones was equally keen (as were Page and Bonham) to take the reunion further, but it should probably come as little surprise that Robert Plant would turn his back on the proposed endeavour.

Instead, Jones hooked back up with Foo Fighters mainman Dave Grohl, with whom he and Page had appeared at Wembley Stadium in 2008 performing 'Rock And Roll' and 'Ramble On'. Jones had previously worked with Grohl on the Foo Fighters' 2005 album 'In Your Honour' and also appeared at the 2008 Grammy Awards with the band. He then formed Them Crooked Vultures alongside Grohl and Josh Homme of Queens of the Stone Age, a supergroup who have taken Zeppelin's early raw blues sound and developed it for a modern rock audience. The band's self-titled debut album was released to much fanfare in 2009.

Perhaps befitting his nature as the more thoughtful member of Led Zeppelin and the most studious musically, Jones eased his way gently back into the limelight over the post-Zep years, all the while maintaining a more than healthy work ethic and remaining in demand. In the past decade his profile could not have been higher and he clearly relishes all the work he's been involved with. Whether the future holds another return to the spotlight with Zeppelin remains to be seen but, as with his time as the band's bassist, Jones has always conducted himself with the utmost dignity. A worthy plaudit for a rock musician in this day and age.

JUNIPER, DAVID

Juniper is the artist and illustrator who designed the cover for Led Zeppelin's second album, 'Led Zeppelin II'.

The cover is based on an old World War One photograph of Jasta 11, the German squadron led by the famous Red Baron (Manfred von Richthofen), dubbed the Flying Circus. The faces of band members were airbrushed into the original photo, along with those of manager Peter Grant, tour manager Richard Cole, actress Glynis Johns and bluesman Blind Willie Johnson.

'In the late sixties in London, anything seemed possible,' Juniper told the email list *Cover Stories*. 'I was employed at the time in a boring Art Director's job, so I got a lot of satisfaction out of moonlighting on speculative stuff. The combination of collage/photography and airbrush illustration was groundbreaking for me, because the traditional airbrush technique was very tricky, especially when compared to today's digital equivalents. The cover imagery was completely experimental and I liked the combination of the abstract ghostly Zeppelin shape along with a faded sepia WW1 photo of German Aviators.

'All the faces were replaced or altered (sunglasses & beards on some of the pilots!). The original photo of the Jasta Division of the WW1 German Air Force came from an old book about the Sopwith Camel, which was a famous British bi-plane from WW1.

'I used bright inks to make the illustration parts really pop. I just presented it to the group and they went for it, with only a few changes to the inside spread. The outside cover went through as it was proposed.

'The inside image is full-on psychedelia, in contrast to the original idea discussed, which had a Zeppelin flying past the Statue of Liberty. They did not want something on the inside with a similar feel to the outside, so I just went for a colourful painting as a complete contrast to the outside. I remembered a documentary film of Twenties/ Thirties German architecture and thought this approach would give the image a heavy rock/blues feel.

'Anyway, from that point forward, the group's management was all very friendly and used me on other covers for some of their other artists, including Donovan and Lulu.

'Another great treat was to be asked down to Olympic Studios in Barnes while they worked on the recording, but what pleased me the most was that cover was nominated at the '68 Grammy Awards!'

Juniper is still highly active in the world of art and his distinctive work can be viewed at *www.davidjuniper.com*

KASHMIR

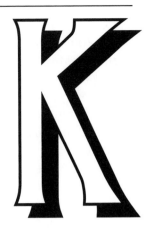

One of the most iconic songs in the Led Zeppelin canon, this was featured as the sixth track on the 1975 album 'Physical Graffiti'.

Robert Plant once described this as the definitive Zeppelin song, and it's not hard to see why. It has a sweeping, majestic feel, a sense of musical adventure. It's heavy without being brusque, haunting without becoming a dreamscape.

Jimmy Page and John Bonham initially worked on the song together, developing its loping, lilting trademark guitar and drum sounds. They demoed it in 1973, with John Paul Jones adding strings in '74. There are, of course, considerable Middle Eastern and Indian influence in the music, brought about by Page: 'I had a sitar for some time and I was interested in modal tunings and Arabic stuff. It started off with a riff and then employed Eastern lines underneath.'

This is also one of the few Zeppelin songs to expand the horizons by use of outside musicians, and Jones spent ages getting the right balance: 'The secret of successful keyboard string parts is to play only the parts that a real string section would play. That is, one line for the First Violins, one line for Second Violins, one for Violas, one for Cellos, one for Basses. Some divided parts (two or more notes to a line) are allowed, but keep them to a minimum. Think melodically.'

Lyrically, Plant wrote this while in the Sahara Desert after the band's 1973 US tour. He was driving from Goulimine to Tantan, and the song was originally called 'Driving To Kashmir'. Plant explained to Cameron Crowe for the latter's notes on 'The Complete Recordings' set: 'The whole inspiration came from the fact that the road went on and on and on. It was a single-track road which neatly cut through the desert. Two miles to the East and West were ridges of sandrock. It basically looked like you were driving down a channel, this dilapidated road, and there was seemingly no end to it. "Oh, let the sun beat down upon my face, stars to fill my dreams..." It's one of my favourites...that, "All My Love" and "In The Light" and two or three others really were the finest moments. But "Kashmir" in particular. It was so positive, lyrically.'

'Kashmir' was part of the band's live set from 1975 onwards. The version performed at Knebworth

Park on 4 August 1979 is featured in the 2003 DVD *Led Zeppelin*. Plant would regularly improvise during this song, which might explain why nobody realised at the time that he had inadvertently sung the second verse twice and omitted the third one altogether!

The song was used in the James Bond movie *GoldenEye* and in the film *Fast Times At Ridgemont High*. It was also the basis for the Puff Daddy song 'Come With Me', which featured Jimmy Page; the latter even appeared in the video. The tune was put together for the film *Godzilla*. Page and Plant recorded their own version for the 1994 album 'No Quarter: Jimmy Page And Robert Plant Unledded'. For this, they brought in Egyptian musicians and an orchestra.

'Kashmir' was released as a single in Thailand in 1975, backed by 'Black Country Woman' and 'Boogie With Stu'. It was released as a download single in 2007 but only made Number 80 in the charts, faring little better in the States where it failed to make the Top 40.

Which only leaves one question: why was it called 'Kashmir' when it had nothing to do with that part of the Indian subcontinent? Ah well, such are the mysteries of Zeppelin.

KNEBWORTH

This park in Hertfordshire surrounding a stately home was the location for what were to be Zeppelin's last ever UK shows

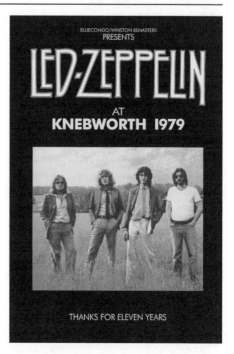

BLUECONGO/WINSTON REMASTERS
PRESENTS

LED·ZEPPELIN

AT
KNEBWORTH 1979

THANKS FOR ELEVEN YEARS

with John Bonham. They happened on the successive Saturdays of 4 and 11 August 1979.

Also on the bill for both occasions were the New Barbarians – a band featuring Keith Richards, Ronnie Wood, Stanley Clarke, Bobby Keys, Ian McLagan and Joseph Modeliste – Todd Rundgren and Utopia, Southside Johnny and the Asbury Jukes, the New Commander Cody band, Chas and Dave and Fairport Convention (who only appeared at the first date). The host was DJ Nicky Horne. Tickets cost £7.50.

It's said that 109,000 came to the first day, but officially around 40,000 came for the second day. However, there have been a number of estimates over the years, some of which claimed that in excess of 250,000 were there on 4 August. However, a major problem arose between Bannister and Zeppelin manager Peter Grant. The latter thought Bannister had misled him on ticket sales for the first date, and so decided to take over manning the gate for the final show. It all led to a lot of unpleasantness, the result being that Bannister lost so much money that his company went into liquidation.

It's also worth noting that on the official posters, the Marshall Tucker Band are advertised, whereas it was the New Commander Cody Band who played.

Zeppelin's set list for 4 August was:
The Song Remains The Same/ Celebration Day/Black Dog/Nobody's Fault But Mine/Over The Hills And Far Away/Misty Mountain Hop/ Since I've Been Loving You/No Quarter/Ten Years Gone/Hot Dog/ The Rain Song/White Summer/Black Mountain Side/Kashmir/Trampled Underfoot/Sick Again/Achilles Last Stand/In The Evening/Stairway To Heaven/Rock And Roll/Whole Lotta Love/Heartbreaker.

The set list for 11 August was: *The Song Remains The Same/ Celebration Day/Black Dog/Nobody's Fault But Mine/Over The Hills And Far Away/Misty Mountain Hop/ Since I've Been Loving You/No Quarter/Hot Dog/The Rain Song/ White Summer/Black Mountain Side/Kashmir/Trampled Underfoot/ Sick Again/Achilles Last Stand/In The Evening/Stairway To Heaven/ Rock And Roll/Whole Lotta Love/ Communication Breakdown.*

There have been a number of bootlegs over the years, while the following were also included on

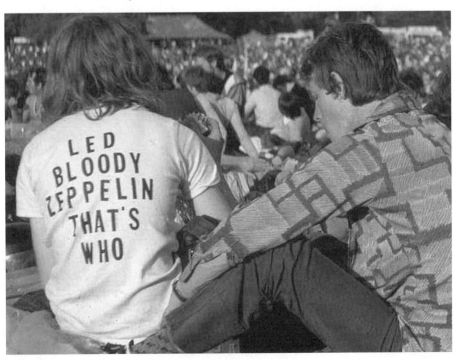

the 2003 DVD *Led Zeppelin*: 'Rock And Roll', 'Nobody's Fault But Mine', 'Sick Again', 'Achilles Last Stand', 'In The Evening' 'Kashmir' and 'Whole Lotta Love'.

KNOBS

This was the name used by the band when they played in Copenhagen on February 28, 1970. The reason for this was a threat of legal action by Frau Eva von Zeppelin, a descendent of Count Ferdinand von Zeppelin who created the Zeppelin airship.

She had been angered the previous year when the band played in the city, but seemed appeased after meeting the band. However, things changed when the aristocrat saw the cover for the first album depicting the Hindenburg disaster in which a Zeppelin explodes.

When the band returned to the city they elected to change their name for one night in order to prevent any legal action. It was one of the few times when they stood down in a confrontation. There was speculation they might call themselves Ned Zeppelin, but in the end they settled for the Nobs (sometimes spelt as the Knobs, hence the inclusion here), inspired by the name of their European promoter Claude Nobs.

Jimmy Page told *Melody Maker* at the time:

'Then we shall call ourselves The Nobs when we go to Copenhagen, the whole thing is absurd. The first time we played we invited her backstage to meet us, to see how we were nice young lads. We calmed her down but on leaving the studio, she saw our LP cover of an airship in flames and she exploded! I had to run and hide. She just blew her top.'

Interestingly, tickets for the show still bore the name 'Led Zeppelin'.

KRAMER, EDDIE

Famed engineer and producer. Kramer was born in Cape Town in 1941, moving to London when he was 19. He relocated to New York in 1968, being employed at the Record Plant Studios. He engineered five Zeppelin studio albums from 'Led Zeppelin II' onwards and also worked on *The Song Remains The Same*.

Kramer is credited as being the person who came up with the celebrated echo effect on Robert Plant's voice during the psychedelically inspired 'Woman…you need it' wail in 'Whole Lotta Love'

He has commented on working with Zeppelin, thus: 'I was very pleased to have worked with Jimmy Page and the band; I did five albums with them. Certainly they were the greatest rock'n'roll band that I'd ever worked with, especially with Bonham being in the band – the greatest heavy rock drummer, I feel.

'There were certain similarities between Jimmy Page and Jimi Hendrix, whom I'd previously worked with, in that they were both very much in control of their own destiny in the studio. They would have this very clear picture and laser-like concentration: "Okay, this is the song and here's where we're gonna go with it." There's a remarkable similarity between the two men. Completely different styles of playing, of course.'

KRAUSS, ALLISON

American bluegrass-country singer and fiddler Alison Krauss has helped to boost Robert Plant's current stock, thanks to their collaborative 2007 album 'Raising Sand'. Mind you, Plant's name has aided Krauss as well.

This album not only sold over a million copies in America, but picked up five Grammy Awards in February 2009, including Album of the Year', Best Contemporary Folk/Americana Album and Record of the Year (for the song 'Please Read The Letter'), Best Pop Collaboration with Vocals and Best Country Collaboration with Vocals.

All the songs on the album were handpicked by producer T-Bone Burnett. In 2010, the pair are working on a second album.

LANGLEY, ROBERT

Robert Langley was an alleged bootlegger who was charged with 12 counts of producing and selling products without permission in July 2007.

Jimmy Page appeared at the Glasgow hearing at the request of the British Phonographic Industry who seized goods at a Glasgow record fair, which included £11,500 worth of Led Zeppelin items, including a £220 Japanese tour box set. Beatles and Rolling Stones items were also confiscated.

Langley, of Buckingham, originally pleaded not guilty to the charges, but after an appearance by Page he changed his plea to guilty of three trademark and two copyright infringements.

'The legitimate part is where fans trade music, but once you start packaging it up and you do not know what you are getting, you are breaking the rules legally and morally,' Page stated after the court appearance, where he happily greeted waiting fans and signed autographs. 'There are some of these type of recordings where it is just a whirring, and you cannot hear the music. If you have something like this that appears legitimate then it is just not right.'

Many of the items recovered from Langley featured footage that was stolen from Page's own

personal collection in the Eighties. Langley was jailed for 20 months.

LATTER DAYS: THE BEST OF LED ZEPPELIN VOLUME TWO

'Latter Days: The Best Of Led Zeppelin Volume Two', released on Atlantic in March 2000, was a companion release to the 1999

'Early Days: The Best Of Led Zeppelin Volume One'.

Like the earlier release it's something of a cash-in job. Where the first volume concentrated on the first four albums, 'Latter Days...' featured material from the albums 'Houses Of The Holy' to 'In Through The Out Door', inclusive. An enhanced DVD of a live performance of 'Kashmir' was also included.

In 2002 'Latter Days...' was paired with 'Early Days...' in a box set titled 'The Best Of Led Zeppelin'. TRACKLISTING:
The Song Remains The Same/No Quarter/Houses Of The Holy/ Trampled Under Foot/Kashmir/Ten Years Gone/Achilles Last Stand/ Nobody's Faulty But Mine/All My Love/In The Evening

LED ZEPPELIN BOX SET

Released in September 1990. 'Box Set' was a six album (or four-CD or cassette) set of Led Zeppelin's most popular songs.

It also featured new live versions of 'Travelling Riverside Blues' recorded at BBC's Maida Vale studios in July 1969, 'White Summer' recorded at London's Playhouse Theatre in June 1969 and a new version of 'Moby Dick' mixed with 'Bonzo's Montreux' which was put together in New York in 1990.

The set featured the same cover as 'Remasters', which was a three-album set released in October 1990, and this led to some confusion. Some territories took to referring to 'Box Set' as 'The Complete Collection', itself a title which should not be confused with 1993's 'The Complete Studio Recordings'.

TRACKLISTING (VINYL):

Side One: *Whole Lotta Love/Heartbreaker/ Communication Breakdown/Babe I'm Gonna Leave You/What Is And What Should Never Be.*

Side Two: *Thank You/I Can't Quit You Baby (live)/ Dazed And Confused/Your Time Is Gonna Come/Ramble On.*

Side Three: *Travelling Riverside Blues/Friends/Celebration Day/Hey Hey What Can I Do/White Summer – Black Mountain Side.*

Side Four: *Black Dog/Over The Hills And Far Away/Immigrant Song/Battle Of Evermore/Bron-Y-Aur Stomp/Tangerine.*

Side Five: *Going To California/ Since I've Been Loving You/D'yer Mak'er/Gallows Pole/Custard Pie.*

Side Six: *Misty Mountain Hop/ Rock And Roll/The Rain Song/ Stairway To Heaven.*

Side Seven: *Kashmir/Trampled Underfoot/For Your Life.*

Side Eight: *No Quarter/Dancing Days/When The Levee Breaks/ Achilles Last Stand.*

Side Nine: *The Song Remains The Day/Ten Years Gone/In My Time Of Dying.*

Side 10: *In The Evening/Candy Store Rock/The Ocean/Ozone Baby/ Houses Of The Holy.*

Side 11: *Wearing And Tearing/Poor Tom/Nobody's Fault But Mine/Fool In The Rain.*

Side 12: *In The Light/The Wanton Song/Moby Dick – Bonzo's Montreux (remix of the two recordings)/I'm Gonna Crawl/All My Love.*

LED ZEPPELIN BOX SET 2

'Led Zeppelin Box Set 2' was a two-CD set that was released on the Atlantic label in September 1993. It was viewed very much as a companion piece to the 1990 four-CD box set 'Remasters' Between the two sets they featured every Led Zeppelin studio track from the band's ten studio albums, the band's only non-LP B-side, two live BBC tracks and one studio outtake. Unique to 'Led Zeppelin Boxed Set 2' is the track 'Baby Come On Home'.

TRACKLISTING:

CD One: *Good Times Bad Times/ We're Gonna Groove/Night Flight/ That's The Way/ Baby Come On Home/The Lemon Song/You Shook Me/Boogie With Stu/Down By The Seaside/Out On The Tiles/Black Mountain Side/Moby Dick/Sick Again/Hot Dog/Carouselambra*

CD Two: *South Bound Suarez/ Walter's Walk/Darlene/Black Country Woman/How Many More Times/The Rover/Four Sticks/Hats Off To (Roy) Harper/I Can't Quit You Baby/Living Loving Maid (She's Just A Woman)/ Royal Orleans/Bonzo's Montreux/ The Crunge/Bring It On Home/Tea For One*

LED ZEPPELIN (ALBUM)

Led Zeppelin's debut album was released on 21 January 1969. Not only was 'Led Zeppelin' truly groundbreaking, but it was recorded under a unique set of circumstances that would help define Led Zeppelin as a business model (for want of a better word), as much as the music contained therein would define both Led Zeppelin and the rock world that developed all around them. That it was one of the first albums to be released in stereo-only form – prior to this, albums would be released in both stereo and mono versions – merely emphasises the point.

Led Zeppelin took shape out of the rapidly disintegrating Yardbirds, who all but ceased to be in the autumn of 1968. This allowed remaining guitarist Jimmy Page to expand on ideas he had been harbouring for some months and which, after tentative approaches to various musicians, he'd settled on fellow session musician, bassist John Paul Jones and Black Country duo Robert Plant on vocals and John Bonham on drums, both of whom had played together in Band of Joy.

The new band, initially working under the name the New Yardbirds, primarily to fulfil live contractual obligations in Scandinavia, first played together as a four-piece under a record store in Soho's Gerrard Street and later at a recording session for Sixties singer PJ Proby.

Undertaking their first tour allowed the band to mix a set of Yardbirds favourites with covers, and some of Page's own compositions that were gradually taking shape. Thus the likes of 'Communication Breakdown', 'I Can't Quit You Baby', 'How Many More Times', 'You Shook Me' and 'Babe I'm Gonna Leave You' all benefited from the quartet having a period of time to develop and rehearse material that would form the basis of their debut album, named 'Led Zeppelin' after the new name given to them upon their return from their touring commitments.

It was this factor that Jimmy Page, who produced the album,

cited as being of prime importance for the speed with which the fledgling band worked their way through their electrifying debut. 'Led Zeppelin' was recorded in a mere 36 hours of studio time at London's Olympic Studios (1976's 'Presence' would take the second shortest time for the band to record and album, clocking in at a relatively epic 18 days!). 'I knew what sound I was looking for,' Page stated. 'It just came together incredibly quickly.'

Glyn Johns was on hand as engineer to help Page, who played a psychedelically painted Fender Telecaster on the album, a gift from Jeff Beck. On later albums Page would switch to a Gibson Les Paul.

'Led Zeppelin' was recorded prior to the band securing a record deal, which was a pretty unique situation for a band to find themselves in, and perhaps another unspecified reason for the economic use of studio time. Page and manager Peter Grant paid for the sessions.

'I wanted artistic control in a vice grip, because I knew exactly what I wanted to do with these fellows,' Page told *Guitar World*. 'In fact, I financed and completely recorded the first album before going to Atlantic. It wasn't your typical story where you get an advance to make an album – we arrived at Atlantic with tapes in hand... Atlantic's reaction was very positive – I mean they signed us, didn't they?'

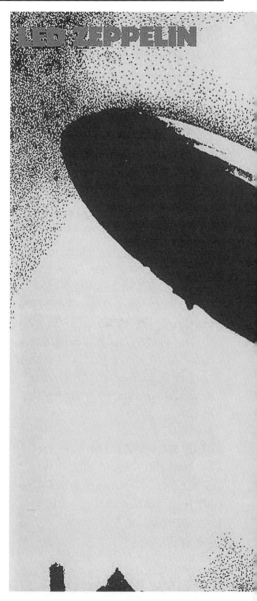

Musically 'Led Zeppelin' offers a supremely confident and hungry young band. And yet for all the take-your-breath away heaviness on offer, the album also showcased elements of the band's make-up that would always help stand them apart from many of their contemporaries.

Thus alongside the primally

explosive, proto heavy metal of 'Communication Breakdown', 'Dazed And Confused', 'I Can't Quit You Baby' and 'You Shook Me', Led Zeppelin were already showing their willingness to incorporate folk ('Black Mountain Side') and blues ('How Many More Times') into their sound, musical threads that would become more prevalent over their next three albums.

Although he didn't get a writing credit on the debut (still being signed to an old solo deal with Columbia), it is widely regarded that Plant was as involved as Bonham and Jones in helping Page map out the musical path of the new band. What is without doubt is that his raw, powerful howl immediately set him out as a vocalist of note as much as Page's intense fretboard interplay suggested he too would become a pioneering talent, as much as the taut industry of Jones and Bonham both underpinned the band's sound and yet still found time for both to display their own not inconsiderable talents.

Amazingly, 'Led Zeppelin' was panned in America, where *Rolling Stone* magazine suggested it lagged behind Jeff Beck's 'Truth' in terms of impact and imagination. Chris Welch at the UK's *Melody Maker* was more impressed, stating 'Jimmy Page triumphs'. The public, however, were impressed from the off. The album spent 79 weeks on the UK charts, where it would reach Number 6. In America it remained on the charts for 73 weeks, and within two months had reached Number 10. By 1975 alone 'Led Zeppelin' had grossed $7 million. Not bad for an album that cost £1,782 to record.

And in 2006, even *Rolling Stone*, with whom, thanks to young journalist Cameron Crowe,

Zeppelin would forge a working relationship in the mid Seventies, saw the error of their ways, re-assessing 'Led Zeppelin thus:

'(The album) was pretty much unlike anything else. The arrangements were more sculpted than those of Cream or Jimi Hendrix, and the musicianship wasn't cumbersome like Iron Butterfly's or bombastic like Vanilla Fudge's. The closest comparisons might be to MC5 or the Stooges – both from Michigan – yet neither had the polish or prowess of Led Zeppelin, nor did Led Zeppelin have the political, social or die-hard sensibility of those landmark bands. What they did have, though, was the potential for a mass audience.'

Hindsight. It's a wonderful thing!

TRACKLISTING:
Good Times, Bad Times/Babe I'm Gonna Leave Me/You Shook Me/ Dazed And Confused/Your Time Is Gonna Come/Black Mountain Side/ Communication Breakdown/I Can't Quit You Baby/How Many More Times.

LED ZEPPELIN II

Considering what Led Zeppelin achieved in their very first year as a band, it is a measure of the supreme talent of the band as individuals and as a unit that not only did they manage to release two records, but two records that made such an unequivocal impact on the rock world at large.

By the time Zeppelin released their second album in October 1969 they'd already undertaken three tours of America, and four more across Europe. A phenomenal level of live activity for any band, especially one in its first year together. But Led Zeppelin didn't just tour the world to spread their word. They also managed to record and release one of the most important albums in the history of hard-rock music.

Much of what would become 'Led Zeppelin II' was recorded at various studios around the world. The band would write on the road, book a studio and head straight in to record what they'd come up with. After the incendiary debut, the band were literally buzzing on a creative high – and, as friendships and writing partnerships developed, the four individuals that made up Led Zeppelin flourished.

'We were touring a lot,' recalled Jones. 'Jimmy's riffs were coming fast and furious. A lot of them came from on-stage, especially during the long improvised section of "Dazed And Confused". We'd remember the good stuff and dart into a studio along the way.'

Songs such as 'Thank You' and 'The Lemon Song' were worked on whilst the band were on the road, whilst the band also mixed 'Whole Lotta Love' and 'Heartbreaker'. Studios used for the recording of 'Led Zeppelin II' included Olympia in London, A&M, Quantum, Sunset, Mystic and Mirror Sound in Los Angeles, Mayfair, Groove and Juggy Sound in New York,

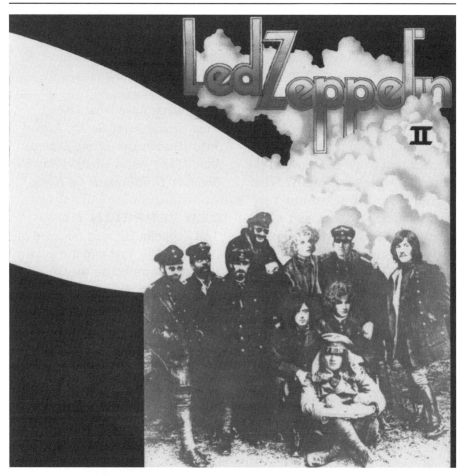

Ardent in Memphis, and what was affectionately credited as 'a hut' in Vancouver.

Page once again handled the production sound, and was aided and abetted by engineer Eddie Kramer. The production sound on 'Led Zeppelin II', as well as the vibrant performances from the band themselves, is one of the reasons the album remains so influential. Kramer himself pointed to his good working relationship with Page as being a major factor when he spoke to *Classic Rock* magazine: 'We did that album piece-meal. We cut some of the tracks in some of the most bizarre studios you can imagine, little holes in the wall. Cheap studios. But in the end it sounded bloody marvellous. There was a unification of sound on 'Led Zeppelin II' because there was one guy in charge and that was Mr Page.'

Musically 'Led Zeppelin II' built upon themes laid down on the band's debut. Towering rockers like 'Whole Lotta Love' and 'Heartbreaker' went even further to suggest no-one in the rock world could work such magic with a riff as Jimmy Page. Robert Plant officially stepped up to the plate with his first writing credits, oozing raw sexuality on 'The Lemon Song', using his love of the blues to imbue the likes of 'Bring It On Home' and adding touches of his early fantasy themes on 'Ramble On'. And the acoustic touches that could be heard on the softer parts of 'What Is And What Should Never Be' pointed to folkier influence that would soon pervade the band's over all sound.

Housed in a grandiose gatefold sleeve, designed by David Juniper [see JUNIPER, DAVID], 'Led Zeppelin II' was an immediate success. Released with the knowledge of 400,000 advance orders, the album was the band's first to reach the coveted Number 1 spot in America (where it knocked the Beatles 'Let It Be' off the top). The UK followed that lead where the album, which spent a grand total of 138 weeks on the UK charts, reached Number 1 in April 1970.

'Whole Lotta Love' was released as a single in America (against the band's wishes) and reached Number 4.

'Led Zeppelin II' is widely regarded as one of the most influential rock albums of all time, its powerful grooves and towering performances of Plant and Page inspiring many a young rock fan across the world, particularly in America where these fans would be propelled to form bands like Aerosmith, Van Halen and even Guns N'Roses. Bands who would,

in the four decades to come, rise up triumphant, yet forever find themselves under the shadow of the mighty Zeppelin.

TRACKLISTING:
Whole Lotta Love/What Is And What Should Never Be/The Lemon Song/Heartbreaker/Living Loving Maid (She's Just A Woman)/Ramble On/Moby Dick/Bring It On Home.

LED ZEPPELIN III

'Led Zeppelin III' was released in October 1970, just under a year after the powerhouse that was 'Led Zeppelin II'. It is noted for its abundance of acoustic material, the band continuing to follow their folkier inclinations.

It is perhaps not surprising that Zeppelin slowed the tempo somewhat on their third album if one bears in mind that, within one year, the band had announced their arrival not only with two hugely expressive and monumental rock albums but also with seven different tours of America and Europe.

Following the band's 1970 US tour, Led Zeppelin took a break, with Robert Plant and family and Jimmy Page and girlfriend decamping to a cottage in Wales that Plant's family had visited, known as Bron-Yr-Aur. Inspired by being cut off from the world and in a cottage with no electricity and running water (can you imagine a band whose second album had hit the top of the charts on both sides of the Atlantic doing this today?), Page and Plant's writing partnership thrived.

'After the intense touring that had been taking place through the first two albums, working almost 24 hours a day, basically, we managed to stop and have a proper break, a couple of months as opposed to a couple of weeks,' Page told *Trouser Press* in 1977. 'We decided to go off and rent a cottage to provide a contrast to motel rooms. Obviously, it had quite an effect on the material that was written... It was the tranquility of the place that set the tone of the album. Obviously, we weren't crashing away at 100-watt Marshall stacks. Having played acoustic and being interested in classical guitar, anyway, being in a cottage without electricity, it was acoustic guitar time... After all the heavy, intense vibe of touring which is reflected in the raw energy of the second album, it was just a totally different feeling.'

With much of the album written, Page and Plant convened with John Paul Jones and John Bonham at Headley Grange in Hampshire, where once more the pastoral surroundings benefited the band's vibe during rehearsals

of the new material. The band also recorded some of 'Led Zeppelin III' at Headley Grange, as well as at Olympic Studios in London with engineers Andy Johns and Terry Manning.

Despite 'Led Zeppelin III's mellow reputation, it includes some fierce rockers none more so than its paean to Norse explorer Leif Ericson, the thundering opener 'Immigrant Song', with its now legendary '…Hammer of the Gods…' refrain, as well as the rowdy 'Out On The Tiles' and 'Celebration Day'. But what truly makes 'Led Zeppelin III' so important in the Zep canon is the band's evident delight in musical exploration.

'Since I've Been Loving You' and 'Friends' hinted at the epic numbers that would evolve later in the Seventies, 'Gallows Pole' played a delightful folk hand, while the likes of 'Bron-Y-Aur Stomp', 'Tangerine' and the sublime 'That's The Way' showed a mastery of folk that anyone raised purely on 'Communication Breakdown' and 'Whole Lotta Love' would have claimed was any other band other than Led Zeppelin.

Maybe this is why 'Led Zeppelin III', housed in its colourful, kaleidoscopic sleeve with turning wheel, confused some upon its release. Some critics dismissed the lighter material as a mere pastiche of Crosby, Stills, Nash and Young, forcing Page to retort to *Rolling Stone*'s Cameron Crowe, 'When the third LP came out and

got its reviews, Crosby, Stills and Nash had just formed. That LP had just come out and because acoustic guitars had come to the forefront all of a sudden: LED ZEPPELIN GO ACOUSTIC! I thought, "Christ, where are their heads and ears?" There were three acoustic songs on the first album and two on the second.'

He was right, too. As Robert Plant seemed to confirm; '"Led Zeppelin III" was not one of the best sellers in the catalogue because the audience turned round and said, "What are we supposed to do with this? Where is our 'Whole Lotta Love Part 2'?" They wanted something like "Paranoid" by Black Sabbath! But we wanted to go acoustic and a piece like "Gallows Pole" still had all the power of "Whole Lotta Love" because it allowed us to be dynamic.'

'Led Zeppelin III' followed its predecessor to the top of the charts in both the UK and America. It would remain at Number 1 in America for four weeks and in the UK for three, returning to the top slot later in the year. But more importantly it proved that Led Zeppelin weren't just about behemoth rock moments. Their musical magic could and, as the band's fourth album would prove, would be woven around a myriad of far-reaching musical styles.

Led Zeppelin pre-empted the release of 'Led Zeppelin III' with a full-page advertisement in *Melody*

Maker that simply said: 'Thank you for making us the world's Number 1 band'. As usual, Led Zeppelin got it spot-on.

TRACKLISTING:

Immigrant Song/Friends/Celebration Day/Since I've Been Loving You/Out On The Tiles/Gallows Pole/Tangerine/ That's The Way/Bron-Y-Aur Stomp/ Hats Off To (Roy) Harper.

LEE, MICHAEL

Michael Lee was the drummer for both Robert Plant's band on 'Fate Of Nations' and subsequently with Jimmy Page and Robert Plant throughout the duration of their work together in the Nineties.

Lee had begun his musical career with Scarborough's Brit-rock hopefuls Little Angels who rose to prominence in the late Eighties/early Nineties. He was sacked by the band when they learned he'd auditioned for the Cult, whom he subsequently joined in 1991. He then hooked up with Plant, working on his 1993 solo album 'Fate Of Nations' and forging a dynamic partnership with bassist Charlie Jones. The pair would become an integral part of the Page/Plant band, appearing on both 1994's 'No Quarter: Jimmy Page And Robert Plant Unledded' and 1998's 'Walking Into Clarksdale' (Lee and Jones would receive writing credits on the latter).

Lee also worked with Echo and the Bunnymen, Ian Gillan and Thin Lizzy, amongst others. Sadly, he died of an epileptic seizure in November 2008.

Plant remembered him thus: 'Michael was the rhythm bridge between the Seventies and the 21st century. On the work which was not original, he had a tough gig to visit Bonham-driven classics and present his own imprint. He mastered and transfigured this, introducing an inherent swing mixed up with his drum-and-bass leanings, he always encouraged.'

LE FEVRE, BENJI

Benji Le Fevre worked behind the scenes for Zeppelin manager Peter Grant. He is listed as a technician on the credits for the 1976 film *The Song Remains The Same.*

He replaced Richard Cole as tour manager after Cole was sacked prior to the band's final European tour of 1980. It was Le Fevre who, along with John Paul Jones, discovered John Bonham dead at Jimmy Page's Old Mill, Windsor residence on 25 September 1980.

Post Zeppelin, Le Fevre has worked as a record producer, recording with the likes of Damned singer Dave Vanian. He also acted as producer and engineer on Robert Plant's 1985 third solo album, 'Shaken 'N' Stirred'.

LEWIS, DAVE

Dave Lewis is the premier Led Zeppelin archivist and chronicler, author and editor of the long-running and hugely respected Zeppelin magazine *Tight But Loose.*

He is the author of such books

as *Led Zeppelin The Final Acclaim, Then As It Was: Led Zeppelin At Knebworth 1979, Led Zeppelin: The Concert Files* and *Led Zeppelin: A Celebration*.

Tight But Loose has been running since 1978: information is available from *www.tightbutlooose.co.uk*. A book about Led Zeppelin's final European tour of 1980 was in the pipeline in 2010.

LIVE AID

Live Aid was the worldwide series of concerts held on 13 July 1985 to raise money to help victims of the famine in Ethiopia. The main concerts, which were held simultaneously at London's Wembley Stadium and Philadelphia's JFK Stadium, were organised by Bob Geldof and Midge Ure, the men behind the 1984 Band Aid charity single.

The remaining members of Led Zeppelin appeared on the bill at JFK, although they were not announced as such. Alongside Jimmy Page, Robert Plant and John Paul Jones, drummer Tony Thompson (Chic) filled the role vacated by the late John Bonham, although Phil Collins had flown from appearing at Wembley Stadium by Concorde so he could also appear. Robert Plant's bassist Paul Martinez also featured.

The band performed 'Rock And Roll', 'Whole Lotta Love' and 'Stairway To Heaven', taking the stage amidst much fanfare. However the reunion did not work well. Page struggled with an out-of-tune Les Paul, whilst lack of rehearsals hampered the timing of the drummers and rendered Plant's vocals largely hoarse. Plant subsequently labelled the band's appearance, their first public reunion 'an atrocity' and laid the blame fairly and squarely at the feet of the two drummers. 'I don't want to blame anyone, but the two drummers hadn't learned their parts,' he said. 'You can get away with that in a pop band, but not with Led Zeppelin.'

When, after over two decades Bob Geldof decided to release the event on DVD, Led Zeppelin specifically requested that their performance be left off, claiming it was 'substandard'. All three surviving members chose instead to donate money to demonstrate their ongoing support for the campaign behind Live Aid. That said, there are plenty of bootlegs available.

LIVE AT THE GREEK

'Live At The Greek' is a double live album featuring Jimmy Page and US rockers the Black Crowes. It was released as a download in February 2000, and on CD via the TVT label in July.

The album, which was produced by Kevin Shirley, was recorded at two shows Page performed with the Crowes at Los Angeles' Greek Theater on 18-19 October 1999.

Originally the band played a mix of traditional blues numbers and Black Crowes and Led Zeppelin material, but contractual reasons meant that the Crowes' own material had to be left off the album. The album was a moderate success, reaching Number 39 in the UK album charts and 64 in America.

TRACKLISTING:

Disc One: *Celebration Day/Custard Pie/Sick Again/What Is And What Should Never Be/Woke Up This Morning/Shapes Of Things/Sloppy Drunk/Ten Years Gone/In My Time Of Dying/Your Time Is Gonna Come*
Disc Two: *The Lemon Song/ Nobody's Fault But Mine/ Heartbreaker/Hey Hey What Can I Do/ Mellow Down Easy/Oh Well/Shake Your Money Maker/You Shook Me/ Out On The Tiles/Whole Lotta Love.*

The Japanese edition also featured 'Misty Mountain Hop' and 'In The Light'. Both 'What Is And What Should Never Be' and 'Ten Years Gone' were released as singles in America.

LIVING LOVING MAID (SHE'S JUST A WOMAN)

'Living Loving Maid (She's Just A Woman)' is the sixth song on 1969's 'Led Zeppelin II'. It doesn't leave much to the imagination, relating the tale of a groupie who had allegedly upset the band.

The song segues almost seamlessly from the preceding 'Heartbreaker', which meant many US radio stations would play the two songs consecutively. However, despite the band regularly performing 'Heartbreaker' in concert, they never performed 'Living Loving Maid (She's Just A Woman)' in its entirety, as it was allegedly Jimmy Page's least favourite Led Zeppelin song (despite the fact he'd written it with Page). One story alleges that Page's then girlfriend, Charlotte Martin, was offended by the song.

A small snatch of the song did follow a live version of 'Heartbreaker' at a show in Dusseldorf in March 1970. And Robert Plant performed 'Living Loving Maid (She's Just A Woman)' on the US leg of his 1990 'Manic Nirvana' tour.

Despite the lack of live performances, the song was released as a single in Japan and Turkey backed with 'Bring It On Home', in Argentina backed with 'Whole Lotta Love' and in Peru backed with 'Ramble On'.

LUCIFER RISING

Lucifer Rising is the title of a 1972 short film from controversial director Kenneth Anger. The film starred British singer and actress Marianne Faithfull.

Jimmy Page was originally asked by Anger to write and record the soundtrack for the film, which was inspired by Anger's long-term fascination with Aleister Crowley and the occult.

Page and Anger fell out, and Anger then asked musician and Manson Family member Bobby Beausoleil to complete the music, which he did in 1979, with permission from the authorities (he was in prison for the murder of Gary Hinman).

The album was released in 1980 on the Disgust label and reissued on CD on the Arcanium label in 2005.

[For the full story concerning Page and Anger see ANGER, KENNETH]

LULU

Lulu is a Scottish singer, actress and television personality who rose to prominence in the Sixties. She was joint winner of the 1969 Eurovision Song Contest

Despite her wholesome image, Lulu mixed with many of the glitterati of the rock world throughout the late Sixties and Seventies. Many of her early hit records utilised the talents of popular session musicians of the day, and her 1968 hit 'Best Of Both Worlds' featured a lush orchestral arrangement courtesy of John Paul Jones.

John Bonham further strengthened the Zeppelin connection by drumming on Lulu's 1971 single 'Everybody Clap'.

McCARTNEY, PAUL

Subsequent to the Zeppelin split, John Paul Jones was involved in several recording and video sessions with the one-time Beatle. He also contributed to the soundtrack for McCartney's 1984 film *Give My Regards To Broad Street*.

Jones, along with John Bonham, also performed on an October 1978 session at Abbey Road studios with Wings. The session, under the title Rockestra, was for Wings' 1979 album 'Back To The Egg'. Two songs were recorded, 'Rockestra Theme' and 'So Glad To See You Here'. Also present at the sessions were the Who's Pete Townshend, the Shadows' Hank Marvin and Pink Floyd's Dave Gilmour.

McCartney also turned up for the band's 2007 reunion show at London's O_2 Arena. There were unsubstantiated allegations that he was seen smoking marijuana at the show!

McCALLUM, DAVID

The father of top actor David McCallum, it was he whom Page credited as giving him the idea of playing his guitar with a violin bow. McCallum Sr, who died in 1972, was, in his time, first violin in three orchestras: the Royal Philharmonic, the London Philharmonic and the Scottish National.

MADDOX, LORI

Also known as Lori Lightning and Lori Mattix, she was part of the Hollywood groupie scene in the Seventies, being one of the GTOs (Girls Together Outrageously). Born in 1958, she's said to have lost her virginity to David and Angie Bowie when aged 13.

Jimmy Page became so intrigued with Lori that he pursued her relentlessly when the band were in Los Angeles, but to no avail. Eventually he's said to have had Zeppelin tour manager Richard Cole 'kidnap' the 14-year-old and bring her to the Continental Hyatt Hotel, where the band were staying at the time. Lori describes the scene in Page's room in the controversial Zeppelin biography *Hammer Of The Gods*: 'It was dimly lit by candles…and Jimmy was just sitting there in a corner, wearing this hat slouched over his eyes and holding a cane. It was really mysterious and weird… He looked just like a gangster. It was magnificent.'

It was the start of an 18-month relationship which was kept secret as Page faced arrest for having sex with an underage girl. And, despite claims that the pair were in love, Page kept on seeing other women as well.

Eventually Page dumped Lori for Bebe Buell, which devastated the teenager who tried in vain to rekindle the guitarist's interest. They did briefly get back together in the Eighties, but this quickly fizzled out.

When last sighted, Lori Maddox was working as a buyer and manager at an LA fashion boutique. She still gives occasional interviews about her relationship with Page.

MANIC NIRVANA

Robert Plant's fifth solo album was released in March 1990, reaching Number 15 in the UK and Number 12 in America – both chart positions a comparative disappointment.

The album featured the band of Doug Boyle (guitar), Phil Johnstone (guitar/keyboards), Charlie Jones (bass) and Chris Blackwell (guitar/drums). It was co-produced by Plant, with Johnstone and Mark 'Spike' Stent.

The big songs on the record were 'Tie Dye On The Highway' and 'Hurting Kind (I've Got My Eye On You)'. Musically, it followed the path of 1988's 'Now And Zen', but also included some of the elements that would come to fruition on the next record, 1993's 'Fate Of Nations'.

TRACKLISTING:
Hurting Kind (I've Got My Eyes On You)/'Big Love/SSS & Q/I Cried/
She Said/Nirvana/Tie Dye On The Highway/Your Ma Said You Cried In Your Sleep Last Night/Anniversary/ Liar's Waltz/Watching You.

MANNING, TERRY

Veteran producer and engineer Terry Manning started out in El Paso, Texas in the early Sixties playing in local bands. After moving to Memphis, he worked for both Stax Records and Ardent Studios, and during this time he got to record such artists as Isaac Hayes, Booker T and the MGs and Ike and Tina Turner. He even released his own album, 'Home Sweet Home', in 1970 through Stax's Enterprise imprint.

In subsequent years, he has worked with such names as Molly Hatchet, ZZ Top, Joe Walsh, Johnny Winter, Lenny Kravitz, Shania Twain and Bryan Adams. He's also a successful photographer.

Manning first met Jimmy Page when the latter was touring America as bassist for the Yardbirds. Manning was then a member of the Memphis group Lawson and Four More. The two bands shared the bill on the Dick Clark Caravan Of Stars Tour in the mid-South, which is when Jeff Beck quit the Yardbirds and Page became lead guitarist

Manning and Page did talk at the time of starting a new project together, but nothing came of these discussions. However, Manning was called in to engineer 'Led Zeppelin III' in 1971, and is credited with adding the Aleister Crowley inscriptions 'Do what thou wilt' and 'So mote it be' to the runoff groove of first pressings.

MARTINEZ, PAUL

So, who has played bass with Led Zeppelin? Full marks for anyone who mentioned Paul Martinez. He augmented the band's live sound on 13 July 1985 when they played the JFK Stadium in Philadelphia – Live Aid.

Born in Casablanca in 1947, Martinez has also played with the likes of the Downliners Sect, the Foundations and Chicken Shack. He once turned down the chance to join Whitesnake, which might explain why Robert Plant hired him in 1982 to play on debut solo album 'Pictures At Eleven'. He also appeared on the Plant albums 'The Principle Of Moments' (1983) and 'Shaken N'Stirred' (1985).

As for his brief stint with Zeppelin, Martinez wryly recalls on his website (*www.paulmartinezmusic.com*): 'Robert Plant still does remember me being there!'

MASSOT, JOE

The writer and director who began work on the 1976 film *The Song Remains The Same*. However, he never got the chance to finish it, being removed from the project and replaced by Peter Clifton. Apparently, there was concern over the slow progress being made under Massot's guidance.

Massot also worked on the 1968 movie *Wonderwall*, which featured a soundtrack from George Harrison, and 1981 ska movie *Dance Craze*.

He died in 2002.

MAYFAIR BALLROOM

It was at this Newcastle venue that Led Zeppelin played their first UK show, even though they were still being billed as the Yardbirds. It was on 4 October 1968, following a run of nine shows in Denmark and Sweden. The band returned to the venue once more, on 18 March 1971.

Tickets for that debut British date were the equivalent of 52p today, and the bill also included Terry Reid fronting a band called Fantasia. Also appearing were Junco Partners and Downtown Faction.

Interestingly one flyer announcing the show mentioned it was the Yardbirds 'featuring Jimmy *Paige*'.

The band's set that night featuring old Yardbirds songs plus a mix of material being worked on for that first album and a cover of Garnett Mimms' 'As Long As I Have You'.

MIDNIGHT FLYER

A band formed in 1980 who were signed to Zeppelin's Swan Song label. The line-up featured Maggie Bell (vocals), Anthony Glynne (guitar), Tony Stevens (bass), John Cook (keyboards) and Dave 'Duck' Dowle (drums).

Between them they'd experience

with Whitesnake, Stone the Crows, Streetwalkers, Savoy Brown, Foghat, Jim Capaldi and Leo Sayer.

Recalls Dowle: 'At the time I joined, Maggie and Tony Stevens were just putting the band together. Maggie had been a solo artist and she was ready to do something different. It did feel like a band, though, as opposed to Maggie's backing band. But you always felt that Maggie was the bee's knees. She was marvellous. Peter Grant loved her. He'd known her for years. They just phoned me up.

'Funnily enough I'd been called by Ozzy Osbourne, who was getting together with Randy Rhodes and I went up and played with them for a little while, but I didn't really like it. Judas Priest phoned me up too. In those days, because I'd been in Whitesnake, I had a bit of a name, and there weren't that many drummers around. Ant Glynne had been recommended to Tony Stevens by a friend of his. The band lasted a couple of years. We had a marvellous time, and Maggie and I are still in contact.

'We rehearsed for quite a long time before recording the album and we were quite relieved when we got signed to Swan Song. Because you never really knew how it was; Swan Song was all about Peter Grant and Led Zep, so it took quite a while to come about. Maggie was signed to them as a solo artist. But in a way that delay was good. By the

time we went into the studio we were really well rehearsed.'

The self-titled, debut album was produced by Bad Company guitarist Mick Ralphs, keeping it in the Swan Song family (Bad Company were also signed to the label). It came out in February 1981, but never really stood a chance of selling, despite touring with AC/DC. The label really went into decline after the death of John Bonham in 1980, Peter Grant suffering from addiction and depression, and Midnight Flyer fell apart in 1982.

MIGHTY REARRANGER

The title of the 2005 album from Robert Plant and Strange Sensation. It was Plant's second record with the band, following on from 2002's 'Dreamland'. The record has a lot of world music influences, plus political and religious comment, many of which are cynical and biting.

'Freedom Fries' is an attack on George W Bush's US administration, which might seem like going with the popular flow among musicians at the time but is still quite overt for someone like Plant. The album title itself is meant to refer to a creature who controls the fate of mankind.

The album was Plant's most successful in the UK since his debut solo record, 1982's 'Pictures At Eleven'. It reached Number 4 in the charts. This also did well in America, making it to Number 22, better than anything since 'Manic Nirvana' in 1990.

Nominated for two Grammys, the album was available in a limited edition with a bonus CD featuring an interview with Plant. But this was only available at Best Buy retail outlets in America.

TRACKLISTING:
Another Tribe/Shine It All Around/ Freedom Fries/Tin Pan Valley/All The King's Horses/The Enchanter/ Takamba/Dancing In Heaven/ Somebody Knocking/Let The Four Winds Blow/Mighty ReArranger/ Brother Ray/Shine It All Around (Girls Mix) – this was a hidden track.

In France, copies were sold with a live bonus CD, recorded at Studio 104 in Paris on 9 June 2005. This had the following tracklisting:
Shine It All Around/Black Dog/ Freedom Fries/When The Levee Breaks/All The Kings Horse/Takamba/ Tin Pan Valley/Gallows Pole/The Enchanter/Mighty ReArranger/ Whole Lotta Love.

MIRROR SOUND STUDIOS

The Los Angeles studio where part of the 'Led Zeppelin II' album was recorded. 'The Lemon Song' and 'Moby Dick' were recorded here.

MISTY MOUNTAIN HOP

The fifth song featured on the 1971 'Led Zeppelin IV' album, this showcased John Paul Jones on electric piano, and a riff that has interplay between Jones and Jimmy Page, the former on piano. Recorded at Headley

Grange, 'Misty Mountain Hop' was the B-side of the single 'Black Dog', released in America and Australia.

The lyrics are said to be about the aftermath of an encounter with the police, involving marijuana. Subsequently, they head for the Misty Mountains, a range which is located in the JRR Tolkien world of Middle-Earth, running a distance of 765 miles north to south.

The band played it live from 1972 to '73, often linked to 'Since I've Been Loving You'. It was also part of their set for the 2007 London reunion show at the O_2 Arena and is featured on the 2003 *Led Zeppelin* DVD.

Jimmy Page played this on his 1999 tour with the Black Crowes and it is a bonus track on the Japanese edition of the 2000 album 'Live At The Greek'.

MITCHELL, JONI

The celebrated Canadian singer-songwriter inspired the lyrics for 'Going To California' from the 1971 album 'Led Zeppelin IV'. Both Robert Plant and Jimmy Page were said to have been obsessed with her at the time. In fact, the story goes that Page went out to dinner with Mitchell soon after this was released, but was so intimidated in her presence that he could hardly speak.

Plant also met her in the mid-Seventies and claimed it to be a highlight of his life. In 2005, talking to writer Camille Paglia, Mitchell said: 'Actually, other artists would cross the street when I walked by! Initially, I thought that was due to elitism, but I later found out they were intimidated by me. Led Zeppelin was very courageous and outspoken about liking my music, but others wouldn't admit it. My market was women, and for many years the bulk of my audience was black, but straight white males had a problem with my music. They would come up to me and say, "My girlfriend really likes your music", as if they were the wrong demographic.'

MOBY DICK

An instrumental piece showcasing the talents of drummer John Bonham, this was known at various times by the alternative titles 'Pat's Delight' and 'Over The Top'.

It was the eighth track featured on 1969 album 'Led Zeppelin II'. It came about because Jimmy Page recorded various studio jams from Bonham, then pieced these together. The intro and outro also feature riffs from Page and John Paul Jones – the rest is pure Bonham.

The guitar riff is heavily inspired by the 1961 Bobby Parker single 'Watch Your Step'. Page so admired Parker, a blues-rock guitarist born in Louisiana, that he tried unsuccessfully to sign to him to Swan Song. Page first used the riff in a BBC recording in 1969, for a song called 'The Girl I Love'.

During the early days, the track was actually known as 'Pat's Delight', named after Bonham's wife, It the became 'Moby Dick', but was called 'Over The Top' during the band's 1977 US tour.

A live Bonham solo tour de force, this was last played at the Seattle Kingdome on 17 July 1977. This could last upwards of 20 minutes, with Bonham dispensing with sticks and using just his hands, more often than not drawing blood. It is the soundtrack to his fantasy sequence in the movie *The Song Remains The Same*, and a 1970 performance at the Royal Albert Hall in London is featured on the 2003 DVD *Led Zeppelin*.

Why was it titled 'Moby Dick' at all? Apparently, that's thanks to Jason Bonham, John's son. According to the late drummer's widow, Pat, one day Jason is said to have asked his father to play 'The long song'. When asked why, the boy said because, 'It's big, like Moby'.

MOON, KEITH

The madcap Who drummer is said to have been the person who recommended Jimmy Page call his new band Led Zeppelin. There are a lot of variations on the story. One is that someone told Moon that Page was going to call the band the New Yardbirds. Moon commented: 'That'll go down like a lead zeppelin'. Another variant is that Moon said this directly to Page, and yet another has him claiming to Page that the New Yardbirds 'would go down like a lead balloon', and it was Page to switched this to Lead Zeppelin, and subsequently to Led Zeppelin.

There's still another one, which comes from the recording sessions for the Jeff Beck single 'Beck's Bolero' in 1966. Moon and the Who's bassist John Entwistle were involved, as was Page plus keyboard-player Nicky Hopkins. At the time, the Who pair were fed up with the infighting in their group and formed a loose alliance with Page and Jones. Moon and Entwistle jokingly called this band Lead Zeppelin, and even created some spoof artwork for a supposed first album.

The Who bassist eventually dropped out of the session, but he, Moon, Beck and Page continued to talk about starting a band. It's claimed that only their failure to land either Steve Winwood or Steve Marriott as the singer scuppered the project. Amusingly, John Paul Jones replaced Entwistle on the session in question.

As if that's not enough, Entwistle himself has laid claim to coming up with the name, though the generally perceived wisdom is to give the credit to Moon.

There is one other connection between Moon and Led Zeppelin. He appeared onstage with them at the Forum in Los Angeles on 23 June 1977.

MORGAN STUDIOS

A north-west London studio where the band recorded 'Thank You' with engineer Andy Johns for their second album. The track 'Sugar Mama' was also recorded during these sessions, but remains officially unreleased.

Morgan Studios, now known as Battery, has had a succession of major names through its doors down the years, from the Kinks to Pink Floyd, AC/DC to Iron Maiden, Def Leppard, Black Sabbath, Yes and Paul McCartney. Bucks Fizz even worked there, which is cachet enough!

Back on the Zeppelin front, there are reports that the band regularly jammed down there with Black Sabbath – something confirmed by the latter's Bill Ward. Whether any recordings were made at the time, and still exist in any meaningful form, is open to speculation.

MOTHERSHIP

The title of a double CD album put out in 2007 tracing the band's career, but with no rare or previously unreleased tracks. The tracklisting was chosen by Robert Plant, Jimmy Page and John Paul Jones.

TRACKLISTING:

CD1: *Good Times Bad Times/ Communication Breakdown/Dazed And Confused/Babe I'm Gonna Leave You/Whole Lotta Love/Ramble On/Heartbreaker/Immigrant Song/ Since I've Been Loving You/Rock And Roll/Black Dog/When The*

Levee Breaks/Stairway To Heaven.
CD2: *The Song Remains The Same/ Over The Hills And Far Away/D'yer Mak'er/No Quarter/Trampled Underfoot/Houses Of The Holy/ Kashmir/Nobody's Fault But Mine/ Achilles Last Stand/In The Evening/ All My Love.*

A deluxe edition with a bonus DVD disc features clips from the 2003 *Led Zeppelin* DVD. This has a tracklisting of:
We're Gonna Groove/I Can't Quit You Baby/Dazed And Confused/ White Summer/What Is And What Should Never Be/Moby Dick/Whole Lotta Love/Communication

Breakdown/Bring It On Home/ Immigrant Song/Black Dog/Misty Mountain Hop/The Ocean/Going To California/In My Time Of Dying/ Stairway To Heaven/Rock And Roll/Nobody's Fault But Mine/ Kashmir/Whole Lotta Love.

A four-LP vinyl edition was issued nearly a year later.

Of particular significance is that the album's release coincided in November 2007 with the band making their entire back catalogue available for download, which was a major move.

The album, with a sleeve designed by artist Shepard Fairey

(who came from the skateboarding scene), got to Number 4 in the UK charts and Number Seven in America. It did top the charts in New Zealand and Norway, and also made the Top 10 almost everywhere else. By 2010, it had sold over two million copies in America and was heading towards the million mark in the UK.

MUSICLAND STUDIOS

The studio in Munich established underneath the Arabella Hotel in the late Sixties by producer/songwriter Giorgio Moroder is where Zeppelin recorded and mixed the whole of the 'Presence' album in late 1975/early 1976, with engineer Keith Harwood.

Other bands to record there include Queen, the Rolling Stones, ELO, Deep Purple, Donna Summer and Elton John. The studio closed in the Nineties, because the sound of passing trains was starting to affect recording quality.

MYSTIC SOUND STUDIO

The Hollywood Studio originally known as Bob Keene's Del-Fi Records Studio where Ritchie Valens recorded his legendary 'La Bamba' and Bobby Fuller did 'I Fought The Law'. It changed name to Mystic Sound Studio in 1969.

Led Zeppelin recorded 'The Lemon Song' for their second album at the studio, stopping off during their second tour of America to do this one song.

NEW YARBIRDS

The New Yarbirds was the name provisionally given to the fledgling Led Zeppelin before they settled on an actual name, although it was never officially the band's name.

The Yardbirds were winding down by 1968. Singer Keith Relf and drummer Jim McCarty were keen to pursue a more folk-orientated musical direction, which would lead them to forming folk-prog act Renaissance. Guitarist Jimmy Page was keen to explore the heavier, more experimental approach the band had been developing over their last couple of tours. Bassist Chris Dreja would pursue a career in photography; it is his photograph that adorns the back cover of 'Led Zeppelin'.

The very last Yardbirds show took place on 7 July 1968, 12 years to the day before the very last Led Zeppelin show with John Bonham in Berlin. However the band were contractually obliged to undertake a Scandinavian tour, and Relf and McCarty gave their blessing for Page and Dreja to undertake the tour with replacements. Page was keen to get vocalist Terry Reid involved, but he was already contracted to do a Rolling Stones tour in America and suggested a young Black Country vocalist who'd impressed him, Robert Plant of the Band of Joy. He also suggested the same band's drummer, John Bonham.

There had been a plan for Page to form a band with fellow Yardbirds guitarist Jeff Beck and with the Who rhythm section of Keith Moon and John Entwistle, with Donovan, Steve Winwood or Steve Marriott in the singer role, but this never materialised. Instead Page began working with Plant and Bonham. When Chris Dreja decided against touring, Page, at the suggestion of session drummer Clem Cattini, got in contact with session bassist John Paul Jones. The four came together to rehearse under a record shop in Gerard Street, jamming on 'Train Kept A-Rollin''.

The quartet, managed by Peter Grant, played their very first show on 7 September 1968 at Gladsaxes Teen Club in Denmark. They had previously recorded one session for Sixties singing star PJ Proby before heading off on tour. Upon return they decided on a name change, not least because Chris Dreja claimed to still own the rights to the Yardbirds name. At Grant's suggestion, Lead was changed to Led, to avoid Americans

mispronouncing the band's name.
Thus Led Zeppelin was born.

NICKY JAMES MOVEMENT

The Nicky James Movement were a band fronted by Brumbeat scenester James, and at one point featured John Bonham on drums.

James (real name Michael Nicholls) had played in bands with fellow Brumbeat musician Denny Laine and was even in a fledgling version of the Moody Blues, then named the Moody Blues 5. He was also in the Diplomats and mod act the Jamesons alongside John Maus (later John Walker of the Walker Brothers).

As the Nicky James Movement, James signed to Columbia Records and released a single, 'Stagger Lee'. As well as Bonham, the band would also feature later Electric Light Orchestra drummer Bev Bevan and Wizzard/Move man Roy Wood.

James would later sign to Threshold, the Moody Blues' own label and would appear on various solo albums by Moody Blues members. He carried on recording and performing live right up until his death in 2007. He had been working on a new album at the time.

NIGHT FLIGHT

The eleventh song on the 1975 album 'Physical Graffiti' was largely written by bassist John Paul Jones. It was originally recorded during sessions at Headley Grange in 1971 but was held back from Led Zeppelin's fourth album, for which it had originally been intended.

The song, which recounts the tale of a young man absconding from military service, was never performed live but does feature as a soundcheck from a Chicago gig on 6 July 1973 on various bootlegs. The song was covered by Jeff Buckley.

NINE LIVES

'Nine Lives' is a 2006 box set containing all eight Robert Plant solo albums, as well as the Honeydrippers' 'Volume One', the R&B album Plant recorded with Jimmy Page and Jeff Beck.

The albums are remastered and feature all extra B-sides from singles. There is also an accompanying DVD that features 20 promotional videos and interviews with the likes of Roger Daltrey, Phil Collins, Tori Amos, John McEnroe and Ahmet Ertegun amongst others.

Tracklisting

Disc One: *Burning Down One Side/ Moonlight In Samosa/Pledge Pin/ Slow Dancer/Worse Than Detroit/Fat Lip/Like I've Never Been Gone/ Mystery Title/Far Post/Like I've Never Been Gone' (Live).*

Disc Two: *Other Arms/In The Mood/Messin' With The Mekon/ Wreckless Love/Thru' With The Two Step/Horizontal Departure/Stranger Here... Than Over There/Big Log/In the Mood (Live)/Thru' With The Two Step (Live)/Lively Up Yourself (Live)/Turnaround.*

Disc Three: *I Get A Thrill/Sea Of Love/I Got A Woman/Young Boy Blues/Rockin' At Midnight/Rockin' At Midnight (Live).*

Disc Four: *Hip To Hoo/Kallalou Kallalou/Too Loud/Trouble For Money/Pink And Black/Little By Little/Doo Doo A Do Do/Easily Lead/Sixes And Sevens/Little By Little (Remixed Long Version).*

Disc Five: *Heaven Knows/Dance On My Own/Tall Cool One/Way I Feel/ Helen Of Troy/Billy's Revenge/Ship Of Fools/Why/White Clean And Neat/Walking Towards Paradise/ Billy's Revenge (Live)/Ship Of Fools (Live)/Tall Cool One (Live).*

Disc Six: *Hurting Kind (I've Got My Eyes On You)/Big Love/S S S & Q/I Cried/She Said/Nirvana/Tie Dye On The Highway/Your Ma Said You Cried In Your Sleep Last Night/ Anniversary/Liars Dance/Watching You/Oompah (Watery Bint)/One Love/Don't Look Back.*

Disc Seven: *Calling To You/Down To The Sea/Come Into My Life/I Believe/29 Palms/Memory Song (Hello Hello)/If I Were a Carpenter/ Promised Land/Greatest Gift/Great Spirit/Network News/Colours Of A Shade/Great Spirit (Acoustic Mix)/ Rollercoaster (Demo)/8.05/Dark Moon (Acoustic).*

Disc Eight: *Funny In My Mind/ Morning Dew/One More Cup Of Coffee/Last Time I Saw Her/Song To The Siren/Win My Train Fare Home/ Darkness Darkness/Red Dress/Hey Joe/Skip's Song/Dirt In A Hole/Last Time I Saw Her (Remix).*

Disc Nine: *Another Tribe/Shine It All Around/Freedom Fries/Tin Pan Valley/All The King's Horses/The Enchanter/Takamba/Dancing In Heaven/Somebody Knocking/Let The Four Winds Blow/Mighty ReArranger/ Brother Ray/Red White And Blue/ All The Money In The World/Shine It All Around (Girls Remix)/Tin Pan Valley (Girls Remix). The Enchanter (UNKLE Reconstruction).*

Disc 10 (DVD): *Nine Lives (Documentary)/Burning Down One Side (Video)/Big Log (Video)/In The Mood (Video)/Rockin' At Midnight (Video)/Sea Of Love (Video)/Little By Little (Video)/Pink And Black (Video)/Heaven Knows (Video)/Tall Cool One (Video)/Ship Of Fools (Video)/Hurting Kind (I've Got My Eyes On You) (Video)/Nirvana (Video)/Tie Dye On The Highway (Video)/29 Palms (Video)/Calling To You (Video)/I Believe (Video)/If I Were A Carpenter (Video)/Morning Dew (Video)/Darkness, Darkness (Video)/Shine It All Around (Video).*

NO QUARTER

'No Quarter' is the seventh song from 1973 album 'Houses Of The Holy' and was written by John Paul Jones, Jimmy Page and Robert Plant.

The song, whose title and lyrics allude to the military option of showing no mercy to a defeated foe, is one of the highlights, not only of 'Houses Of The Holy' but Led Zeppelin's entire output. It stands as a masterclass of the arranging skills of bassist Jones, who developed the song into a showcase for his piano and organ skills in the live arena. The original version had been faster before Page slowed the entire song down a semitone in the studio.

'No Quarter' became an immediate live favourite and would be lengthened to at least double its original seven minutes, primarily to allow Jones to improvise at the piano. From the band's 1975 tour onwards Jones would take the opportunity to perform classical pieces on the piano during the song, frequently Rachmaninoff but occasionally Rodriguez's 'Concerto de Aranjuez'. A 1977 Seattle performance is said to have clocked in at 36 minutes, with Jones leading the band in an impromptu R&B-inspired jam.

The song was also used in the film *The Song Remains The Same* for Jones' fantasy sequence, which featured him as a masked huntsman.

The song was re-recorded by Page and Plant for 1994's 'No Quarter: Jimmy Page And Robert Plant Unledded', a move which surely would have rankled with the absent Jones, and Plant himself recorded a re-worked version live which can be seen on his *Soundstage: Robert Plant And The Strange Sensation* DVD. Led

Zeppelin performed the song at their O_2 reunion gig in 2007.

'No Quarter' has been covered by artist such as Crowbar, Dread Zeppelin, Tool, Aryeon, Sly and Robbie, Gov't Mule and the Flaming Lips. It has been sampled by Apollo 440.

NO QUARTER: JIMMY PAGE AND ROBERT PLANT UNLEDDED

'No Quarter: Jimmy Page And Robert Plant Unledded' is an album from the pair as released on the Fontana label in 1994. The album came about on the back of the pair's reunion for an MTV *Unplugged* show titled *Unledded*, at the time the closest thing to a much-desired Led Zeppelin reunion outside of the Live Aid and Atlantic 40th Anniversary shows, that there had been (although John Paul Jones was left out of the reunion, allegedly not even being informed of it – a move traced back to supposed altercations with Plant during their days together).

The influence of Plant is writ large, not only over quite drastic re-workings of the Led Zeppelin material, but also over the Eastern and Moroccan musical styles to be heard on four new tracks recorded by the pair. The show and subsequent album were recorded in London (at MTV's Camden studios), Wales and Morocco.

Bassist Charlie Jones and drummer Michael Lee from Robert Plant's solo band feature on the album, as they did on the subsequent tour along with guitarist Porl Thompson, who had been a member of the Cure. The album also features a host of Moroccan and Egyptian musicians.

The album, not surprisingly, performed very well, reaching Number 4 in the US charts and Number 7 in the UK. The subsequent world tour was also a huge success. The duo would go on to record another album of all new studio material, 'Walking Into Clarksdale', in 1996.

TRACKLISTING:
Nobody's Fault But Mine/Thank You/ No Quarter/Friends/Yallah/City Don't Cry/Since I've Been Loving You/Battle Of Evermore/Wonderful One/That's The Way/Gallows Pole/ Four Sticks/Kashmir.

NOBODY'S FAULT BUT MINE

The fourth song on Led Zeppelin's 1976 album 'Presence' is credited as being written by Jimmy Page and Robert Plant, although musicologists have pointed to the similarity between this and Blind Willie Johnson's 1927 blues 'It's Nobody's Fault But Mine'.

There are, however, significant differences between the two versions, not least a completely different rhythm to the Zeppelin version and radically different lyrics. Nevertheless the fact the band had, on 1969's 'Led Zeppelin II', featured a photograph of Johnson on the cover merely added weight to conspiracy theories.

'Nobody's Fault But Mine' is a

tale of giving in to the sins of the flesh whereas Johnson's was more a tail of religious and spiritual enlightenment. The song became a live favourite from the off and featured in most Led Zeppelin live sets until 1980 and was also performed at the 2007 O_2 reunion show.

It has been covered by Dread Zeppelin, John Corabi, the Black Crowes and Paul Gilbert.

THE NOBS
[See THE KNOBS entry]

NOW AND ZEN
'Now And Zen' was Robert Plant's fourth solo album, released on the Es Paranza label in 1988.

After the stylistically weak 'Shaken N'Stirred', on which Plant had seemed to betray much of his Zeppelin heritage, on 'Now And Zen' he seems to openly embrace his past. As a result, it was hailed as his finest solo album since his 'Pictures At Eleven' solo debut. The fact that it also featured some contributions from Jimmy Page goes a long way to explaining the reason 'Now And Zen' is rated so highly.

Musically, 'Now And Zen' mixes flashes of Zeppelin-esque heaviosity with technology very much in keeping with Eighties recording techniques. Indeed Plant told Uncut magazine in 2005: 'If I listen to ("Now And Zen") now, I can hear that a lot of the songs got lost in the technology of the time.'

However, in sampling old Zeppelin tunes such as 'The Ocean',

'Whole Lotta Love', 'Custard Pie' and 'Black Dog' on the rocking 'Tall Cool One' it seemed that Plant had laid to rest the ghost of Zeppelin's past that seemed to haunt his early career – alas, they would return sporadically throughout his ensuing career, most recently causing him to spurn the chance of a further Zeppelin reunion following the well-received 2007 O_2 reunion show. Still, at the time, fans were more than happy to revel in the likes of the excellent 'Heaven Knows', 'Helen Of Troy' and 'Ship Of Fools'.

With a revitalised new band featuring Charlie Jones on bass, Phil Johnstoneon keyboards and Doug Boyle on guitar, 'Now And Zen' was a critical and commercial success for Plant, reaching Number 10 on the UK charts and Number 6 in the US. Plant performed 'Tall Cool One', 'Heaven Knows' and 'Ship Of Fools' during his solo set at the Atlantic 40th Anniversary show at Madison Square Garden in New York in 1988. 'Ship of Fools' also featured heavily in the final episode of the hit TV show *Miami Vice*.

TRACKLISTING:
Heaven Knows/Dancing On My Own/ Tall Cool One/The Way I Feel/Helen Of Troy/Billy's Revenge/Ship Of Fools/Why/White Clean And Neat/ Walking Towards.
The 2007 remastered reissue also had three live bonus tracks: *Billy's Revenge/Tall Cool One/Ship Of Fools.*

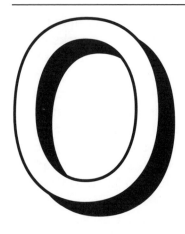

OCEAN, THE

The eighth and final song from the band's 1973 album 'Houses Of The Holy', this song was dedicated to Zeppelin fans, who provide an 'ocean' of support at every gig.

Right at the start, you can hear drummer John Bonham declare: 'We've done four already but now we're steady, and then they went 1, 2, 3, 4!' This refers to the fact that Zeppelin had already done four takes of the song, without nailing it. However, following this pep talk, the band got it right next time around.

Another point of interest is that there's the very faint sound of a telephone ringing twice during the song. Some have tried to suggest that this was deliberate, although quote what they would have been trying to achieve with such an effect is hard to understand. On the other hand, it's also difficult to imagine that the band would allow a telephone ring to interrupt them, and then leave it in. It's more likely that, having struggled a little to capture the sound in the way they wanted, the band got on a roll; a telephone did go off but they just kept going, not wanting to lose the flow. And when this was mixed, it may well have been that the decision was made to keep it in there, as the effect worked.

The last line of the song refers to Robert Plant's daughter Carmen. She is 'The girl who won my heart', as the lyric goes. Right at the end, during the last minute or so, Plant seems to intone the line 'I'm sorry, I'm sorry, yeah' in a very soft tone. Some have suggested he's actually saying 'I'm so, I'm so, I'm so glad'.

The reference in the lyrics to 'The Hellhound' was inspired by Robert Johnson, who is alleged to have sold his soul to the Devil at the crossroads. The band played this first during their 1972 US tour, but dropped it after 1973. It never returned to the set.

A performance from Madison Square Garden in 1973 is featured on the 2003 DVD *Led Zeppelin*. Part of this song turns up in Plant's solo song 'Tall Cool One', while the Beastie Boys sampled it for 'She's Crafty'.

OLD HYDE, THE

The house in Cutnall Green, Worcester owned by drummer John Bonham. Part of his fantasy sequence in the film *The Song Remains The Same* was shot here, including the game of snooker. Bonham bought this in 1972, and it would be his home for the rest of his life. He is actually buried at Rushock Parish Church near the Old Hyde Farm.

Bonham's sister, Deborah, recorded a song called 'The Old Hyde'. This is the title track of her 2004 album and has her nephew Jason, John's son, on drums.

If you go to: *www.ledzeppelin.com/video/john-bonham-old-hyde*, you will hear the song as the soundtrack to footage showing you around the house.

OLD MILL HOUSE

The house in Clewer, Windsor where Led Zeppelin officially split up in 1980, following the death of drummer John Bonham. It was owned by Jimmy Page. The guitarist only bought this at the start of 1980. He still owns it.

It was the Old Mill House to which Led Zeppelin returned following a days rehearsals at Bray Studios on 25 September 1980. Bonham had been drinking heavily all day. At the Old Mill House Bonham fell asleep and was put to bed. In the morning he was discovered dead by Zeppelin's new tour manager, Benji LeFevre and bassist John Paul Jones.

OLYMPIC STUDIOS

This is where Zeppelin worked on some of the songs for 'Led Zeppelin I', 'Led Zeppelin IV', 'Houses Of The Holy' and 'Physical Graffiti'.

Here is a list of songs connected with this studio:

From 'Led Zeppelin I' – The whole album was recorded and mixed there, with engineer Glyn Johns.

From 'Led Zeppelin IV': 'Rock And Roll' was partially mixed there by engineer Andy Johns. 'Misty Mountain Hop', 'Going To California' and 'The Battle Of Evermore' were all fully mixed there by Andy Johns.

From 'Houses Of The Holy': 'The Song Remains The Same', 'The Rain Song' and 'No Quarter' were all mixed there by Andy Johns.

From 'Physical Graffiti': 'Custard Pie', 'In My Time Of Dying', 'Trampled Underfoot', 'Kashmir'; 'In The Light', 'Ten Years Gone' and 'The Wanton Song' were all mixed there by engineer Keith Harwood.

Glyn Johns considers working at Olympic on 'Led Zeppelin I' 'a milestone. That was unbelievable, quite extraordinary. I think that's got to be one of the best rock'n'roll albums ever made, and I'm just grateful that I was there. I've never got off quite as much, and that record was made in nine days, which shows you. They'd rehearsed themselves very healthily before they got near the studio.

'I can't single out one track more than any other in my mind, but I remember that it was tremendously exciting to make that album. 'I'd never heard arrangements of that ilk before, nor had I ever heard a band play in that way before. It was just unbelievable, and when you're in a studio with something as

creative as that, you can't help but feed off it. I think that's one of the best-sounding records I've ever done.'

The original Olympic Studios was located inside a disused synagogue in Carlton Place, London. Many major recordings were made there, including the first ever Rolling Stones single 'Come On'. Many significant and celebrated artists trawled through the doors, and a number of now top producers (including Chris Kimsey and Terry Brown) first cut their teeth there.

In 1966 Olympic was relocated to Barnes in Surrey, where it stayed until shut down in 2009. Celebrating its history, Pierre

Perrone wrote the following eulogy in *The Independent* newspaper:

'First established in the late Fifties near Baker Street in central London, the original Olympic employed future Elton John producer Gus Dudgeon as a tea boy and was the place where the Yardbirds cut "For Your Love" and Millie Small recorded "My Boy Lollipop" in 1964. Two years later, Cliff Adams and Keith Grant bought Olympic from owner Angus McKenzie and moved to the current address at 117 Church Road in Barnes, south-west London. A former theatre built in 1906, the premises had already been converted into a film studio and, with a bit of acoustic tweaking by Grant and architectural work by Robertson Grant, easily adapted to become what was generally acknowledged as the best UK studio by its many clients.

'Olympic kept its connections with the film and TV industries and the theatre and hosted sessions for the soundtracks to *The Italian Job, The Rocky Horror Picture Show, Joe 90* and the original album version of the Tim Rice and Andrew Lloyd Webber musical *Jesus Christ Superstar* featuring Ian Gillan of Deep Purple. The news of Olympic's likely end has prompted Lloyd Webber to comment: 'I have fond memories of my first-ever recording session there when I was just 21. The closure of Olympic is the end of an era in rock'n'roll. I wonder whether the music industry has changed for ever.

'Traditionally, major labels such as EMI, Pye and Decca each had their dedicated studio but the pop explosion of the mid-Sixties, combined with the rise of the record producer and the development of the album as a format, created a demand for rooms with a vibe more in tune with the musicians' needs. Olympic was always a hipper place than Abbey Road, whose EMI employees rather resembled civil servants in their outlook and demeanour. Glyn Johns and his brother Andy in particular fitted in with the more dissolute lifestyles of the Stones while the state-of-the-art mixing desks built

by Grant and Dick Swettenham were the envy of the competition.

'Olympic still thrived in the age of residential studios like the Manor in Oxfordshire or Rockfield in Wales and when acts became tax exiles and began recording in exotic locations such as Compass Point in Nassau, Air in Montserrat or Miraval in the South of France in the Eighties. Olympic Studios even survived the drastic redesign which followed their acquisition by Virgin but now they seem to have reached the end of the road.'

OLYMPICS 2008
Jimmy Page joined British singer Leona Lewis during the closing ceremony of the Beijing Olympics. Lewis performed 'Whole Lotta Love' in a soft ballad style before Page joined in and the song was taken up a tempo or two.

The duo were part of a celebration of not just the Beijing games but the fact that the 2012 games would be held in London. The fact a Zeppelin song was chosen to help represent the finest qualities of London – and, by implication, Britain – shows how far things have changed from the days when the band were outcasts as far as the mainstream was concerned.

However, there were still problems. The line 'I'm gonna give you every inch of my love' was altered to 'I'm gonna give you every bit of my love' at the request of Lewis, who felt it would make more sense that way for a female – which is reasonable. The third verse was dropped altogether, because it was thought be too racy for the global audience.

OUT ON THE TILES

A song from the 1970 album 'Led Zeppelin III', this was the fifth track on the record.

The inspiration for it all came from John Bonham, who would often talk about going 'out on the tiles', which is a phrase meaning going out on the town. He'd also go on about visiting 'rubbers' and picking up 'scrubbers'. 'Rubbers' comes from cockney rhyming slang. 'Rubber' is 'Rubadub', which is a 'pub'. And 'Scrubbers' refers to ladies of a 'dubious distinction', to be delicate about it all. What Jimmy Page did was take this blunt reference from Bonham, clean it up a bit and up popped 'Out On The Tiles'.

There's a strange rhythm to this rather aggressive song, which might explain why someone can be definitely heard shouting 'Stop!' just after the one minute and 23 seconds mark. This is generally thought to be Page acting as a verbal guide, giving out instructions. There's also someone commenting 'All right' eleven seconds in, again thought to be Page.

'Out On The Tiles' was rarely played in its entirety during Zeppelin shows. One of the most famous occasions was on 4 September 1970 in Los Angeles.

The reason it's so well known is that it is featured on the famous bootleg 'Live On Blueberry Hill'.

More often the intro was used to lead into 'Black Dog'; on the 1977 US tour this introduced Bonham's drum solo, 'Moby Dick', although on that tour the solo was known as 'Over The Top'. Page played this song on his 1999 tour with the Black Crowes, and this is featured on the album from that tour, 2000's 'Live At The Greek'.

A number of covers over the years include Megadeth on their 2007 album 'United Abominations', and Blind Melon for the 1995 album 'Encomium: A Tribute To Led Zeppelin'.

Incidentally, if you've a Japanese version of the seven-inch 'Black Dog' single with 'Out On The Tiles' on the B-side, then you've something rare. Some were pressed up like this when 'Hey Hey Want Can I Do' should have been on the flip.

OUTRIDER

This was Jimmy Page's first, and so far only, solo album, released in 1988 by Geffen Records. The guitarist recorded it as his own Sol studio and has Robert Plant guesting on one song, 'The Only One'. Jason Bonham is also featured.

This was intended to be a double album, but Page's house was broken into and demos were taken. Some of these songs have apparently turned up on various bootlegs, and it is said that the break-in had an adverse effect on Page, with the result being that the album didn't out as well as everybody hoped. Whether this is a convenient excuse is open to speculation.

The album also featured Chris Farlowe and John Miles on vocals, Tony Franklin and Durban Laverde on bass and Barriemore Barlow on drums. It was released in June 1988 but didn't do particularly well in the US or the UK, It only made it to Number 26 in the former, and Number 27 in the latter. However, it has now sold over 500,000 copies in the States.

TRACKLISTING:

Wasting My Time/Wanna Make Love/ Writes Of Winter/The Only One (co-written by Page and Plant)/Liquid Mercury/Hummingbird (written by Leon Russell)/Emerald Eyes/Prison Blues/Blues Anthem (If I Cannot Have Your Love…)

OVER THE HILLS AND FAR AWAY

The third song from the 1973 album 'Houses Of The Holy', this was pieced together by Robert Plant and Jimmy Page while at Bron-Yr-Aur, the isolated location in Wales to which they retreated after the 1970 US tour.

Page explained how the song was constructed to *Guitar World* magazine:

GW: 'There's an acoustic guitar running throughout the song. Did you play a main acoustic and then overdub an electric?'

Page: 'No, we played it through entirely as you know it, but I was playing electric.'

GW: 'So you simply edited out of the beginning?'

Page: 'Yeah, that's right. Presumably. It sounds that way. It sounds like the acoustic is going straight through.'

The song was released as a single in the US, reaching Number 51, with 'Dancing Days' on the B-side. The band regularly played this live from 1972 to 1979, but dropped it for the 1980 European tour. Plant would frequently reference Acapulco Gold (a type of marijuana) onstage, when the line 'A pocketful of gold' came up.

OZONE BABY

This was one of three songs recorded during sessions at Polar Studios for the 'In Through The Out Door' album, but left off the final tracklisting. The others were 'Wearing And Tearing' and 'Darlene'. Eventually the song turned up on the 1982 outtakes album 'Coda'.

Never performed live by Zeppelin, it's an unexceptional straightahead rocker made more interesting because Robert Plant used harmonised vocal effects which he had rarely done in the studio.

American band Fuel referenced this for the song 'Ozone (Sucker)', which appeared on their 1998 debut album 'Sunburn'.

PAGE, JIMMY

The magus. The wizard. The occultist. The conductor of the Zeppelin experience. So much has been postulated about Jimmy Page, yet in this era of Internet and ready access to information about anyone, Page remains something of an enigma. Was he (is he) really a practitioner of the black arts? Was he responsible for the bad karma that led to the death of Robert Plant's son, Karac, and ultimately to the end of the band? Who can say? Page has stayed tight-lipped on the matter over the decades and unless he decides to write his autobiography, and tell the truth, we shall forever be in the dark.

'Jimmy is incredibly shrewd and talented,' said Peter Grant, Zeppelin's late manager, in 1990. 'I always saw him as my business partner in the band. I took care of the finances, while he dealt with the music. I always enjoyed his company, but even I have to say there was a darkness about him. Call it an aura if you want, but it

was something I could never quite get to grips with. Jimmy has a side to him that he allows few to see. Is he something of a Satanist? I don't believe so. But he has a real interest in the subject, and where you draw the line between interest and indulgence…well, I'm not sure.

'But that's why everyone holds Jimmy in awe, because he's more than a brilliant musician. He does have this unique charisma, and he found a way of channelling it through the songs. Do I believe that he brought bad karma into Zeppelin, and that led to tragedies? No, of course not. But it doesn't matter how many times I might say that, the majority will always choose to believe that he did.'

As the saying goes, when the legend becomes fact print the…legend.

So, what do we really know about Jimmy Page? He was born James Patrick Page on 9 January 1944 in the West London suburb of Heston, now part of the London borough of Hounslow. It was when

living in Epsom, Surrey that Page first picked up the guitar. He was 13 years old and, mainly through his own efforts, the budding talent began to emerge. He told *Trouser Press* magazine in 1977:

'Very early, once I started getting a few chords and licks together, I did start searching feverishly for other musicians to play with, but I couldn't find any. It wasn't as though there was an abundance. I used to play in many groups… anyone who could get a gig together, really.'

Inspired by the likes of Scotty Moore and James Burton, two rockabilly guitarists who played with Elvis Presley, Page began to explore his own abilities. Staring off on a Futurama Grazioso, before quickly graduating to a Telecaster, the teenage prodigy made his TV debut in 1957, on a show called *All Your Own*, a BBC TV talent show which was, one could say, the forerunner for *The X Factor* and such programmes. Page was in a skiffle quartet at the time. The foursome played two songs: 'Mama Don't Want To Skiffle Anymore' and the more bluesy 'In Them Ol' Cotton Fields Back Home'. But when asked by host Huw Weldon what his ambitions were, Page surprisingly didn't opt for becoming a rock god, but claimed that he wanted to find a cure for cancer!

However, the muse would not be denied. When he left Danetree Secondary School in West Ewell, he elected to try his hand at becoming a full-time musician. It wasn't easy. But his big break came when he was asked to join Neil Christian's band, the Crusaders. At the time, they were making a name for themselves on the live circuit.

'It was Neil Christian who saw me playing in a local hall and suggested that I play in his band. It was a big thing because they worked in London, whereas I was from the suburbs. So there I was, the 15-year-old guitarist marching into London with his guitar case. I played with him for a couple of years.

'We used to do Chuck Berry and Bo Diddley numbers, bluesy things, before the blues really broke. In fact, half the reason I stopped playing with Neil was because I used to get very ill on the road, glandular fever, from living in the back of a van.

'We were doing lots of travelling, the sort of thing I'm used to doing now. I was very undernourished then. It wasn't working right either; people weren't appreciating what we were doing. At that time they wanted to hear Top 20 numbers. I guess you could put pretty much akin to the pre-Beatles period in America, except that this was a couple of years before that. I was at art college for 18 months after I left Neil Christian, which was still before the Stones formed, so that dates it back a way.

'The numbers we were doing were really out of character for

the audiences that were coming to hear us play, but there was always five or ten percent, mostly guys, who used to get off on what we were doing because they were into those things themselves as guitarists, record collectors. You'll find that nearly all the guitarists that came out of the Sixties were record collectors of either rock or blues. I used to collect rock and my friend collected blues.'

After falling ill with glandular fever, Page temporarily gave up the guitar and enrolled in Sutton Art College to indulge his other passion, painting. As he said in 1975: 'I was travelling around all the time in a bus. I did that for two years after I left school, to the point where I was starting to get really good bread. But I was getting ill. So I went back to art college. And that was a total change in direction. That's why I say it's possible to do. As dedicated as I was to playing the guitar, I knew doing it that way was doing me in forever. Every two months I had glandular fever. So for the next 18 months I was living on ten dollars a week and getting my strength up. But I was still playing.'

While at college, Page would regularly go down to the Marquee Club in Wardour Street, Central London, where he'd get the chance to play with Alexis Korner's Blues Incorporated, Cyril Davies' All Stars, and even Jeff Beck and Eric Clapton. It was while doing this that he was

spotted by John Gibb from Brian Howard and the Silhouettes. As he explained in 1977 to *Trouser Press*: 'I was jamming at night in a blues club. By that time, the blues had started to happen, so I used to go out and jam with Cyril Davies' Interval Band. Then somebody asked me if I'd like to play on a record, and before I knew where I was I was doing all these studio dates at night, while still going to art college in the daytime. There was a crossroads and you know which one I took.'

His first session commission to was to play on a record by Jet Harris and Tony Meehan in 1963. '(It was called) "Diamonds" by Jet Harris and Tony Meehan, but that didn't mean anything to me. It was a hit (reaching Number 1) and that gave me impetus to keep on doing it. If "Your Momma's Out Of Town" (by Carter Lewis and the Southerners, his next session) hadn't been a hit, though, I might have abandoned it then and there.

'Doing sessions kept me off the road until such time as it became stagnant and it was time for a change. I was doing pretty well with Neil Christian, as far as money went, and to come out of that and go to art college on $10 a week would seem like insanity to a lot of people, but I'd do it anytime if it were necessary – make a drastic change if it had to be.'

Known at the time as Little Jim, to distinguish him from another session guitarist of the time, Big Jim Sullivan, Page became a prolific sessioneer, working with such names as Marianne Faithfull, the Rolling Stones, Dave Berry, Brenda Lee and Them – all in 1964. He recalled this period in 1977: 'I was mainly called in to sessions as insurance. It was usually myself and a drummer, though they never mention the drummer these days, just me. On the Them session (which included the single "Baby, Please Don't Go"), it was very embarrassing because you noticed that as each number passed, another member of the band would be substituted for a session musician. Talk about daggers! God, it was awful. There'd be times you'd be sitting there – you didn't want to be there, you'd only been booked – and wishing you weren't there.'

Being the preferred choice of producer Shel Talmy meant that Page got the chance to work on records by both the Kinks and the Who. And in 1965, Andrew Loog Oldham started up the Immediate label and brought in Page to both play on and produce records by the likes of Eric Clapton and John Mayall. He also began writing songs with singer Jackie DeShannon, of whom Page said in 1977:

'Just happened to be on a session. She was playing guitar and she said, "I've never found a guitarist who could adapt so quickly to the sort of things I'm doing". She had these odd licks and she said, "It's usually a big struggle to get these things across." I didn't know what she was talking about, because I'd been quite used to adapting.

'We wrote a few songs together, and they ended up getting done by Marianne Faithfull, PJ Proby, and Esther Phillips or one of those coloured artists did a few. I started receiving royalty statements, which was very unusual for me at the time, seeing the names of different people who'd covered your songs.'

If you want to check out just some of the records on which Page played, then there are two albums worth acquiring. These are 'James Patrick Page: Session Man Volume One' and 'James Patrick Page: Session Man Volume Two'. These were released in 1989 and 1990 respectively. Page had even recorded his own single, 'She Just Satisfies'.

'I did it because I thought it would be fun. I played all the instruments, except drums, which was Bobbie Graham. The other side was the same story. I wanted to do "Every Little Thing" as the follow up with an orchestra, but they (the label) wouldn't let me do it.'

Back in 1964, Page had been asked to join the Yardbirds when Clapton quit, but had turned down the offer. He recalled to *Trouser Press* in 1977:

'Giorgio Gomelsky (the band's manager/producer) approached me and said that Eric wasn't willing to expand and go along with the whole thing. I guess it was probably pretty apparent to them after they did the single "For Your Love". Clapton didn't like that at all. By that time they had already started using different instruments like harpsichords and at that point Clapton felt like he was just fed up. The rest of the band, especially Gomelsky, wanted to move further in that direction.

'The very first time I was asked to join the Yardbirds, though, was not at that time, but sometime before then. Gomelsky said that Eric was going to have a "holiday", and could I step in and replace him. The way he put it to me, it just seemed really distasteful and I refused. Eric had been a friend of mine and I couldn't possibly be party to that. Plus Eric didn't want to leave the band at that stage.'

Page at that juncture wanted to concentrate on his lucrative session work, so recommended Jeff Beck to step in for Clapton. Two years later, though, things were moving – fast. Page had just played on the session for the Jeff Beck solo single 'Beck's Bolero'. Also involved with Nicky Hopkins on keyboards, Keith Moon on drums and John Entwistle on bass. The Who pair were getting a little fed up with the way things were moving in their band, and when Page suggested that he, the Who duo and Beck form a new band, it was given serious thought. And it's said to have been during these talks that the

name 'Led Zeppelin' first sprang up. Subsequently, Entwistle opted out of the project, with another session man, John Baldwin (aka John Paul Jones), coming in. The band, though, never got off the ground, And Page received yet another offer to join the Yardbirds, one this time that he grabbed.

'It was at a gig at the Marquee Club in Oxford which I'd gone along to. They were playing in front of all these penguin-suited undergraduates and I think Paul Samwell-Smith (bass), whose family was a bit well-to-do, was embarrassed by the band's behaviour. Apparently Keith Relf had gotten really drunk and he was falling into the drum kit, making farting noises to the mike, being generally anarchistic. I thought he had done really well, actually, and the band had played really well that night. He just added all this extra feeling to it.

'When he came offstage, though, Paul Samwell-Smith said, "I'm leaving the band." Things used to be so final back then. There was no rethinking decisions like that. Then he said to (guitarist) Chris Dreja, "If I were you, I'd leave too." Which he didn't. They were sort of stuck.

'Jeff (Beck) had brought me to the gig in his car and on the way back I told him I'd sit in for a few months until they got things sorted out. Beck had often said to me, "It would be really great if you could join the band." But I just didn't think it was a

possibility in any way. In addition, since I'd turned the offer down a couple of times already, I didn't know how the rest of them would feel about me joining. It was decided that we'd definitely have a go at it; I'd take on the bass, though I'd never played it before, but only until Dreja could learn it as he'd never played it either. We figured it would be easier for me to pick it up quickly, then switch over to a dual guitar thing when Chris had time to become familiar enough with the bass.'

But Page was joining a disintegrating band. Beck was fired during an American tour, and then both Keith Relf and Jim McCarty quit, leaving Page and manager Peter Grant to totally reconfigure the line-up to meet outstanding live commitments, Led Zeppelin was born.

'Well, we still had these dates we were supposed to fulfil. Around the time of the split John Paul Jones called me up and said he was… interested in getting something together. Also, Chris was getting very into photography; he decided he wanted to open his own studio and by that time was no longer enamoured with the thought of going on the road. Obviously, a lot of Keith and Jim's attitude of wanting to jack it in had rubbed off on him, so Jonesy was in.

'I'd originally thought of getting Terry Reid in as lead singer and second guitarist but he had just signed with Mickie Most as a solo artist in a quirk of fate. He suggested I get in touch with Robert Plant, who was then in a band called Hobbstweedle. When I auditioned him and heard him sing, I immediately thought there must be something wrong with him personality-wise or that he had to be impossible to work with, because I just could not understand why, after he told me he'd been singing for a few years already, he hadn't become a big name yet. So I had him down to

my place for a little while, just to sort of check him out, and we got along great. No problems.

'At this time a number of drummers had approached me and wanted to work with us. Robert suggested I go hear John Bonham, whom I'd heard of because he had a reputation, but had never seen. I asked Robert if he knew him and he told me they'd worked together in this group called Band of Joy.'

During the 12 years that Zeppelin flew higher and further than any other rock band on the planet, Page's influence was dominant. Not just as a guitarist, but also as a composer and producer. He shaped the band's sound and perhaps had the vision and the ingenuity to introduce new recording techniques, and to drive the style and feel of Zeppelin. One of these innovations was the use of reverse echo, whereby the echo comes before the actual sound itself.

Page has claimed that he constantly switched engineers on different albums, in order to maintain his own reputation. He told *Guitar World* in 1998: 'I consciously kept changing engineers because I didn't want people to think that they were responsible for our sound. I wanted people to know it was me.'

After Zeppelin's split in 1980, Page didn't touch a guitar for about a year, eventually being coaxed onstage to join old pal Beck at the Hammersmith Odeon in 1981. Since then, it must be said his output has been patchy. A brief alliance with Paul Rodgers in the Firm followed an aborted attempt at getting the XYZ project off the ground with the Yes rhythm section of Alan White (drums) and Chris Squire (bass). But two albums with the Firm really did no justice to either Page or Rodgers.

He worked on the *Death Wish II* soundtrack album in 1982, recorded several tracks with the almost reunited Yardbirds, under the project name of Box of Frogs, contributed to the Rolling Stones single 'One Hit (To The Body)' and even did some session work for Crosby, Stills and Nash.

But nothing really replaced his love and passion for Zeppelin. In 1988, he released the solo album 'Outrider' and guested on Plant's album 'Now And Zen'. And in the early Nineties, he surprised everyone by hooking up with David Coverdale for a project called Coverdale-Page, which was responsible for one decent, self-titled album in 1993. Many thought Page had deliberately chosen to work with Coverdale, because he knew it would rile Plant, who had a healthy disdain for the former Deep Purple singer.

Eventually, Page and Plant resumed their collaboration for the 'No Quarter: Jimmy Page And Robert Plant Unledded' acoustic album, which saw them refashion some of the most iconic Zeppelin material. And the pair even recorded an album of original songs called 'Walking Into Clarksdale' in 1998.

But it would appear that the hold Zeppelin has on the rest of the world is even stronger with Page. He seems to be most at home when trawling through the vast recesses of unreleased material, both audio and visual. This led to the live album 'How The West Was Won' and the DVD *Led Zeppelin*, both of which were released in 2003.

There have been hints at a new album, probably solo, and it appears at the time of writing that he wants to play live again. His status was augmented when he was chosen to perform at the closing ceremony of the Beijing Olympics in 2008, doing a version of 'Whole Lotta Love' with Leona Lewis. And he was awarded an OBE in 2005, not for services to music but for his tireless charity efforts on behalf of Task Brazil and Action For Brazil's Children's Trust.

All of which leaves the thorny subject of his interest in the occult. This is still an unclear area, but while he has an abiding interest and fascination with Aleister Crowley, going so far as to purchase the latter's house (Boleskine) and starting up the occult company the Equinox Bookshop and Publishers, based in West Kensington, London, it's doubtful that this ever went further than a keen enthusiasm. In 1978 he said: 'I feel Aleister Crowley is a misunderstood genius of the 20th century.

Because his whole thing was liberation of the person, of the entity, and that restrictions would foul you up, lead to frustration which leads to violence, crime, mental breakdown, depending on what sort of makeup you have underneath. The further this age we're in now gets into technology and alienation, a lot of the points he's made seem to manifest themselves all down the line.'

Page sold the bookshop, due to increasing demands on his time from Zeppelin, and has since sold Boleskine. He now seems content to live a semi-quiet family life and devote his time to projects which capture his imagination.

That Jimmy Page is one of the all-time greats of rock, and particularly of the guitar, is taken as read. But he is more than this. Without question his greatest triumph is Led Zeppelin, at least on a professional scale. But, to some extent, it has also become a trap. More than anyone else closely associated with the band, it appears he is the one most tied to the history and heritage of Zeppelin. What he created has become his concubine, addiction and jailer.

And still those sordid stories of Seventies excess follow and daunt him. Sexually, drugs-wise, musically and in his pursuit of occult knowledge, Page displayed an appetite that was allegedly voracious and unquenchable. Now, he is the keeper of his own legend – and perhaps we should hope he

never decides to reveal everything about his past. The magic of Page lies as much in the speculative ignorance as in his legacy of great works.

'If I had to sum up Jimmy, then I'd call him an unrequited genius,' said Peter Grant. That is, perhaps, a fitting accolade.

PAGE, SCARLET

Scarlet Page (born 24 March 1971) is the daughter of Jimmy Page and Charlotte Martin, the French model who was in a long-term relationship with Page between 1970 and 1986.

Page is briefly seen with her mother during one scene in *The Song Remains The Same*, in the closing seconds of the 'Scarecrow' sequence. She was also involved in the August 1975 car accident on the Greek Island of Rhodes, which injured Robert Plant and his wife Maureen, although Page escaped unhurt.

An unreleased tribute to the then three year-old Scarlet was recorded by Jimmy Page, Keith Richards and Ian Stewart on 15 October 1974 at Island Studios, simply titled 'Scarlet'.

Having graduated from the University of Westminster with a degree in Photography, Film and Video, Scarlet Page worked with legendary rock photographer and humanitarian (sic) Ross Halfin as an assistant before branching out on her own.

Page's first commission was for the now defunct *Raw* magazine in

1993, shooting Soundgarden's Chris Cornell. She has since worked for a variety of magazines such as *Q, Blender, Kerrang!* and *Spin*, and her work adorns album covers for the Verve and Robbie Williams.

More recently she has been used by MTV and the veterinary charity PDSA. Her work can be viewed at: *www.scarletpage.com*.

PAGE AND PLANT
Jimmy Page and Robert Plant reunited in 1994 as a duo, initially to record an unplugged event for MTV. This in turn led to the release of 'No Quarter: Jimmy Page And Robert Plant Unledded' and a subsequent world tour.

Initial discussions for the MTV event began in 1993, broached initially by Plant's manager Bill Curbishley. 'By that time I didn't feel like I was even a rock singer any more,' Plant told *Uncut* in 2005. 'Then I was approached by MTV to do an *Unplugged* session. But I knew that I couldn't be seen to be holding the flag for the Zeppelin legacy on TV. Then mysteriously Jimmy turned up at a gig I was playing in Boston, and it was like those difficult last days of Led Zep had vanished. We had this understanding again without doing or saying anything. We talked about the MTV thing and decided to see where we could take it.'

Deliberately sidestepping the idea of what would have been a hugely lucrative and much-longed for Led Zeppelin reunion, John Paul Jones was not asked to take part, much to his annoyance. However the pair made their first tentative steps in April 1994, appearing at a tribute for the late Alexis Korner in Buxton, Derbyshire. In August of that year, the pair recorded various performances of reworked Zeppelin songs, as well as some new, Eastern themed material with North African musicians at MTV's studios in Camden, London; they also revisited Bron-Yr-Aur cottage in Wales and Morocco, the latter due to Plant's increasing fascination with indigenous music from the area.

The performance aired to great fanfare on 12 October 1994 and the resultant album was released two days later, reaching Number 7 in the UK album charts and Number 4 in America. A world tour kicked off in February 1995, the closest thing to a full-blown Zeppelin reunion the rock world had yet seen.

Following a creative and commercially successful tour, the pair entered London's Abbey Road studios with Jesus Lizard/Nirvana producer Steve Albini mixing the album. The resultant work was the 1998 album 'Walking Into Clarksdale' which charted even higher than the '...Unledded' project, at Number 3 in the UK and 8 in the US.

Another successful tour ensued, following which Plant decided to call time on the project.

'There could have been a follow-up (to 'Walking into Clarksdale'),' Page told *Uncut* in 2009. 'I certainly had about a dozen numbers written for a third album. Robert heard them and said that some of them were really good, but he just wanted to go in another direction. That's fair enough.'

Plant would release a new solo album, his seventh, in 2002's 'Dreamland'. Page worked with Puff Daddy on the Kashmir'-sampled single 'Come With Me' (from the *Godzilla* soundtrack) and later would also tour with the Black Crowes.

Page and Plant did reunite in 2001 for a performance at the Montreux Jazz Festival. The live DVD *No Quarter Unledded* appeared in 2004.

PHYSICAL GRAFFITI

The sixth album from Led Zeppelin, this is their only official double studio album discounting compilations. It was released in 1975, and is regarded by some as the apogee of their artistry, wizardry and sheer individual brilliance. And yet it is something of a mongrel.

While the core of the album was recorded at Headley Grange, the new recordings actually stretched beyond the length permissible on a single vinyl album. Instead of paring down what they had, the band elected to add extra tracks left over from other recording sessions, thereby making this a double release.

Recording started in November 1973, using the Rolling Stones' mobile studio, but these were rapidly halted when John Paul Jones was allegedly taken ill; Zeppelin decided to let Bad Company (signed to their Swan Song label) take over the sessions to work on what was to become their self-titled, debut album. Jimmy Page told Cameron Crowe in 1975:

'It took a long time for this album mainly because when we originally went in to record it, John Paul Jones wasn't well and we had to cancel the time…everything got messed up. It took three months to sort the situation out.'

However, there is an alternative story, whereby Jones wasn't actually ill but wanted to quit the band to become choirmaster at Winchester Cathedral! Manager Peter Grant partially admitted this to be the case when he talked to co-author Dome in 1990.

'I think John Paul was fed up with the touring schedule we had at the time. It was murderous, and he was agitating to do something else. He didn't actually threaten to leave, but a number of options were open to him. He never actually told me about the Winchester Cathedral offer, and I am a little sceptical as to whether this was a serious proposition. But I felt that we should take a break from recording, to see whether John Paul would settle back down again. Which he fortunately did – all that was needed was a little

time for him to realise how special Led Zeppelin were to him.'

So, the band returned to Headley Grange at the start of 1974, and quickly recorded eight songs, with engineer Ron Nevison. 'To be honest, I think the whole band benefited from the break,' said Grant. 'But once we'd got those done, there had to be a decision as to what we did. If this was to be a single album, then some editing would be required. But, as it was to be the first album from Zeppelin on Swan Song, we agreed to go for a double – to make it something special.'

Instead of carrying on the recording process, it was decided that the band would investigate their own archives and look at previously unreleased songs.

'The musicians decided that was the route they'd take,' said Grant. 'We had so many strong songs left off previous records for no other reason than space. I know Jimmy was anxious that these should be heard. The others felt the same way, so we extended the record with these.'

So, out came 'Bron-Yr-Aur', an instrumental originally recorded for 'Led Zeppelin III' in 1970 at

Island Studios. Then there were 'Night Flight', 'Boogie With Stu' (both recorded at Headley Grange) and 'Down By The Seaside' (taped at Island Studios), all from the sessions for 'Led Zeppelin IV'. Both 'The Rover' and 'Black Country Woman' came from the recordings done at Stargroves on the Rolling Stones Mobile in May 1972 for the 'Houses Of The Holy' album, while the song 'Houses Of The Holy' itself was cut in May 1972 at Olympic Studios.

The album was mixed by Keith Harwood at Olympic Studios in October 1974, with the album being released in February 1975. Interestingly, Nevison claims he never knew this was to be a double album until it was actually released. He told *Classic Rock* magazine in 2007: 'I never knew that 'Physical Graffiti' was going to be a double album. When we started out we were just cutting tracks for a new record. I left the project before they started pulling in songs from "Houses Of The Holy" and getting them up to scratch. So I didn't know it was a double until it came out.'

One reason why the album is regarded as perhaps the pinnacle of the band's recording career is that it spans the whole gamut of their range. There are hard-rockers ('The Rover', 'Houses Of The Holy'), eastern mysticism ('Kashmir'), funk ('Trampled Under Foot'), acoustic imagery ('Boogie With Stu'), Blues ('In My

Time Of Dying') and an instrumental ('Bron-Yr-Aur'). No other album can claim to have such a diverse spectrum, and it's all so cohesive. The band didn't just slam down several offcuts, but carefully chose the additional material to complement what was already recorded. Use of extra overdubs and the overall mix ensured that nothing sounded out of place. The result is a stupendous representation of a band arguably at the height of their considerable powers.

Both Robert Plant and Jimmy Page have expressed their belief that this is the best of all Zeppelin records, and it is hard to disagree. The album works as a flowing entity, being sequenced to realise the potential of each song as part of the audio tapestry. Yet, the individual tracks themselves also work as separate components standing alone. It is truly a triumph.

The album received huge critical acclaim when released, and was the first album ever to go platinum in America on advance orders alone. Platinum means sales of one million copies, but as this was a double album sales of 500,000 were needed to go platinum. It has now sold over eight million copies in the States alone, making it 16 times platinum. The record topped the charts in the US, UK charts and Canada, while its success drove the other five Zeppelin albums back into the US charts.

TRACKLISTING:
Custard Pie/The Rover/In My Time Of Dying (the longest studio song the band ever recorded)/Houses Of The Holy/Trampled Under Foot/ Kashmir/In The Light/Bron-Yr-Aur (the shortest studio song the band ever recorded)/Down By The Seaside/ Ten Years Gone/Night Flight/The Wanton Song/Boogie With Stu/Black Country Woman/Sick Again.

At the time, 'Bron-Yr-Aur' was placed straight after 'Kashmir' on cassette versions, to give an even running time on both sides. The running times on the original vinyl pressings are wrong for both 'Kashmir' (down at 9:41 and not 8:32) and 'Ten Years Gone' (down as 6:55 and not 6:32).

PICTURES AT ELEVEN
'Pictures At Eleven', released on 28 June 1982 on the Swan Song label, was Robert Plant's first solo album.

It was the most obvious hard-rock offering amongst Plant's first three solo albums. Always seeming to deny and then embrace his heritage, often only to try and deny it again, Plant opened his solo career with the strongest of those three albums. Much of 'Pictures At Eleven' hints at the hard-rock majesty conjured up by Led Zeppelin, yet strips away some of the bombast that clouded some of the band's later works.

The addition of original Honeydrippers guitarist Robbie Blunt helps here, with some delightfully understated guitar work. Plant also enlists drummers Phil Collins and Cozy Powell to add some serious input – an area that must have been one of the most emotional for him, bearing in mind his closeness with John Bonham. Jezz Woodroffe plays keyboards and Paul Martinez, who would appear with Led Zeppelin at Live Aid, adds bass.

The end result was a solidly pleasing start to Plant's solo career. Vocally he sounds in fine fettle too. Less histrionic than his Zeppelin days,this is a fine introduction to the solo Robert Plant of the early Eighties. The album reached Number 2 in the UK and Number 5 in America.

A reissue on Rhino in 2007 added the track 'Far Post', as well as a live version of 'Like I've Never Been Gone'. 'Far Post' featured on the soundtrack to the 1985 film *White Nights*.
TRACKLISTING:
Burning Down One Side/Moonlight In Samosa/Pledge Pin/Slow Dancer/ Worse Than Detroit/Fat Lip/Like I've Never Been Gone/Mystery Title/Far Post/Like I've Never Been Gone (Live).

PLANT, KARAC
Karac was the son of Robert and Maureen Plant, and was born on 22 April 1971. He was their second child after daughter Carmen (born 21 October 1968). Both children can be seen in the film *The Song Remains The Same*.

Sadly Karac Plant was taken ill on 26 July 1977. Following the band's two appearances at the Oakland Coliseum at the Day on the Green they'd travelled to New Orleans for a show at the Louisiana Superdome on 30 July. On arrival Plant received news from his wife that Karac, then six, had been taken ill. Two hours later Plant received the devastating news that his son had died from a stomach virus.

Plant immediately flew back to England with John Bonham and tour manager Richard Cole. They were the only two members of the Led Zeppelin entourage to attend Karac's funeral.

Plant was later inspired to write 'All My Love' on 'In Through The Out Door' in memory of his late son.

PLANT, ROBERT

There are two sides to Robert Plant. One is the man who in the early Eighties, when one swooning and devoted female fan told him that she'd admired him for so long, turned around and retorted 'Yes, you and a million other women, love.'

The other is the man who, in 2003 when he headlined the short-lived Canterbury Fayre Festival, carried his own suitcase into the hotel and politely waited his turn in the queue, never showing even the merest hint of rock-star histrionics. The looks of shock on the faces of the gathered throng told its own story.

This is the man who once confided to co-author Dome that the biggest thrill of his life was meeting Steve Bull, a goalscoring legend for his beloved Wolverhampton Wanderers football team. 'I have never been so nervous. This man is a hero to me, and to get the chance of shaking his hand was just incredible,' recalled Plant.

Plant, like any other celebrity fan, is reduced to becoming a one-eyed naïve imbecile when discussing the sport. He is no longer the rock icon, but just another fan hoping his own club can do the impossible.

'I flew on a private plane to the Canterbury Fayre in 2003,' Plant said a few months later. 'I had to go and see Wolves play. We lost 4-0, and I spent most of the time on the flight drowning my sorrows with a consoling bottle of brandy. Yes, that's how much it means to me.'

This is the same Robert Plant who is so passionate about music. The late, great broadcaster Tommy Vance recalled one particular night spent in the company of Robert Plant.

'We went out and got very drunk, then went back to his place, and spent the night listening to old Fifties singles on his jukebox. It was two fans just talking excitedly about music, and he knows so much about that era. Even down to catalogue numbers!'

Yet, this is the man whom late Led Zeppelin manager Peter Grant once described as 'capable of being a bit of an arse, if I'm

Photo licensed from Getty Images

honest. It all depends what mood you catch him in. He can be the sweetest man around. But then he can turn. I suppose it what makes him unique, and a truly remarkable vocalist'

There are numerous examples to back up both sides of Plant, but one thing is certain. He is the sole member of Led Zeppelin who has constantly stood against the band reforming. While both Jimmy Page and John Paul Jones have made it clear that they'd be happy, even delighted to put the beast back on the road, Plant has always blocked the concept. More than anyone else in the band, he moved on when Zeppelin declared the last rites in 1980. The first to release a solo album, 1982's 'Pictures At Eleven', and step back into the real world, one far removed from the comfort and company of the Zeppelin zephyr.

But just who is this man, who has been described as the ultimate rock god? Robert Anthony Plant was born on 20 August 1948 in West Bromwich, but he was brought up in Halesowen, which is now part of the Metropolitan Borough of Dudley. He nurtured an interest in singing from a very young age.

'I recall hiding behind the curtains in the lounge, and pretending I was Elvis,' he would recall years later. 'That wasn't due to shyness – there just seemed to be a real ambience in that gap between the curtains and French windows, one in which I could

develop my vocals.'

By the time he was 16, Plant had left school, King Edward's in Stourbridge, and determined to follow a musical path. He even threw over a promising career as a chartered accountant to follow his dream – well, when we say a 'promising career' that might be something of a leap of faith; he only spent two weeks on the course before deciding it wasn't for him.

'When I was 16 I was in and out of local bands. But it all helped me to gain a greater understanding of the blues, which I had grown to love, and what it meant to sing this sort of music. For me, it was an unrivalled education, one that stood me in great stead down the years.'

It was perhaps this peripatetic tendency which prevented Plant from coming to the attention of higher-profile bands, and therefore being snapped up before Zeppelin came into the frame – or the New Yardbirds as they were back then.

Plant recorded three singles for the CBS label, all of which flopped mightily. These were 'You Better Run'/'Everybody's Gonna Say' (released in 1966 under the band name of Listen), 'Our Song'/'Laughing Crying Laughing' and 'Long Time Coming'/'I've Got A Secret' (both put out in 1967 under Plant's own name). But the band which really set him on the right path were the Crawling King Snakes – not because they were a sensational band destined for greatness, but it teamed up Plant with a certain drummer called John Bonham, and the pair subsequently joined the Band of Joy. Now, this had been an outfit Plant had formed in 1966, but he quit a few months later, only to return, this time with Bonham in tow.

The new line-up recorded some demos early in 1968, as guitarist/vocalist Kevyn Gammond recalled when talking in 1992 to the website www.ledzeppelin.org:

'Denny Cordell, who produced all the Move records, picked up on the demos, and Robert said, "Okay, I'm going to London with the demos." And Denny was really over the moon about them.

'The next we heard Robert was knocking on the door saying, "Yeah, they love it!" But then somehow it got messed up. Robert said, "Come on, and let's go meet Denny," and he didn't come back. So we went down, and he said, "Great, let's go in the studio." And Denny said, "There's a guitar." He stuck it in my hand and said, "Write something." At that age we really hadn't started writing, so he said, "Okay, I'll give you a tenner and put you up at the Madison Hotel, go write a song and come back in the morning."

'So, there was Robert and I with a borrowed guitar. And we said, "Well, we better come up with something." So, we did this wild thing with, like, one bar and we went back the next day. Of course that killed us (laughs). And Paul (Lockey, bass/vocals) picked

us up coming back off the motorway about 10.30 that night. We had no money for train fare, he met us and we gave him the exciting news.'

One of the tracks from the demo, 'Adriatic Sea View', was released on a charity record which got limited distribution in the Midlands. It was later made available through *Nirvana* magazine.

In 1968, Jimmy Page was finally putting together the band of his vision. He wanted Terry Reid to join on vocals, but the latter famously turned down the offer, believing that his career was going in a different direction entirely. However, as fate would have it, Reid didn't merely walk away from Page's offer, but recommended that the guitarist check out a young singer called... Robert Plant. By this time, he was fronting a band called Hobbstweedle, and Page duly checked him out.

Now, there are those who've insisted that Plant wasn't a total unknown to Page. In fact, members of the Band of Joy say that the guitarist saw them several times with Plant and was fully aware of their singer's potential. Whether Page initially chose to ignore Plant's obvious abilities because he felt his new band needed someone with gravitas and experience is hard to judge. But, there was a bonding between the two on Page's houseboat, moored on the Thames,

Page is said to have played Plant the Joan Baez version of the Anne Bredon song 'Babe I'm Gonna Leave You' and explained that his dream was to find a way of heightening the contrasts in the song, and to put it into a new context – this was where his musical mind was wandering.

'We were dealing from the same pack of cards,' Plant said in 2005. 'You can smell when people... had their doors opened a little wider than most, and you could feel that was the deal with Jimmy. His ability to absorb things and the way he carried himself was far

more cerebral than anything I'd come across before and I was so very impressed.'

Throughout their 12-year relationship in Zeppelin, Plant and Page were very much the twin axis – one with his musical anticipation and exploratory aptitude, the other with his imposing charisma, charm and lyrical skills – not to mention a voice that could comfortably deal with all manner of styles. It was this union that drove the band.

Oddly, Plant never got any songwriting credits on the first Zeppelin album, ostensibly because he was still under contract to CBS, although it might well betray a sense from Page that he didn't yet trust the young singer to come up with anything worthwhile. However, on 'Led Zeppelin II', the frontman dived straight in, the first lyrics being written for his wife Maureen in the song 'Thank You'.

As a lyricist, there was a clear dichotomy in Plant's approach. On the one hand, he would delight in bombastic, barely disguised sexuality, which betrayed his own love of the blues. Yet, on the other hand, he was fascinated by mythology and the works of JRR Tolkien. He was particularly enthralled by the legends of Wales. Plant bought a sheep farm in Wales during 1973, began to learn Welsh and thence to explore the folklore of the land. Even his son Karac was named after early Welsh chieftain Caractacus.

As time passed, he also began an enduring relationship with Eastern philosophies and ideas, something that he's retained to this day. But this isn't to suggest that Robert Plant was an intellectual looking to make his lyrics more meaningful than mere sounds to complement the power and bravura of Zeppelin. He had a sly humour as well, and would never get so bogged down in his own word play that he couldn't appreciate a good chuckle. This was most obvious onstage, when his spontaneous asides were often clever and quick-witted.

As a performer, Plant quickly became iconic. While the musicianship of Page was flamboyant and elegant, the frontman had a raw sensuality that appealed to both sexes. With his trademark flowing blond locks and bare chest, Plant came to typify the archetypal rock god, even though he himself never saw this as something deliberate:

'I took something from Elvis, a little from Howlin' Wolf, and also a touch of Roger Daltrey and simply threw them all together. It came out the way it did, and that seemed to work. Did I take it all seriously? How can you possibly do that? The more that you try to analyse it, the more you appreciate and understand that it was all a bit daft.'

However, in an era where the concept of stadium rock was only starting to get into its stride, Plant was one of the few who realised that in order to make yourself a focal point onstage in front of tens of thousands, then you had to project your persona as a larger-than-life almost caricature of yourself, while also making everyone there believe you are talking directly to them. This is where his sense of humour and of the ridiculous helped. He had a softly spoken, almost off-kilter way of talking to an audience that made them listen. Watching Plant's easy manner live was to witness a master of his craft. He learnt quickly how to sustain and maintain a crowd's commitment, how to make between-song banter part of the rhythm of a show. All too often, frontmen allow the energy levels to dip with mundane song introductions, but Plant rode off the back of the musical dynamic and therefore made himself more than the singer in a rock'n'roll band.

Much has been said over the years about the supposed bad karma which struck the band down. Mostly, the blame is put on Page for his alleged tampering with the dark forces, and it would appear that Plant was the one to suffer more than anyone in the band during the Seventies. In 1975 he has badly injured in a road accident while in Rhodes, Greece. This forced the band to cancel all planned tour dates and set back recording plans for the 'Presence' album. Worse was to follow two years later when his son Karac died from a stomach infection. At the time, Zeppelin were on tour in America, but Plant flew straight home, and for months contemplated whether he wanted to carry on with the band.

Of course, all the black magic claims were really irrelevant. Whether Plant ever took the 'karmic theory' seriously remains open to doubt, but there's little question that he in particular had no energy to carry on with Zeppelin after the death of John Bonham in 1980. The pair had been childhood friends, and it was Plant who got him the chance to audition for Zeppelin in the first place. For Plant, the loss of Bonham signified that a chapter in his life – a long and hugely successful one – had come to an end. To him, Led Zeppelin were about four people, giants in their own right who became more than the sum of their individual parts.

Of the three remaining members, it's been Plant who has consistently proved to be the stumbling block for planned reunion tours. Maybe this is because he was being true to the memory of his dead friend, and felt that while there were many candidates to play drums for the band – and there are a lot who could do a great job – nonetheless John Bonham would always be missed.

Another theory suggests that Plant believes the band were of their time, the magic and myth having become so vast any performance would pale when put up against the legend. Plant, Page and Jones were members of Led Zeppelin, but are no longer those people, and it is possible that Plant appreciates the importance of preserving Zeppelin's reputation through avoiding showing they now have feet of clay, Certainly their brief performances at Live Aid (1985) and the Atlantic 40th Birthday Party (1988) were bordering on dire, although the set in December 2007 at the O$_2$ Arena in London helped to restore the balance.

Cynics have also suggested that

Plant has continually rejected Zeppelin overtures because he can. While the band, he was very much under the thrall of Page and Grant, who ran things their way. Now, he has the power to turn down offers, and exercises this as a way of frustrating Page's supposed visions of a reunion tour, and even a possible new album.

Certainly, of all those closely associated with the band, he was the one who got himself quickly back on his feet with a solo career, releasing the album 'Pictures At Eleven' in 1982, and immediately showing everyone that he wasn't scarred or overshadowed by Zeppelin. While John Paul Jones retreated into production, and Page seemed to be blinded and blighted by what Zeppelin had achieved, Plant had the strength of will and the music fortitude to press on.

He has retained a distinct work ethic ever since, releasing a succession of well-received solo albums that proved that he was prepared to explore so many new ideas in music. Plant has embraced his own delight in world music, and has also come to terms with his Zeppelin heritage and baggage. For a long while, he was reluctant to play any songs from his Led catalogue, but now has found ways of re-imagining these for a modern age and a fresh era.

Not that he has cast adrift old friendships. He and Page worked together on the successful album 'The Honeydrippers: Volume 1', released in 1984, and Plant guested on Page's 1988 album 'Outrider'; the latter returned the favour with an appearance on Plant's 'Now And Zen'.

In 1994, Page and Plant fully reunited for the 'No Quarter: Jimmy Page And Robert Plant Unledded' album, wherein they found ways of taking classic Zeppelin material into a different dimension. This collaboration came right after Page had worked on an album with Whitesnake frontman David Coverdale, something about which Plant was openly hostile and scathing. The one-time Zeppelin singer always felt that Coverdale had taken imitation a little too far and become a copy of him.

Whether this has any veracity at all, the fact remains that Plant and Page not only got back together for the 'No Quarter...' project, but for the 1998 album 'Walking Into Clarksdale', a comparative commercial disappointment.

Following this, Plant returned to his solo career, but also found time to guest on the Afro Celt Sound System album 'Volume 3: Further In Time' (2001), duetting with Welsh singer Julie Murphy on the song 'Life Begins Again'.

Of course, the Zeppelin accolades have kept on coming. In 2005 they received a Lifetime Achievement Award at the Grammys, and won the Polar Music Award a year later in

Sweden. In addition, he received the CBE in 2009 for services to music. He accepted the honour at Buckingham Palace from Prince Charles, saying at the time: 'I owe everything to the musicians I work with. From the UK to Africa to Tennessee, it is their brilliance that I bounce off. Alone I'm nothing.'

In August 2009, he was made a vice president of Wolverhampton Wanderers Football Club, an honour with which he was particularly pleased. He said at the time to the Wolves official website: 'I must say that, despite following innumerable players and teams around the world over the last 50 years, I feel no more a vice president, in truth, than every other deranged punter who trundles through the turnstiles week in, week out, with fingers crossed.'

And his collaboration with bluegrass singer Alison Krauss has reinvented Plant and taken him even further away from those Zeppelin days. The album 'Raising Sand' was released in 2007, not only becoming a massive commercial success but also bringing the pair a whole clutch of awards, including no less than five Grammys in 2009, amongst them Album of the Year. It was even nominated for a Mercury Music Prize in 2008.

Robert Plant is now very much his own man, in charge of his destiny and the one former Zeppelin member who neither craves nor desires a return to those halcyon days, After the O$_2$

Arena show, Plant made his thought very clear on a mooted reunion tour – if it happened it would be without him. In 2008, as rumours of a tour grew, he said: 'I will not be touring with Led Zeppelin or anyone else for the next two years. Anyone buying Led Zeppelin tickets will be buying bogus tickets.'

The diversity and range of Plant's work over the past 30 years or so has been staggering. Away from the demands of Zeppelin he has become a musical nomad, delighting in tasting all manner of exotic fruits and trying to see if he fits into their parameters. What he has done is immerse himself in the artistry and subtlety of the music, never agreeing to compromise. He appears to have the gift of knowing that, if anything is to work, then it must be kept intact. His musical output has betrayed a surprising lack of ego and self-affectation. What matters to him are the songs, the instrumentation and, of course, the singing within the context of the arrangements.

'To me, singing isn't a way of making my fortune. It's what I'd be doing, even if I wasn't paid for it. I am in love with singing and singers, and I love listening to great performances, I whatever sphere, I know people expect me to be a heavy rock vocalist, but anyone who understood what Led Zeppelin were all about will know that this was only a small part of what we did. If that band gave me only one thing, then it is the knowledge that there are no barriers in music, no boundaries. Try anything.'

That appears to be the Plant ethos: try it, because it might just work. Here is a giant of rock who wants more than anything else to be respected as an artist. He's succeeded. Led Zeppelin were his life for 12 years, but that was then, this is now.

PLOUGH, THE

The Plough in Shenstone was a pub nearby to John Bonham's the Old Hyde residence in Rushock, Droitwich, which Bonham used to own. So the story goes, the area behind the bar was rebuilt so that Bonham could ride his beloved motorbikes.

The Plough is not the pub that features in *The Song Remains The Same*, which was the nearby New Inn, now closed down.

POLAR MUSIC PRIZE

The Polar Music Prize was set up by Abba manager Stig Anderson (named after his record label Polar Music) and awarded to individuals, groups and institutions in recognition of exceptional achievements in music. It is one of the most prestigious musical awards in Sweden; previous winners were BB King, Bob Dylan, Burt Bacharach, Paul McCartney, Bruce Springsteen, Elton John and Stevie Wonder.

Led Zeppelin were honoured alongside the Russian composer Valery Gergiev in 2006. The King of Sweden, King Carl Gustaf XVI, presented the award to Jimmy Page, Robert Plant and John Paul Jones, with John Bonham's daughter Zoe also in attendance.

This is how the BBC reported the event at the time: 'The surviving members of Led Zeppelin have received an award recognising them as "great pioneers" of rock music.

'The king of Sweden presented the group with the Polar Music Prize in Stockholm, where they recorded their final studio album 27 years ago. They shared the award – which is split between pop and classical musicians – with Russian conductor Valery Gergiev. In his acceptance speech, Plant recalled that Led Zeppelin recorded their album "In Through the Out Door" in the Swedish capital towards the end of 1978. "It's a long time ago," he said. "Music has been a fantastic passport to us all."'

POLAR STUDIOS

Polar Studios are recording studios in Stockholm, Sweden, founded by Bjorn Ulvaeus and Benny Andersson of Abba. They opened on 18 May 1978, and in November and December of the same year, Led Zeppelin recorded their 1979 album 'In Through The Out Door' there.

The studios have since been used by the likes of Genesis, Abba, Beastie Boys, Roxy Music, the Ramones and Roxette.

PONTIAC SILVERDOME

The Pontiac Silverdome was an indoor arena in Pontiac, Michigan which was home to both the Detroit Lions American Football team and the Detroit Pistons basketball team.

Led Zeppelin broke the world record for attendance at a solo indoor attraction when they performed there in April 1977, playing to an audience of 76,229. This beat the previous record of 75,962, set by the Who in December 1975. The largest crowd ever recorded at the Silverdome was a visit by the Pope in 1987 which attracted an audience of 93,682.

The Silverdome was the arena where Pink Floyd performed the whole of 'Dark Side Of The Moon' for the first time since 1975 when they appeared there in 1994.

POOR TOM

'Poor Tom' was the second track from 'Coda', Led Zeppelin's first release since their demise in 1980.

Written by Jimmy Page and Robert Plant at Bron-Yr Aur in 1970 and recorded at Olympic Studios in May of that year, the song was originally recorded for 'Led Zeppelin III' but left off the album at the last minute.

Led Zeppelin never performed 'Poor Tom' live.

PRESENCE

'Presence' is Led Zeppelin's seventh studio album, released on 31 March 1976. Like 1973's 'Houses Of The Holy', the album was comprised of all band-written material, six of the album's seven tracks penned by Jimmy Page and Robert Plant and one, 'Royal Orleans', by the whole band.

The writing and recording of the album was somewhat fraught, with Robert Plant convalescing following a car accident in Rhodes in 1975 that had prevented Zeppelin from touring. Plant began his recovery in Jersey before moving to the warmer climes of Malibu in California, and it was here that he was joined by Jimmy Page to begin writing the material for the album.

The band rehearsed for a month on the new material at SIR Studios in Hollywood before travelling to Musicland in Munich to begin recording. It was here that things became fraught. Plant was still confined to a wheelchair and felt claustrophobic using the studio which was located in the basement. Equally, the band were working at a frenetic pace, as the Rolling Stones were booked into the studio to begin work on 'Black And Blue'.

'I spent the whole process in a wheelchair, so physically I was really frustrated,' Plant explained. 'I think my vocal performance on it is pretty poor. It sounds tired and strained. The saving grace of the album were "Candy Store Rock" and "Achilles Last Stand". The rhythm section on that it was so inspired... I was furious with

Page and Peter Grant. I was just furious that I couldn't get back to the woman and the children that I loved. And I was thinking, "Is all this rock'n'roll worth anything at all?"'

To a certain extent this explains the taut and muscular hard rock that pervades the entire album. With Page dominating, there was less room for the band's more experimental and acoustic moments; indeed there is only one acoustic guitar, which features quietly on 'Candy Store Rock'.

'I think it was just a reflection of the total anxiety and emotion of that period,' commented Page. 'There's a hell of a lot of spontaneity about that album. We went in with virtually nothing and everything just came pouring out.'

The album was completed in a mere 18 days – the quickest since their 1968 debut. Opening with the colossal 'Achilles Last Stand' the album rocks hard, and despite the straightforward nature of the material, the likes of 'For Your Life', 'Nobody's Fault But Mine' and 'Tea For One' are intricately woven songs, whilst 'Royal Orleans', 'Candy Store Rock' and 'Hots On For Nowhere' recalled the primal nature of the young Led Zeppelin.

The album sleeve, designed by George Hardie (who had worked on the band's debut sleeve) and Hipgnosis, showed scenes of people interacting with a dark obelisk-like figure, referred to as The Object, is supposed to convey the force of the band.

Although 'Presence' reached top spot in the UK and American album charts, it met with a mixed critical reaction and is not one of the biggest-selling Zeppelin albums. And while it remains one of Page's favourites, Plant is less complimentary. 'It was really like a cry of survival,' he told *Rolling Stone*. 'There won't be another album like it, put it like that. It was a cry from the depths, the only thing that we could do.'

Perhaps unsurprisingly, only two songs from 'Presence' were performed live by the band. The tour de force of 'Achilles Last Stand' and the blues-based 'Nobody's Fault But Mine' were featured on the band's 1977 world tour, and remained in the set until 1980. Jimmy Page and Robert Plant featured 'Tea For One' on their 1996 Japanese tour. The reunited Led Zeppelin played 'For Your Life' at their 2007 O_2 show.

Despite the album's lukewarm critical response – it tended to get overshadowed by the release of the film *The Song Remains The Same* in the same year – time has served 'Presence' well and it remains one of Led Zeppelin's great albums. and a defiant and muscular reaction to troubled times.

TRACKLISTING:
Achilles Last Stand/For Your Life/ Royal Orleans/Nobody's Fault But Mine/Candy Store Rock/Hots On For Nowhere/Tea For One.

PRETTY THINGS

The Pretty Things were a British rock band who, along with the Rolling Stones, the Yardbirds and Them, helped pioneer the British beat invasion of America in the mid to late Sixties and received a certain amount of critical and commercial success in the UK.

The band's 1968 concept album 'SF Sorrow' saw them embrace psychedelia in a major way and is widely regarded as their finest recording. The follow-up, 1970's 'Parachute', was nominated as *Rolling Stone* magazine's album of the year.

In the mid Seventies the Pretty Things' were managed by Peter Grant and they subsequently signed to Led Zeppelin's Swan Song label. Their 1974 album 'Silk Torpedo' was the first UK release on the label in November (Bad Company's self-titled debut had been Swan Song's inaugural release in America) and was celebrated with a huge party held in Chislehurst Caves in Kent.

The Pretty Things also released 1975's 'Savage Eye' on Swan Song but would not release another album until 1980's 'Cross Talk' which appeared on the Warner Bros label. The band remain an active unit, regularly touring, and released 'Balboa Island' in 2007.

PRINCIPLE OF MOMENTS

'The Principle Of Moments' was the second Robert Plant solo

The Pretty Things

album, released in July 1983 on his own Es Paranza label.

Musically 'The Principle Of Moments' was a lighter affair than his debut album, featuring softer rock, a path that would continue would continue with 1985's lacklustre 'Shaken N'Stirred'. However the album remains a compelling listen and in the laid back groove of 'Big Log' Plant found himself in the singles chart in the UK, reaching Number 11 (the song peaked at Number 20 in America).

Plant was again joined by Phil Collins on drums for six of the album's eight tracks, with ex-Jethro Tull drummer Barriemore Barlow on the remaining two (Collins would tour with Plant in support of the album). Again guitarist Robbie Blunt was on hand, as were Paul Martinez and Jezz Woodroffe.

The album, which was recorded at Rockfield Studios in Monmouth, was a commercial success for Plant, reaching Number 7 in the UK and Number 8 in America. 'The Principle Of Moments' was reissued on the Rhino label with five extra tracks, including a live cover of Bob Marley's 'Lively Up Yourself'.

TRACKLISTING:
Other Arms/In The Mood/Messin' With The Mekon/Wreckless Love/ Thru With The Two Step/Horizontal Departure/Stranger Here...Than Over There/Big Log/In The Mood (live)/Thru With The Two Step (live)/ Lively Up Yourself (live)/Turnaround/ Far Post

PRIORY OF BRION

A folk-rock band started by Robert Plant that toured around the UK in 1999 and 200. and grew out of a reunion between Plant and his one-time Band of Joy pal Kevyn Gammond (guitar). Their setlist consisted of songs which had influenced and inspired the pair, with Them's 'Gloria' always a highlight, as were songs by Arthur Lee. The name, Plant explained, was a combination of French secret society the Priory of Zion and the Monty Python film *The Life Of Brian*.

Aside from Plant and Gammond (the latter was also known as Carlyle Egypt in the band), the rest of the line-up was Paul Timothy (aka Owain Glyndwr) on keyboards, Paul Wetton (aka Eric Bloodaxe or Brian) on bass and Andy Edwards (aka Aleister Crowley) on drums.

PROBY, PJ

PJ Proby was an American-born pop singer, real name James Marcus Smith, who rose to fame in the UK in the early Sixties. His best-known hit was 1964's 'Hold Me', although he is perhaps more famous for his trousers splitting during a performance at a 1965 show in Luton (of all places!). He also portrayed Elvis Presley in a 1977 version of *Elvis - The Musical*.

Jimmy Page played on a recording session for Proby's single 'Together'. His 1969 album 'Three Week Hero' featured the line-up for what were then called the New Yardbirds. It was the first recording session to feature all four members of the fledgling Led Zeppelin, who played on the final day of recording.

'Come the last day we found we had some studio time, so I just asked the band to play while I just came up with the words,' Proby is quoted as saying. 'They weren't Led Zeppelin at the time, they were the New Yardbirds and they were going to be my band.'

PUFF DADDY

Puff Daddy, better known as Sean Combs, or even P-Diddy, is the well-known American rap star, record producer and entrepreneur.

Jimmy Page supplied guitar to Puff Daddy's 1998 single 'Come With Me', which featured in the hit film *Godzilla*. The song is heavily influenced by and samples Led Zeppelin's own 'Kashmir'. This was approved by Jimmy Page, who along with the producer Tom Morello (guitarist with Rage Against The Machine) supplied live guitar to the record. Page also featured in a video.

The song did not go down too well with some Zeppelin fans, and former Megadeth drummer Nick Menza cited the song as being 'blasphemy'.

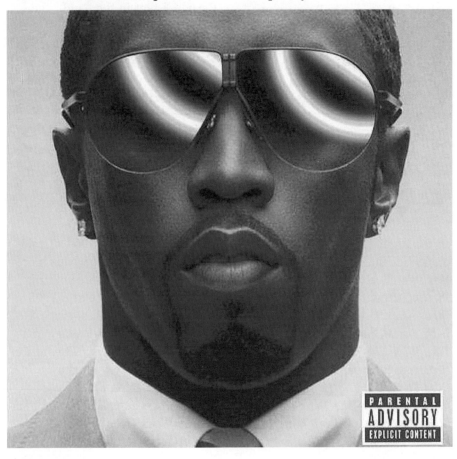

QUANTUM STUDIOS

The Los Angeles recording facility where Zeppelin did some of the work on 'Led Zeppelin II'.

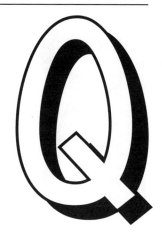

Photos taken by Ron Raffaelli during sessions in the studio were featured in *Good Times, Bad Times: A Visual Documentary Of The Ultimate Band*. This was put together by Jerry Prochnicky and Ralph Hulett and published in 2009 by Abrams.

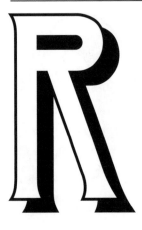

RAIN SONG, THE

'The Rain Song' is the second track on Led Zeppelin's fifth album, 1973's 'Houses Of The Holy'. Originally known by its working title of 'Slush', itself a tongue-in-cheek reference to the gentle, easy-listening nature of the song's music, it was inspired by a comment made by the Beatles' George Harrison, who mentioned to drummer John Bonham that Led Zeppelin never wrote any ballads. In tribute, the opening two chords of 'The Rain Song' are directly lifted from the melody of Harrison's own Beatles song 'Something'.

Seven minutes long, 'The Rain Song' had music supplied by Jimmy Page with lyrics added by Robert Plant (he considered them to be some of his very best). Page wrote and arranged the melody of the song at his then Plumpton residence on a set of new studio equipment, some of which came from the Pye Mobile Studio which had recorded Zeppelin's own 1970 Royal Albert Hall show, as well as the Who's celebrated 'Live At Leeds' album. John Paul Jones added some haunting Mellotron.

'The Rain Song' proved to be an enduring live favourite, which would be performed live directly following 'The Song Remains The Same', as both songs required Page to use his legendary double-neck Gibson, but was eventually dropped from the band's 1977 tour. It returned for the band's dates in 1979 and 1980, and was re-recorded by Jimmy Page and Robert Plant for their 1994 'No Quarter: Jimmy Page And Robert Plant Unledded' album. Although it failed to make the tracklisting of the original album, it did appear on the 2004 edition.

The song is also rare in that it has been authorised to appear in two films, aside from Zeppelin's own *The Song Remains The Same*, in which it accompanied Robert Plant's fantasy sequence. It features in Cameron Crowe's *Almost Famous* and Davis Guggenheim's *It Might Get Loud*, the documentary which looked at the history of the electric guitar, focusing on the careers of U2's the Edge, The White Stripes' Jack White and Led Zeppelin's Jimmy Page.

RAISING SAND

'Raising Sand' is the Grammy-winning 2007 album from Led Zeppelin singer Robert Plant and bluegrass singer Alison Krauss.

Under the aegis of roots producer T-Bone Burnett, the seemingly unlikely pairing traverse their way through a delightful selection of bluegrass and folk with songs from the likes of Gene Clark, Mel Tillis, Townes Van Zandt, the Everly Brothers and even a new take on the Page/Plant track 'Please Read The Letter'.

The album was a critical and commercial success, reaching Number 2 on both the UK and US album charts. The song 'Gone Gone Gone (Done Moved On)' won the duo the Grammy for Best Pop Collaboration with Vocals in 2008 and a year later, at the 51st Grammy Awards 'Raising Sand' won five awards, including the Grammy for Album of the Year.

The ensuing 2008 tour undertaken by the duo was largely seen by many as the main reason Plant turned his back on the proposed Led Zeppelin reunion tour that had been mooted after Led Zeppelin's triumphant reunion show at London's O$_2$ Arena for the Ahmet Ertegun tribute show in December 2007.

TRACKLISTING:

Rich Woman/Killing The Blue's/ Sister Rosetta Goes Before Us/Polly Come Home/Gone Gone Gone (Done Moved On)/Through The Morning, Through The Night/Please Read The Letter/Trampled Rose/Fortune Teller/ Stick With Me Baby/Nothin'/Let Your Love Be Your Lesson/Your Long Journey.

Raising Sand
Robert Plant | Alison Krauss

RAMBLE ON

This groove-laden rocker, the seventh track from 'Led Zeppelin II', is a prime example of how Robert Plant would use the influence of Tolkien in his lyric writing, something he has since expressed a certain amount of embarrassment about.

Not only do the opening lines of the song seem to echo Tolkien's own poem 'Namarie' (also known as 'Galadriel's Lament'), but later in the song such lyrics as "Twas in the darkest depths of Mordor/I met a girl so fair/But Gollum and the evil one crept up/And slipped away with her' are more than clear about where Plant is drawing his inspiration.

'Ramble On' was never performed in its entirety during Led Zeppelin's original tenure, but a complete version of the song received its inaugural live airing at the O_2 show on 10 December 2007.

'Ramble On' was sampled on the 1989 Donald D track 'A Letter I'll Never Send' and has been covered by Vanilla Fudge, Dread Zeppelin, the String Cheese Incident and Rick Derringer and was one of the songs performed by the Foo Fighters with Jimmy Page and John Paul Jones at Wembley Stadium in 2008.

Interestingly, throughout the entire song John Bonham is heard hitting an upturned plastic bin.

RED SNAPPER INCIDENT

[See EDGEWATER INN entry]

REID, TERRY

Terry Reid is an English rocker whose main claim to fame is that he was allegedly Jimmy Page's first choice as singer for Led Zeppelin following the disbandment of the Yardbirds and when Page turned his attention to what was originally called the New Yardbirds.

The truth of the matter is that, whilst Reid has remained a hugely respected figure in the British rock scene, commercial success never matched the critical plaudits that came his way.

Indeed, even by the time he came to Page's attention his debut album, 1968's 'Bang Bang, You're Terry Reid' had failed to capitalise on his initial promise. An American tour with Cream, and subsequent UK tours supporting Fleetwood Mac and Jethro Tull, helped boost his status when Page came calling.

'We'd done a gig at Albert Hall – a great bill: us (the Yardbirds), the Stones, the Ike and Tina Tuner Revue, and this band Peter Jay and the Jaywalkers, which had Terry Reid in it,' Page told *Mojo* magazine. 'I remembered him as a really good singer, so I told Peter (Grant), that I wanted to start a group with Terry Reid, so could he get the office to find him. I had all these ideas and I wanted to get it right. So I'm back in England after the end of this Yardbirds tour, and Peter said, "Well I've located Terry, but he's just signed a solo deal." I said,

"Who with?" He said "Mickie Most!" Now you know their (Most and Grant) two desks faced each other, right?!'

Fate, however, would conspire against Reid, who'd just signed an agreement to tour with the Rolling Stones in America, which obviously seemed like more of an opportunity for Reid's fledgling solo career than re-starting with a brand new act, not to mention the potential legal implications pulling out of the deal might have. He did, however, remember seeing a young vocalist who had impressed him.

'I was doing a gig. I think it was in Buxton with the Band of Joy,' Reid recalls. 'I'd seen them before, and I knew Robert Plant and John Bonham. And this time, as I watched them, I thought: "That's it!" I could hear the whole thing in my head. So the next day I phoned up Jimmy. He said, "What does this singer look like?" I said, "What do you mean, what does he look like? He looks like a Greek god, but what does that matter? I'm talking about how he sings. And his drummer is phenomenal. Check it out!"'

And so it was that Robert Plant and his drummer, John Bonham, would join the New Yardbirds, subsequently Led Zeppelin, and rocket into the fame stratosphere.

'We were good friends because we seemed to be on the same circuit...we always seemed to be playing on the same bill together,' Plant told *Uncut* magazine of Reid.

'He was one of those stellar vocalists along with Steve Winwood, Jess Roden and Steve Marriott, and he got the offer from his connection with Mickie Most, who shared an office with Peter Grant... So Terry said to Peter and Jimmy, "No I've go this thing going. But you should see my mate. Go and have a look at The Wild Man From The Black Country."'

Reid fell out with Mickie Most following his return from the Stones tour – Most wanted to turn him into a crooner – and despite eventually singing with Atlantic, his career fell into a commercial doldrum from which it has never truly recovered. He became a respected session singer during the Eighties, working with the likes of Don Henley, Jackson Browne, Bonnie Raitt and UFO.

Subsequent attempts to revive his solo career never achieved the desired results, although he continues to tour and a new EP was expected for 2010 release. *www.terryreid.net*

REMASTERS

This was the title of a three-album (vinyl) box set released in 1990, which was essentially a scaled down version of the four-CD Led Zeppelin 'Box Set', also put out in 1990. It was also available as a two-CD or two-cassette collection. It stalled at Number 10 in the UK charts, but topped the listings in Finland.

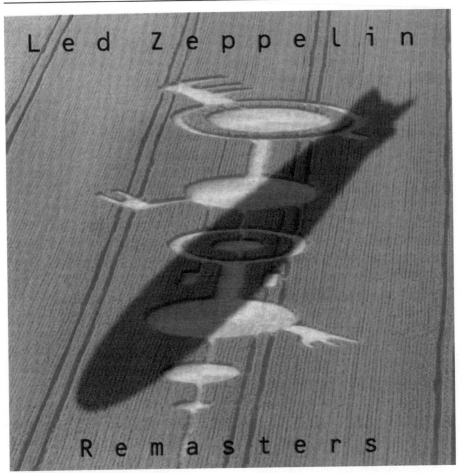

TRACKLISTING:

Side One: *Communication Breakdown/Babe I'm Gonna Leave You/Good Times Bad Times/Dazed And Confused/Heartbreaker.*

Side Two: *Whole Lotta Love/Ramble On/Since I've Been Loving You/Celebration Day/Immigrant Song.*

Side Three: *Black Dog/Rock And Roll/The Battle Of Evermore/Stairway To Heaven.*

Side Four: *The Song Remains The Same/D'yer Mak'er/No Quarter/Houses Of The Holy.*

Side Five: *Trampled Under Foot/Kashmir/Nobody's Fault But Mine.*

Side Six: *Achilles Last Stand/All My Love/In The Evening.*

In 1992, a three-CD version was released (also available as a triple cassette). The bonus disc featured promotional interviews with Robert Plant, Jimmy Page and John Paul Jones.

ROCK AND ROLL

The second track from Led Zeppelin's hugely popular 1971 fourth album remains one of the band's most enduring and popular songs.

Structured in a simple 12-bar format, the frenetic rocker is a spontaneous celebration of the joys of the early rock music that inspired the members of Led Zeppelin in the first place, name-checking old rock'n'roll standards such as 'The Stroll', 'Walking In The Moonlight' and 'The Book Of Love'.

The song came about from a jam session whilst the band were attempting to complete the song 'Four Sticks', when drummer John Bonham suddenly struck up the drum beat to the Little Richard song 'Good Golly Miss Molly' and the rest of the band joined in, Plant apparently even joining straight in with the lyrics. Subsequently, all four members of Led Zeppelin received co-writing credits for the song.

The song was an enduring live favourite, and by 1972 had become the opening number of the set, Plant, for reasons best known to himself, would often rename the song 'It's Been A Long Time' in reference to the opening line of the song, and would often switch the second and third verses.

'Rock And Roll' was also featured in the band's 1985 Live Aid set and the final number performed at the 2007 O_2 show, as well as being one of the Led Zeppelin numbers Jimmy Page and John Paul Jones performed with the Foo Fighters at Wembley Stadium in 2008.

'Rock And Roll' was one of the few Led Zeppelin songs to be released as a single outside of the UK. It reached Number 47 on the US singles chart and Number 14 in Germany in 1972. It has been covered by Heart, Van Halen, Sheryl Crow, Roger Daltrey, Jerry Lee Lewis, Stevie Nicks, KMFDM, Steve Lukather and Alvin and the Chipmunks.

ROCK AND ROLL HALL OF FAME

'Combining the visceral power and intensity of hard rock with the finesse and delicacy of British folk music, Led Zeppelin redefined rock in the Seventies and for all time. They were as influential in that decade as the Beatles were in the prior one. Their impact extends to classic and alternative rockers alike. Then and now, Led Zeppelin looms larger than life on the rock landscape as a band for the ages with an almost mystical power to evoke primal passions. The combination of Jimmy Page's powerful, layered guitar work, Robert Plant's keening, upper-timbre vocals, John Paul Jones' melodic bass playing and keyboard work, and John Bonham's thunderous drumming made for a band whose alchemy proved enchanting and irresistible. "The motto of the group is definitely, 'Ever onward'," Page said in 1977, perfectly summing up Led Zeppelin's forward-thinking philosophy.'

With these words, from the Rock and Roll Hall of Fame website, the legendary quartet of Jimmy Page, Robert Plant, John Paul Jones and John Bonham

were inducted into America's annual, rock backslapathon. In direct contrast to the UK, which, for many years, astonishingly seemed to view Led Zeppelin and their huge achievements through quizzical eyes whilst lauding whatever throwaway pop phenomenon was force-fed them, America has long worshipped at the Zeppelin altar. So it came as no surprise when, on 12 January 1995, the band were inducted into the Rock and Roll Hall of Fame (alongside the Allman Brothers Band, Frank Zappa, Al Green, Janis Joplin, Neil Young and Martha Reeves and the Vandellas.

The band were inducted by Aerosmith (perhaps America's closest representation of a rock band with the might of Zeppelin) members Steven Tyler and Joe Perry. Jason and Zoe Bonham, John's son and daughter, were in attendance to receive the award on behalf of their father alongside Page, Plant and Jones. Jones seemed to cause some consternation when he stated: 'Thank you, my friends, for finally remembering my phone number', an apparent reference to his being ignored by both Page and Plant over their '...Unledded' project and subsequent tours.

Following the event, the remaining members of Zeppelin jammed with Jason Bonham and both Tyler and Perry, and later with Neil Young (with Plant's own drummer Michael Lee replacing Bonham).

ROYAL ORLEANS

'Royal Orleans' is the third track from Led Zeppelin's 1976 album 'Presence' and the subject of an enduring rumour behind its supposed subject-matter.

The band would stay at the Royal Orleans Hotel when travelling through New Orleans on tour. So the story goes, during the early Seventies whilst staying at the hotel, one member of the band's entourage picked up a transvestite (unknown to them), repaired to their room, wherein both smoked marijuana and fell asleep, the transvestite having a still-lit joint in their hand which proceeded to burn down the room, all parties managing to escape.

The lyrics allude to the incident, with lines such as: 'And when the sun peeked through/John Cameron with Suzanna/He kissed the whiskers, left and right.' The use of the name John Cameron seemed to point the finger as bassist John Paul Jones being the protagonist from the band's entourage (Cameron had been a session rival to Jones).

When quizzed on the incident by *Mojo* magazine in 2007, Jones quipped: 'The transvestites were actually friends of Richard (Cole's); normal friendly people and we were all at some bar. That I mistook a transvestite for a girl is rubbish; that happened in another country to somebody else... Anyway "Stephanie"' ended up in my room and we rolled a joint or two and I fell asleep and set fire to the hotel room, as you do, ha ha, and when I woke up it was full of firemen!'

The only song from 'Presence' to be credited to all four members of Led Zeppelin, 'Royal Orleans' was never performed live by the band. It was released as a single in 1976 in France and New Zealand as the B-side to 'Candy Store Rock'.

ROVER, THE

The second track from Led Zeppelin's 1975 album 'Physical Graffiti' was originally written at Bron-Yr-Aur cottage in Wales in 1970 and was recorded in 1972 during sessions for 'Houses Of The Holy'. However it was left off of that album, and when it appeared on 'Physical Graffiti' the song had taken on a much heavier feel, driven by John Bonham's drums and a precise Jimmy Page riff.

The title refers to the age-old wanderer and, although the band never performed the song live, snippets would occasionally crop up on parts of other songs. Bootlegs of a 1973 Chicago soundcheck show that the band did rehearse 'The Rover', two years prior to it appearing on album.

The song was released as a single in Thailand, backed by 'Tramped Under Foot'.

RUSHCOCK PARISH CHURCH

This is the small parish church in the graveyard of which the ashes of John Bonham are interred after he was cremated on 12 October 1980. His headstone reads: 'Cherished memories of a loving husband and father, John Henry Bonham who died Sept. 25th 1980. aged 32 years. He will always be remembered in our hearts, Goodnight my Love, God Bless.'

ST MARK'S PLACE, NYC

96 and 98 St Mark's Place are depicted on the front cover for the 1975 album 'Physical Graffiti'.

The front cover of the album shows the two buildings during the day, while the back depicts them at night. However, there were certain adjustments to the reality. The actual location has five visible storeys, whereas on the cover it's down to four, thanks to some touching-up. This was done to fit the perspective of the artwork. The other slight alteration comes from the fact that, although you are supposed to be seeing the buildings from the opposite side of the street, this is not the real view.

Number 96 is now the location for the Physical Graffiti boutique,

while number 98 houses Starfish & Jelie clothing, accessories and gifts.

It's also worth noting that Mick Jagger and Keith Richards were filmed there in the video for the Rolling Stones song 'Waiting On A Friend'.

SAD CAFÉ

This Manchester band started out in 1976, fronted by Paul Young (not the solo star) and also featuring Ian Wilson and Ashley Mulford on guitar, John Stimpson on bass, Tony Creswell on drums and Vic Emerson on keyboards.

Initially signed to Chrysalis, the band recorded an album which was then inexplicably shelved. Sad Café then switched to RCA for 1977's 'Fanx Ta-Ra', their actual debut, which was followed by 'Misplaced Ideals' ('78) and 'Facades' ('79). It was the last-named that gave the band their biggest hit single, with 'Every Day Hurts' making it to Number 3 in the UK charts.

However, the band split in 1981 after releasing the 1980 self-titled album (which gave them their only other UK Top 20 single, 'My Oh My') plus 'Live' and 'Ole' (1981). It was the self-titled album that provided Sad Café with their sole connection to Swan Song, this being released in America by the Zeppelin-run company.

The band did return in the mid-Eighties, with Young splitting his time between the reactivated band and Mike and the Mechanics. However, the singer's

death in 2000 from a heart attack ended the band.

SCARLET

The title of an unreleased song said to have been recorded at Island Studios in London on 15 October 1974 and named after Jimmy Page's daughter.

According to one source, this session has Page on guitar, Keith Richards on guitar and vocals, Ian Stewart on keyboards, Ric Grech on bass and Bruce Rowland on drums. Grech is known for his stints with Family, Traffic and Blind Faith, while Rowland was with Fairport Convention.

Another report claims this was solely an instrumental.

SCREAM FOR HELP

This was the 1984 movie for which John Paul Jones recorded the soundtrack. Jones' first full post-Zeppelin album was released in its own right in 1985.

Apparently Michael Winner, the film's director, had originally asked Jimmy Page (a neighbour of his in Berkshire) to do the soundtrack, but he was too busy and suggested Jones. At the time, he had just upgraded his home studio in Devon and was keen to take on the task.

At Winner's insistence, a 70-piece orchestra (the Royal Philharmonic) was used, plus vocals from Yes' Jon Anderson and Madeline Bell. Celebrated folk guitarist John Renbourn is also featured, while Page co-wrote the songs 'Crackback' and 'Spaghetti Junction'.

TRACKLISTING:

Spaghetti Junction/Bad Child (co-written by Jones with his daughter, Jacinda Baldwin)/Silver Train/ Crackback/Chili Sauce/Take It Or Leave It/Christie/When You Fall In Love (co-written by Jones and Jacinda Baldwin)/Here I Am.

SENATORS

In 1964, John Bonham recorded his first ever record. It was the single 'She's A Mod' with a band called the Senators.

Bassist Bill Ford recalled those days and Bonham's role when talking to *Brum Beat* magazine: 'I joined the Senators in 1962-63. At that time we were called Bobby Child and the Sidewinders, the personnel being Barry Goodchild, aka Bobby Child (vocals), Trevor McGowan (lead guitar), Graham Dennis (rhythm guitar), a guy called Mick on drums and John Hunt on bass guitar, who I replaced.

'This line up continued for a while until Barry left and we auditioned for a replacement singer. After many auditions we chose Terry Beal, an extremely talented singer and composer, as well as being a multi-instrumentalist Terry had originally played in Terry Webb and the Spiders, along with his old pal John Bonham.

'Terry Beal had played in a band called the Nighthawks between 1960 and 1962 with bass guitarist Mike Ellis with whom he formed the Reddich group the Blue Star Trio along with drummer Bill Harvey. John Bonham replaced Bill on drums at the end of 1962 and the group performed all over the area. They backed Roy Edwards who was a professional singer and also made some recordings for the BBC at their Broad Street studios in 1963. Mike Ellis went on to join Johnny Neal and the Starliners.

'At this stage the Senators still had an unreliable drummer and were let down by him on a number of occasions. We had to call on other drummers to gig with us, and one of these was Alan Eastwood. He was a great drummer but also a mean blues singer and used to take the mike sometimes and do a couple of R&B numbers with us.

'Our drummer let us down again one night when we had a double gig. Terry played drums on the first set at the first gig at Perry Hall, Bromsgrove. During the break, he shot off in his car to fetch his mate who he said could play the drums. He came back 20 minutes later with this lad named John Bonham. We started the second half and it was as if someone had stuck rocket fuel in our drinks! We went down a storm, and John joined us as our drummer there and then.

'With this final line-up, we played regularly at many of the Birmingham venues and pubs. Ma Regan's places – the Ritz, the Plaza and the Cavern, the West

End Ballroom and the Moat House Club, just to mention a few. Terry took on the name of 'Bobby' because we had a professionally signwritten van! Also, because of our connections with Redditch where John and Terry came from, we had a big following there as well – regularly playing Redditch Youth Club, Alcester Trades and Labour Club and other pubs and clubs in the Worcestershire area.

'We won many talent competitions (to no avail) but were selected in 1964 along with 13 other groups to be on the "Brum Beat" album with a track called "She's A Mod", an original composition by Terry Beal and recorded at Hollick and Taylor Studios in Birmingham. Soon afterwards, we were approached to re-record this song at, I think it was, Decca Studios in London, to be released as a single. Another song called "I Know A Lot About You" was chosen to be recorded as the B-side.

'The Senators single was released the same week as "Tell Me When" by the Applejacks, which became a hit with the help of Mickie Most's backing. Our single, due to lack of funds, was withdrawn from sale. The music was published by Dick James Music and "She's A Mod" was used in the soundtrack of a film called *Steppin' Out* featuring the latest dance and fashion trends.

'"She's A Mod" was picked up by an Australian band called Ray Columbus and the Invaders who recorded their own version that was at Number 1 in their charts for about 14 weeks! We made many other demos but never managed to get that elusive deal. We turned down offers to play the clubs in Hamburg so who knows what might have happened? After some time, when gigs were getting harder to get because of the number of bands around, we decided to call it a day and the Senators broke up.

'I kept in touch for a short while with Graham Dennis and I used to see John Bonham occasionally right up to a few weeks before his death. I still treasure the autographed Led Zeppelin albums he gave me and still have the two complimentary tickets (face value £1 each!) he gave me when they played at the Odeon in Birmingham.'

SHAKEN N'STIRRED
This is the title of Robert Plant's third solo album, released in 1985. It featured guitarist Robbie Blunt, bassist Paul Martinez, drummer Richard Hayward, keyboard-player Jezz Woodroffe and vocalist Toni Halliday.

Co-produced by Plant, with Tim Palmer and Benji Le Fevre, it reached Number 19 in the UK charts and Number 20 in America. The single 'Little By Little' was a Number 1 hit in the States, and made it to Number 36 in Britain.
TRACKLISTING:
Hip To Hoo/Kallalou Kallalou/Too Loud/Trouble Your Money/Pink And

Black/Little By Little/Doo Doo A Do Do/Easily Led/Sixes And Sevens.

The album was originally on the Es Paranza label, but was reissued in 2007 by Rhino with a remix of 'Little By Little' added as a bonus track.

SHE JUST SATISFIES

A garage rock-style single from Jimmy Page released by Fontana in 1965 with the instrumental 'Keep Movin'' on the B-side. 'She Just Satisfies' (sometimes known as 'She Just Satisfies Me') and 'Keep Movin'' were among the tracks on the compilation album 'Session Man Volume One', which was released in 1989, and showcased mostly Page's session work between 1963 and 1965.

SICK AGAIN

The fifth song from the 1975 Zeppelin album 'Physical Graffiti' was written by Robert Plant about the groupies in America who used to flutter around the band. In 1975, he explained to *Rolling Stone* magazine:

'If you listen to "Sick Again", the words show I feel a bit sorry for (the girls). "Clutchin' pages from your teenage dream in the lobby of the Hotel Paradise/ Through the circus of the LA Queen how fast you learn the downhill slide." One minute she's 12 and the next minute she's 13 and over the top. Such a shame. They haven't got the style that they had in the old days…way back in '68.'

Musically, it has a certain bluesy echo, expounded upon by some intricate guitar moments from Jimmy Page and heavy drums courtesy of John Bonham. In a way it is a battle between the pair, with Plant's vocals often disappearing somewhere in the mix, but that actually gives it a mysterious quality.

This is the last song on the album, ending with a Page pick scrape before someone (thought to be Bonham) coughs in the background.

Regularly played live by the band from 1975, it was dropped from the set list for their final European tour, in 1980. Page performed it with the Black Crowes on their 1999 tour, captured on the 2000 album 'Live At The Greek'.

SINCE I'VE BEEN LOVING YOU

The fourth song featured on the band's third album, 1970's 'Led Zeppelin III', this is the only track from that record that the band had played live prior to the studio sessions, but it's said to have been the hardest to record. Legend has it that Jimmy Page was having so much trouble nailing the solo that he went for a walk and found an unplugged amplifier lying outside the studio. He used this for the next take, and got the sound he wanted.

Zeppelin played it live in the studio, with John Paul Jones on Hammond organ, using bass pedals. Because it was recorded live, you can hear the squeak of John Bonham's bass-drum pedal. This is also audible on six other tracks: 'The Rain Song', 'The Ocean', 'Dancing Days', 'Ten Years Gone', 'I Can't Quit You Baby' and 'Bonzo's Montreux'.

'Since I've Been Loving You' was a regular part of the band's live set from 1970-73, and was then brought back for tours in 1977, 1979 and 1980. It was meant to have been included for the 1975 American tour but was only performed a few times. Page broke the tip of his left ring finger just prior to the tour starting, when it got jammed in a door. Therefore the song, along with 'Dazed And Confused', was dropped until this healed.

The band had this in their set for the O$_2$ Arena reunion gig in December 2007, and Page and Plant recorded it for the 1994 album 'No Quarter: Jimmy Page And Robert Plant Unledded'. Plant also sampled it for his own 1988 song 'White, Clean And Neat'.

SIRIUS XM ZEPPELIN STATION

At 6pm EST on 1 November 2008, Sirius XM Radio in America launched a station dedicated solely to the music of Led Zeppelin.

Called Led Zeppelin Radio, it was 24/7 on Sirius channel 12 and XM channel 39. Totally commercial-free, it ran rare interviews and other archive material, as well as the iconic catalogue of the band.

The official press release on this innovation said: 'Led Zeppelin is one of the most important rock bands in history,' said Scott Greenstein, President and Chief Content Officer, Sirius XM Radio. 'We are thrilled to broadcast Led Zeppelin Radio for our subscribers and provide Led Zeppelin fans the only place to go for a comprehensive experience of their music and interviews with one of rock's most iconic bands.

'Led Zeppelin Radio will be a non-stop broadcast of virtually every song from Led Zeppelin's music catalogue. The channel will also provide Led Zeppelin fans with archived interviews with Jimmy Page, Robert Plant, John Paul Jones and John Bonham and unique content that celebrates Led Zeppelin's musical contribution to rock music. This channel will provide fans exclusive access to the sounds and insights that have made Led Zeppelin rock legends.

'Led Zeppelin Radio is the latest limited run artist-branded channel dedicated to iconic musicians offered by Sirius XM Radio. In addition to the current broadcast of Bruce Springsteen's E Street Radio and AC/DC Radio, Sirius XM has previously offered limited run channels such as Mandatory Metallica, Rolling Stones Radio, The Spectrum of John Mellencamp, the Who Channel, Radio REM, Coldplay Nation, Abba Radio, Neil Diamond Radio, Jay-Z Nation, Michael

Jackson's XM Thriller, George Strait's Strait Country, Garth Brooks Radio, Kenny Chesney's No Shoe Radio, and Duran Duran's Red Carpet Radio among many others.'

The station ran until 31 December 2008.

SIXTY SIX TO TIMBUKTU

The title of the 2003 compilation from Robert Plant, showcasing his pre- and post-Led Zeppelin careers. It starts in 1966 and ends at the Festival in the Desert in Mali – hence the title.

Taking at the time, Plant said: 'For me, being able to sing is a joy. I just love doing it. I'd be singing even if it was as a hobby. What I wanted to do with this compilation was to capture the expressions of emotion that I believe have coloured my career to date. Everybody knows the Zeppelin stuff, so it was important for me to complete the picture.

'Nothing gives people an insight into my character more than my singing. So, this is something close to being my autobiography. It shows you where I came from, and where I've gone.'

The album only got to Number 27 in the UK charts, and fared even worse in America, where it stumbled to Number 134.

TRACKLISTING:

CD One: *Tie Dye On The Highway/Upside Down/Promised Land/Tall Cool One/Dirt In A Hole/ Calling To You/29 Palms/If I Were A Carpenter/Sea Of Love/Darkness, Darkness/Big Log/Ship Of Fools/I Believe/Little By Little/Heaven Knows/Song To The Siren*

CD Two: *You'd Better Run/Our Song/Hey Joe/For What It Is Worth/Operator/Road To The Sun/Philadelphia Baby/Red Is For Danger/Let's Have A Party/Hey Jayne/Louie, Louie/Naked If I Want To/21 Years/If It's Really Got To Be This Way/Rude World/Little Hands/ Life Begins Again/Let The Boogie Woogie Roll/Win My Train Fare Home (live)*

SOL STUDIOS

Located in Cookham, Berkshire, this studio was built in the early Eighties by celebrated producer Gus Dudgeon who subsequently sold it to Jimmy Page. It was here that the latter recorded the soundtrack album for the *Death Wish II* album. Page also reworked the songs 'Poor Tom' and 'We're Gonna Groove' at the studio. These were originally recorded in 1970, but then finessed for the 'Coda' album.

The Firm, featuring Page and vocalist Paul Rodgers plus drummer Chris Slade and bassist Tony Franklin, recorded their self-titled, debut album there, plus its follow-up, 'Mean Business'; it was also where Page worked on his solo album 'Outrider'.

Other artists to work at Sol include Jeff Beck (1989's 'Guitar Shop' album), Mick Fleetwood (he mixed and did overdubs for his 1981 album 'The Visitor'),

Elton John (1985's 'Ice On Fire' was recorded at the studio, as was 1986's 'Leather Jackets'), Wishbone Ash ('Twin Barrels Burning', released in 1982, was done there) and Vandenberg (the Dutch band's 1982 self-titled debut).

SOMETHIN' ELSE

One of Fifties rocker Eddie Cochran's most famous songs. Released in 1959, it was co-written by the man with his elder brother Bob and then-girlfriend Sharon Sheeley.

Led Zeppelin recorded a version on 16 June 1969 at Studio 2 at Aeolian Hall in Bond Street, London. This was broadcast six days later on the BBC Radio 1 show *Chris Grant's Tasty Pop Sundae*, although it was originally intended for the *Symonds On Sunday* show, hosted by Dave Symonds. It was one of five tracks recorded that day, the others being 'You Shook Me'. 'Communication Breakdown', 'The Girl I Love She Got Long Black Wavy Hair', and 'What Is And What Should Never Be'.

'Somethin' Else' was included on the 1997 compilation album 'BBC Sessions'. There's also a clip on the 2003 DVD *Led Zeppelin*. This was filmed at the Royal Albert Hall in London on 9 January 1970. The song they played that night before 'Something Else' was another Cochran hit, 'C'mon Everybody'.

Zeppelin's version isn't too far removed from the original, although the sound is thicker and heavier and Plant's vocals have a more stirring inflection.

SON OF DRACULA

Released by Apple, this 1974 musical comedy film starring Ringo Starr and Harry Nilsson featured cameo appearances from both John Bonham and Keith Moon, who play drums in Count Dracula's band.

The idea for the film was developed by Starr, who wanted to make a rock'n'roll version of *Dracula*. Nilsson thought the former Beatles drummer got the idea from his own 1972 album 'Son Of Schmilsson', which had spoofed classic horror-movie ideas. But Ringo insisted this was coincidental.

This is the way the movie is described on the official Harry Nilsson website (*www.harrynilsson.com*): 'Count Down (Harry Nilsson), the son of Dracula, is into just about every kind of music there is. The Count is about to be crowned the Overlord of the Netherworld, when he has a change of heart. Dr Van Helsing (Dennis Price) proposes an operation which will make the Count mortal and give him the capacity to love – and force him to relinquish the Netherworld throne. Throw in Baron Frankenstein (Freddie Jones), "Daybreak", and some tracks from "Nilsson Schmilsson" and "Son Of Schmilsson" and you have *Son Of Dracula*.

"It is not the best film ever made, but I've seen worse." – Ringo Starr.'

Of the nine songs in the soundtrack, only 'Daybreak' was written especially for the film. Jay Fairbank, who is credited with the screenplay for *Son Of Dracula*, is actually actress Jennifer Jayne.

SONG REMAINS THE SAME, THE (SONG)

The first track on the 1973 album 'Houses Of The Holy'. According to an interview Jimmy Page did with *Guitar World* magazine in 1993: 'It was originally going to be an instrumental – an overture that led into "The Rain Song". But I guess Robert Plant had different ideas. You know, "This is pretty good, Better get some lyrics – quick!" I had all the beginning material together, and Robert suggested that we break down into half-time in the middle. After we figured out that we were going to break it down, the song came together in a day... I always had a cassette recorder around. That's how both "The Song Remains The Same" and "Stairway To Heaven" came together – from bits of taped ideas.'

The song was to be called 'The Overture', the title proposed when it was still an instrumental. Then it became 'The Campaign', before finally settling down to life as 'The Song Remains The Same'. Incidentally, the lyrics are Plant's celebration of music as a global unifying force.

The band first performed this on their 1972 Japanese tour. From 1972 until 1975, this actually led into 'The Rain Song', reflecting the original intentions of the song when it was still an instrumental. It remained in the set until being dropped for the 1980 European tour. However, this was revived for the reunion show at the O$_2$ Arena in London in December 2007.

Not only was this song also used during Plant's fantasy sequence in the 1976 movie, but it also provided the title for the film.

SONG REMAINS THE SAME, THE (ALBUM)

The title of the 1976 live album, which was also the soundtrack to the film of the same name.

The tracks were recorded at Madison Square Garden from 27-29 July 1973 by Eddie Kramer, and then mixed at Electric Ladyland (New York), plus Trident Studios (London). However, there were big differences between the album tracklisting and that of the film. 'Celebration Day' was on the album but not in the film, while the record also lacked the hurdy-gurdy piece 'Autumn Lake', 'Bron-Yr-Aur', 'Since I've Been Loving You' and the introduction to 'Heartbreaker'. Of the rest, recordings from different nights are used occasionally for the album and the film.

The album topped the UK charts, and got to Number 2 in the States, selling over four million copies there.

TRACKLISTING:
Rock And Roll/Celebration Day/The Song Remains The Same/The Rain Song/Dazed And Confused/No Quarter/Stairway To Heaven/Moby Dick/Whole Lotta Love.

The album was reissued in 2007, with the album and DVD finally in sync, and the whole performance restored to the audio. The tracklisting was now:
Rock And Roll/Celebration Day/Black Dog (including Bring It On Home)/Over The Hills/Misty Mountain Hop/Since I've Been Loving You/No Quarter/The Song Remains The Same/The Rain Song/The Ocean/Dazed And Confused/Stairway To Heaven/Moby Dick/Heartbreaker/Whole Lotta Love.

In 2008, a four-LP edition of the 2007 reissue was released on 180-gram audiophile vinyl. It was housed in a deluxe two-piece box with foil stamping and included a 12-page full colour booklet with loads of previously unseen stills from the film, as well as four individual jackets with new and unique artwork. A special white vinyl edition was also printed in very limited numbers. Just 200 were produced, with only 100 being made available to the public (only from *www.ledzeppelin.com*).

Incidentally, the album's sleeve showed an old cinema in Old Street, London, where the band rehearsed before the 1973 tour.

SONG REMAINS THE SAME, THE (FILM/DVD)

The 1976 movie which mixed fantasy sequences with footage of the band live was described by manager Peter Grant to co-author

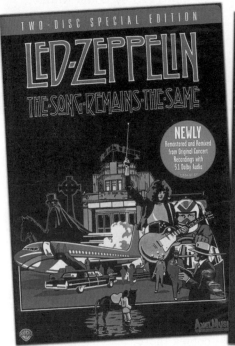

Dome in 1989 thus: 'I always knew we should do something on screen. Now, at the time that usually meant doing something on TV – but I believed that we were much bigger than that. And to capture what Zeppelin was all about would take a cinematic release.

'We first tried it at the Royal Albert Hall in London in 1970 (on 9 January). We had these guys Peter Whitehead and Stanley Dorfman come in and shoot the show. But the problem was the lighting was not up the standard we needed so the film footage was shelved.' This was to emerge finally on the 2003 DVD *Led Zeppelin*.

Back to Grant: 'The idea of doing what was to be a feature film never went away, but it was a case of finding the right time and approach. It finally all came together on our 1973 tour of America. There was a guy called Joe Massot, a film-maker who lived near Jimmy (Page) in Berkshire, who had wanted to do Zeppelin stuff for a few years. We'd always turned him down, but with the huge success we were having in America at the time we decided to go for it.'

Massot hurriedly assembled a film crew at just three days' notice, to shoot the shows in Baltimore (23 July 1973, the first night of the last leg of the tour) and then at Madison Square Garden from 27-29 July. The band also had their arrival in Pittsburgh on 24 July filmed, as they came in

by their own private plane, the *Starship*, and travelled in a motorcade to the Three Rivers Stadium.

Because progress appeared too slow, Massot was fired from the project, with Aussie director Peter Clifton hired. This then led to problems when attempts were made to get back the footage from Massot.

'I sent someone round to his house,' recalled Grant in 1989. 'But he'd hidden it somewhere else. Now, this was footage we'd paid for in good faith – I'm not sure what his game was. So, we took an editing machine as collateral and eventually negotiated a settlement. Let me be clear about this: Joe Massot was offered decent compensation for his contract being terminated. He finally got a lot more than he was entitled to, but we had to settle otherwise the film would have been scuppered.'

Clifton suggested additional filming in order to fill obvious gaps in the footage. So, the 1973 stage was mocked up at Shepperton Studios, where close-ups could be done, and dropped in as and when necessary. Clifton was also ready to shoot on the band's 1975 US tour, which was of course abandoned after Plant was injured in a car accident in Rhodes, Greece.

Adding to the interest in the film were fantasy sequences depicting all four members of the band, plus Grant and tour manager Richard Cole.

'Joe Massot wanted Richard and I to be seen as hit men in a gangster sequence,' said Grant. 'That was fun. Robert went for something romantic and medieval, becoming a knight, and there was even a sword fight (Plant is also seen as the family man on his farm in Wales). Jimmy went for something mystical, climbing up a mountain by his home (Boleskine House). He had a hermit waiting at the top with a lantern, which was supposed to represent knowledge and enlightenment (he is also seen playing a hurdy-gurdy by a lake at his home in Plumpton, East Sussex). John Paul played a highwayman of sorts; he based this on the film *Doctor Syn* (he's also depicted reading *Jack And The Beanstalk* to his two daughters). John (Bonham) wanted to go racing, so we went to Santa Pod Raceway in Northampton and he loved driving around (he's also seen as a family man, at his home, the Old Hyde, in Worcestershire, with his wife and children).'

Each member of the band also had specific music during their fantasy sequences: Page had 'Dazed And Confused', Plant went for 'The Song Remains The Same' and 'The Rain Song', Jones had 'No Quarter' and Bonham was filmed against 'Moby Dick'.

The film was finally finished in 1976, 18 months behind schedule and well over budget, Its first screening was a midnight one organised by Atlantic Records, where label boss Ahmet Ertegun allegedly fell asleep!

Despite something of a critical panning, the film did well at the box office in America, grossing $10 million in its first year. It has retained a fascination for fans ever since, being regarded as not so much a classic but more an interesting insight into the world's biggest band during that period. And, it must be said, Zeppelin allowed a lot of footage to be used that didn't necessarily show them in the best possible light, with Grant showing his dark side on screen as he dealt with promoters. It also depicts the aftermath of the theft from the safe of the Drake Hotel in New York when the takings for the Madison Square Garden shows in 1973 were stolen.

'I had no qualms about this being filmed,' admitted Grant. 'I'm there on my way to the police station to be questioned. But I knew I had nothing to hide, so why not put it on screen? The case was never solved, but I know who did it – however, I have no proof, so it will remain something I shall never be able to reveal.'

The movie is something of a hotch-potch – but because of this, it actually adds to the lustre and mystique of Zeppelin. Released on DVD in 2007, this still has an appeal, if only because despite all the problems, the charisma of the band shines through – and for years it was the only official footage of them out there.

Jimmy Page told *New Musical*

Express in 1976: *'The Song Remains The Same* is not a great film, but there's no point in making excuses. It's just a reasonably honest statement of where we were at that particular time. It's very difficult for me to watch it now, but I'd like to see it in a year's time just to see how it stands up.'

Not quite a live performance movie, not a fly-on-the-wall insight, not a fictional inference, *The Song Remains The Same* is all three.

The full listing of scenes for the DVD is:
Mob Rubout/Mob Town Credits/ Country Life/Bron-Yr-Aur/Rock And Roll/Black Dog/Since I've Been Loving You/No Quarter/Who's Responsible?/The Song Remains The Same/The Rain Song/Fire And Sword/Capturing The Castle/No Quite Backstage Pass/Dazed And Confused/Strung Out/Magic In The Night/Gate Crasher/No Comment/ Stairway To Heaven/Moby Dick/Country Squire Bonham/ Heartbreaker/Grand Theft/Whole Lotta Love/End Credits.

SOUNDSTAGE: ROBERT PLAND AND STRANGE SENSATION

A live DVD from Robert Plant and Strange Sensation, this was filmed at the Soundstage Studios in Chicago on 16 September 2005 and released in October 2006.
TRACKLISTING:
No Quarter/Shine It All Around/ Black Dog/Freedom Fries/Four Sticks/Tin Pan Valley/Gallows Pole/ The Enchanter/Whole Lotta Love.

There were also bonus clips, these being covers of 'Hey Joe' and 'Girl From The North Country', the promotional videos for '29 Palms' and 'Morning Dew', *Top Of The Pops* performances of '29 Palms' and 'Big Log', plus a jukebox facility.

SOUTH BOUND SAUREZ

The second track from the 1979 album 'In Through The Out Door'. 'Saurez' is a wine-producing region in Uruguay. The lyrics certainly suggest a South American feel, even though there are some who believe this is a misspelling of the French word 'Soiree', which means a party in the evening.

The song was co-written by John Paul Jones and Robert Plant, with no involvement from Jimmy Page; this is only one of two Zeppelin songs on which Page isn't included in the writing credits the other being 'All My Love' from the same album.

Never played live, the studio version features one or two minor mistakes from Page, which were deliberately kept in. This perhaps underscores how distant he felt from a song in which he had no writing input.

SPRINGFIELD, DUSTY

Without the advice of the great British soul singer, Led Zeppelin might never have been signed to

Atlantic. Springfield strongly urged the label to snap them up, mainly because John Paul Jones had not only been involved with some of her records (including arranging her rendition of 'Piece Of My Heart', so associated with Janis Joplin), but also played bass with her live. At the time, Dusty Springfield was working on what was to become one of her most acclaimed albums, 1969's 'Dusty In Memphis'.

To reinforce the connection between Dusty Springfield and Led Zeppelin, in 1969 Atlantic Records pressed up a promotional LP featuring selected tracks from both 'Led Zeppelin 1' and 'Dusty In Memphis'. This was sent to various records stores in America to help highlight both albums.

STAIRWAY TO HEAVEN (SONG)

The fourth song from the 'Led Zeppelin IV' album. Such is the power, the charisma and the unbreakable magic of the song that, in 1991, *Esquire* magazine calculated that, by that point, 'Stairway To Heaven' has already spent the equivalent of 44 years on the radio.

So many tens of thousands of words have been spilt in an effort to appreciate and dissect its hold on all of us. Perennially voted the greatest rock song of all time, that particular epithet has become mundane simply because repeated exposure to this remarkable, epic journey has

misled us into believing that we never need to hear it again. Wrong! This is one of the iconic songs of the 20th Century for a reason. Listen again to the way it builds from a gentility that tells of Shakespearian forests and Poe-fuelled everglades.

It tells of myths, legends, aspirations, hopes and dark endeavours. Then, it opens up with all the bravura of a Wagnerian opera, as it reaches towards crescendo and climax.

Some, like Erik Davis (in his book analysing 'Led Zeppelin IV') suggest there is an alchemy at work on this track because it's the fourth song on the fourth album from the four-piece who invoke the four elements. That's perhaps going a little too far into the realms of magick and metaphysics. However, what has held everyone in thrall is the rather enigmatic ones which have been interpreted and reinterpreted to considerable effect over the last four decades. But, as Robert Plant has so succinctly pointed out: 'The only thing that gives "Stairway To Heaven" any staying power at all is its ambiguity.'

Plant has said that Jimmy Page brought the tune for the song virtually complete to Headley Grange, where the band would record it. Plant was in something of a sour mood when, seated one night at a fire, he started to write the lyrics; 'There was something pushing it (the pen) saying, "You guys are okay, but you want to do something timeless, here's a wedding present for you.'"

By stating this, Plant was reaffirming an old belief that all music and lyrics exists in a dimension to which we can all reach out. However, only the very few are 'chosen' to be the conduits, through which these elements of music are brought down to earth. Whether you believe this or not, the fact is that 'Stairway To Heaven' is certainly an inspired moment in the history of music.

However, Page had actually begun to piece this together at Bron-Yr-Aur cottage in Wales during 1970. Many feel that what's described in this song is a journey across a bridge connecting two worlds: ours and the afterlife. That what Plant is describing is a religious awakening of sorts.

But, one can overcomplicate the lyrics and, as Plant himself says, maybe it's best not to over-emphasis the Gnostic beauty of the words. In part, though, Plant has said he got ideas from the book *Magic Arts In Celtic Britain*, written by 19/20th Century Scottish antiquarian Lewis Spence, and the lyrics do mix various mythic and religious symbols and symbolism.

Whatever the truth about the origins of the songs and the way it was created, Page told Cameron Crowe in 1975 that it '...crystallised the essence of the band. It had everything there and showed the band at its best...as a band, as a unit. Not talking about solos or anything, it had everything there. We were careful never to release it as a single. It was a milestone for us. Every musician wants to do something of lasting quality, something which will hold up for a long time and I guess we did it with 'Stairway...' (Pete) Townshend probably thought that he got it with "Tommy". I don't know whether I have the ability to come up with more. I have to do a lot of hard work before I can get anywhere near those stages of consistent, total brilliance.'

The whole way the song builds, Page's guitar solo...everything about this is magical, in the musical sense if no other. It was the song that crossed Zeppelin over from being a giant band to becoming iconic.

Ironically, the song was first played live on 5 March 1971 – to an indifferent response! This was at the Ulster Hall in Belfast. It got its first radio airplay on 4 April 1971 on Radio 1. This was a version recorded three days earlier in London at the Paris Theatre.

The band inevitably played 'Stairway To Heaven' on every tour from 1971. It has also been part of the set for each reunion. Plant would sometimes try to freshen up the song with occasional ad-libs, the most famous of which was, 'Does anybody remember laughter?' For a while, Plant seemed to be fed up with the song, as he told the *Los*

Angeles Times in 1988: 'I'd break out in hives if I had to sing ('Stairway To Heaven') in every show. I wrote those lyrics and found that song to be of some importance and consequence in 1971, but 17 years later, I don't know. It's just not for me. I sang it at the Atlantic Records show because I'm an old softie and it was my way of saying thank you to Atlantic because I've been with them for 20 years. But no more of "Stairway To Heaven" for me.'

This phase passed, even though Plant is perhaps still kicking against the beast that is this song.

Talking of the 'Beast', there have been allegations that there are backwards messages in the song, which purport to state 'Here's to my sweet Satan' and 'I sing because I lie with Satan'. These claims began to emerge in 1981, when a Michigan minister called Michael Mills used his radio show to put forward the idea that 'sinful' rock bands were putting in backwards messages that would be picked up by the subconscious mind. This notion spread quickly, and there are still those who believe this to be the case, despite the obvious nonsense of such accusations.

'It's part of the myth of the song, isn't it?' said Peter Grant in 1989. 'If I were to refute these claims, then I won't be believed anyway. So, let's leave it for people to make up their own minds. All I would say is that to go as far as rigging up a device to play the record backwards at the so-called correct speed (he was talking about vinyl) is so complex and problematic, you have to wonder at the sanity of such people!'

King Diamond, of Mercyful Fate fame, is one avowed Satanist who says that such messages exist 'I have a cassette of this,' he claimed in 1983, 'and you can certainly hear Robert Plant saying, "My sweet Satan".'

Amazingly, the song wasn't released as a single until November 2007, when it was made available as download, reaching Number 37 in the UK charts, and 30 on the US Digital Singles chart. A version by the Far Corporation was released as a single in Britain in 1985, getting to Number 8, while Rolf Harris' 1993 version (complete with didgeridoo and wobbleboard) got to Number 7. In America, a promo-only single was made available in 1972, with 'Stairway To Heaven' on both sides.

Whatever happens in the next century or so, 'Stairway To Heaven' has its unrivalled place in rock iconography. Many millions more words will be used up in trying to understand and appreciate the song, while the tune and lyrics will remain tantalisingly out of reach of mere mortals. The way it should be.

STAIRWAY TO HEAVEN (BOOK)
Published in 1992, this was a book co-written by one-time Led

Zeppelin tour manager Richard Cole with journalist Richard Trubo.

The book deals with his experiences working with Zeppelin, but didn't exactly receive a massive thumbs-up from anyone connected with the band. Peter Grant was typically scathing: 'I'm not sure if all the drugs have messed up Richard's memories, but a lot of those stories and supposed recollections are simply not true. I am sorry for Richard, because his supposed expose has only damaged himself.'

STARGROVES

This was the country estate of Mick Jagger in Newbury during the Seventies where Led Zeppelin recorded part of 'Houses Of The Holy' (all of the songs bar 'The Ocean', 'The Crunge' and 'No Quarter') and 'Physical Graffiti'.

Jagger bought the estate in 1970, and the Stones recorded there on a mobile studio, including tracks which would subsequently appear on the albums 'Exile On Main Street', 'Sticky Fingers' and 'It's Only Rock'n'Roll'. Other bands to record there included Iron Maiden, Status Quo, the Who, Deep Purple and Santana.

The exterior of the house and the grounds were used in the *Doctor Who* stories *Pyramids Of Mars* and *Images Of The Fendahl*. Rod Stewart bought the estate from Jagger in 1998 for £2.5million.

STARSHIP

A Boeing 720B airliner used by Led Zeppelin from 1973 to 1975 on their North American tours.

The band had used a small falcon plan in 1972 and early '73 to get from city to city, but after encountering some severe turbulence en route from San Francisco to Los Angeles, after a show at the Kezar Stadium, they decided to hire the *Starship* for the rest of that tour, at a cost of $30,000.

The plane belonged to American singer/actor Bobby Sherman and his manager Ward Sylvester. They acquired it from United Airlines, who'd taken delivery in 1960. The *Starship*, registration N7201U, had been customised by Sherman and Sylvester, with a reduced seating capacity, plus the introduction of a bar, a TV and video set-up, two rooms at the back (one acting as a bedroom and shower facilities, the other with a low couch and pillows), revolving armchairs, 30-foot couch and an electronic organ housed within the bar.

The band had the plane resprayed with their logo down the side of the fuselage and that of Swan Song Records on the tail.

'We loved using the *Starship*,' Grant said in 1989. 'It meant that we weren't having to check constantly into and out of hotels – we could base ourselves at specific locations, and just fly to the venues and then back. John Bonham was something of a pilot, and was in the co-pilot's seat all the way from New York to Los Angeles in 1975.'

There were the inevitable stories of debauched behaviour on the plane during Zeppelin's tenure – one involved a very drunk Bonham demanding that American photographer Neal Preston strip naked and crawl down the aisle. It was the snapper's price for being allowed on the plane.

Others to use the plane were Deep Purple, Rolling Stones, the Allman Brothers and Alice Cooper. The last person to hire it was Peter Frampton before the plane was finally scrapped in 1982.

Zeppelin decided to discontinue use of the plane on the 1977 US tour, by which time it had started to suffer from engine problems. The band elected to hire a 45-seat Boeing 707, instead. This was known as *Caesar's Chariot*, being owned by Caesar's Hotel in Las Vegas.

STEWART, IAN

Known as the so-called 'sixth member' of the Rolling Stones, Ian Stewart was a renowned keyboard player who was an original member of that band. He was fired in 1963, but stayed on as tour manager and also to contribute keyboard parts.

He appears on two Led Zeppelin songs, these being 'Rock And Roll' from 'Led Zeppelin IV', and 'Boogie With Stu', from 'Physical Graffiti'. Both feature the type of boogie-woogie piano-playing which Stewart had become renowned for.

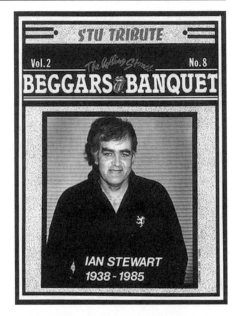

STU TRIBUTE

Vol. 2   The Rolling Stones   No. 8

BEGGARS BANQUET

IAN STEWART
1938 - 1985

Both came out of a jam session recorded at Headley Grange on the Rolling Stones mobile in 1971.

STRANGE SENSATION

This was the name of Robert Plant's backing band for two albums in the 21st Century, these being 2002's 'Dreamland' (albeit solely credited to Plant) and 2005's 'Mighty ReArranger'. There is also one live DVD, 2006's *Soundstage: Robert Plant And Strange Sensation*.

The band featured Plant on vocals, Liam 'Skin' Tyson on guitars (ex-Cast), Billy Fuller on bass, John Baggott on keyboards and synthesisers (a member of Portishead's touring line-up), Justin Adams on lap steel guitar, bass, bender and mandolin (who had worked with Jah Wobble) and Clive Deamer on bass and drums (another member of the Portishead live band).

SUNSET SOUND STUDIOS

The studio on Sunset Boulevard, West Hollywood that was acquired by Walt Disney in 1958 was where Led Zeppelin mixed 'When The Levee Breaks'; from 'Led Zeppelin IV'. There are suggestions that 'Going To California' was also mixed there. However, this doesn't appear to have been the case.

SUTCH, SCREAMING LORD

The wacky, irreverent and highly individual Screaming Lord (David) Sutch was a rock'n'roller, pop star and budding politician. In 1970, he released an album called 'Lord Sutch And Heavy Friends'. It included contributions from Jimmy Page and John Bonham, as well as Jeff Beck, Nicky Hopkins and Noel Redding. Page also produced the album and co-wrote the following songs on it: 'Wailing Sounds', ''Cause I Love You' (Bonham also gets a writing credit here), 'Flashing Lights', 'Thumping Beat', 'Union Jack Car' and 'Baby, Come Back'.

The album got to Number 84 in the American charts, while ''Cause I Love You' made it to Number 80 in the US singles charts. Sadly, many of the musicians on the record were unhappy with the sound quality (it was recorded at Mystic Studios in Hollywood), and distanced themselves from it, which didn't exactly help sales. The album has also been reissued under the title of 'Smoke And Fire'.

In 1998, a BBC poll named this the worst album of all time.

SWAN SONG

The label set up by Led Zeppelin in May 1974 in order to release their own records and those of other artists. It was overseen by manager Peter Grant, who told co-author Dome: 'There were several reasons for us going down this route. Firstly, we wanted total artistic control over what we did. Not that Atlantic (the band's label at the time) interfered, but this would put the seal on our independence.

'Secondly, we wanted to have more financial control. When you are signed to a record company, however much power and success you have there is only so much you can involve yourself in the financial dealings. You are still reliant on what they give you, and this in turn is dependent on so many variables.

'Thirdly, we felt that what this band had achieved could be a good template for others. So, we set out to directly sign bands and artists to Swan Song, because who better to understand and appreciate what musicians need than other musicians – and the guys in Zeppelin were all heavily involved. We saw what the Beatles had done with Apple, and felt we could learn lessons from where they'd gone wrong and apply these to Swan Song.'

The band decided to launch their own label once the five-year deal with Atlantic had run out, but still used Atlantic to market and distribute their records. The label launched itself with lavish parties in New York and Los Angeles, while a celebration was held at Chislehurst Caves in Kent on 31 October 1974 to commemorate the first UK album release, 'Silk Torpedo', from the Pretty Things; the debut American release had been the first, self-titled album from Bad Company.

With a logo based on a 19th-Century painting by William Rimmer called *The Fall Of Day*, which represented the Greek god Apollo, the label appeared to be going from strength to strength by 1977, when Jimmy Page told *Trouser Press* magazine:

'We'd been thinking about it for a while and we knew if we formed a label there wouldn't be the kind of fuss and bother we'd been going through over album covers and things like that. Having gone through, ourselves, what appeared to be an interference, or at least an aggravation, on the artistic side by record companies, we wanted to form a label where the artists would be able to fulfil themselves without all of that hassle. Consequently the people we were looking for the label would be people who knew where they were going themselves. We didn't really want to get bogged down in having to develop artists, we wanted people who were together enough to handle that type of thing themselves, like the Pretty Things. Even though they didn't happen, the records they made were very, very good.'

'We also saw this as more than a musical company, which is why we helped to fund the film *Monty Python And The Holy Grail*,' recalled Grant in 1989.

But things didn't quite work out the way everyone had hoped. A consistent lack of success, outside of their own releases, and a tendency to overstretch themselves eventually put the proverbial skids under the dream. 'We were too generous with a lot of artists, and even signed some just for the hell of it,' sighed Grant. One of the latter were the Message, with guitarist Richie Sambora and bassist Alec John Such, who went on to join Bon Jovi. Inevitably, the label collapsed and closed in 1983.

'We were the victims of our own enthusiasm,' believed Grant. 'But what we forgot was that, if you are as big as Zeppelin were then it takes up all of your time. You have nothing left to offer others on the label. So, we tried to overcompensate by throwing money at them, and that's not the way forward. We also made the mistake of signing young talents without thinking about how best to take them forward. I believe in many ways Swan Song failed because we cared too much about music and musicians. We lost sight of the strong business sense, which had helped to make this band so powerful.

'Ultimately, we ended up making the same mistakes as the Beatles. But if you are going to be a band and own a label, then you have to be prepared to give the latter time as the former.'

The full discography for the label is as follows:

LPs

June 1974 – SS-8410
Bad Company – Bad Company.
November 1974 – SS-8411
Silk Torpedo – Pretty Things.
February 1975 – SS-2-200
Physical Graffiti – Led Zeppelin.
April 1975 – SS-8412
Suicide Sal – Maggie Bell.
April 1975 – SS-8413
Straight Shooter – Bad Company.
December 1975 – SS-8414
Savage Eye – Pretty Things.
February 1976 – SS-8415
Run With The Pack – Bad Company.
March 1976 – SS-8416
Presence – Led Zeppelin.
September 1976 – SS-2-201
The Song Remains the Same (soundtrack) – Led Zeppelin.
March 1977 – SS-8500
Burnin' Sky – Bad Company.
April 1977 – SS-8417
Detective – Detective.
April 1977 – SS-8418
Get It – Dave Edmunds.
April 1978 – SS-8504
It Takes One To Know One – Detective.
September 1978 – SS-8505
Tracks On Wax 4 – Dave Edmunds.
March 1979 – SS-8506
Desolation Angels – Bad Company.
July 1979 – SS-8507
Repeat When Necessary – Dave Edmunds.
August 1979 – SS-16002

In Through the Out Door – Led
Zeppelin.
February 1981 – SS-8509
Midnight Flyer – Midnight Flyer.
April 1981 – SS-16034
Twangin' – Dave Edmunds.
August 1981 – SS-16048
Sad Café – Sad Café.
November 1981 – SS-8510
Best Of Dave Edmunds – Dave
Edmunds.
February 1982 – SS-11002
Rock'n'Roll Party (mini LP) –
Midnight Flyer.
February 1982 – SS-8511
Death Wish II (soundtrack) – Jimmy
Page.
June 1982 – SS-8512
Pictures At Eleven – Robert Plant.
August 1982 – 790001-1
Rough Diamonds – Bad Company.
November 1982 – 790051-1
Coda – Led Zeppelin.
April 1983 – 790078-1
Wildlife – Wildlife.
Singles
November 1974 – SSK-19401
Is It Only Love/Joey – Pretty
Things.
April 1975 – SS-70102
*Trampled Underfoot/Black Country
Woman (US only)* – Led Zeppelin.
May 1975 – SSK-19403
I'm Keeping.../Atlanta – Pretty
Things.
July 1975 – SSK-19401
Joey/Bridge Of God – Pretty Things.
November 1975 – SD-18144
Mirabai – Mirabai.
January 1976 – SSK-19405
Sad Eye/Remember The Boy –
Pretty Things.
May 1976 – SSK-19406

Tonight/It Isn't Rock'n'Roll – Pretty
Things.
June 18 1976 – SS-70110
*Candy Store Rock/Royal Orleans
(US only)* – Led Zeppelin.
July 1976 – SSK-19408
*Here Comes The Weekend/As Lovers
Do* – Dave Edmunds.
October 1976 – SSK-19409
*When Or Where/New York's A
Lonely Town* – Dave Edmunds.
April 1977 – SSK-19410
Ju Ju Man/What Did I Do Last Night
– Dave Edmunds.
June 1977 – SSK-19411
*I Knew The Bride/Back To
Schooldays* – Dave Edmunds.
March 1978 – SSK-19412
Hazell/Night Flighting – Maggie
Bell.
September 1978 – SSK-19413
Deborah/What Looks Best On You –
Dave Edmunds.
November 1978 – SSK-19414
Television/Never Been In Love –
Dave Edmunds.
March 1979 – SSK-19416
Rock'n'Roll Fantasy/Crazy Circles –
Bad Company.
April 1979 – SSK-19417
*A1 On the Juke Box/It's My Own
Business* – Dave Edmunds.
May 1979 – SSK-19412P
*Hazell/Night Flighting (picture disc
reissue)* – Maggie Bell.
August 1979 – SSK-19418
*Girls Talk/Bad Is Bad (clear vinyl
issue)* – Dave Edmunds.
September 1979 – SSK-19419
*Queen Of Hearts/Creature From The
Black Lagoon* – Dave Edmunds.
October 1979 – SSK-19420
Crawling From The Wreckage/As

Lovers Do – Dave Edmunds.
December 1979 – SS-71003
Fool In The Rain/Hot Dog (US Only) – Led Zeppelin.
January 1980 – SSK-19422
Singing The Blues/Boys Talk – Dave Edmunds.
March 1981 – SSK-19423
Rough Trade/Midnight Love – Midnight Flyer.
April 1981 – SSK-19424
Almost Saturday Night/You'll Never Get Me Up – Dave Edmunds.
June 1981 – SSK-19425
The Race Is On/(I'm Gonna Start) Living If It Kills Me – Dave Edmunds with the Stray Cats.
October 1981 – BAM-1
Hold Me/Spring Greens – B A Robertson and Maggie Bell.
April, 1982 – SSK-19426
Waiting for You/Rock'n'Roll Party – Midnight Flyer.
September, 1982 – SSK-19428
Goosebumps/Key To Your Heart – Maggie Bell.
September, 1982 – SSK-19429
Burning Down One Side/Moonlight In Samosa – Robert Plant.
September, 1982 – SSK-19429T
Burning Down One Side/Moonlight In Samosa/Far Post (12 inch) – Robert Plant.
January, 1983 – MB-1
Crazy/All I Have To Do Is Dream – Maggie Bell.
September, 1983 – B-9842
Somewhere In The Night/Sun Don't Shine – Wildlife.
Promo discs
1978 – LAAS-002
Live From The Atlantic Studios – Detective.

1978 – PR-230
College Radio Presents Dave Edmunds – Dave Edmunds.
July, 1982 – SAM-154
Pictures At Eleven – Interview with Alan Freeman – Robert Plant.

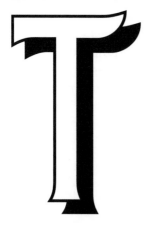

TAMPA STADIUM

Tampa Stadium was a sports arena built in Florida in 1967. It originally played host to the University of Tampa, whose Tampa Spartans American football team used to play there. The American Soccer League's Tampa Bay Rowdies, who featured amongst their playing staff over the years the Brazilian Mirandinha and UK players such as Sam Allardyce, Rodney Marsh and Frank Worthington, were the stadium's first professional tenants (the team was dissolved in 1993) and they were joined by the Tampa Bay Buccaneers, the American football team, in 1976.

The Buccaneers were purchased by the American billionaire Malcolm Glazer in 1995, who promptly changed the name of the stadium to Houlihann's after the Glazer-owned restaurant chain. It remained the Houlihann's Stadium until its demolition in 1998, when it was replaced by the newly built Raymond James Stadium (a move instigated at taxpayer's expense by new owner Glazer, who threatened to move the Buccaneers to another city unless a new stadium was built). Glazer is currently also the owner of Manchester United Football Club in England. The site of the Tampa Stadium is now a parking lot.

Led Zeppelin set a new box-office record when they appeared at Tampa Stadium on 5 May 1973, as they kicked off their record-breaking 'Houses Of The Holy' tour. The audience figure was recorded at 56,800, which bettered the previous record of the Beatles, whose 1965 performance at Shea Stadium in New York had attracted an audience of approximately 55,000. Zeppelin grossed $309,000 for the performance.

The set-list on the night was: *Rock And Roll/Celebration Day/ (Bring It On Home intro) Black Dog/Over The Hills And Far Away/ Misty Mountain Hop/Since I've Been Loving You/No Quarter/The Song Remains The Same/Rain Song/ Dazed And Confused (including San Francisco)/Stairway To Heaven/ Moby Dick/Heartbreaker/Whole Lotta Love (including Let That Boy Boogie)/The Ocean/Communication Breakdown.*

The band returned to the Tampa Stadium for their 1977 tour, appearing at the venue on 3 June. This time, however, the band's performance was cut short due to a severe thunderstorm. Tickets had been printed suggesting that the band would perform come 'rain or shine' and a riot of some 3,000 fans, according to the local Cleveland press, broke out. For the record, the band had only performed 'The Song Remains The Same', 'Sick Again' featuring an intro from 'The Rover' and 'Nobody's Fault But Mine'.

TANGERINE

Once referred to by Robert Plant on stage at Earl's Court in 1975 as, 'A song of love in its most innocent stages', 'Tangerine' is the seventh track from 1970's 'Led Zeppelin III' album. In keeping with much of the album, the song is in a more acoustic vein than the rampaging rock of album opener 'Immigrant Song' and the kind of music the band had indulged in on both of their previous albums.

'Tangerine' was written solely by Jimmy Page, and his use of pedal steel on the song lends 'Tangerine' an almost country feel. The song's roots are in the Yardbirds song 'Knowing That I'm Losing You' – a track the latter band had worked on in spring 1968, but never recorded.

Led Zeppelin would feature 'Tangerine' as a part of their acoustic set in their live shows in 1971-72 and re-introduced the song to their set for the Earl's Court shows in 1975. It has been covered by, amongst others, Life Of Agony, Great White, Dave Matthews and Big Head Todd and the Monsters. The song also appears in the film *Almost Famous*.

TEA FOR ONE

'Tea For One' is the seventh and final track from Led Zeppelin's 1976 album 'Presence'.

The song is a slow blues number which echoes 'Since I've Been Loving You' from 'Led Zeppelin II', as pointed out by Jimmy Page in an interview with *Trouser Press* magazine in 1977. 'It was the only time I think we've ever got close to repeating the mood of another of our numbers, "Since I've Been Loving You". The chordal structure is similar, a minor blues. We just wanted to get a really laid-back blues feeling without blowing out on it at all. We did two takes in the end, one with a guitar solo and one without. I ended up sitting there thinking, "I've got this guitar solo to do", because there have been blues guitar solos since Eric (Clapton) on the "Five Live Yardbirds" album and everyone's done a good one. I was really a bit frightened of it. I thought, "What's to be done?" I didn't want to blast out the solo like a locomotive or something, because it wasn't conducive to the vibe of the rest of the track. I was extremely aware that you had to do something different than just some BB King licks.'

Lyrically, 'Tea For One' echoes the loneliness of life on the road, the title taken from a Robert Plant comment regarding being alone in a hotel room on a US tour with 'tea for one'. Plant wasn't the only member of the Zeppelin entourage to suffer from homesickness, and both John Paul Jones and, in particular, John Bonham would suffer at times throughout the band's career.

'Tea For One' was never performed live in its entirety by Led Zeppelin, although the guitar solo would occasionally be incorporated into 'Since I've Been Loving You' on the band's 1977 tour. The song was performed thre times by Page and Plant on their 1996 tour of Japan.

TEN YEARS GONE

'Ten Years Gone', a song written by Jimmy Page and Robert Plant, is the tenth track on the band's 1975 'Physical Graffiti' album.

The song, which some have speculated was actually the unused Zeppelin song 'Swan Song', was originally intended as an instrumental, and Jimmy Page uses no less than 14 separate guitars. However Robert Plant eventually added some lyrics, inspired by an ex-girlfriend.

Plant explained in a 1975 interview: 'Let me tell you a little story behind the song "Ten Years Gone" on our new album. I was working my ass off before joining Zeppelin. A lady I really dearly loved said, "Right. It's me or your fans." Not that I had fans, but I said, "I can't stop, I've got to keep going." She's quite content these days, I imagine. She's got a washing machine that works by itself and a little sports car. We wouldn't have anything to say

anymore. I could probably relate to her, but she couldn't relate to me. I'd be smiling too much. Ten years gone, I'm afraid. Anyway, there's a gamble for you.'

'Ten Years Gone' was performed live on the band's 1977 tour, which would feature John Paul Jones playing a triple-neck guitar. The band also performed the song at the first of their two Knebworth shows in 1979, after which it was dropped.

More recently Jimmy Page and Robert Plant performed the song once, at a 1996 Osaka show, and Page performed 'Ten Years Gone' with the Black Crowes on their 1999 tour. A version appears on the Jimmy Page/Black Crowes 'Live At The Greek' album, released in 2000.

TERRY WEBB AND THE SPIDERS

Terry Webb and the Spiders were a Brumbeat quartet who were the first band that Led Zeppelin drummer John Bonham joined, aged 16 in 1964. He performed with the band for approximately a year, before joining the Senators.

THANK YOU

The mellow, balladic 'Thank You' is the fourth track on Led Zeppelin's second album, 1969's 'Led Zeppelin II'.

It is a hugely important song in the Led Zeppelin canon, being the very first that Robert Plant wrote all the lyrics for, allowing Jimmy Page to realise that his singer was more than capable as a lyricist. In this instance, the lyrics take the form of a tribute to Plant's then wife Maureen.

The song was frequently performed live, swiftly becoming a showcase for John Paul Jones's organ playing, and although it was dropped from the band's main set following their 1973 tour it made occasional returns to the set. However the song clearly remained close to Page and Plant, who performed the song on their 1994 '...Unledded' tour and subsequent 1996 and 1998 tours. Plant also sang a few lines of 'Thank You' prior to his performance of 'Crazy Little Thing Called Love' at the 1992 Freddie Mercury Tribute Concert at Wembley Stadium.

'Thank You' is one of Led Zeppelin's most widely covered songs, having been undertaken by Tori Amos, Duran Duran, Great White, Sly and Robbie, Tesla, Chris Cornell and the Flaming Lips, amongst others.

THAT'S THE WAY

One of the most delightful tracks from 'Led Zeppelin III', 'That's The Way' is the eighth song on the album.

It is also one of the many Led Zeppelin songs written at the Welsh cottage retreat Bron-Yr-Aur, so favoured by the band. In this instance, the song was written by Robert Plant and Jimmy Page whilst the pair had been out enjoying a long walk. Stopping to rest upon their return, Page played the melody to Plant, who sang the opening verse straight off, the results captured on a portable cassette recorder they were carrying. At the time the pair were joined by their respective partners, Plant's wife Maureen and their daughter Carmen, and Page by his then partner Charlotte Martin. During the Plant/Page '...Unledded' reunion tour Plant announced that Page's daughter Scarlet was conceived within half-an-hour of the song being written.

Originally known as 'The Boy Next Door', the song is a gentle acoustic number which, despite Page's use of pedal steel, features more of a folk flavour than country, and also features John Paul Jones on mandolin and only light tambourine from John Bonham. Lyrically the song echoes Plant's feelings on the environment, hardly surprising given the situation of the song's inception, although certain lines, such as: 'I can't believe what people saying/You're gonna let your hair hang down/I'm satisfied to sit here working all day long/You're in the darker side of town...' seem to display a certain resentment to the manner in which the band had been treated on visits to America, as well as the way they had seen what they perceived as kindred spirits being treated by various authorities.

The band performed 'That's The Way' in concert between 1970 and 1972 and live renditions can be heard on 'How The West Was Won' and 'Led Zeppelin BBC Sessions' as well as visually on the DVD *Led Zeppelin*. The song also features on 'No Quarter: Jimmy Page And Robert Plant Unledded', both on CD and DVD.

'That's The Way' is also one of the few Led Zeppelin songs authorised to appear on a film soundtrack. It is one of six to feature in Cameron Crowe's 2000 film *Almost Famous*, although it is the only one that features on the official soundtrack.

THEM CROOKED VULTURES

John Paul Jones got together with Foo Fighters frontman Dave Grohl and Queens of the Stone Age's Josh Homme in 2009 to form a supergroup.

Although Jones, along with Jimmy Page, had appeared with the Foo Fighters at their 2008 shows at Wembley Stadium, performing 'Rock And Roll' and 'Ramble On', the roots of Them Crooked Vultures go back to a 2005 interview Grohl gave to *Mojo* magazine where he announced the next album he was planning was him on drums, Homme on guitar

and Jones playing bass, stating, 'That wouldn't suck!'

The trio began recording in Los Angeles during the summer of 2009 and made their live debut at Chicago's Metro on 9 August. In the UK their first show was on 26 August supporting The Arctic Monkeys at London's Brixton Academy (Homme had recently produced the Monkeys' third album, 'Humbug'.

Debut album 'Them Crooked Vultures' was released in the UK on the Sony label (it was released via Interscope in America) on 16 November to generally good reviews; the band's blend of Zeppelin-like beats and Queens of the Stone Age's alternative rhythms and melodies finding favour with most rock critics.

The band's subsequent live UK tour sold out quickly, despite no music actually being available to the public at the time tickets went on sale.

TRACKLISTING:

No One Loves Me And Neither Do I/ Mind Eraser, No Chaser/New Fang/ Dead End Friends/Elephants/ Scumbag/Bandoliers/Reptiles/ Interludes With Ludes/Warsaw Or The First Breath You Take After You Give Up/Caligulove/Gunman/ Spinning In Daffodils.

THOMPSON, TONY

Tony Thompson is best known as the drummer for disco act Chic who also drummed with Led Zeppelin when they appeared at the JFK Stadium in Philadelphia for their much-publicised reunion show at Live Aid in 1985.

Despite their perceived background as a dance/disco-orientated act, it is worth noting that Thompson, along with Chic mainmen Bernard Edwards and Nile Rodgers, started out in a hard rock band called the Bad Boys and later the Big Apple Band. But, much like similar black hard-rock act Mother's Finest, they met music-industry resistance.

Thompson, widely acknowledged as being one of the hardest-hitting drummers, was asked to fill John Bonham's role for the Live Aid show – the much-publicised appearance by Phil Collins was only ever as an additional drummer. So highly regarded was Thompson that it is alleged he was asked to fill in on an ultimately aborted 1986 Led Zeppelin reunion.

Thompson also drummed for

disco act LaBelle, as well as David Bowie, Madonna, Rod Stewart, Robert Palmer and Mick Jagger. He was also a member of the Eighties funk-rock supergroup the Power Station, alongside Duran Duran's John and Andy Taylor and singer Robert Palmer. He also drummed with melodic rock bands Crown of Thorns and Distance.

Thompson was diagnosed with kidney cancer in October 2003 and died within the month on 12 November, two months after his Power Station bandmate Robert Palmer had died of a heart attack.

THORGERSON, STORM

Although best known for his pioneering album cover work with Pink Floyd, Storm Thorgerson was a mainstay of the Hipgnosis design group alongside Aubrey Powell, who undertook a wide array of spectacular album sleeve designs. Alongside the work of Roger Dean with Yes, they made the concept album cover their own throughout the Seventies with their abstract approach and fascinating use of photographed visuals.

The first Led Zeppelin album Hipgnosis worked on was 1973's 'Houses Of The Holy', although the company's relationship was almost soured from the off when Thorgerson's initial submission, an electric green tennis court with a tennis racquet, was rejected by a furious Jimmy Page, who thought the designer believed Led Zeppelin's music was just a racket. Thorgerson was fired and his partner Powell brought in, who based his work on the ending of the Arthur C Clarke novel *Childhood's End*.

Hipgnosis and Thorgerson were brought back into the Zeppelin fold for 1976's 'The Song Remains The Same' and would also work on 1976's 'Presence' and 1979's 'In Through The Out Door', as well as the posthumous 1982 collection 'Coda'.

Although the Hipgnosis partnership dissolved in 1983, Thorgerson has continued to work on the album sleeve medium and his easily recognisable stylistic images can be seen on covers for bands such as Muse, the Mars Volta and Audioslave.

His work can be viewed at his website: *www.stormthorgerson.com*

THUNDERTHIEF

'The Thunderthief' was John Paul Jones' second solo outing proper, following on from 1999's 'Zooma'.

Released in 2001 on the DGM label, it followed on stylistically from 'Zooma' but was the first time that Jones had applied some lyrics to his music as a solo artist

Best of all is a splendid cover of the bluegrass standard 'Down To The River To Pray'. While Jones' own lyrics on the title track and the faux punk of 'Angry, Angry' don't exactly match the quality of his musicianship and arrangement skills, the likes of 'Hoediddle' and the Eastern-themed 'Freedom Song' display the kind of towering approach fans were used to from his work in Zeppelin.

Jones himself supplies the vocals, four, six, 10 and 12-string bass, bass steel guitar, acoustic and electric guitars, mandolin, piano, organ, synthesiser and ukulele, and is joined by Nick Beggs on Chapman stick, Teri Bryant on drums and Robert Fripp on guitar.

TRACKLISTING:
Leafy Meadows/The Thunderthief/ Hoediddle/Ice Fishing At Night/ Daphne/Angry Angry/Down To The River To Pray/Shibuya Bop/Freedom Song.

TOWER HOUSE

The Tower House is a Grade 1 listed building in Melbury Road, Kensington London which has served as a residence to Led Zeppelin guitarist Jimmy Page since 1972.

The house was built between 1876 and 1878 in a gothic style by William Burges, the Victorian artist and architect. The house features an array of previously used Burges features, including a cylindrical tower and conical roof in the style of Castell Coch in Wales, and fireplaces from Cardiff Castle.

Burges himself had used the residence as his own home and the actor Richard Harris had lived there before Page, an admirer of Burges's style, purchased the property. 'I had an interest going back to my teens in the pre-Raphaelite movement and the architecture of Burges,' Page has said. 'What a wonderful world to discover.'

TRAMPLED UNDER FOOT

'Trampled Under Foot', written by Jimmy Page, Robert Plant and John Paul Jones, was the fifth song from the band's 1975 album 'Physical Graffiti'.

The song evolved out of a 1972 jam session and was inspired by Stevie Wonder's rockier workouts, with a guitar lick similar to that used in the Sam and Dave classic 'Soul Man'. John Paul Jones played the rhythm of the song on a clavinet. Lyrically, Robert Plant sought his inspiration from Robert Johnson's 'Terraplane Blues', although Zeppelin's more carnal offering has little to do with cars, as Johnson's did.

'Trampled Under Foot' was a popular addition to Led Zeppelin's live set, allowing Jones to showcase his keyboard skills, and was often used for lengthy jam sequences, as can be seen from the version from the 1975 Earls Court gig on the DVD *Led Zeppelin*. Robert Plant, for whom 'Trampled Under Foot' was a particular favourite, added the song to his live set on the 'Now And Zen' tour. He also performed the song, with Jason Bonham on drums, at his daughter Carmen's 21st birthday.

'Trampled Under Foot' was released as a single throughout the world, backed with 'Black Country Woman', and reached Number 38 in the US charts in 1975. With the band's Earl's Court shows coming up, there were plans to release 'Trampled Under Foot' as a single in the UK. There were similar plans for 'D'yer Mak'er', from 'Houses Of The Holy', suggesting a slight softening of attitude to releasing UK singles. As it was, despite promotional copies of the single being pressed up, neither song would be released in the UK, meaning these promo singles are rare finds.

UK MUSIC HALL OF FAME

The UK Music Hall of Fame opened its doors in 2004 as a way of celebrating and acknowledging important contributors to music. Led Zeppelin were inducted in November 2006 in a ceremony at Alexandra Palace in London. Roger Taylor of Queen inducted the band, while Australian band Wolfmother performed 'Communication Breakdown' as a tribute.

In his induction speech, Taylor said, 'They don't make bands like this any more. Britain should be proud of them. True legends.'

Jimmy Page accepted the award on behalf of Zeppelin. At one point, he said: 'We played in this building in the early Seventies. In those days it had a glass ceiling and sounded absolutely unbelievably bad. We played well, but it just sounded bad.'

He also dedicated the award to Ahmet Ertegun, co-founder of Atlantic Records, who at the time was unwell at home in New York and was to die shortly afterwards.

Other inductees that year were James Brown, Rod Stewart, James Brown, Bon Jovi, Dusty Springfield, Brian Wilson and Prince. Sir George Martin received honorary membership, presented by the then UK Chancellor of the Exchequer Gordon Brown.

This was the last time that the ceremony was actually held. Seemingly, it's been scrapped, due to lack of interest It must be said that the UK Music Hall of Fame has failed to capture the imagination in the way that American Rock and Roll Hall of Fame has done.

UNIVERSITY OF SURREY

This is where Led Zeppelin played their first ever show under that name. All previous shows had been under the name of the New Yardbirds.

It happened in the Great Hall on 25 October1968, the band's third actual gig together in the UK. The other two were under the old name. Some have tried to suggest the band's first date as 'Led Zeppelin' was on 9 November at the Roundhouse in Chalk Farm, London, when they were billed as 'The Yardbirds Now Known As Led Zeppelin' – very unwieldy! But this isn't correct, although this was the first time they were to be advertised as Led Zeppelin in any form.

The decision to change the band's name was made so late that all posters for the gig still advertise them as the New Yardbirds. Tickets cost the equivalent today of just 37p! Supporting were a band called the Gass.

Jimmy Page was given an honorary doctorate by the University of Surrey on 20 June 2006 at a ceremony conducted at Guildford Cathedral. He got this for services to the music industry. The official press release from the university said:

'The University of Surrey is proud to confer the honorary degree of Doctor of the University to Jimmy Page for services to the music industry. The award was made on Friday, June 20 at Guildford Cathedral... Through his work with Led Zeppelin, Jimmy Page, a major creative force within the band, became universally recognised as being one of the greatest and most versatile guitarists of all time.

'Away from music, he has been involved in the Action for Brazil's Children Trust, or ABC Trust. His commitment to this cause goes back to 1994 where he witnessed first hand unrest in the largest of Rio de Janeiro's shanty towns. He resolved there and then to do something to help, which led to the establishment of "Casa Jimmy", a shelter for abandoned street children, which continues to be

run successfully today and has helped over 250 children to find a better life. Building on this, the ABC Trust was set up with Jimmy Page as the founding patron. In 2005 he was awarded an OBE in recognition of his charitable work, and also made an honorary citizen of Rio de Janeiro later that same year.'

UNTITLED

This is one of the alternative titles for 'Led Zeppelin IV', released in 1971. The band took a massive risk in not putting their name or the title of the record on the sleeve. But it worked, because this heightened the mystery that seemingly enveloped Zeppelin.

These days, most people assume the album is actually called 'Led Zeppelin IV', but it also has been called 'Four Symbols' after the individual symbols created to represent each member of the band.

VALENS, RITCHIE

Valens (real name Steven Richard Valenzuela) was a pioneering West Coast rock'n'roller who helped pioneer the Chicano, or Hispanic rock movement, which would eventually see artists such as Carlos Santana and Los Lobos rising to prominence. His recording career was short, lasting a mere eight months, but still yielded two major hits.

His first single, 'Come On Let's Go' reached Number 42 in the US during 1958, but it was his second, the plaintive ballad 'Donna', which propelled him to Number 2 in the US charts in the same year. However, it was the B-side to 'Donna', the effusive 'La Bamba', which was sung entirely in Spanish and featured some startlingly unique guitar-work.

Valens' music was an inspiration to early Led Zeppelin, and they showed their appreciation with the song 'Boogie With Stu' which appeared as Track 13 on the 1975 album 'Physical Graffiti'. The song borrows heavily from Valens' own 'Ooh, My Head', a song on his 1959 self-titled debut album.

The credits for 'Boogie With Stu' include 'Mrs Valens'.

However, there was an attempt by the Valens family to sue Zeppelin over the song, which led to the following comments from Page to *Guitar World* magazine: 'Curiously enough, the one time we did try to do the right thing, it blew up in our faces... What we tried to do was give Ritchie's mother credit, because we heard she never received any royalties form any of her son's hits, and Robert did lean on that lyric a bit. So what happens? They tried to sue us for all of the song! We had to say bugger off.'

Valens died in the tragic 1959 plane accident that also took the lives of Buddy Holly and the Big Bopper. Valens took his place on the charter flight, which was required because a tour bus had broken down, having won a coin toss with Buddy Holly guitarist Tommy Allsup. The accident was immortalised in the Eddie Cochrane song 'Three Stars', and also on Don McLean's 1971 hit 'American Pie' which included the legendary refrain 'The day the music died'.

WALKING INTO CLARKSDALE

The one studio album that was recorded by Robert Plant and Jimmy Page, when the one-time Led Zeppelin pair reunited in the mid-Nineties.

Having explored their joint legacy and heritage in 1994 with the live album 'No Quarter: Jimmy Page and Robert Plant Unledded', they decided to go one step further in 1998 by releasing a studio album of new songs. In all honesty, it is a patchwork affair that showed up the reality that the duo were, if anything, now pulling in different musical directions.

While some songs – like 'Most High' and 'Please Read The Letter' – were rather cohesive

and impressive, there were also some songs that were among the most confused and anodyne of their illustrious careers. It would seem that, without the balance of the rest of Zeppelin, Page and Plant struggled to find any meaning in working together in an original capacity.

The other musicians on the record were Charlie Jones (bass), Michael Lee (drums), Tim Whelan (keyboards), while the whole thing was recorded and mixed (in 35 days) by Steve Albini.

The album charted well around the world, following its release in April 1998. It got to Number 3 in the UK and Number 8 in America. The single, 'Most High', made it to Number 26 in Britain. 'Shining In The Light' was also put out as a single, but failed to chart significantly. Incidentally, 'Please Read The Letter' was re-recorded by Plant with Alison Krauss for their 2007 album 'Raising Sand'.

Bernadette Giacomozzo, reviewing for *In Music We Trust*, said of the album: 'The good news is: Jimmy Page and Robert Plant really don't have that much to prove. This dynamic duo was, as any halfway coherent rock fan knows, one-half of the original, legendary Led Zeppelin line-up. The better news is: They don't *try* to prove anything...

'The bottom line? Though Page and Plant embrace their past, they live in the present. They can see that rock today needs a real kick-start to get going again, and if means giving the kids a dose of the original formula, so be it. Be warned – if you want a Led Zeppelin album, don't come to "Walking Into Clarksdale" (you want my advice on the definitive Zeppelin album? "Physical Graffiti", thank you very much). But if you want some back-to-basics rock, from two of the pioneers, by all means, come to this album.'

Tracklisting:

Shining In The Light/When The World Was Young/Upon A Golden Horse/Blue Train/Please Read The Letter/Most High/Heart In Your Hand/Walking Into Clarksdale/Burning Up/When I Was A Child/House Of Love/Sons Of Freedom

An extra track, 'Whiskey In The Glass', featured on the Japanese edition. All songs were written by Plant, Page, Charlie Jones and Michael Lee. Clarksdale itself is a town in the Mississippi Delta, which is regarded as the cradle of delta blues – a major influence on Page and Plant.

WALTER'S WALK

One of those songs which only saw the light of day on the 1982 'Coda' collection of previously unavailable tracks; this was the fourth song on that record. It was actually recorded at Stargroves during the sessions for the 'Houses Of The Holy' album. However, it has also been suggested that Robert Plant did the vocals at Jimmy Page's Sol Studios in 1982.

Whatever, the truth, 'Walter's Walk' was never given a proper live airing by the band. The closest they got was to include snippets during performances of 'Dazed And Confused' on the 1972 and 1973 tours.

WANTON SONG

The 12th song from the 1975 album 'Physical Graffiti', it is usually suggested that it's all about having sex with a wanton woman, although there have been the occasional hint that the title itself was a play on Chinese phonetics. Think about it: Wan Ton could be a Chinese dish!

Musically, it came out of a jam session, with Page employing both a backwards echo (one where the echo comes before the note itself) and also put his guitar through a Leslie speaker to create a Doppler effect with a Hammond organ. It's a technique, he first explored with the Yardbirds.

'The Wanton Song' was played during the 1975 tour by Zeppelin, before being dropped. It was revived by Robert Plant and Jimmy Page for their 1995 and 1998 tours. Most recently, Jimmy Page played this with the Black Crowes on their 1999 tour and it subsequently turned up on their 2000 album 'Live At The Greek'.

WEARING AND TEARING

A song recorded during sessions for the last Led Zeppelin Studio album, 1979's 'In Through The Out Door'. But, like 'Ozone Baby' and 'Darlene', it was left off the album due to space restrictions.

It finally showed up in 1982 on the 'Coda' album of outtakes and previously unreleased material; it was the eighth and final track on the record. A tough rocker, most people consider this a statement from the band that they could outdo any of the younger bands starting to make their mark. Considering the general style of 'In Through The Out Door', maybe it didn't fit the atmosphere of the record.

The band did consider releasing this as a commemorative single for the two shows at Knebworth Park, England in August 1979, but ran out of time to do so. This was never performed live by the band.

WHAT IS AND WHAT SHOULD NEVER BE

Second song from the 1969 album 'Led Zeppelin II'. The lyrics are said to be about a romance between Robert Plant and his wife's younger sister – it's one of the first songs on which Plant received a writing credit. It was also one of the first on which Jimmy Page used his Gibson Les Paul guitar.

This was a regular part of the Zeppelin live set from 1969 to 1972, and a performance from 1970 at the Royal Albert Hall is featured on the 2003 DVD *Led Zeppelin*.

WHATEVER HAPPENED TO JUGULA?

The eventual title of the 1985 album from Roy Harper and Jimmy Page, released on the Beggars Banquet label. This was originally going to be called 'Rizla' (the album sleeve is based around an open packet of Rizla cigarette papers), then 'Harper And Page' (but Roy Harper felt that was playing too much on Jimmy Page's reputation to sell the album). The idea of '1214' (the year the Magna Carta was signed) was then conceived, but dismissed as being too esoteric.

Finally it was decided to go for 'Whatever Happened To Jugula?', which was a phrase Harper connected with the then-popular Trivial Pursuit board game.

Almost all the songs on the record were written by Harper alone. The exception was 'Hope', a collaboration with David Gilmour. Here's what Harper said about this song to Pink Floyd fanzine *The Amazing Pudding* in 1985:

'One day I'd gone in and done the demo of the vocal on their track (this referred to the fact that Harper had written a song for Gilmour's solo album 'About Face') and the producer, Bob Ezrin, thought it was a good song – I really like Bob, by the way; he's a good guy, very bright, very intelligent – and a month or so later Dave said, "Roy, I've got bad news for you: we're not going to use the track on the record." I'd

given it to him for free anyway, as a token of friendship; like a debt I owed him. He wasn't gonna have to pay me any royalties on it as far as I was concerned. So I said, "Why not?" He said, "Well, I can't sing it the way that you sang it – I can't get the conviction into the lyrics." So I said, "Oh, um, well, I'm gonna use it," and he said, "Alright then".'

Despite popular theory, Gilmour doesn't play on this track. It is, in fact, Harper's son Nick, who was 16 at the time.

The album was a beautiful exposition of styles, with Page and Harper complementing one another perfectly on a series of songs that most definitely fit Harper's slightly idiosyncratic catalogue. But the Page input is very obvious in places. The album reached Number 44 in the UK and Number 60 in America.

Apart from Harper, his son and Page, the record also featured bassist Tony Franklin, drummers Steve Broughton, Ronnie Brambles and Preston Heyman and keyboard player Nik Green.

Pete Townshend covered the song 'Hope' on his 1985 album 'White City: A Novel', although he retitled it 'White City Fighting'. Merseyside band Anathema also covered it on their 1996 album 'Eternity'. Harper and Page appeared together in 1984 at the Cambridge Folk Festival, with a subsequent tour to promote the album.

There was also a famous interview with the pair on the BBC TV show *The Old Grey Whistle Test* in November 1984, when Harper and Page are filmed on Scafell Pike in the Lake District, playing acoustic guitars on 'Hangman' and 'The Same Old Rock'.

Tracklisting:
Nine Forty Eight-ish/Bad Speech/ Hope/Hangman/Elizabeth/Frozen Moment/Twentieth Century Man/ Advertisement (Another Intentional Irrelevant Suicide).

WHEN GIANTS WALKED THE EARTH: A BIOGRAPHY OF LED ZEPPELIN

Written by Mick Wall, this was published in 2008 by Orion Books and is his insight into the story of the band. It has received widespread acclaim and positive reviews.

WHEN THE LEVEE BREAKS

The final song on 1971's 'Led Zeppelin IV', this is a cover of the 1929 number made famous by blues duo Kansas Joe McCoy and Memphis Minnie. It dealt with the Great Mississippi Flood of 1927 which devastated the Mississippi basin and led to a huge migration of African Americans to the Midwest in search of work and shelter.

Primarily, the song concerns itself with the evacuation of 13,000 people from Greenville, Missouri to an unaffected levee (which is a natural or artificial slope used to regulate water flow). The fear of what might happen should this break down is what drives the lyrics.

Zeppelin tried to record this at Island Studios during early sessions for their fourth album, but couldn't make it work. Eventually, they nailed it at Headley Grange in December 1970. Their version does differ significantly from the original, in that is has both rearranged and newly written lyrics, and uses drums and harmonica in a relentlessly heavy style. There's also a backwards echo on Robert Plant's vocals.

This is the only track from the album not to undergo a remix. The band had originally had the record mixed in America, but hated the results so much they had it redone – all except for this track.

Talking about the song, Page said to *Trouser Press* magazine: '"When The Levee Breaks" is probably the most subtle thing on the album as far as production goes because each 12 bars has something new about it, though at first it might not be apparent. There's a lot of different effects on there that at the time had never been used before. Phased vocals, a backwards-echoed harmonica solo.'

The song was performed briefly on the band's 1975 US tour, but proved difficult to recreate live because of the production values. However, Page and Plant performed it live, as has John Paul Jones. Plant and Alison Krauss also included it as part of their 2008 touring set. In addition, Jeff Buckley, WASP and A Perfect Circle have all covered it.

Incidentally, the Zeppelin version is credited to Page, Plant, Jones and John Bonham, as well as Memphis Minnie. But Kansas Joe McCoy is not credited.

WHITE SUMMER/BLACK MOUNTAIN SIDE

This was a combination of 'White Summer', an instrumental worked out by Jimmy Page during the last days of the Yardbirds, and 'Black Mountain Side', an instrumental from the 1969 debut album.

Page had originally conceived the first piece for the 1967 Yardbirds album 'Little Games' and subsequently developed it live. This was captured towards the end of the Yardbirds' career, when recorded live in New York on 30 March 1968. This show was released as the 1971 album 'Live Yardbirds With Jimmy Page', and underscored the way the band's musical direction was slowly changing under Page's guidance. The album was swiftly withdrawn at Page's behest.

In the early days of Zeppelin, Page would play 'White Summer' and segue this into 'Black Mountain Side'. This happened from 1968-70. Later on, he would play the whole of this piece, going into 'Kashmir'.

Cult folk guitarist Davey Graham was said to be annoyed

that Page allegedly borrowed heavily from his own 1963 instrumental 'She Moved Through The Bazaar' for 'White Summer' without any effort at acknowledgement. In a fit of revenge, he is said to have gone up to Page at a music awards ceremony and said, 'Hello, Robert'.

WHOLE LOTTA LOVE

One of the most recognised songs in rock history – not just in the story of Led Zeppelin. This first featured on the 1969 album 'Led Zeppelin II' (track one), but was also a hit single for them in America, where it sold over a million copies and reached Number 4 in the charts, Germany (where it topped the charts), Holland (reaching Number 4), France, Belgium and Japan, among others. The single was backed with 'Living Loving Maid (She's Just A Woman)'.

The song is credited to Jimmy Page, Robert Plant, John Paul Jones and Willie Dixon. The reason the last-named is there is because this is based to a large extent on the 1962 song 'You Need Love', which was written by Dixon for Muddy Waters. Dixon, though, had to sue the band to get due credit and be financially recompensed, which happened in 1986.

Oddly, Dixon never sued the Small Faces, despite the fact that they had done a song called 'You Need Loving' for their 1966 debut album. If anything, this borrowed even more from the Dixon original, but he never got any credit.

The song opens with one of the famous riffs of all time, which Page explained to *Uncut* magazine came about when 'we were rehearsing some music for the second album. I had a riff, everyone was at my house, and we kicked it from there. Never was it written during a gig.'

The middle section, in which Plant appears to have an orgasm against a backdrop of psychedelic freakouts, came about says engineer Eddie Kramer almost by accident: 'At one point there was bleed-through of a previously recorded vocal in the recording of "Whole Lotta Love". It was the middle part where Robert screams, "Wo-man. You need it." Since we couldn't re-record at that point, I just threw some echo on it to see how it would sound and Jimmy said, "Great! Just leave it".'

Plant did his vocal parts in one take, despite the fact that the song itself was recorded at various studios in New York and Los Angeles on the band's second American tour, Page then constructed the song at Olympic Studios in London.

In the past 40 years, the song has taken on a life of its own and was even used as the theme on the famed BBC TV show *Top Of The Pops* from 1972 to 1981, and again from 1998 to 2003. This wasn't the Zeppelin original, but a cover by CCS.

'Whole Lotta Love' was part of

the band's live set almost throughout their career and was the last song they played live with the original line-up. It also featured in every subsequent reunion. Jimmy Page also played the song with Leona Lewis during the closing ceremony for the 2008 Beijing Olympics, albeit with slightly altered lyrics.

The enormous list of covers includes Jimmy Page with the Black Crowes, plus Perry Farrell, Ben Harper, Sly and Robbie, Tori Amos and Prince. It's also been sampled by the Prodigy, among others.

WILDLIFE

Short-lived English band who were signed to Swan Song Records. The band in their Swan Song era featured Steve and Chris Overland on guitar and vocals (they'd go on to form FM), Phil Soussan on bass (he'd subsequently join Ozzy Osbourne's band) former Bad Company/Free drummer Simon Kirke and Mark Booty on keyboards.

The band was actually started by the Overland brothers with drummer Pete Jupp, recording the album 'Burning' in 1981 for Chrysalis. A change of drummer and label led to the release of the 'Wildlife' album on Swan Song two years later, produced by Bad Company guitarist Mick Ralphs.

The album has the 'distinction' of being the last released on the Swan Song imprint. A single, 'Somewhere In The Night'/'Sun Don't Shine' taken from the record was the last ever single on the label.

WILLIAMSON, SONNY BOY

Aleck 'Rice' Miller was bluesman Sonny Boy Williamson II, following on from the original Sony Boy Williamson, whose real name was John Lee Williamson. He became known as 'Sonny Boy Williamson' in the early Forties, something seemingly forced on him by the sponsors of the King Biscuit Time radio show, broadcast on radio station KFFA in Helena, Arkansas.

There is confusion as to why this happened, but Miller embraced the name, even going so far as to claim he'd thought it up first! This was patently untrue, but he has probably gone on to become the more famous of the pair.

In 1963, Sonny Boy Williamson II recorded the song 'Bring It On Home', written by Willie Dixon. Zeppelin recorded their version, drawing heavily from the original for the intro and outro although not crediting Dixon until forced to do so by a lawsuit.

Williamson II, who was born on a plantation in Tallahatchie Country, Mississippi, died on 25 May 1965. His exact date of birth remains a mystery, Some have put it as early as 1899, while some have suggested he was actually born 13 years later, His headstone has it as 11 March 1908.

He gained significant status with a series of European tours in

had such a reputation for inventing and exaggerating stories that nobody back home in the Delta area ever believed he'd played in Europe!

WOOD, ROY

One of the great and enigmatic figures of British pop and rock, Wood made his name with the Move before co-founding the Electric Light Orchestra. He subsequently quit to form Wizzard.

In 1979, he released solo album 'On The Road Again' with a guest appearance from John Bonham, an old pal of Wood's from their formative days in Birmingham.

Wood remains a brilliant yet unpredictable character, capable of innovative songwriting and performance as well as periods of complete silence.

WOLFMOTHER

The Australian band were chosen to perform 'Communication Breakdown' during Led Zeppelin's induction into the UK Music Hall of Fame in November 2006 at Alexandra Palace.

Wolfmother have always cited Zeppelin as a significant influence. Says mainman Andrew Stockdale: 'I grew up listening to bands like Led Zeppelin. To me, they're very special.'

WOLVERHAMPTON WANDERERS

The Premier League (at the time of writing) football club, who have the undying devotion of Robert

the early Sixties, backed by bands such as the Yardbirds and Animals, whom he'd influenced. His combination of sharp suits, bowler hat, rolled-up umbrella and an attaché case in which he carried a selection of harmonicas made the man a major figure on the blues-rock circuit. He even recorded a live album with the Yardbirds, then featuring Eric Clapton on guitar, called 'Sonny Boy Williamson With The Yardbirds'. Things went sour for him in the UK, however, when he was accused of stabbing a man in a fight.

His influence is quite considerable, with the Who, Aerosmith, Van Morrison, New York Dolls, Ten Years After, Doobie Brothers and Joe Bonamassa among those to cover his songs.

It is amusing to note that he

Plant, who's been a lifelong supporter, and sufferer. He told the *Sunday Mercury* newspaper in 2008: 'I know what I'm doing every other Saturday is masochism, and it's the nearest thing to actually walking under a bus. Well, I suppose it is a bit like a religion, but I don't carry the crucifix right through the weekend these days, although I used to.'

'It played havoc with my marriage for a while. When we won the League Cup in 1974, it took me three days to get home from Wembley to Worcestershire. I haven't got a clue where I was. I know the Mayor of Wolverhampton received the team in official form, and I remember being there for a minute or two.'

Plant is now a vice president of the club. He had this to say of the honour in August 2009 to the *Express & Star* newspaper: 'First of all, I'm flattered, but I'm embarrassed to be honest. There are so many other people who are so important and relevant to the club, especially the people I sit next to at Molineux (the club's home ground) in the Steve Bull Stand.

'They've seen so many more games than me and they're able to keep a closer eye on what's going on.'

XYZ

XYZ was the name of what could have been a major rock supergroup featuring Jimmy Page and Robert Plant, plus bassist Chris Squire and drummer Alan White from progressive rock band Yes. With both Zeppelin and Yes on hiatus, the name alluded to ex-members of Led Zeppelin and Yes – hence XYZ.

The seeds for the potential union formed in the aftermath of the death of Led Zeppelin drummer John Bonham in September 1980 when Page moved near to where Squire was living in Virginia Water, Surrey during 1981.

Drummer White has said: 'I met Jimmy quite a few times because he lived pretty close to Chris, he lived in the same area. We used to meet at parties in London and all that kind of stuff and basically Chris called me on day and said, "Jimmy wants to go and play in the studio…" So we all just turned up one day and started playing and it started sounding pretty good. We got the engineer in there and they started putting down the XYZ tapes as it were. Quite a lot of it was stuff that I'd been writing with Chris and we had, I think it was like four, five, six songs.'

With Page feeling the need for a strong vocalist for the project, it seems only natural thoughts turned to Plant and the singer is said to have attended a rehearsal in April 1981. However Plant wasn't keen on the complex, progressive nature of the music, and that, combined with the difficulties in Zeppelin manager Peter Grant reaching any kind of agreement with Yes manager Brian Lane, meant the project was short-lived.

Plant continued with what would become his debut solo album, 'Pictures At Eleven', whilst Page worked on the soundtrack for the film *Death Wish II*, directed by Michael Winner. Squire and White went on to record a Christmas single, 'Run With The Fox' at the end of 1981, and would eventually form Cinema with South African guitarist Trevor Rabin and original Yes keyboard player Tony Kaye. The band would evolve into a new line-up of Yes with the arrival of vocalist Jon Anderson mid-way through recording sessions, leading to the successful 1983 album '90125'.

Some XYZ material was worked on by the early Cinema line-up, with Rabin attempting to incorporate it into his own repertoire. Some material from the recording sessions has appeared on various bootlegs, believed to have come from tapes stolen from Page's Berkshire residence in 1987. These include two untitled instrumentals; the riff from one would materialise in the Firm's 'Fortune Hunter', the other in the 1997 Yes song 'Mind Drive'. Of the two vocal tracks, 'Telephone Hunter' came from an idea Yes had toyed with during sessions for their 1980 album 'Drama', and 'And (Do) You Believe It' would appear as 'Can You Imagine' on Yes's 2001 album 'Magnification'.

Says White: 'Jimmy kept calling Robert saying how great it was and he should get involved, but Robert thought (the music) was too complicated. He came and listened to it and I think he thought it was too complicated; or else there could have been the kind of a Yes Zeppelin band at that time. I think that kind of either frightened a lot of people off at that time or it was a too-good-to-be-true kind of thing. But the management thing got involved and they really screwed it up, and it just all went haywire, that's what really dissipated the whole thing.'

YARDBIRDS

There would be no Led Zeppelin without the Yardbirds – stylistically and logically. Not only did Jimmy Page find his niche when he joined the band, but they also had the flair, acumen, insight and vision to see the possibilities of taking blues-rock further than ever – and might have succeeded had circumstances not been against them.

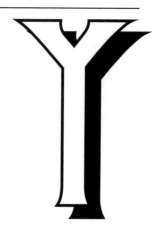

The Yardbirds started out in 1962 as the Metropolitan Blues Quartet, a somewhat pretentious name for a bluesy young band born out of Kingston Art College in Surrey.

By September 1963, they'd taken over from the fast-rising Rolling Stones as house band at the Crawdaddy Club in Richmond, Surrey, and had made the name change to the Yardbirds. With a line-up of Keith Relf (vocals), Anthony 'Top' Topham (lead guitar), Chris Dreja (rhythm guitar), Paul Samwell-Smith (bass) and Jim McCarty (drums), they played a selection of classic blues numbers to great acclaim.

In October of that year, Topham left, with a young Eric Clapton taking over. By this time, Giorgio Gomelsky (impresario at the Crawdaddy) had taken over managing the band, got them signed to Columbia (then part of EMI) and produced their first album, 1964's 'Five Live Yardbirds', which was recorded live at the Marquee Club in London. A second live album was recorded when the band backed the legendary Sonny Boy Williamson II on a European tour, the cunningly titled 'Sonny Boy Williamson With The Yardbirds'.

The band made their commercial breakthrough with third single 'For Your Love', written by Graham Gouldman, who would go on to join 10CC. But Clapton, horrified the Yardbirds had forsaken some of their blues roots for a chart-friendly approach, quit to join the altogether more purist John Mayall's Bluesbreakers, where he would become an iconic guitar figure. He recommended young sessionman Jimmy Page to replace him.

Page told *Trouser Press* magazine in 1977: 'Giorgio Gomelsky approached me and said that Eric wasn't willing to expand and go along with the whole thing. I guess it was probably pretty apparent to them after they did "For Your Love". Clapton didn't like that at all. By that time they had already started using different instruments like harpsichords, and at that point Clapton felt like he was just fed up. The rest of the band, especially Gomelsky, wanted to move further in that direction.

'The very first time I was asked to join the Yardbirds, though, was not at that time, but some time before then. Gomelsky said that Eric was going to have a "holiday", and I could step in and replace him. The way he put it to me, it just seemed really distasteful and I refused. Eric had been a friend of mine and I couldn't possibly be party to that. Plus Eric didn't want to leave the band at that stage.'

So, Beck took over from Clapton. And the band soon began to thrust forward, propelled by Beck's experimental, almost raw approach. Classic singles like 'Heart Full Of Soul' and 'Shapes Of Things' were followed by the 1966 album 'Roger The Engineer' (also called 'The Yardbirds'), which suggested the band were taking massive leaps towards embracing a much more progressive and psychedelic approach, not only in keeping with the times but ahead of them. Co-produced by Samwell-Smith and new manager Simon Napier-Bell, it was something of a revelation for anyone brought up on the much more regimented, albeit flamboyant ambivalence of 'For Your Love'.

In June 1966, Samwell-Smith elected to quit the Yardbirds, to concentrate on his talents as a producer. At which point Page

stepped in, as he told *Trouser Press* in '77:

'It was at a gig at the Marquee Club in Oxford which I'd gone along to. They were playing in front of all these penguin-suited undergraduates, and I think Samwell-Smith, whose family was a bit well to do, was embarrassed by the band's behaviour.

'Apparently Keith Relf had gotten really drunk and he was falling into the drum kit, making farting noises to the mike, being generally anarchistic. I thought he had done really well, actually, and the band had played really well that night. He just added all this extra feeling to it. When he came offstage, though, Paul Samwell-Smith said, "I'm leaving the band."'

In October 1966, the band released the landmark single 'Happenings Ten Years Time Ago'. This had both Page and Beck on guitar, with John Paul Jones on bass; Dreja was on rhythm guitar. The B-side had 'Psycho Daisies', with Page reverting to bass, leaving Beck on lead guitar. This line-up also revamped and recorded 'Train Kept A-Rollin'' for the film *Blow Up*. They even appeared in the film (one of the hippest movies of the time, starring David Hemmings, Vanessa Redgrave and Sarah Miles) after the Who had turned the chance down, and a band called the In Crowd (featuring future Yes guitarist Steve Howe) were unable to make the filming schedule. At the end of the scene, Beck smashed up a cheap guitar, a la Pete Townshend, on instructions from director Michaelangelo Antonioni.

Little was recorded during this era of the Yardbirds, although they did do the music for a commercial for a milkshake product called Great Shakes – they used the riff from 'Over Under Sideways Down'! Beck was astonishingly fired from the band while they were in Texas in October 1966:

'It was on the Dick Clark tour when there were a few incidents,' recalled Page in 1977. 'One time in the dressing room I walked in and Beck had his guitar up over his head, about to bring it down on Keith Relf's head, but instead smashed it on the floor. Relf looked at him with total astonishment and Beck said, "Why did you make me do that?" Fucking hell. Everyone said, "My goodness gracious, what a funny chap."

'We went back to the hotel and Beck showed me his tonsils, said he wasn't feeling well and was going to see a doctor. He left for LA where we were headed in two days time anyway. When we got there, though, we realised that whatever doctor he was claiming to see must have had his office in the Whisky club. He was actually seeing his girlfriend, and had just used the doctor bit as an excuse to cut out on us.

'These sort of things went on, and it must have revived all the previous antagonism between him and the rest of the band. I think that that, and a couple of other things, especially the horrible wages we were being paid, helped bring about his behaviour, which had obviously stewed behind everybody's back. That quote that Keith Relf had said, "The magic of the band left when Eric left", I think really has to be taken into account. They were prepared to go on as a foursome, but it seemed that a lot of the enthusiasm had been lost Then Simon Napier-Bell called up with the news that he was selling his stakes in the band to Mickie Most I think they must have cooked it up, actually, the three of them: Napier-Bell, Most and Beck. This way Beck could have a solo career, which he had already begun in a way with the recording of the single "Beck's Bolero".'

Now down to a four-piece with Page on lead guitar, the band's fortunes were fast failing. At which point Peter Grant was brought into the frame. Here's Page's take on it: 'Peter was working with Mickie Most and was offered the management when Most was offered the recording... I'd known Peter from way back in the days of Immediate Records, because our offices were next door to Mickie Most and Peter was working for him. The first thing we did with him was a tour of Australia and we found that suddenly there was some money being made after all this time.

'I was only on a wage, anyway,

with the Yardbirds. I'd like to say that because I was earning about three times as much when I was doing sessions and I've seen it written that, "Page only joined the Yardbirds for the bread." I was on wages except when it came to the point when the wages were more than what the rest of the band were making and it was cheaper for Simon Napier-Bell to give me what everybody else was getting.'

By March 1968, Relf and McCarty were ready to leave, to pursue something altogether heavier, while Dreja was keen on taking up a career in photography. A final single was recorded, 'Goodnight Sweet Josephine', with the proto-Zeppelinesque 'Think About It' on the B-side. But it was all so fragile and volatile that, on 7 July 1968, the line-up fell apart.

'It just got to a point where Relf and McCarty couldn't take it any more,' recalled Page. 'They wanted to go and do something totally different. When it came to the final split, it was a question of begging them to keep it together, but they didn't. They just wanted to try something new. I told them we'd be able to change within the group format, coming from a sessions background I was prepared to adjust to anything. I hated to break it up without even doing a proper first album.'

At first Page and Dreja tried to put together a new line-up. But the latter soon bowed out, And, after various alternatives were considered, the Yardbirds emerged

with Page, old session pal John Paul Jones on bass, the tyro Robert Plant on vocals (Terry Reid had turned down the job, and Plant was recommended by Mickie Most) and John Bonham on drums (after Procol Harum's BJ Wilson and top sessionman Clem Cattini had been considered).

Said Page: 'We still had these dates we were supposed to fulfil. Around the time of the split John Paul Jones called me up and said he was interested in getting something together. Also, Chris was getting very into photography; he decided he wanted to open his own studio, and by that time was no longer enamoured with the thought of going on the road. Obviously, a lot of Keith and Jim's attitude of wanting to jack it in had rubbed off on him, so Jonesy was in.

'I'd originally thought of getting Terry Reid in as lead singer and second guitarist but he had just signed with Mickie Most as a solo artist in a quirk of fate. He suggested I get in touch with Robert Plant, who was then in a band called Hobbstweedle...'

The result was the band who would soon become Led Zeppelin. Relf and McCarty started folk rockers Renaissance, with Relf forming Armageddon in the mid-Seventies. They did one very impressive album, mixing progressive music folk and hard rock, before Relf was electrocuted and died on 14 May 1976. McCarty went on to form Illusion with Relf's sister, Jane. In 1983, Dreja, McCarty and Paul Samwell-Smith got some form of Yardbirds reunion together, under the name of Box of Frogs.

In 1992, the Yardbirds were inducted into the Rock and Roll Hall of Fame, with Page and Beck present: Clapton was unable to attend. And shortly thereafter, Dreja and McCarty revived the Yardbirds with a reunion tour. They were still going strong in 2010, with a line-up of the two originals, Andy Mitchell (vocals/harmonica), Ben King (lead guitar) and David Smale (bass).

There's little doubt that the Yardbirds were, at their best, one of the great British bands of the Sixties – and if there's anything that can be said of the connection between they and Zeppelin, it is that the latter fulfilled the potential the former showed but were never able to capitalise on.

YES

In 1981, following the Led Zeppelin split, Jimmy Page briefly teamed up with the Yes pair of Chris Squire (bass) and Alan White (drums), with the intention of forming a band called XYZ (see XYZ entry). Page would subsequently, after this project fell apart, join Yes onstage in 1984. This was at the Westfalenhalle in Dortmund, for the song 'I'm Down'.

Of course, both bands were also signed to the Atlantic label.

YOU NEED LOVE

The 1962 song that Willie Dixon wrote for Muddy Waters which was then used as the basis for Led Zeppelin's own 'Whole Lotta Love'. In 1985, a lawsuit was filed by Dixon, claiming that Zeppelin had plagiarised his song.

A comparison of the opening verse in each case suggests he had a very good point. Zeppelin's opens with the following: 'You need coolin', baby, I'm not foolin'/I'm gonna send ya back to schoolin'/Way down inside, honey, you need it/I'm gonna give you my love.'

Dixon's begins with 'I ain't foolin', you need schoolin'/Baby you know you need coolin'/Baby, way down inside, woman you need love'.

Right at the end, Plant intones: 'Shake for me, girl/I wanna be your back door man'. This is said to celebrate two Howlin' Wolf songs: 'Shake For Me' and 'Back Door Man'. However, both were written by Willie Dixon. Inevitably, Dixon got his way as the case was settled out of court and he was duly given a writing credit alongside Jimmy Page, Robert Plant, John Paul Jones and John Bonham.

Oddly, the Zeppelin song was based more on the Small Faces' 1966 track 'You Need Loving' than on the Muddy Waters original. And the former was credited only to Steve Marriott and Ronnie Lane – even more strange is that the Small Faces were never sued!

Perhaps that's because the Zeppelin songs went on to become such an acknowledged masterwork, whereas the Small Faces' one remained comparatively undiscovered.

It must also be asked why it took Dixon over 15 years to take legal action.

YOU SHOOK ME

A song recorded by the band on their 1969 debut album; it was track three and was written by Willie Dixon and JB Lenoir. The latter, who died in 1967, is principally recalled these days for the fact that many of his songs were outspoken commentaries on social and political ills of the time.

It was first recorded as an instrumental by Earl Hooker before Muddy Waters did a version with vocals in 1962. Joining him on the recording with Dixon himself on bass, Earl Hooker on guitar, Casey Jones on drums, JT Brown and Ernest Cotton on saxophones and Johnny 'Big Moose' Walker on organ.

Zeppelin's version came out months after Jeff Beck had released his own take on it for the 1968 album 'Truth'. The similarities between the two versions led to Beck accusing Zeppelin of ripping him off.

Page responded in *Trouser Press* magazine: 'We had done our first LP with "You Shook Me", and then I heard Beck had done "You Shook Me". I was terrified because I thought they'd be the same. But I

hadn't even known he'd done it, and he hadn't known that we had.

'Beck had the same sort of taste in music as I did. That's why you'll find on the early LPs we both did a song like "You Shook Me". It was the type of thing we'd both played in bands. Someone told me he'd already recorded it after we'd already put it down on the first Zeppelin album. I thought, "Oh dear, it's going to be identical", but it was nothing like it, fortunately. I just had no idea he'd done it. It was on "Truth", but I first heard it when I was in Miami after we'd recorded our version. It's a classic example of coming from the same area musically, of having a similar taste.'

Beck himself is quoted as saying the following about the whole affair: 'He (Page) said, "Listen to this. Listen to Bonzo, this guy called John Bonham that I've got". And so I said I would, and my heart just sank when I heard "You Shook Me". I looked at him and said, "Jim, what?", and the tears were coming out with anger. I thought, "This is a piss-take, it's got to be". I mean, there's "Truth" still spinning on everybody's turntable, and this turkey's come out with another version. Oh boy…then I realised it was serious, and he did have this heavyweight drummer, and I thought, "Here we go again" – pipped at the post kind of thing.'

It must be said there are inevitable similarities between the

two versions, although Zeppelin's
is far more rampant and the call-
and-response style admirably suits
them. The band played this
regularly in their live set from
1969 to 1973, eventually being
dropped for more recent material.

Jimmy Page did play this on the
1999 tour with the Black Crowes,
captured on the album 'Live At
The Greek' released a year later.

YOUR TIME IS GONNA COME

The fifth song from the 1969 'Led
Zeppelin' album. Jimmy Page
actually had to learn steel guitar
to play on this recording, while
John Paul Jones created a bass
effect with the organ.

The lyrics are about an
unfaithful woman, with a nod
towards Ray Charles by quoting
from his song 'I Believe To My
Soul'. Oddly, many feel that Page
(who co-wrote this with Jones)
was expressing his belief at the
time that women were inferior to
men – a highly dubious
supposition. And, a rarity, all four
members of the band sing on the
chorus.

Zeppelin only performed this
song in its entirety live on their
1968 Scandinavian tour, although
a brief snippet is patched in
'Whole Lotta Love' during a show
in Tokyo on 24 September 1971.
There may also be other instances
around this period when the band
did something similar.

ZACRON

Zacron is the working name of the artist, poet, art journalist and broadcaster who is best known for designing the captivating sleeve for 'Led Zeppelin III'.

Zacron had originally met Jimmy Page through the Kingston College of Art, where he had studied alongside Eric Clapton, in 1963. In 1970 Page asked Zacron to work with him on designing the cover for the third Led Zeppelin album. The result was the collection of seemingly random images that grace the outer and inside sleeves of the album's gatefold cover; close inspection suggests the images are all connected by the theme of flight (ie Zeppelin). The cover is notable for its revolving inner wheel.

Zacron would not work with Led Zeppelin again, but he has remained active in the art world ever since. He was a lecturer at Leeds Metropolitan University, and currently runs his own Zacron studios. He was interviewed by *Classic Rock* magazine for their December 2007 issue about his work on 'Led Zeppelin III', in which he stated that Page had telephoned him to announce that he considered the sleeve 'looked fantastic'. This directly contrasted with Page's own view, which he aired in *Guitar World* magazine in 1998 that he was disappointed with the work and felt it looked 'teenybopperish'.

Zacron's work can be viewed at his own website: *www.zacron.com*

ZEPPELIN, COUNTESS EVA VON

Countess Eva Von Zeppelin was the great granddaughter of Ferdinand Graf Von Zeppelin, the German aviator and aircraft manufacturer best known for founding the Zeppelin Airship company, from which Led Zeppelin took their name.

Eva threatened to sue Led Zeppelin in 1968 for illegal use of the family name and for using the image of the *Hindenberg* crashing into flames on the cover of the 'Led Zeppelin' album. She is alleged to have stated: 'They may be world famous, but a couple of shrieking monkeys are not going to use a privileged family name without permission'. The action was taken, unsuccessfully as it happened, to prevent a live Danish television performance recorded in Copenhagen in October 1969.

ZOSO

Zoso, sometimes misconstrued as Zofo, is the apparent

pronunciation of Jimmy Page's chosen symbol for Led Zeppelin's fourth album, sometimes known as the Four Symbols album.

Each member of the band chose specific symbols. Robert Plant chose a circle containing a feather, John Bonham three connecting circles and John Paul Jones a single circle with three connecting single *vesica pisces* – the shape made by the intersection of two circles of the same radius – (Sandy Denny, who featuring alongside Plant on the track 'Battle Of Evermore', was acknowledged by three triangles).

Given Page's known interest in the occultist Aleister Crowley, much speculation fell upon his symbol and its meaning. The very fact that Page himself has never spoken about the meaning itself merely added to speculation that the symbol hid some alleged Satanic connection.

Perhaps the best and most detailed explanation of Page's symbol can be found at the New Zealand based website *In The Light* (*www.inthelight.co.nz*), in which it is concluded that the symbol reflects Page's star sign Capricorn and its astrological ruler Saturn.

ZOOMA

'Zooma' was the first solo album proper from bassist John Paul Jones. Since Led Zeppelin's demise Jones had worked with a variety of artists ranging from Diamanda Galas through the Mission and the Butthole Surfers to Heart, as well as scoring the soundtracks for the films *Scream For Help* (1985) and *The Secret Adventures Of Tom Thumb* (1993), but 'Zooma' saw him step out of the shadows and into the rock'n'roll limelight once more.

The album was released on Robert Fripp's (King Crimson) DGM label in September 1999 and is a nine-track wholly instrumental album. Musically, it mixes the expected Zeppelin hard-rock bombast with orchestral, world, jazz and blues styles. Sonically many of the individual pieces take a single theme and slowly build and expand on it building it to its ultimate climax. The piece 'Nosumi Blues' is the most stylistically similar to Jones' work with Led Zeppelin, whilst 'Snake Eyes' is a simple organ solo.

Jones himself played bass, double bass, guitars, keyboards, electric mandola and Kyma. He is joined on the album by an array of musicians including Trey Gunn (rhythm guitar), Paul Leary (guitar), Pete Thomas (drums) and the London Symphony Orchestra.

The album was met with widespread critical acclaim and Jones toured in support of it. It was followed by Jones' second and, to date, last solo album, 'The Thunderthief', in 2001.

TRACKLISTING:
Zooma/Grind/The Smile Of Your Shadow/Goose/Bass N'Drums/B Fingers/Snake Eyes/Nosumi Blues/Tidal.

BIBLIOGRAPHY

The Complete Guide To The Music Of Led Zeppelin – Dave Lewis
Then As It Was: Led Zeppelin At Knebworth 1979 – Dave Lewis
Led Zeppelin Dazed And Confused: The Story Behind Every Song – Chris Welch
The Man Who Led Zeppelin – Chris Welch
When Giants Walked The Earth – Mick Wall
Hammer Of The Gods – Stephen Davis
Stairway To Heaven: Led Zeppelin Uncensored – Richard Cole
Classic Rock
Mojo
Uncut
Q
New Musical Express
Trouser Press
Raw
Rolling Stone
Guitar Player
Musician
Spin
http://www.ledzeppelin.com
http://www.jimmypageonline.com
http://www.robertplant.com
http://www.johnpauljones.com
http://www.jasonbonham.net
http://www.deborahbonham.com
http://www.themcrookedvultures.com
www.wikipedia.org
http://www.turnmeondeadman.com
http://www.furious.com/perfect/most

MALCOLM DOME

MALCOLM DOME IS A VETERAN — ANOTHER WAY OF SAYING 'OLD GIT' — OF OVER 30 YEARS' SERVICE AT THE ROCK'N'ROLL MAST. HE STARTED OUT HIS JOURNALISTIC 'CAREER' (IF YOU CAN CALL IT THAT!) IN 1979, WRITING FOR THE NOW DEFUNCT RECORD MIRROR, BECOMING THEIR SO-CALLED ROCK AND METAL EXPERT. ALL OF WHICH WAS FAIR TRAINING IN GETTING UP AND DOWN THE COUNTRY TALKING TO COUNTLESS BANDS AND REVIEWING ENDLESS GIGS AND ALBUMS.

BY 1982, HE WAS ENSCONCED ON A MOST UNPROMISING COLOUR FORTNIGHTLY MAGAZINE CALLED KERRANG!, A YOUNG BUCK THAT WAS TREATED WITH SUCH DISDAIN BY ITS OWN PUBLISHERS THAT IT WAS SHOVED INTO A COAL HOLE. STILL, THAT PUBLICATION WENT ON TO DO SOME DAMN FINE THINGS AND REMAINS A SPECIAL ERA.

SINCE THEN, HE'S WORKED ON NUMEROUS MAGAZINES — METAL HAMMER, CLASSIC ROCK, CLASSIC ROCK PRESENTS PROG, RAW — AS WELL AS WRITING (OR CO-WRITING) VARIOUS BOOKS AND BROADCASTING ON THE ROAD (HE HAS A WEEKLY SHOW ON INTERNET STATION TOTALROCK) AND ON TV. HE ALSO RECENTLY MADE A CAMEO APPEARANCE (IS THAT THE RIGHT DESCRIPTION?) IN THE HIT MOVIE ANVIL: THE STORY OF ANVIL, AND HAS ALSO APPEARED IN VARIOUS OTHER DVDs.

DOME ONLY SAW ZEPPELIN ONCE — AT EARL'S COURT IN 1975 — BUT THEY ARE STILL HIS FAVOURITE BAND OF ALL TIME.

HE AND JERRY EWING HAVE WRITTEN TWO PREVIOUS BOOKS TOGETHER, AND WHEN NOT TAPPING AWAY ON KEYBOARDS, THEY CAN USUALLY BE FOUND TAPPING ON GLASS AT THE CROBAR. THERE, THE SECRET'S OUT!

SO, WHY IS DOME STILL WRITING AND WAFFLING ABOUT ROCK? TOO DAFT AND STUPID TO STOP, PROBABLY.

JERRY EWING

JERRY EWING IS EDITOR OF CLASSIC ROCK PRESENTS PROG, A
MAGAZINE THAT DOES PRETTY MUCH WHAT IT SAYS ON THE COVER.
HE LAUNCHED THE MAGAZINE FOR FUTURE PUBLISHING IN JANUARY
2009 AND STILL DONS HIS CAPE AND SETS OFF TO WORK EACH
MORNING TO LISTEN TO ALBUMS THAT LAST FOR THREE WEEKS.
EWING'S WRITING CAREER BEGAN WITH METAL FORCES MAGAZINE IN
1989, WHEN HE EVENTUALLY REALISED A PASSION FOR AC/DC –
THE BY-PRODUCT OF A YOUTH SPENT IDLING AWAY HIS DAYS
LISTENING TO MUSIC ON THE BEACHES OF SYDNEY – WAS MORE
CONSUMING THAN A DEGREE IN MANAGEMENT SCIENCE WOULD
REALLY EVER BE.

SINCE THEN HE'S WORKED FOR METAL HAMMER, VOX, STUFF
AND BIZARRE AMONGST OTHERS. HE SET UP CLASSIC ROCK
MAGAZINE FOR DENNIS PUBLISHING BACK IN 1998 AND THEN SPENT
A HUGELY ENJOYABLE SIX YEARS TOYING WITH IMAGES OF SCANTILY
CLAD WOMEN AND MAKING UP CRUDE JOKES FOR MAXIM. HE ALSO
WORKS AS A BROADCASTER, FREQUENTLY FOR INTERNET RADIO
STATION TOTALROCK AND IS THE AUTHOR OF AN EVER-INCREASING
AMOUNT OF BOOKS ON MUSIC AND FOOTBALL.

HIS FAVOURITE LED ZEPPELIN SONG IS 'ACHILLES LAST
STAND' FROM 'PRESENCE', ALTHOUGH WHEN THE PURISTS AREN'T
LISTENING HE'LL ADMIT TO STILL HAVING AN ENORMOUS SOFT SPOT
FOR 'STAIRWAY TO HEAVEN'.

AWAY FROM MUSIC HE STILL INDULGES A NOW 40-YEAR ODD
PASSION FOR CHELSEA FOOTBALL CLUB, THE SYDNEY ROOSTERS
AND VEGEMITE. HE HAS ALSO BEEN KNOWN TO ENJOY THE ODD DROP
OF GREEN LABEL JACK DANIEL'S. BUT LIKE THE ADVERTS TELL YOU,
HE DOES SO RESPONSIBLY.

EWING HAS ALSO BEEN REFERRED TO AS A VETERAN SCRIBE,
ALTHOUGH HE IS MUCH YOUNGER THAN MALCOLM DOME.

ACKNOWLEDGEMENTS

Richard Anderson and everyone at Cherry Red.

Roxy and Adair.

All at TotalRock: Tony Wilson, Talita, Holly, Fist, The Bat, Mad Maz, Chloe, Ratchetto, Chris G, Tina, Sara, PMQ, Zed, Joel, TP, Gillian, Barnett!

Everyone at the Crobar: Rich, Steve, Johanna, Ben, Joey, Mitch, Olivia, Nicola, Steve Hammonds, Sir Hugebert, Dave Everley, Emma 'SF' Bellamy, Harjaholic, Curt, The Do, The Scamp, Keith, The Unique One, Isa, Richard Thompson, Belinda, Martamaria, Jacques, Anna Maria, The Crazy Bitch, Philip Wilding, Nuala, Jonty, Lauren and Xerxes.

And The Ship: Charlotte, Suski, Hannah, Dani Julius, Josh, Gill, Paul T, Paul H, Colm, Blaise, Arren, Mona, Nana and Fatty.

The Prog Posse: Ang, Jo Prog.

The Metal Hammer Mob: Chris Ingham, Alexander Milas, Caren Gibson, Jamez Isaacs, Hards, Lewis Somerscales, Gill, Jonathan Selzer, The Beez, Ester S, Tina K.

The Classic Rock Crew: Scott Rowley, Sian Llewellyn, Alex Burrows, Geoff Barton, Paul Henderson, Ian Fortnam, Brad Merrett, Mark Gillman. Dave Ling is light on his loafers.

Other titles available

Rockdetector: A To Zs of '80s
Rock/Black Metal/Death
Metal/Doom, Gothic & Stoner
Metal/Power Metal and Thrash
Metal
Garry Sharpe-Young

Rockdetector: Black Sabbath –
Never Say Die
Garry Sharpe-Young

Rockdetector: Ozzy Osbourne
Garry Sharpe-Young

The Motorhead Collector's Guide
Mick Stevenson

Fucked By Rock (Revised and
Expanded)
*Mark Manning (aka Zodiac
Mindwarp)*

Prohets and Sages: The 101 Greatest
Progressive Rock Albums
Mark Powell

Johnny Thunders – In Cold Blood
Nina Antonia

All The Young Dudes: Mott The
Hoople & Ian Hunter
Campbell Devine

Good Times Bad Times – The
Rolling Stones 1960-69
Terry Rawlings and Keith Badman

The Rolling Stones: Complete
Recording Sessions 1962-2002
Martin Elliott

Embryo – A Pink Floyd Chronology
1966-1971
Nick Hodges And Ian Priston

Those Were The Days – The Beatles'
Apple Organization
Stefan Grenados

The Legendary Joe Meek – The
Telstar Man
John Repsch

Truth... Rod Steward, Ron Wood
And The Jeff Beck Group
Dave Thompson

You're Wondering Now – The
Specials from Conception to
Reunion
Paul Williams

Kiss Me Neck – A Lee 'Scratch'
Perry Discography
Jeremy Collingwood

Our Music Is Red – With Purple
Flashes: The Story Of The Creation
Sean Egan

Quite Naturally – The Small Faces
Keith Badman and Terry Rawlings

Irish Folk, Trad And Blues: A Secret
History
Colin Harper and Trevor Hodgett

Number One Songs In Heaven –
The Sparks Story
Dave Thompson

from Cherry Red Books:

Random Precision – Recording The Music Of Syd Barrett 1965-1974
David Parker

Bittersweet: The Clifford T Ward Story
David Cartwright

Goodnight Jim Bob – On The Road With Carter Usm
Jim Bob

Tamla Motown – The Stories Behind The Singles
Terry Wilson

Block Buster! – The True Story of The Sweet
Dave Thompson

Independence Days – The Story Of UK Independent Record Labels
Alex Ogg

Indie Hits 1980 – 1989
Barry Lazell

No More Heroes: A Complete History Of UK Punk From 1976 To 1980
Alex Ogg

The Day The Country Died: A History Of Anarcho Punk 1980 To 1984
Ian Glasper

Burning Britain – A History Of UK Punk 1980 To 1984
Ian Glasper

Trapped In A Scene – UK Hardcore 1985-89
Ian Glasper

The Secret Life Of A Teenage Punk Rocker: The Andy Blade Chronicles
Andy Blade

Best Seat In The House – A Cock Sparrer Story
Steve Bruce

Death To Trad Rock – The Post-Punk fanzine scene 1982-87
John Robb

Deathrow: The Chronicles Of Psychobilly
Alan Wilson

Hells Bent On Rockin: A History Of Psychobilly
Craig Brackenbridge

Music To Die For – The International Guide To Goth, Goth Metal, Horror Punk, Psychobilly Etc
Mick Mercer

Please visit www.cherryredbooks.co.uk for further information and mail order.

CHERRYRED.TV

Cherry Red's Internet TV station

Featuring fantastic interviews with several of Cherry Red Books' key authors, including Terry Wilson discussing the Motown story, Paul Williams on The Specials and the legend that is Ian Glasper discussing his Punk trilogy, CRTV is a must for any fan of our publications.

The site also features a huge selection of concert footage from an ever expanding list of artists including Alien Sex Fiend, Black Flag, Dead Kennedys, ENT, Marc Almond, Exploited, The Fall, Felt, GBH, Hanoi Rocks, Robyn Hitchcock, Jim Bob, Meteors, Monochrome Set, Nico, Spizz, Thompson Twins and Toyah amongst others.

In-depth interviews with some fascinating characters from the industry, including both musicians and business figures. Monochrome Set's Bid, Morgan Fisher, Claire Hamill, Hawkwind's Harvey Bainbridge, John Otway, Bridget St John, Alvin Stardust, Jim Bob and representatives from Cooking Vinyl, El Records, Glass, Midnight Music, No Future, Nude, Oval, Esoteric Records, RPM and, of course, Cherry Red's own Iain McNay all contribute to this incredible resource for anybody interested in the world of independent music.

The station grows every month, and we are always interested to hear your ideas and suggestions - please contact: *crtv@cherryred.co.uk* **with your comments.**

www.cherryred.tv

CHERRY RED BOOKS

Here at Cherry Red Books we're always
interested to hear of interesting titles looking for
a publisher. Whether it's a new manuscript or an
out of print/deleted title, please feel free to get
in touch if you've written, or are aware of, a book
you feel might be suitable.

richard@cherryred.co.uk

www.cherryredbooks.co.uk
www.cherryred.co.uk

CHERRY RED BOOKS
A division of Cherry Red Records Ltd
Power Road Studios
114 Power Road
London
W4 5PY